KEY TO [...]

"Talia Gryphon is a master [...]
Her diverse group of chara[...]
imagination long after the l[...]
are strong and independent, and her men are alpha [...]
led. Talia is a developing master of the word who has an amazing
grasp of human nature and the ability to craft tales that will engage the mind as well as thrill the soul."

—Stephanie Burke, author of *Keeper of the Flame*

"Fun and imaginative, this rock-'em, sock-'em vampire tale puts
a hard-as-nails military twist on the ole wooden stake. Oh, you
want some erotic spice? Here's a whole rack!"

—David Bischoff, author of *Farscape: Ship of Ghosts*

KEY TO CONFLICT

"A kick-ass blond vampire-therapist, two sexy vampire brothers
and an evil Dracula looming in the offing. I dare you to put this
book down."   —Rosemary Laurey, author of *Midnight Lover*

"A fast-paced adventure tale set in a fascinating new alternate
reality."   —Robin D. Owens, author of *Heart Fate*

"Kick-butt attitude, sassy dialogue and steady action make this a
light, fast read. Gryphon puts a refreshingly different spin on Anubis, Osiris, Dionysus, Jack the Ripper and elves, while giving a
nod to J. R. R. Tolkien."   —*Monsters and Critics*

"Urban fantasy readers will welcome Talia Gryphon, whose thriller
will appeal to fans of Charlaine Harris and Kelley Armstrong."

—*The Best Reviews*

"With a story that is just complex enough to be attention-grabbing,
rich locales, vibrant characters and multifaceted mythology inter-
woven with current cultural icons, this book will draw you in and
not let you put it down."   —*The Eternal Night*

"Gill is a wonderful character, full of conflicts . . . interesting
twists and turns . . . The story was strong, the characters were intriguing and . . . the prose really took off. I think that we'll see
some really great writing from this author in the future."

—*SFRevu*

Ace Books by Talia Gryphon

KEY TO CONFLICT
KEY TO CONSPIRACY
KEY TO REDEMPTION

Key to Redemption

TALIA GRYPHON

ACE BOOKS, NEW YORK

THE BERKLEY PUBLISHING GROUP
Published by the Penguin Group
Penguin Group (USA) Inc.
375 Hudson Street, New York, New York 10014, USA
Penguin Group (Canada), 90 Eglinton Avenue East, Suite 700, Toronto, Ontario M4P 2Y3, Canada
(a division of Pearson Penguin Canada Inc.)
Penguin Books Ltd., 80 Strand, London WC2R 0RL, England
Penguin Group Ireland, 25 St. Stephen's Green, Dublin 2, Ireland (a division of Penguin Books Ltd.)
Penguin Group (Australia), 250 Camberwell Road, Camberwell, Victoria 3124, Australia
(a division of Pearson Australia Group Pty. Ltd.)
Penguin Books India Pvt. Ltd., 11 Community Centre, Panchsheel Park, New Delhi—110 017, India
Penguin Group (NZ), 67 Apollo Drive, Rosedale, North Shore 0632, New Zealand
(a division of Pearson New Zealand Ltd.)
Penguin Books (South Africa) (Pty.) Ltd., 24 Sturdee Avenue, Rosebank, Johannesburg 2196,
South Africa

Penguin Books Ltd., Registered Offices: 80 Strand, London WC2R 0RL, England

KEY TO REDEMPTION

An Ace Book / published by arrangement with the author

PRINTING HISTORY
Ace mass-market edition / October 2008

Copyright © 2008 by Talia Gryphon.
Cover art by Judy York.
Cover design by Annette Fiore DeFex.
Interior text design by Kristin del Rosario.

ISBN: 978-0-441-01644-0

ACE
Ace Books are published by The Berkley Publishing Group,
a division of Penguin Group (USA) Inc.,
375 Hudson Street, New York, New York 10014.
ACE and the "A" design are trademarks belonging to Penguin Group (USA) Inc.

PRINTED IN THE UNITED STATES OF AMERICA

10 9 8 7 6 5 4 3 2 1

For Uncle Walter. Your courage during your time as a POW in Hirohata during World War II and your tolerant, noble heart continue to be an inspiration.

To Tim Frasier, my fencing master and dear friend.

To Uncle John and Aunt Virginia. You always made me laugh.

To Max and Desiree', my childrens' best friend and his fiancée. May you have a wonderful life together.

To Bill Paisley. No one has ever looked better in a kilt.

To Mary and Tom Wallbank. Hooray for Captain Mother and Tom.

Thank you to Louis Kellerman, for his help with the translations of French and Italian in the books.

To GerardButler.net and GerardButlerGALS.com, for the charitable work they and Gerard Butler do for many worthwhile causes.

As always, to Ginjer Buchanan, my wonderful editor, and Joe Veltre, my fabulous agent.

Special thanks to my military advisors: Charles Randolph, Sgt. U.S. Army Special Operations Command, Retired; Jon Eppler, Sgt. U.S. Army Reserves Intelligence Analyst; Steven Mills, Sgt. USMC, Retired; Donald Akina, Corpsman Second Class U.S. Navy, Retired.

*Disclaimer—Licensed sex therapist and licensed sexual surrogate are highly specialized, scrupulously screened and meticulously trained professions. Most are under the auspices of Masters and Johnson, the Kinsey Institute, AASECT or similar legitimate groups. Gillian's training, ethical code and mentors are in regard to the study of Human and Paramortal relationships in her world. This does not infringe on the practices of these professionals in our world.

Talia Gryphon

CHAPTER

1

CASTLE Rachlav was becoming a boardinghouse of sorts to all the Paramortals who had come out of the forest, fields, hills, dales and the occasional closet. Romania's location and Aleksei's connections with Osiris and Dionysus and his diplomatic ties to more than half of the known Fey, Sidhe and Elf worlds made it a logical place to hold meetings and Court and to discuss their collective next moves.

Dracula had been busy. There were murders, missing persons, decimated populations of Paramortals and not so thinly veiled threats toward those who would sign the now-famous Osiris Doctrine. The fact that all the murders, abductions and misdeeds were carried out quietly so that they had no way to prevent anything was a constant source of irritation for investigation teams everywhere. The Human world was in collective fear, wondering why in hell they had ever legalized the Paramortals and invited them into their homes and offices in the first place. Things were not looking cheery, even with Gillian and company's valiant rescue effort of some months back.

Gillian was out of sorts since she couldn't turn a corner in the castle without nearly tripping over one of the Fey, Brownies or the occasional Elf. The Vampires were far less obtrusive, even before the Egyptian Vampires had gone home. Anubis reasoned that Aleksei had plenty of muscle and that he and Sekhmet could better serve the cause by traveling on as Emissaries for Osiris. Noph and Montu had offered to stay but Aleksei graciously assured them that they could go with a clear conscience.

Daed and Kimber were wrapping up their little Russian expedition with the earthquake survivors and planned on joining the rest of the party at Castle Rachlav. The reality that no one from the various governments, the IPPA, and the newly formed Alliance had any semblance of a plan was driving Gillian into a highly agitated state. Aleksei was, for the most part, a rock, an anchor, in the subliminal chaos, but Gillian couldn't find it in herself to lean on him to any extent. That made Aleksei irritable.

Centuries-old Vampires had difficulty mastering flexibility. They tended to hang on to their old ways, old habits, old ways of thinking. Aleksei, while fairly progressive for a four-hundred-year-old Vampire and newly evolved Lord, still clung to some rather inflexible ideas. One of them being the notion that Gillian needed to be sheltered and taken care of—a concept she refused to entertain. She continued to see clients, meet with the local brass of the various councils, go hunting for Dracula's associates, sometimes alone, and she wouldn't take a dime from him to meet her own expenses. That most of all got under his luminous skin. He wanted to take care of her, and she wasn't having it.

When she saw they were getting on each other's last nerves, Gillian often left, taking Trocar, Jenna, Tanis or Pavel with her, on scouting expeditions around the province. It deflected a lot of arguments, caused more than a few, but usually accomplished easing tension between the Romanian Lord and herself. She was on her way out on just such an excursion, when her thigh vibrated and she had to fight not to scream.

Stupid cell phone. She'd forgotten she'd left it on vibrate. The damn thing felt like a rattlesnake in the loose pocket of her olive khaki cargo pants. Already annoyed, she yanked it out and flipped it open with an expert snap of her wrist.

"Key here."

"Gillian? It's Helmut. I have a rather delicate question to ask you, if you don't mind." Her mentor, boss and friend's voice sounded pretty clear.

"Jeez, Helmut, I'm not a fragile flower, just ask the question." Shouldering her backpack and balancing the phone between chin and collarbone, she hurried down the stairs toward Trocar, Dalton and Pavel. They were about to head East, toward another small village, deeper into the Carpathian Mountains, and Gillian had her mind on the road trip.

"Very well." He sighed audibly into the phone.

Dr. Helmut Gerhardt had been her professor, committee chairman, mentor and friend for years. He knew her better than she knew herself, but he still hated to stir up her ire. "I need to know if your certification credentials from the Miller-Jackson Center for Intimacy are up to date."

That stopped her dead in her tracks. "What? What the hell do I need that credential for, here and now? Wait, hang on a moment." Her voice dropped into a low, hissing whisper as she turned on the stairs and bolted back up to her room and away from prying pointy ears. Reaching the safety of her room, she locked the door, turned on the shower and the bathroom fan, then asked again, "Okay, I'm back. What do I need *that* for?"

Helmut's voice was calm and level, a sure sign that he was going to ask her something that she wouldn't like one damn bit. "I have a client for you, Gillian. Well, actually several, but this one individual, I believe, can benefit from your expertise in this area."

Dead silence. He waited, knowing it was better not to speak too much, too soon. "Helmut, you do realize Aleksei and I have been trying to have a relationship, right?"

"Of course, Gillian. I do pay attention when you share with me, dear." Helmut's gruff voice softened a little. He'd been a father figure for her in many ways. Not having a good relationship with her own male parent, she relied on Helmut to be a rock of support and encouragement whenever she faltered in her belief that a former Marine Captain could make an outstanding psychologist to the Paramortal.

"What the hell am I supposed to tell him about this? He's four hundred fucking years old, Helmut! He's going to have a Vampire heart attack, if that's possible!" She was pacing back and forth in the sumptuous bathroom, tapping her teeth with the nail of her index finger.

"Gillian, you are a trained professional. If you don't want to take the case, that's one thing. But you cannot refuse a client merely because your boyfriend might get jealous." That was an admonishment. She could recognize them with astonishing regularity anymore.

Exasperated, she wilted against the expensive wallpaper and slid down, legs extended, until she wound up sitting on the tiled floor. "I know, I'm sorry." Her free hand raked through her gleaming golden hair. "I don't have the certificate on me, Helmut. As far as I know, they mailed it directly to IPPA for my permanent file, where it's been ever since I got it."

"I will obtain a copy and bring it with me when I come so that it and you are in the same location," Helmut replied.

"Why are you coming here?"

"There are several clients who requested you. One is the gentleman I spoke earlier of, who is French; one gentleman travels a great deal but heard about you by referral; and one says she knows you from your Russian expedition." He paused a moment. "Perhaps 'says' is a misnomer. The poor creature, when she is able to communicate verbally, made it clear that she wished to have you as a therapist. She's convinced you can work a miracle with her.

"I am bringing the lot of them down to you. It's far too dangerous right now for you to go country hopping. The Board met and decided that it would be better to bring what clients were willing to travel to you. The nonlocals anyway." Helmut sounded like he always did, calm and matter-of-fact.

"Fine," Gillian bit off.

"Gillian . . ." Helmut allowed a slight warning tone to enter his voice.

"I said, fine." Her voice was strained. "When are you coming?"

"Day after tomorrow. We'll take the train into Brasov, then I'll rent a van or SUV to drive down to you. Do you have a place for them to stay in the area? And a place for private therapy with the French gentleman?"

"All right, I'll see you then. Just come straight to the castle. Make sure you arrive in daylight. No wait, I'll have one of my former Lieutenants come pick you up; it'll be safer. I'll notify the pack not to rip your heads off, and yes to both: we have accommodations and I have a private bungalow I can access." All business, Gillian was mentally already making notes and trying to figure out what the hell she was going to tell Aleksei about this.

Helmut said his good-byes and hung up. Gill snapped the phone shut and swore, "Fuck." This wasn't going to go well, she already knew that. Climbing to her feet, she turned off the shower, light and fan and went off to find Aleksei and a very private room.

After telling Trocar, Dalton and Pavel to go on without her, she found Aleksei, discussing the resurveying of the province for patrols with Finian, the Twilight Court Prince, and the two Wood Elves. The silvery light in his eyes when he saw her should have been chilly but it was warming and filled with immediate interest when she entered the room.

Watching him cross the room toward her after she beckoned to him, she was amazed how he rivaled the Fey and the Elves in sheer physical beauty. Vampires were generally stunning but Aleksei was certainly in a class by himself. His smile was warm as he kissed her hand formally, the gleam in his eyes betraying his decorum. Gillian could have just contacted him mentally now that they shared a blood bond again, but she wasn't comfortable with that level of intimacy on a regular basis. He knew it and left her alone about it. He didn't want to do anything to spook her in this relationship. They'd waited nearly two years before consummating their relationship, and he didn't want to push her faster than she was ready to go.

"I am yours, *angela*. What is it?"

"Let's go somewhere private, I have to tell you something

and I would rather our aesthetically eared friends not hear everything we discuss." She let him take her hand and guide her to a private area in the little-used kitchen.

Vampire senses were firing with alarming rapidity. Something was wrong. Gillian's blood pressure was slightly elevated; she was tense and her hand was a bit damp where he had held it. She moved a little away from him and turned back, putting the corner of the stainless steel island between them. Frowning slightly, Aleksei leaned a hip against the island, folded his arms and tried to appear casual while he waited for her to speak. Being a six-foot seven-inch, drop-dead-gorgeous Vampire made it difficult to appear casual, but hey, he gave it a shot.

"What is it, *piccola*? You know you may discuss anything with me."

Gill swallowed hard and met his icy gray gaze head-on. "You know, you would think I could, but this might be stretching your tolerance level just a little."

That got his complete attention. "My tolerance level?" An elegant eyebrow rose. "And what could you possibly tell me that would stretch my tolerance level further than it already has been?" He smiled warmly at her.

That warm and wicked smile that made her go all gooey inside. Shit. She had to focus and not let him affect her or she'd never get this said.

"Helmut called and is bringing a van load of clients down for me tomorrow," she ventured, trying to stay as far away from the actual point as she could for a while.

"That is the problem?" Aleksei's eyes widened slightly. That couldn't be it; she was far too nervous for that to be the complete story.

"No, I knew you wouldn't mind lodging them here. But I will need to borrow the guesthouse for one of the clients."

"Gillian." The black velvet voice rolled over her, a slight warning entering his tone. "Nothing you have told me is so overtly out of the ordinary that you could not have spoken about it among our guests. You already know that everything

I have is yours to use or take as you will." He was discovering that he had a bullshit detector where Gillian was concerned and it was registering high on the scale at the moment.

A small hand tucked an errant strand of golden hair behind her shell ear, a sure sign that she was very uncomfortable with what she wanted to talk about. "You're right, but I needed to tell you that first so that I could tell you this next part. And that's the part I'm afraid you're not going to be happy about."

He was suddenly standing closer, much too close. She could smell the uniquely clean cardamom and nutmeg that seemed to emanate from him. His large, warm hand covered hers where it lay on the steel island. "Gillian, talk to me. What is wrong?"

"Aleksei, one of the clients is a man with a particular problem. That particular problem requires a very specially trained therapist who is credentialed and certified to handle it." She cringed a little internally at his use of her given name.

"And you are trained in this skill?"

She felt the blush coming before it hit her cheeks and wished that she were armed so she could just shoot herself and be done with it. "Yes I am. I had to take specific post-graduate study for it, train for two extra years and be specifically credentialed in this area in addition to my regular licensure."

Blushing. Gillian blushing. Aleksei's mind was whirling. There wasn't a great deal which made Gillian blush . . . unless . . .

"What exactly do you need to do for this . . . man?" His voice had dropped to a deeper register as it often did when he felt she was right on the verge of not telling him the entire truth about something. "Be specific, Gillian. Be very specific."

Her eyes snapped up again to meet his at his tone. "I am a licensed sex therapist, Aleksei. This particular client has some real issues with sex and personal closeness. I will need to work on a very close and very delicate level with him, which is why I will need the guesthouse for his lodging."

She searched his face to see if that was sinking in. "I have training and credentialing from the Miller-Jackson Center for Intimacy, which hosts the foremost authority and most widely respected program of this type in the world."

Understanding flooded his beautiful features, and his eyes lightened to almost white, giving them an eerie glow. "Sex therapist," he repeated incredulously. "You are a mental health professional who is also trained to provide a sort of sexual healing?" His eyes were locked on her face, and his hand, which had been stroking hers, was rock still, effectively trapping her.

"Yeah, I guess that's the best way to put it," she said brightly, seeing that he understood, "Thanks, Aleksei, I was afraid that we would be here for hours just explaining what a sex therapist was, and that you'd be really upset about this, but you're really being an adult about it and I can't tell you how much I appreciate that." She took a deep breath after her hurried, run-on sentence, patted the hand over hers warmly, stepped around the corner of the island and leaned upward to kiss him. His other hand against her shoulder stopped her.

"Am I to understand that you expect me to sit here, in the castle, knowing that you are down in the guesthouse, making love with a stranger? Someone who has, as you put it . . . mental problems and sexual issues?"

Boy, it had sure gotten chilly in there suddenly. All trace of warmth was gone from Aleksei's voice. It was pure ice to match his eyes.

"Not making love, Aleksei, and maybe not having sex either, although that is very likely. I don't know what the man's issues are. All I know is that he came to the IPPA and asked for a qualified, credentialed sex therapist. Then Helmut called and told me that they really needed me on this case because they thought I would be the best therapist for the client. That's all there is to it. This is business, Aleksei, not a personal relationship. A sex therapist simply helps clients resolve problems that otherwise might emotionally cripple them for life, or a million other issues.

"There isn't a clear answer here because I haven't talked to this client yet. I don't know why he needs my services or what exactly he needs from me. I just wanted to be honest with you before it became an issue."

Gillian was rambling, trying to be diplomatic and take Aleksei's feelings into consideration. After all, if she didn't care, she would have simply taken the client and the hell with how her Vampire lover felt. No, she was trying to be nice, be part of a couple. Recognize that this was all very new to him: her, her modern ideals, her profession, their relationship. He was bound to be a little jumpy about something like this.

Now that she had taken the time to explain, things should go smoothly. Uh-huh. Sure they would. And Captain Smith on the *Titanic* said, "Where is all this fucking water coming from?"

She moved closer, putting a small hand against his broad chest, not trying to pull her other hand out from under his. "Look, this is why I wanted to talk to you privately. No one else needs to know what's going on. This is just between us, understand? I am being paid to help a client. That's it. Period."

Wisely, he waited a minute before he answered her. Four hundred years brings a lot of wisdom if you pay attention. Jealousy, anger, betrayal, confusion, all swept across his expressive and lovely face. He didn't want to feel those things, but just the thought of her being with someone else, touching him, being potentially held in his arms, shook Aleksei to the core.

Knowing he was being irrational and illogical didn't help the way his heart was feeling one bit. She was telling him the absolute truth; he could have sensed that from across the room. This was her job. She helped heal people's minds and souls. Gillian was a very sensual, passionate woman who had no problems with her own sexuality. It was horrifying to her that someone could exist who didn't know the upside of sex and intimacy between two beings who cared for each other.

She would want to help him, need to help him. Her empathy was cell deep. She couldn't sit by and let another be in pain. She couldn't *not* help. Aleksei knew all those things and more, having been inside the upper levels, at least, of Gillian's complicated and brilliant mind. It still didn't help. This bothered him. A lot. Progressive, modern Vampire— like hell. Now how to convey that without pissing her off to the point that she either staked him or just walked away.

He took a deep breath and realized he hadn't been breathing for the past few minutes. "I cannot share you, *piccola*. Please do not ask this of me. Certainly there is another therapist somewhere who could help this man resolve his problems. I do not wish you to take this client, either here on our property or elsewhere. In fact, I would prefer if you never took a client who has need of this type of therapy."

There, he had said it. Direct and to the point. No hedging, no sugarcoating, no power struggle, just the exact words to convey his feelings to her. Honest. Just as she would expect him to be . . . maybe not.

Gillian's eyes narrowed ever so slightly. What? Was he telling her that she couldn't do her job? She completely missed him calling the residence "our" property or that he was being very succinct about his feelings. Okay, so he was being polite about it. Extraordinarily polite, in fact. Hell, both of them were being so diplomatic and were so far up on the High Road that her teeth ached and she felt a nosebleed coming on.

"I know you did not just tell me not to do my job. I know you did not just say something to indicate that you are jealous because you don't trust me to know what I am doing or that you don't approve of my professional abilities." Her voice was clear, cold, professional and flat.

Aleksei hadn't missed the flash in her Nile green eyes. He was treading very thin ice at the moment and he knew it. He also knew he wasn't going to gracefully approve of his . . . What was she anyway . . . his girlfriend? That sounded so trite. His mistress? No, too cheap. His lover? Definitely. His lover and friend, in fact. He was not going to condone this aspect of her job. Not now, not ever. "I said I would not share you with anyone for any reason." He never blinked, never altered his tone, never moved.

Absolute Vampire stillness is creepy when it's done right, and Aleksei was doing a hell of a job using it as an intimidation factor. It set Gillian's teeth right on edge.

"You don't have a choice as to whether or not I do my job." Every word was enunciated with alarming clarity. "I only told you this privately as a courtesy and because I cared about your feelings. You aren't sharing anything, Aleksei. I am with *you*. This man is a patient and it has nothing to do with our relationship. I thought it would be better to let you know ahead of time what this part of my job might entail but I wasn't asking your permission."

Both winged eyebrows shot up over icy silver eyes that now harbored a red flame in their depths. "Then you have made your choice." Deep, hollow, cold; his voice echoed through her like the wind from a graveyard. None of the black velvet warmth that usually came with his anger.

"What fucking choice?" Now she was angry. It sounded an awful lot as though he were deliberately being obtuse.

"I'm not choosing one over the other, Aleksei. This is my profession. It isn't about either doing my job or being in a relationship with you. It's asking you to understand that sometimes my job might entail me doing something that you might find objectionable, while it is perfectly ethical. It's asking you to be a goddamn adult about this and realize that whatever I need to do for or with this particular patient has nothing to do with us as a couple." She searched his face, looking for some response, something besides this wax figure standing motionless before her.

"You do not need to do this job, Gillian. We are together. I have more than enough money to support us for the rest of our very long lives. It is not necessary that you continue this profession at all if you would only desire it." Involuntarily his hand tightened over hers, warm and firm.

Then he made a mistake. "There is no reason for you to

become what amounts to a paid courtesan for some stranger with sexual problems."

White-hot anger shot through her with a force that made her tremble. She couldn't have heard him right. "Did you just call me a prostitute?"

"What else would you call it? You are going to provide sexual intimacy for a man you do not know and you are going to be paid. Is there another more progressive term for it?" Okay, now he was being a smart-ass.

His second mistake was dropping his eyes for a moment so she wouldn't see how deeply this cut him. Truthfully, male Vampire pride didn't want her to see the tears he felt beginning to burn. Pride often goeth before a fall.

Since he was looking down, he didn't see it coming. Gillian did him the courtesy of waiting until his eyes rose again to meet hers before belting him in the mouth. She missed the tears gathering in his eyes. Unfortunately for Aleksei, she didn't miss his sculpted jaw. Gill was strong for a Human female. Seven years in the U.S. Marine Corps will do that. Couple that with the small infusion of awesome mystical Vampire foo Aleksei had bestowed upon her the one time they had exchanged blood, and she packed quite a punch.

It was so totally unexpected that he truly was caught off guard. The blow rocked him backward and bowed his back over the table. "Fuck you, you antiquated, unreasonable, archaic son of a bitch! And to think I was actually trying to consider your feelings! You can go straight to Hell."

Gillian pushed past him and stalked out of the kitchen, not stopping or acknowledging Tanis and Jenna's cheerful greetings as she blew by them in the main foyer. She stomped out the door and down toward the car Aleksei had purchased for her personal use, got in, locked the doors and alternately cried and swore for the next few minutes.

It was Jenna, with Tanis, Pavel and Trocar in tow, who knocked on the car window. Gillian's head snapped up from where she had laid it on her arms, leaning against the steering wheel.

"Sweetie? Talk to us. What happened?" Jenna's concerned chocolate brown eyes were level with hers outside the window as she leaned down to peer in at her friend.

Gill loved Jenna. Jenna didn't ask stupid questions like "Are you all right?" or "Are you crying?" when she could clearly see tears and snot on someone's face.

Wiping her face on her sleeve, Gillian got out of the car. Jenna didn't wait; she hugged her friend. Tanis was at Gillian's back instantly, his hands on her shoulders, offering a wall of Vampire strength. Trocar gently took her hand, waiting for her to speak, and Pavel paced worriedly behind them.

"Sorry, guys," Gillian said softly, none of the recent anger in her voice, "I just have to do a job and Aleksei is being difficult. Difficult and insulting."

"Aleksei deliberately insulted you, *piccola sorella*?" Tanis asked gently, taking Gillian out of Jenna's arms and turning her to face him. Gillian didn't let go of Trocar's hand and was obliged to turn him with her. She met Tanis's golden eyes with impunity.

"Yeah, you could say that. It can't be helped. I have to do a job and he doesn't like it. I tried to explain why and what it was but he wouldn't listen." She wiped angrily at her eyes again as more tears threatened to spill. "I can't blame him really, but it pissed me off enough that I actually decked him."

There was a collective intake of breath, then Tanis chuckled, pulling her against his hard chest and stroking her hair. He was with Jenna now but Gillian was his friend, despite being his former lover. They'd lost the attraction but not the affection for each other.

"You seem to be accruing similar experiences with both of the Rachlav brothers." He hugged her and kissed the top of her head. "To date, we've both insulted you enough to cause you to lose your temper, we've both been your friend and lover, and you have, as you put it, 'decked' both of us."

He put her away from him a little and tipped her face up so she would look at him. "All that is left is a spanking from Aleksei and everything will be even. I'm still one up on him in that area." Tanis winked at her and grinned.

Gillian stared at him a moment, then the realization that

he was teasing to cheer her up filtered through her hurt feelings and she had to laugh. "Yeah, you're right."

Trocar was incredulous. "You," he said, pointing at Tanis, "spanked her?" He pointed to Gillian and looked at her for confirmation. When she nodded, giggling, he turned back to Tanis. "You are braver than I thought, my friend."

CHAPTER
2

AFTER they heard Gillian's version of the story, Tanis went off to confront Aleksei, swearing under his breath. He understood Aleksei's feelings in the matter, but dammit, his brother knew what Gillian did as a psychologist. Granted, the sex therapist part was a surprise, but neither of them had any reason to know about that part of her job since neither of them had any sexual issues.

More than any of that, Tanis trusted Gillian. They'd been together for several months before his kidnapping. He knew that she was a professional, honorable and damn good at her job; he'd seen the difference she'd made with his brother and Pavel. Aleksei of all people should trust her, let her do her job, support her in it and leave his judgmental, archaic feelings the hell alone.

What he was angry about was Aleksei comparing Gillian to a prostitute. That, his brother would answer for if what Gillian had said was accurate. Several things had pissed her off about that remark, as she'd told Tanis, Jenna, Pavel and Trocar. First, she'd had patients, back in the days when she still saw the occasional Human client, who were prostitutes. Most were single mothers with extenuating circumstances; yes, some were drug addicts, but none of them were bad or evil or women with scarlet letters on their chests. She had tremendous compassion for those women, and it bothered her to have what they did vilified.

Second, there was a world of difference between what they did and what she would be required to perform as a licensed sex therapist. Third, she was proud of her profession—every aspect of it, from regular therapy to sex therapy.

There were only a handful of legitimate, licensed sex therapy professionals in the world. Gillian was one of them and an august company it was. They were highly regarded by all branches of the mental health professions. Their training was intense, demanding and very, very structured. The guidelines of the practice were rigid and uncompromising. The Miller-Jackson Center for Intimacy had long been a pioneer in the field of sexual disorders and compatibility for Humans, and was world renowned for turning out professionals who entered at the top of the game and stayed there.

Gillian had brought in the Paramortal perspective since that was her specialty. They developed new coursework and credentials just for her and applauded the journal articles she wrote during the course of her training and research. Now others were coming to apply for certification and specialization in Paramortal sexual disorders and compatibility. They had even renamed the Institute to include "Paramortal Intimacy" in the title. A lot of cross-cultural marriages and cohabitations were occurring since Paramortals had been recognized as "people."

Having Gillian as codeveloper of such a popular program was a windfall of credibility for the newly founded IPPA. They were training and turning out therapists to work with all levels and needs of their very mixed bag of clientele. Paramortals occasionally had sexual issues too. Who knew?

The actual number of therapists was small because it was a very minute, very highly screened patient population that would actually need those specific services. They were exhaustively screened because some saw the profession just as Aleksei did: sort of a form of condoned, legalized prostitution and as a branch of psychology that was better swept under the proverbial rug, unspoken about in polite company.

Some sex therapists went for years without actually seeing a patient, which was why the IPPA's members usually kept up their other specializations and credentials. There just wasn't a large number in either the Human or the Paramortal world who were willing to admit failure in the lovemaking department. Gillian herself had had only two other opportunities to use that particular skill, though she'd been credentialed for several years. Until now.

Tanis stopped by the library, which thankfully was deserted, and pulled up the website for the Miller-Jackson Center for Intimacy on the computer, then bellowed for Aleksei, verbally and mentally. *"Get your sorry backside in here, brother. I have a bone to pick with you."* The entire castle vibrated a moment with the force of his voice thundering through the passageways, and everyone froze in whatever he or she had been doing, wondering what the hell was going on now.

Aleksei was rather shocked by Tanis's attitude so he didn't reply right away, waiting until he got to the library. As he entered, Tanis, who was across the room, looking out a window at the night sky, turned and waved a hand, crashing the door shut behind him. Aleksei glanced over his shoulder at the door, which was trembling in its resting place from the force of the slam.

"I take it you are angry with me about something, but must you punish the door?"

With blurring speed, Tanis was across the room and punched the unprepared Aleksei in the mouth, slamming him back against the already abused door. "What the hell is wrong with you, Aleksei? You have everything you have ever dreamed of: a home you love, a village to protect, a Line to establish and a beautiful, brilliant woman who is strong enough to love you through it all, yet you are ready to throw it all away with an idiotic remark."

Aleksei righted himself, the back of his hand going to his mouth and dabbing at the blood from a split lip. He'd heal in minutes so the injury wasn't the problem. His brother had just "cleaned his clock," as Gillian would have said, and he was perplexed. Perplexed and getting angry.

"What the hell was that for?" he shouted, glaring at his brother as though he'd never seen him before. Tanis's eyes blazed gold and he started forward again but Aleksei held up a hand.

"First, tell me what we are about to be fighting over, and what has already gotten you this angry." He straightened to his full height and was eye to eye with his powerful and angry brother.

"How can you speak disrespectfully to Gillian or about her profession," Tanis hissed, moving forward slowly and deliberately like a panther stalking its prey. Aleksei didn't back up but he began circling, mirroring Tanis's movements.

"She is about to offer herself up to a disturbed patient for money, Tanis. How can you condone that?"

Tanis, circling Aleksei right back, offered, "It is her job, brother. She is the woman you love. The reason you love her is for her bravery and compassion. Yet you name her 'courtesan.' I find that to be a very derogatory term for someone whom I love as a friend and once held in high esteem as a lover." Tanis stopped abruptly and punctuated his sentence by poking Aleksei in the chest.

Aleksei's lovely face radiated his confusion. "Of course I do not think of her as a courtesan, Tanis. But if you were still with her, what would your opinion of this situation be?"

Pain flashed through those icy eyes, all anger gone. He wasn't being arrogant, Tanis realized. Aleksei was terrified. Specifically of losing Gillian. Too bad he might already have accomplished that.

"If I were still with her, I would try to remember that the very core of her being is what I love. Not what she does or does not do in the course of her job, but what she does or does not do in the course of our relationship."

Tanis regarded his brother, eyes still blazing, arms folded. "She tried to explain this out of courtesy and love for you. She feared you would react badly if this were suddenly sprung on you. You have asked her to confide in you, you have asked her to share things with you, and when she does, how have you reacted?"

Aleksei raked his hand through his thick, shimmering black hair, a gesture he shared with Gillian when he was agitated. "She trusted me, came to me with this to discuss it. Exactly as I have often asked her to do." Ding. Elevator to Tact, now arriving.

Realization filtered through and his face became stricken with fear. Gillian had finally confided in him, and he repaid her by being difficult. Oh yes, and grievously insulting her and her profession. She was never going to speak to him again; of that he was sure.

It was very sad to watch a normally rational, intelligent Vampire suddenly have an epiphany, which he should have had sometime *before* he opened his mouth and said something stupid, Tanis decided. "And you very deftly severed that trust, betrayed your confidence in her and made her feel as though you count her value as a person and her love cheaply, unless you have your way."

Tanis was still angry enough to turn the screw a little more. "Very interesting indeed, Aleksei. When we first encountered the good doctor, I seem to recall you telling me that my attitude and behavior were antiquated and unfair." He turned to go, tossing over his shoulder, "Now it is the kettle's turn to call the pot black," as he swept out of the room, leaving Aleksei alone with his churning thoughts.

While Aleksei was receiving the verbal thrashing via Tanis, Gillian was hanging out with the Elf Twins. After the night of the meeting, Gillian made an effort to introduce herself and establish communication directly with those who were in the area. It turned out that Aisling and Gunnolf had heard of Mirrin, the High Elf Prince who had been under her command during their stretch in the USMC, and knew Hierlon, the Golden Elf guide who had brought Mirrin, Trocar and Kimber across the Doorway.

It was nice to connect with the First People again, as the Elves referred to themselves. They were warm, open, very wise, but retained a freshness and purity about them despite living for millennia, fighting horrific battles, and watching the rise and fall of Human civilizations.

Among the Elves there was an ancient saying: "When Hope falls, so does the World." Elves never gave up hope on anything. They believed with every cell of their bodies that even a tragedy of epic proportions would have something good and positive be the ultimate result. Sometimes you just had to look really, really hard for it. Since Gillian was Jewish by heritage, she understood that concept quite well and felt a definite kinship with her First People friends.

Gillian came away from her visit with them with a more positive perspective. She wasn't given to sharing normally. Talking to Tanis, Jenna, Pavel and Trocar was out of character for her, but there wasn't a way she could graciously have avoided it. Aleksei, she evaded deliberately. Archaic prick. Instinctively, she had decided to leave well enough alone. If they were to try and resolve things right now, they would wind up enemies and she knew she didn't want that. In her heart, through her empathy, she knew he truly didn't think the worst of her; that didn't mean his temporary lapse of linguistic judgment hurt any less.

She dragged herself up to her room close to dawn. Since she'd been on Vampire Standard Time, she was pretty well beat by the time the first streaks of light appeared in the sky. Pausing in the hallway outside the door, she thought about going into what was probably an empty room or, worse, one with Aleksei in it. He had been a constant presence in there for the last few weeks and she didn't know if he would realize that the last thing in the world she wanted right now was company.

Well, shit. She needed sleep and didn't want to talk with Aleksei, let alone fight with him. And there would most definitely be a fight if she opened that door and found him in her bed. There was no way she could assure herself that he wasn't already in there. She had been avoiding him all night but hadn't even glimpsed him for the past hour.

After a few minutes of searching the upper hallways, she

managed to locate a linen closet and grabbed a pillow, sheets
and a couple of blankets, then headed back downstairs. There
was still a bustling of activity with all the new houseguests
and campers. Briefly she wondered where they were going to
put the new patients Helmut was escorting to her and how
they were going to manage confidentiality and privacy. She
opened the massive front door and stepped out into the night.
Cezar's Wolves were on patrol, but they were familiar with
her now and didn't give her so much as a glance as she turned
left and headed toward the nearby forest.

Straight ahead there was a brief flash and she went toward
it. As she neared, Trocar stepped out of the trees, crystalline
hair all white and sparkly in the night. Gratefully, she went
to him. He smiled and took her bedding from her, tucking it
under his left arm and her under his right. "Come and be
with the Elves tonight, Captain."

Elves' voices were almost on par with a Vampire's, but
Gillian didn't want to think about that or Aleksei. Still, by
addressing her by her former rank, Trocar was unobtrusively
inserting a boundary between them for tonight at least, one
that he would not cross. He meant for her to join them for
comfort and companionship, not sex. Gillian wanted to kiss
him for being astute and understanding, but she didn't.

He escorted her a little farther into the forest, where she
could see a campfire ahead. Aisling and Gunnolf were
seated by the fire, as was Dalton, the Fey Prince of the Light
Court. They waved at her and she returned it, but didn't really feel like conversation. Trocar quickly spread her blankets near his, a curiously comforting act to her at the
moment. He rose and looked down at her from his six-foot
two-inch height. "Rest, Gillyflower. You are among friends
and will not be disturbed."

Wordlessly, she nodded and lay down, scooting around to
keep the bedding beneath her before Trocar, smiling and
shaking his head, knelt to rearrange the blankets and tuck
her in. She glowered up at him. "I am not a kid, Trocar,
knock it off."

In response, he turned and dragged his sleeping pallet

close to hers. With a swirl of his cape, he removed the garment and laid it next to the bedding, then, with effortless grace, slid into his own bedroll. Gillian yelped when a strong arm pulled her against an even stronger chest and she rolled over to stare at him. "What the hell do you think you're doing?"

"I am comforting you, Gillyflower. Now be still and rest easy. I will watch you this night, as will the others. You must be fresh for your new clients tomorrow." Trocar's voice was lovely but she felt like he was mocking her.

"I know your thoughts, Mellina. I am not making sport of you. You need a friend tonight, and I am that friend."

Tears burned in her eyes for a moment and she whispered, "Thanks," then turned and let him pull her close. Exhaustion took her and she slept.

Trocar waited until her breathing was level and steady, then adjusted his own position so he could mold around her body more, giving her his warmth, and closed his own eyes. Her scent of sun-kissed clover meadow and snow was in his nostrils.

"Sleep well, Gillyflower, and pray that your Vampire Lord and I do not have a disagreement anytime soon," he murmured, half to himself, as he fell asleep.

Once a Marine, always a Marine. You stand by your Captain and your fellow soldiers. Period. Trocar had been furious with Aleksei's reaction to Gillian when he had learned of the incident. He afforded her a respect that he gave few others. As his commanding officer, she had never been his lover, though he had wished it, but they had been stalwart friends. There was a Blood Oath between them and they would be friends until their dying day.

No one insulted Gillian—only he got to do that . . . well, and Kimber . . . and Jenna . . . and Daed . . . but that was beside the point. The team had earned the right to pick on each other. These newcomers had not.

Aleksei might have been in a bad way tonight if Trocar had been true to his nature. Serving in the USMC had tamed him a little and made him less reactionary than his fellows.

Gillian wasn't letting the insult slide, by any means, but she hadn't killed Aleksei either. By Trocar's standard, she had every right to but chose not to do it.

The Vampire Lord would apologize to her and learn to curb his tongue or Trocar would cut it out. The Vampire would heal. Meanwhile, Trocar would be Gillyflower's friend and comfort her. He knew what she needed tonight and provided it. His last thought before sleep was that Aleksei should make it his business to develop a better understanding of Gillian—of who and what she was—if he wanted to remain in her life.

CHAPTER

3

HELMUT Gerhardt and his charges arrived just when Gillian told him to—right after dusk the following evening. The rented van pulled into the courtyard while the sun hung low on the horizon, like a bloody red ball. Having gotten some sleep, thanks to Trocar, and been fed, thanks to the Elves, Gillian was ready to take on her responsibilities again. Her issues with Aleksei could wait until later; right now she had a job to do.

As the van came to a stop, she unconsciously shifted into parade rest. It was a leftover defense mechanism from the Service. When she felt she would be evaluated, she became more formal with everything she did: speech, mannerisms and even her stance.

"Dr. Gerhardt, welcome to Castle Rachlav," Gillian said with a smile she didn't really feel as her boss and mentor exited the van. Aleksei would be out in a moment to greet the guests. She had successfully avoided him since their fight and wasn't looking forward to seeing him now but she couldn't avoid not being there to greet everyone.

"Dr. Key, how nice to see you," Helmut replied, shaking her hand then drawing her into a hug and whispering in her ear, "I have credentials with me that state this is the Rachlav

Institute of Paramortal Healing, to keep everything legal and aboveboard. The patients are aware of this and have all signed waivers in case their confidentiality is violated accidentally here." He pulled back to look into her eyes. "They all specifically requested you, Gillian. Your reputation precedes you."

"Indeed it does, Dr. Gerhardt."

Shit and double shit. Aleksei. He'd come up while Helmut was whispering to her. Sneaky bastard. Nowhere to run now.

"Allow me to welcome you to Castle Rachlav." The tall, breathtaking Vampire glided up to the clinical director of IPPA and shook his hand without giving Gillian so much as a glance. Well, that was just fine with her. Two could play this game.

"Helmut, if you will introduce me to our patients, I will direct them to their rooms. You can talk to Count Rachlav in a moment about your solution. I am sure he will be most agreeable to anything you have to say."

With that, she moved to the van, avoiding Aleksei's gaze and presence with Helmut following close behind her. She felt the slightest brush on her mind and slammed her barriers shut. That should give him the message. It did. She heard the crunch of his boots on the gravel as he turned away from her and the van. Aleksei could walk without a sound on any surface, so she knew he made noise for her benefit so she'd know he was gone.

"Dr. Key, may I introduce Samuel Frank." Helmut opened the van's door and stepped back to allow an enormous cloaked figure to unfold itself out of the van's interior to stand next to them. Whoever he was, he was *huge*. Easily the tallest male of any species that she had ever seen. Well over seven and a half feet tall, his height was only slightly more impressive than the bulk. She couldn't get a good look, he was completely covered from head to feet by the heavy black hooded cloak, which also obscured his face from view.

"I'm glad to meet you, Samuel." Gillian offered her hand and kept the surprise off her face when an enormous gloved hand engulfed hers. His grip was tentative, as if he knew he had great strength and could hurt her. Her empathy flared and she could feel his physical pain and fear. Projecting comforting feelings back was easy. She didn't want him on edge.

"Thank you, Dr. Key."

Ye gods, the voice emanating from under that spooky hood was deep and thick with a hollow fluid sound. Gillian knew from the file Helmut had faxed her that Mr. Samuel Frank had once hailed from Germany. He was basically the failed experiment of two doctors, Frankenstein and Clerval, who thought they could create life from lifelessness, using lightning and the sewn-together parts from a number of corpses, over a hundred years before.

Fortunately or unfortunately, depending on your point of view, they had been successful. Samuel had been brought unceremoniously and painfully to life. Rumor had it that Viktor Frankenstein had removed Clerval's brain when his friend died of a heart attack and placed it in Samuel's skull so his creation would be assured of brilliant intellect.

When Viktor was arrested, he stated that his friend had ordered him to use the brain, citing scientific intent. The magistrate's opinion diverged on that issue and Viktor was ordered to stand trial for murder, corpse theft and the desecration of several bodies, including that of his friend, Dr. Clerval. Viktor opted to run for it.

Having booked passage on a ship going up into the Arctic Circle to hide what remained of the evidence that could put him in prison for the rest of his life, Viktor thought he was safe. Samuel, however, stowed away, intending to see that his remaining creator was brought to justice, one way or another.

There was an accident with a lantern one night. A sailor who was lubricated against the cold tried to refill an already lit lantern with whale oil. The resulting fire ignited the merchant ship and the crew panicked, abandoning both passengers and vessel, leaving Samuel alone with his nemesis. Both were horribly burned; Samuel from trying to salvage his creator so that justice would be meted out and Viktor from trying to escape both the flames and his creation.

Despite Samuel's efforts to save him, Viktor died of his

injuries and exposure to the bone-chilling cold soon after. Before the human died, the two of them had a discussion that resolved a few questions Samuel had about the reason for Viktor's experiments. Samuel was moved enough by his dying creator's honesty to bestow his forgiveness, letting the past die with the Human.

After studying Viktor's remaining journals, notes and books that hadn't been destroyed in the fire, he dug a tomb, deep in the permanent ice. All the research materials were laid next to Viktor, then Samuel sealed the grave, obliterating the entrance so it would never be found. He never wanted another to suffer the folly of men who tried to play God.

After eking out a meager existence in the Arctic for years, he'd made his way back to Germany, traveling mostly at night, keeping well away from civilized areas. Once back in his homeland, he spent an interminable amount of time alone in a forgotten cave in the craggy mountains. He had never fully recovered from either his emotional or his physical wounds. Scarred, alone, despondent, Samuel spent his time looking a bleak immortality in the face, still unable to come to terms with his existence and wishing his iron body would allow him to end it all.

News will travel to even the remotest locations, and a local Fey he discovered on one of his long walks through the forest became his liaison for the occasional book, newspaper or magazine. Paramortal psychology and Gillian were profiled in one of them. Samuel read the article with interest, wondering if this new type of science could possibly help him. He decided he had nothing to lose but his loneliness and sadness, so he contacted the IPPA, asking about their star therapist.

Gillian knew his history, knew what lay under that hood was horror personified. It wasn't simply his appearance; it was the fact that he was literally made out of reanimated pieces of cadavers. Sewn together like garments, the pieces trapped a feeling, thinking soul inside them. She sensed the horror he felt about himself, and it left her vaguely queasy.

Thankfully, Samuel only wanted treatment for his ongoing

depression and body dysmorphic disorder. No problem there. Gillian called Pavel and another young Werewolf named Radu over since they were in Human form. She asked Radu to escort Samuel to his room to unpack, then back to the great hall for an introductory group session. The two of them ambled off slowly. Samuel making large strides but obviously in great pain.

Next out of the back of the van was another tall misshapen figure. This one was as tall as Samuel but with much less bulk. Again the cloak covered the face but the entire cloth seemed pulled and stretched over the outlandish shape underneath.

"This is Tuuli, Dr. Key," Helmut informed her.

This file was unusual. Tuuli was a female Sidhe of the Twilight Court but had been subjected to hostile magic and had been under a polymorph spell for the past several hundred years. Gillian knew some magic, every Paramortal shrink worth their credentials did, but it was only enough to briefly defend herself, help her with contacting reluctant ghosts and keep her from getting herself abruptly killed in a few predictable situations.

She told Helmut that she didn't know how she could help this poor creature, other than to try to come to terms with her altered shape. He had assured her that Tuuli was only there for the same reason as Samuel: to have her depression treated. Well, that, Gill could do.

"Welcome, Tuuli, I am looking forward to our sessions together," Gillian said warmly, again extending her hand. A huge, misshapen limb extended slowly. It looked a lot like a hoof. A very familiar hoof. Gill's empathy sparked and she knew. With the hoof came a scent that Pavel recognized. The great body swayed as Tuuli nodded, still unable to speak. She honked once, sadly.

"Moose?!" Gillian and Pavel said together. The hooded creature honked an affirmative again.

"She continued contact with Daed after you left Russia, Gillian. Through a process of hit and miss in translation, they finally figured out that she wanted to work with you. Daed called me and arranged her to be in this group," Helmut said in explanation.

"Thanks, Helmut. I am looking forward to working with Moo . . . er . . . Tuuli." Gillian patted the cloaked figure in an area she hoped was its shoulder. "Go with Pavel now, please, and I will see you shortly." The huge being ambled off with Pavel, who used his paranormal people skills to brag about Gillian and the area.

Finally, the last figure in the van moved. Gillian glanced at Helmut, who smiled at her, then devoted his attention to whoever was coming out. Black knee-length military-style boots adorned the long, long, masculine legs stepping from the van. He was clothed in a perfectly tailored, retro-fitted black suit. His vest was heavily embroidered with scarlet thread and hung open against a gleaming white linen, ruffled poet-style shirt.

The shirt itself was open at the neck, exposing a strongly columned throat and the upper part of what had to be a fabulous chest if the glimpse of it was any indication. A full-length black cape settled over the broad but lean shoulders and completed his silhouette somehow. This figure wasn't hooded, but he had his face down and away as he unfolded from the van, and she couldn't quite make him out in the growing darkness.

"Dr. Gillian Key, may I present Erik Perrin Talbot Garnier. He prefers to be known as 'Perrin Garnier' and addressed as 'Perrin,'" Helmut said formally, giving Gillian a look that said this was the patient he wanted her to pay particular attention to.

The notes in his file said that this man had seen an article about her in a *Paramortal Psychology Today* magazine, which he had picked up at a coffee shop in Rouen, France. He too had contacted the IPPA and requested her personally.

She looked. Hard. As the man straightened to stand next to them, she caught her breath, empathy kicking in, screaming at her to comfort him. Six feet three inches of devastatingly gorgeous, spectacularly handsome male stood in front of her. Well, the left half of his face was anyway. Part of the other half was covered with a molded white leather mask from his forehead to below his cheekbone, with a line directly down the middle of his perfect nose, ending above his upper lip and back across his cheek to his ear.

The mouth was full, sensual and very male. His hair was a thick midnight black, slightly wavy, cut in layers, combed in waves so that it framed his face in inky whorls, falling over his collar all the way round; tousled but elegant. Perfect black sideburns added to the natural line of his strong jaw; the single visible ebony winged eyebrow lending perfect definition to his sculpted face.

From what she could tell in the fading light, his eyes were an unusual gray green. His skin was alabaster, as if he rarely saw the sun. Even with the distracting mask, he was easily one of the most noble-looking, elegant, purely beautiful males she'd ever seen.

"Hello, Perrin. I'm Gillian." She slowly offered her hand, her eyes never leaving his face.

Surprise lit his eyes as he looked at her proffered hand. Slowly, gracefully, elegantly, he extended his own black leather–encased hand and gently took hers in a tentative grasp. He bowed formally to her, breaking her gaze, then looked up but not quite at her face. "Thank you, Dr. Key. I appreciate you and Dr. Gerhardt allowing me to come."

His voice was deep, sensual, nearly melodic in its quality, with a light French accent overlaid with almost musical tones. He had mixed blood, she was sure. He was registering very oddly on her empathy as if there was something inherently magical leaking from him. No pure Human spoke like that and no pure Human ever looked like that.

Curiouser and curiouser, Alice, Gillian thought to herself. Helmut didn't have a completed file on Perrin, just the basics of how and why he had contacted the IPPA. He wanted her to do the full intake on this man herself. This was her sex therapy patient. *Why would a man who looked like* that *need a sex therapist?* she wondered.

As if reading her mind, Helmut interrupted her thoughts and she realized she'd been staring at Perrin. Oops, but damn the man was attractive, almost mesmerizing.

"Gillian, Perrin . . . Well, I'll let you explain everything to him. If you don't mind, I'll just go inside, get things straightened out with Count Rachlav and find my room while you show Perrin where he will be staying."

"Sure, Helmut. I'll talk to you later." Turning back to her new patient, she smiled and gestured toward the guesthouse. The Wolves would bring everyone's baggage to the rightful owner so she could focus on this new patient.

"We are glad to have you with us, Perrin, and please call me Gillian." She smiled as she walked, going slowly, almost as if she were having to coax him to follow her. He followed hesitantly, but he did follow.

"One moment," she said, holding up a hand to stop him. "Helmut! I thought there was one more!" she called.

"There was. We dropped him off at the Inn! He said he preferred privacy so he'll wait until you can go to him!" Helmut yelled back.

The other file, on this last patient, wasn't put together either. All she knew was what Helmut had told her: that he was an expatriate Romanian Vampire who had fangxiety issues coupled with paranoia. That was almost certainly why he had elected to stay at the Inn rather than the castle. Aleksei or Tanis would probably know him and he wanted to remain anonymous to them. She'd have to do his intake as well and keep the private counseling at the Inn. It would have to wait till later—she wanted to get Perrin settled, spend some time with him, then get the welcoming group going tonight.

She turned back and gestured to Perrin, who had frozen at her command and was watching her closely. He followed her, cape fluttering gently, almost docilely, as if he were afraid to make any wrong moves and risk her disapproval. Her empathy was giving her fits, though they were several feet from each other. The level of emotional pain that was radiating from him was overwhelming, and she had to tone her own network of senses down or she'd wrap him in her arms on the path and rock him like a child. That would be awkward for them both.

Happily the guesthouse was just ahead and she still had her key. She opened the door, slapped on the light and moved aside so Perrin could enter before her. He stopped at the door, frozen again.

"Perrin? You can go inside. This is where you'll be staying and where we will have our sessions together."

Those remarkable eyes looked at her tentatively. "Thank you . . . Gillian." Good, he'd tried out her name.

"Come on." She smiled and walked in. He followed, hesitating long enough for her to hand him the key, then continued into the house.

She shut the door and turned back. "If you want to get settled, I can come back later, or if you prefer, we can start with me getting your background information and then move into our first session together. It's your choice, I don't want to pressure you, your first night here."

Perrin had moved all the way into the room and stood with his back toward her. The tension in the carriage of his shoulders was obvious. The man, or whatever he was, was terrified and trying to be calm and polite. Her empathy was on overload as she began to be swamped with his emotional pain. She needed to get out of there for a few minutes, but she'd given him his choice and would grit her teeth and stick it out if he wished it.

To her horror, she realized that his broad shoulders were beginning to shake. He was crying softly. What the hell? Her feet moved of their own accord and she found herself behind him, not sure how she'd gotten there but her hand pressed against his back, the other going to clasp his arm.

"Perrin? What's the matter?"

"Please," he managed in an agonized voice. "This may have been a mistake. I am afraid my true appearance will disgust you, mademoiselle." Shaking his head, he moved away from her, drawing his cape closer around him. He turned just enough so that she could see the flawless, uncovered side of his face.

Shit. This was going to be tough already. Either he was thinking they were going to start off by jumping each other's bones or he was worried about removing his mask.

"Perrin, you do not disgust me. Let me assure you of that right now."

She moved parallel to him, so that the distance between them remained the same but she could see both sides of his face. "I don't know if you understand how this works so please let me explain. Nothing is going to happen of a sexual nature tonight."

Her smile lit up her face and she focused warmth, calm and acceptance in his direction, hoping like hell that her instincts were correct, that he was sensitive enough to respond to her. "Perrin, this is just a getting to know each other session, all right? I'm not going to ask you to remove your mask, nor will I push you further or faster than you want to."

She took a tentative step closer to him, using his name over and over in a familiarization tactic to help him become acclimated and comfortable with her. He stiffened but didn't move away. Encouraged, she moved closer still. "Please come and sit down, and we'll just talk. This is just time to let you get comfortable with me and vice versa. I won't even touch you without your permission if it makes you uncomfortable."

Seeing him watching her warily, she moved from her spot to the large couch that was now in the room. Aleksei had had the guesthouse redecorated at some point since she'd arrived in Romania, and now it had a lighter feel to it. The overstuffed couch and chairs had light coral- and peach-toned fabric coverings, the dark paneling had been painted a soothing periwinkle blue, the moldings and framing were painted white; the entire place had a more country look and feel.

Gillian sat on one end of the couch, drawing her legs up under her and settling down in a casual position. Perrin watched every move she made. Finally when she was settled, he took the long way around the couch and stood for a moment as if to decide to sit near her or in one of the huge chairs. She waited, wanting him to make his own choice.

After an awkward silence, he moved to the other end of the

couch. With the theatrical flair born of long practice, he removed his cape and tossed it over one of the chairs, then sat on the couch, gracefully crossing then uncrossing his legs. Finally he sat stiffly, both feet on the floor, hands folded in his lap, gloves still on. He looked utterly miserable, so very out of place in even this dimmest of twilight before the stars shone.

Gillian realized he had the mask side toward her and asked, "Would you prefer if we switched sides? You seem uneasy with me on the side where you are masked."

He turned his head toward her without meeting her eyes. "I am sorry. I do not mean to make you ill at ease with my disturbing appearance. You are so lovely, and I do not know why you would give consent to help me." His voice was so musical and rich but so soft and sad it twisted her heart.

"You have nothing to apologize for, Perrin. I was staring at you and I am sorry if I have embarrassed you. It's just that you are such a remarkably attractive man, I have to look at you."

She meant it and let it show on her face, let him feel it from her. He lifted his gaze and saw that her smile reached her eyes; that she did not find him repulsive filled him with amazement.

Gillian saw it. The instant adoration that slid behind his eyes. She felt it. His entire aura shifted. Terror and fear of her rejection were rapidly being replaced by waves of desire and need. Pure sex magic. It was a living thing in the room with them, as though he'd flipped a switch, covering her, filling her. It should have overwhelmed her; he could have used it as a device to overpower her and blind her to his intentions, but he didn't. He continued to sit opposite her on the couch and stare with adoring eyes, still as a statue.

The level of power was something that he could manipulate, she knew instinctively. Perrin was now fully aroused by her: hard, hot, pulsing, aching-for-release aroused. He could have had her at that very moment, because she'd never been more ready for sex in her life. He could have, but he didn't. That was a conscious choice. Points for Perrin. He kept turning the metaphysical dial down until it was more comfortable for them both.

Yes, Perrin sat perfectly still, watching her; a tall elegant compelling male, with pure sexuality to rival a Vampire's. It radiated from him like the deep thrumming of a nuclear reactor—contained, controlled but dangerous as hell. Why he didn't have females throwing themselves at his feet while ripping their clothes off, Gillian couldn't say. All she knew was that if he crooked his finger at her right now, she would tear off their clothes and fuck his brains out on the couch. That was bad. Very bad.

Therapy. This was supposed to be therapy.

Right.

Focus, Gillian.

Dear, sweet, timid, inhibited Perrin was about one lapsed ethical moment away from being a sexual predator. Gillian found herself fighting down panic against his power. He hadn't done a damn thing, and she was wet and hot, palms sweaty, breasts aching for the touch of his hand, breathing rapidly, and seconds away from orgasm.

She slammed her own barriers home and tried to focus on "what" he was. Mind racing, she clicked off the possibilities while she tried to slow her body's response to him. The level of inherent sexual magic was actually deeper than a Vampire's, more on the same level as a natural satyr . . . or part and parcel of Fey glamour.

Dammit. She knew.

"You're part Sidhe, aren't you?"

He said softly, *"Oui."*

Gillian's eyebrow rose. That wasn't the whole truth; she felt him shrink back from her empathy's probing. "What else, Perrin? That's not all you are."

"Non." The word was whispered but she felt the shift again. Utter and absolute loathing washed over him. He hated himself with a passion. The overwhelming sensual sensation was instantly gone, replaced by a cold, tight feeling of revulsion.

"I need your honesty if you want me to help you. I have to be accurate in my perception and diagnosis, Perrin. Please tell me what I need to know to help you."

She didn't move. Didn't lean toward him or touch him to comfort him. Right now, she was busy instinctively erecting her own shields and barriers for him in particular and couldn't afford the added distraction. He would have to suffer for a moment until she got herself under control.

Gillian was an empath in every sense of the word. Sensing her patients' needs and fears, their truth and lies, was an inherent gift. Touching of any kind brought a new level to it. She could calm fears, induce a desire to improve, enhance sensuality or sex, even perform some minor light spiritual healing. Right now, she was too open to him and couldn't afford physical contact for both their sakes. His ability had surprised her and she didn't like being surprised. It wasn't good for either him or her.

Touching him would be very bad right now for both of them. Gillian had no doubt they would have fallen on each other like starving beasts. She wanted to help him; this was just a new and uncharted area of Sex Therapist 101. *Shit, shit and double shit*.

Perrin turned from her and rose, walking toward the now open kitchen area of the house. The way he moved was elegant, poised; he drew the eye to him. He was six feet three inches tall, but his frame, though powerfully built, was lean and stylish: broad shoulders, lean waist, tight, sculpted butt and long, muscular legs. He moved with the refined poise of a dancer, masculine and predatory. He was compelling to watch.

"My parentage is mixed, as you have presumed, Dr. Key." He took a single rose from the vase of flowers that sat on the small dining table and turned back to her. "My mother was half Human and half Sidhe or Fey as some call them. I do not know from what Court, only what I was told, much later . . ." His voice trailed off and he looked lost.

"Go on, Perrin, and please call me Gillian."

"My mother was in Paris, with a troupe of performers who were all of mixed blood. She was a singer, a music Fairy, and was known for the delight she brought to the Humans who came to hear her sing." He touched the petals of the rose delicately with his gloved hand. "She had been warned to stay away from Notre Dame. Gargoyles reside there, you see. There were rumors of a particular Gargoyle who preferred females of Faerie as his prey."

Even with the mask, Gillian could see the pain that flashed across his face. She waited until he collected his feelings. "One night, the story goes, she was carried off by some revelers and taken to the cathedral area. She managed to escape and was trying to make her way back to her troupe when she was set upon by the Gargoyle." Perrin lifted his eyes to hers. "I am the result of that pairing."

That certainly explained a lot of things, Gillian thought. The Fey glamour was what was naturally pouring out of him. The Gargoyle blood . . . Well, that could do a lot of things besides cause a physical deformity. Gargoyles were generally hideously ugly but had their own glamour they could use on unwilling partners: making them believe they were being courted by a creature of great beauty. They were also renowned for their vicious and exhaustive sexual appetites. A sadistic, oversexed stone creature who could become literally rock-hard flesh and had no morals to speak of . . . that getting hold of anyone wasn't a comforting thought.

"Your mother was raped, Perrin. That isn't her fault or yours." Gillian rose and went to him, unable to bear his pain for another moment.

"She didn't want me. Not with *this*." He gestured toward his masked face, his voice low, angry and brimming with eons of anguish. "She abandoned me, to another troupe of gypsy players. Only they were nowhere near as genteel as the group she performed with. They put me on display . . . a performance freak who did magic tricks and who could sing . . . even with this face. I helped make them wealthy . . . They fed me, clothed me, made me sleep among the beasts."

Gray green eyes turned toward her. "In over a hundred and fifty years, I have only experienced the gentle touch of another on three occasions, Gillian." He tried out her name again. "I was rejected by my mother at birth, raised like an animal in a sideshow until a sympathetic soul rescued me and led me beneath the streets of Paris, into the catacombs. No one wanted me. Not my mother, not her people, not anyone!"

The magical voice was harsh with unshed tears as he turned away again. She was afraid he would stop talking but wondered if they should take a break from the enormity of emotions that were pouring from him.

"Perrin, if you would like to continue this later . . ." she began, but he waved her off.

"No, I would like to continue. It is the first time I have told this story to anyone." He turned slightly back and looked at her from the corner of his unmasked eye, imploring her. "I feel safe with you, Gillian, I want you to know my story. Perhaps there is a chance you can help me."

She knew why he felt safe—she was bombarding him with comfort and warmth—but the level of pain he had was still off the scale. "Come and sit with me, please. I want to hear it if you want to tell it." Holding out her hand, she waited.

Slowly he took her hand and she led him back to the couch, sitting closer to him than she had before, and she didn't let go of his hand. She was also trying to put his story together— there was something familiar about it and it was kicking at her to understand. Something obvious. Something she *should* know.

"My rescuer was a young woman, who couldn't bear to see even a young disfigured man tormented," he continued. "Out of the thousands of people who jeered and mocked me, only one took pity. She helped me creep away one night into the darkness with her own cloak over my head. I couldn't see so I had to trust her. Finally she stopped and we were before a grate which led to the underground of Paris. After the fall of the Bastille, there had been a prison built down there, but it had fallen into disuse.

"Networks of tunnels, caves, canals run under the City even to this day. She opened the grate, gave me her own key to it and said that she would return to bring me food and supplies. I spent the first quiet night of my life in utter terror that someone might have seen where she'd led me, but no one came. The next day I began to explore, but returned every evening to the original grate to wait for her to bring me supplies, conversation, just a brief moment of companionship.

"Her family had money and supported the arts, so she brought me things she thought would help me pass the time. Drawing pencils, paper, books she gave to me, freely and happily. I fashioned a mask, out of her cloak, determined never to let her see my face again, not wanting to frighten my benefactor. Then one day on one of my searching expeditions, I heard sounds. Beautiful sounds echoing through my dank prison. I made my way toward them and came upon a lake deep beneath the surface of the streets. It was a large chamber and the acoustics amplified the noise."

Gillian watched as Perrin's face reflected his remembered joy of the moment. He was truly beautiful. She hoped she could help him see it. Alarm bells were clanging in her head . . . a lake, deep beneath the streets of Paris . . . music . . . a lonely disfigured genius . . .

"There was singing. It was the opening of the season for the theatre and they were beginning rehearsal."

Gill gasped as her memory clicked and she knew. If she was correct . . .

"Odin's hells, Perrin, *you're* the actual Phantom of the—" Gillian blurted out, but he interrupted her.

"*Oui*, but I do not want to be him anymore. I do not want to be a legend, a shade, a shadow; thought of as a vengeful ghost. I want to feel the sunlight on my unmasked face. I want to live as a man, not as a creature."

He finished, looking straight at her for the first time. "I lost more than one love to this face and to my social ineptitude. I do not want to live my entire life alone. I would rather die. If this therapy with you does not work, I shall not continue in this existence."

Oh, swell. He was potentially suicidal too. This just kept getting better and better.

CHAPTER

4

ONCE breached, the dam Perrin had built up for his own sanity gave way and he told Gillian everything. He had rather liked the idea of being the Opera Ghost at first. "Haunting" the theatre had given him a sense of purpose, of entitlement. With his extended lifespan, he was easily able to foster his own legend with the players and management staff.

Fear and intimidation were only part of his arsenal. However, he assured her, he had never murdered or harmed anyone, despite what some might say. Displaying an unstable temperament, dire threats and promises of retribution were all smoke and mirrors, like the medium of the theatre or opera itself. He loved the opera, loved to sing, to play his own music and the music of the masters . . . demanded discipline and perfection from the staff and players, just as he required it of himself.

Gillian was impressed as hell that he seemed to be reasonably sane, despite his hang-ups and loneliness. The fact that, despite his unlikely abilities, his obvious intellect, his treatment as a child and his isolation, he had not actually become a killer or an opportunistic rapist was astonishing. He had managed to develop a sense of right and wrong. He had morals, he was ethical. He might have been a predator, but he wasn't.

Overseeing the opera house behind the scenes was also

the only control he had in his life. He felt lonely and guilty for being what he considered a visual aberration, but was desperate for genuine contact with anyone.

Perrin was blessed with perfect pitch, a glorious voice of his own, which he could never share with anyone, and was nearly frantic for companionship. A discarded pipe organ, discovered in an abandoned church, was retrieved so he could amuse himself by playing the songs he heard. He secreted it away beside his lake and built his own little kingdom, learning to play, mastering the classics he heard from above.

Soon, he began to compose his own scores, self-teaching orchestration, stealing sheets of music to learn what the black dots and lines on the barred paper meant. Then with almost obsessive observation, he studied the workings of the backstage of the theatre from the fly-walks and catwalks. He learned how they created their special effects, made their magic, created the delightful world of lights, scenery and music that was to become the only world he knew. The only society that he would ever see.

Perrin's intellect was genius level, but he didn't know it. He assumed that everyone was on par with his own intelligence, could instantly understand things as he did. He loved music, architecture, literature. They were vehicles to finally express all the secret longings of his heart, beautifully, poignantly, safely.

One night, a young, lovely chorus singer caught his attention with her merry tune as she swept the stage after a rehearsal. Her voice was beautiful but untrained, and as an unseen voice in the darkness, using his own legend at first, he'd taken her under his wing, coaching her in her singing. His original benefactor turned up as the Ballet Mistress for the theatre and they too continued their tenuous friendship though they had little further direct contact.

His protégée was a sweet, docile little thing who would have been on the street had she not had such a compelling voice. Trusting and naive, she listened to his whispered words of encouragement, allowing him to direct her voice and her life. Finally able to control something instead of being controlled, Perrin was a strict taskmaster. He demanded her obedience to his schedule and his teaching methods.

The girl wanted to be recognized, wanted to break out of the chorus and become a diva. She loved music too. It was a method to ease her own pain. In her own way, she was as dark and troubled as Perrin. Orphaned young, she had been sent to live with a succession of relatives who abused her. Finally she was taken in by the very woman—now the Ballet Mistress—who had rescued Perrin years before, and she was brought to the opera as a dancer and singer for the chorus.

In the late eighteen hundreds in Paris, physical beauty was honored, almost worshipped. There was a moment of terrible miscalculation on Perrin's part when he thought that she might be mature enough to love him as he was.

The girl had begged him for a glimpse of her teacher. Perrin taught her from his secluded alcoves beneath, around and above the opera. He had never allowed her to see him, fearing her reaction, even with his mask. When she was chosen for a lead role, finally, it was a triumph for them both, and led to his second great tragedy. The young woman wanted to see him, to know him. Perrin refused over and over, leaving her in tears, hurt and bewildered.

But she was persistent, and finally Perrin agreed but not before fashioning several masks to hide the upper-right side of his face. He had taken her with him to his home. Half frightened and half excited, she'd gone willingly with her brilliant master. He kept his masked side turned away from her so that all she saw was the remarkable beauty of his left profile.

The dank room with the enormous lake was lit entirely by scores of candles held in sconces and candelabras that had been thrown away by the theatre. He'd furnished it with discarded furniture, mirrors; built bookshelves, a pipe organ and a private lavatory with his architectural skill and perfect pitch. The lair looked like a magical realm to her innocent eyes; Perrin, like a romantic hero she'd read about and seen portrayed on stage, masked, mysterious, exciting.

He sang to her a song he'd written, pouring his soul into

the piece and watching the wonderment cross her features. The mask he wore only added romance and mystery to her youthful infatuation. Impishly, she had looked around his home, finding the great bed he'd erected behind filmy draperies. Everything he owned, wore, slept on or used was from the opera or his own hands. The whole lot had an unearthly, theatrical, supernatural quality. She teased him, stretching out on his bed, arms open, beckoning with a smile of delight on her face.

Perrin went to her, allowed her to draw him down to kiss him. It was her first kiss, and his. Her small hands moved over his chest, down to his waist and below; she had gasped in shock as he stopped her roughly, astonished by her behavior. All he knew of love and life was from the opera. A young lady did not try to seduce a man. No play he'd seen was ever written that way.

He knew she was innocent, as virgin as he was, though she was eighteen and he closer to thirty. If he made love with her, he wanted it to be perfect, romantic and after they were properly married.

Puzzled, she had tried again, wanting to gift him for all that he had given her with the only thing she could pay him with: herself. He wasn't having it. Perrin was a monster in appearance, but he was honorable even after all he had suffered, because of what he'd learned from the heroes of the theatre. He had inborn powers to seduce and deceive; he knew that instinctively.

He could have lain with her, taken her innocence, but he didn't though she offered it freely. Perrin did nothing but hold her hands away from his body and scold her for her brazen behavior. He loved her. To use her body, then send her back into the light where he could not follow was something he would not do to his angel, though she begged him to take her.

Sadly he had turned away, held out his hand to take her back to the dormitory where she lived. Furious with his rejection and embarrassed by her own actions, she had ripped the mask from his face, exposing the horror beneath. Screaming, she backed away and fainted. Perrin, in shock and humiliated, replaced his mask, then carried her back to her safe little room, leaving her untouched and as innocent as she had been.

He never tried to see her again, nor taught her another note; he ignored her pleas to come back to her and turned away from her voice as the pleas became threats. Lost in misery, he retreated into the darkness of his lair; to the myriad of tunnels beneath Paris, unwittingly perpetuating his own myth of being a ghost. He traveled for a while, under the cover of darkness, revisiting some of the towns and cities he had performed in when with the gypsy troupe. Always separate, always alone; he read, wrote his music, worked on his own structural designs to improve the acoustics of the opera house.

Years passed before Perrin returned to his subterranean home. Soon after, he found a new protégée to focus his attention on. It was another aspiring young singer whose soaring soprano tore through his soul with its beauty. Determined that things go well this time, he judiciously avoided all personal contact with her for several years. He remained a disembodied voice, instructing her in music, guiding her vocal talent, allowing and encouraging her belief that he was truly an angel or ghost who was protecting and teaching her. Despite her gentle requests to meet, Perrin refused to allow a meeting. Better an esoteric love than none at all.

He finally caved when he followed her one snowy afternoon to a cemetery outside Paris, where she went to visit her father's grave. It had become his habit to follow her whenever she went out alone, a watchful eye in the stillness. No family members ever came to see her. He assumed she was alone in the world, and he could not bear the thought of harm coming to her. Silent, unseen, he had always stayed far enough away so that she had only glimpses of him. Rather than being alarmed, she was warmed to think that her brilliant teacher thought so well of her as to follow her into the streets of the city to assure her safety.

On that day, feeling lonelier than usual, she decided she wanted to know him and for him to know her. Pretending to fall on the icy steps of the tomb in a hastily thought out plan, she cried out for help, and he had come to her—a black-cloaked figure, tall and elegant—to offer his gloved hand and steady her as she rose.

Stabilizing herself on his arms, she asked gently if he would remove the hood of his cape so that she might see the face of her teacher. It had been a revelation to him that she had found him out when he had been so careful. When she asked again, he pushed back the hood with shaking hands so that she might see what he was.

Revealing himself to her by the mausoleum, he was over-come by her gratitude and sweetness as she curtsied before him, kissing his leather-encased hands with glad tears in her eyes. She wanted the mask off too, to see the true face of her teacher and benefactor.

Terrified, trembling and ashamed, Perrin stood stock still, unable to do anything but let her peel it slowly back, braced for the screams that he knew would come. Predictably, she was rather shaken at first to see such hideousness, but she didn't scream. The knowledge that this was still her teacher, still the man she respected and admired, still the man who watched over her like a guardian angel, slid into her warm eyes and she smiled. Perrin had expected utter rejection. When instead, standing on tiptoe, she took his face in her small hands and kissed him on his disfigured cheek, then fully on the mouth, he was undone.

They had kissed in the snow, in the shadow of her father's tomb. Her acceptance of him as he was, was a healing balm to his broken spirit. Walking back to the theatre together, his mask placed back on his face by her dainty hands, he felt like a man for the first time, instead of a creature. She proudly took his arm, insisting he leave off at least the cowl, and smiled pleasantly at the passersby who had the gall to stare at her escort.

It turned out she was from a wealthy family and had been raised in a rather bohemian household for the time. Her family remained liberal nonconformists, even after her father's death, and encouraged her independent, charitable spirit.

They honed her idealistic beliefs of everyone being equal, that everyone was entitled to love and acceptance no matter what their social standing, that people should not be judged on how they appeared. They also never dreamed that she might actually act on their teachings.

Several weeks later, at her insistence, he agreed to meet her family. Perrin was firm in his principles that they would not make love or live together until they were married; so married they would be, she decided.

The hope and altruistic nature of youth are unparalleled. Believing her progressive family would accept her brilliant mentor as a suitor no matter what he looked like on the outside, she asked him home. Having been raised to be kind and accepting to everyone, especially the less fortunate or those less than attractive, she honestly believed in her family's benevolent teachings. It was to be the affirming conclusion of the family meal when she reached up, casually peeling away his mask at the dinner table as proof to Perrin of their acceptance of him as a suitor. If her family had truly practiced what they preached, the two of them might have had a joyous life together.

She was not prepared for what came next, but while not prepared, he was very familiar with her family's response. The immediate, utter horror of her mother, uncle and grandfather, the rage of her brother, was swiftly directed at him and a complete shock to her. He blundered from his seat at the table, cowering against the wall.

Creature. Monster. Beast. Inhuman. Those were the kinder things they said before they chased him from the house, his little soprano sobbing and clinging to him in desperation until they pulled her away. He was literally thrown into the street, after they flung his mask into it first, and the door slammed in his face. He was not to contact her again and to forget he had ever known her. She would not be back to the theatre.

Fearing that their headstrong, radical girl would defy them in their demand never to see this "thing" again, her family had packed her up that night and sent her away to live with relatives in Italy. There, she soon contracted pneumonia and died despite the efforts of the best doctors the family could afford. Some said she died of a broken heart more than of the illness since she was forbidden to sing or to contact her former teacher and true love.

When she did not return to the theatre for several weeks, he had made inquiries. Getting no answer, Perrin had finally summoned his courage and gone to their home again in the dead of night, demanding to know where she was. Grieving, her family didn't care anymore that he might know. She was beyond his reach—that was all that mattered—so they cruelly told him the news of her death and lay the blame at his feet. If he had never been in her life, she would have still been alive.

He stumbled back through the darkened streets of Paris, his own heart broken, hope shattered. He had gone away then, taken himself deeper beneath the streets to avoid all contact; into the sewers, hiding from all things which reminded him of that night. Soon, he left Paris, making a home for himself on a secluded estate in Rouen, which he purchased with the money he'd made being the Opera's resident Ghost.

Eventually he returned to his home by the lake when he thought he could face the pain again, and at the opera manager's urging. The Phantom added a mystique to the palatial building; he was a popular draw for the patrons and they wanted him back in his trademark box for performances. His time remained divided between his lair and his estate in the off season of the opera. Perrin was financially very well off; he had all the material things he could possibly need. The only things missing from his life were acceptance and love.

On one of his forays in Paris to the surface streets for supplies, he found a discarded end table set out as trash and brought it down to his home. As he cleaned it up, he opened the top drawer and found a book titled *The Phantom of the Opera*, by Gaston Leroux.

Intrigued, he had read it and was appalled to find that it was about him. It was a story about him and his original angel, the first girl he had tutored. She must have sought out the author and had him pen the story. Most of it was completely false and portrayed him as an aged, shabby, skeletal recluse, an egocentric, murdering monster.

Perrin was beyond despair. The wench had betrayed him, after all he had given her, done for her, after he had left her alone and not taken advantage of her. It nearly destroyed him, this news coming on the heels of his beloved's death. He resolved never again to have contact with another being.

But alas, the life of a mixed blood Gargoyle-Sidhe-Human is long, though he daily prayed for death. Living as he did, completely isolated from the world and its influences, Perrin had no teacher himself. No one told him how to get through a day he didn't control. No one had ever heard him, listened to him, wanted what he had to share, but his two angels. He had reveled in the power and authority he was able to wield as he taught them; enjoyed the level of his influence the way he enjoyed the complete control he had over his own lonely world.

When that control was shattered, the finality of it rocked him so completely that he believed he went mad for a while. There were missing pieces in his memories of the days following the discovery of that book. Reading it, seeing the girl's depiction of him, almost convinced him that he truly was that monster. He played his part of the watchful ghost for the theatre managers well, drawing in more crowds than ever just being the lurking phantom presence with the booming voice when a performance displeased him. Every show where he guaranteed personal attendance was a sellout.

Time eventually will heal even the deepest cut. In due course Perrin found the courage to play, to compose and to sing again, but never again would he allow another being into his life; he never dared to hope that he might be something other than an outcast. It never occurred to him that he might actually ask for help.

He lived surrounded by mirrors that he kept covered up. Once in a while when he could bear it, he would examine his reflection. Always, it was the same. A fit and handsome figure would greet him. Always impeccably dressed, always perfectly correct in its movements. Then he would see his face. Sometimes he looked with the mask on and sometimes he took it off to ply his fingers around the horror. The mirror would once more be covered, and he wouldn't look again for a very long time.

Finally about a year ago, after allowing himself the luxury of a television set at his home in Rouen, he had heard about people like Gillian: therapists who could help Paramortals. People who cared about the life inside the shell, not about the shell itself. After watching news reports about her and her accomplishments, he had seen her picture with Dr. Gerhardt's on the magazine which Jenna had dropped on the table of a coffee shop in Rouen.

The article was about the IPPA and her. It talked about her as one of the pioneers in the field of Paramortal psychology. The reporter mentioned all the advancements and progressions in the science, including sex therapy. Mostly, he remembered it praising her for demystifying psychology for Paramortals and for treating her patients as people, rather than oddities. In other words, he thought she would treat him like a man, rather than a creature.

Finally he had an avenue to pursue. It had been so long since he'd had any hope. At last gaining the courage to come forward, he had entered one of the opera's offices one night and called the IPPA. Fortunately he had gotten transferred to Helmut, who was working late. Helmut, a psychologist himself with years of experience, knew exactly what to do with this broken man he was speaking to, so he made the arrangements to bring Perrin to Gillian.

There was complete silence for several minutes after Perrin finished his tale and sat expectantly, waiting for Gillian's reaction. When he finally turned to look at her, thinking perhaps he had bored her to sleep, he was stunned to see tears on her face.

"Dr. Key? Have I upset you?" he asked anxiously.

Gillian shook her head as if to clear it, then felt the tears on her own face and reached for a tissue to dry it off. "Perrin, I'm sorry, it's just that it was such a moving story. Such a sad story. I am so very sorry that you have had to live with this much pain." She reached out again and he took her hand willingly this time. "I hope you will allow me to help you," she said earnestly.

A slight smile ghosted over his perfect mouth, the sculpted face framed by that perfect hair and sideburns.

"You really are Human, after all. The tears on your face prove your empathy. I could have told my tale to another Sidhe and they would have walked away from this. The Gargoyles would have laughed. But you . . . you have the courage even after what I have said about my true appearance to stay here and ask if you are 'allowed' to help me."

"I want to help you, Perrin," Gillian said, smiling through the tears, which still sparkled in her eyes. "What has to happen is that you let me."

Dalton, Lord of the Light Court, found Gillian sprawled in a chair in the library, swearing at her laptop as she meticulously entered data on a private session, an hour before. "What ails you, my lady?" Dalton said brightly, not really expecting an answer.

Gillian spared him a glare, then went back to typing furiously. "I hate computers. That's what ails me."

He plopped down on the couch near her and peered intently in her direction with eyes that were the lavender of a twilight sky. As he hoped, she looked up. "Can I help you with something, Dalton, or did you just come in to spread Fairy dust and joy around?"

Rich, musical laughter was his response. "You are a delight, little Human. I am glad of this crisis we are all having or I would not have had the opportunity to become acquainted with you."

Blazing green eyes looked at him from over the lid of the laptop. "I can't tell you how much that thrills me," she snapped back in a sarcastic tone.

Hell's bells, couldn't he just shut up? Go play Happy Fun Time Fairy somewhere else? She was trying to focus on Perrin's case. He had disclosed today how he heard about his heritage by cruel accident from a Fey of the Dark Court who had once braved the shadowy halls of the catacombs to meet the Theatre Ghost.

Perrin. Fey. Shit, she was an idiot.

She sat up suddenly, spilling notes on the floor. "Dalton, you're Fey!"

"As am I," purred another silky voice, "but not of the Court of Light."

"Hi, Finian, come in, please, this might be something you both can give me an opinion on."

The purple-haired Prince joined Dalton on the couch. Gillian was momentarily speechless in the presence of two spectacular specimens of Sidhe beauty, then caught herself staring and got back to her train of thought.

"What are the rules and standards for a mixed-blood Fey?" There. That was to the point.

The two Sidhe looked at each other, then back to her. Finian spoke. "I am not sure what you mean, Gillian. Could you explain further?"

"Sure, what I mean is, what happens to mixed-blood babies and children? Are they discarded? Left with their mother? Do you take them into your Courts and raise them? I am not that familiar with Sidhe traditions, and I would like to learn more."

"In truth, it depends on which Court they are born into," Dalton offered cautiously.

Finian snorted inelegantly. "What our Lord of the Light means is, and to answer your question more completely, the Light Court does not often care to gaze on those whose blood is not pure. The Twilight Court and the Dark Court are far more forgiving of one's origins, but even they have a tolerance level."

"You're saying that you're racists?" Gillian asked, rather surprised. She thought the older tribes and magic nations were more progressive than Humans. Maybe not.

"That is exactly what they are saying." Trocar glided in, cape swirling, and deliberately took a seat next to Finian, who nearly blanched but didn't move away.

"The business of the Sidhe Courts does not concern the Grael, Trocar," Dalton admonished the Dark Elf.

Trocar affixed him with an icy stare. Easy, since his eyes were like faceted diamonds, iridescent with every color sparkling in them. "Are you really that stupid, Dalton, or is this an acquired skill?"

Now it was Dalton's turn to blanch. "How dare you, you insufferable assassin!"

"Knock it off, all of you, or get out because I'm busy trying to help a patient and I don't have time for Fairy-versus-Elf Supremacy fights! And Trocar, you're not one to talk about racial snobbery, given what you told me about Grael philosophy on interbreeding when we were in Finland."

Gillian had risen without realizing it and faced the three breathtaking males, clearly angry. "If you can't or don't want to contribute helpful dialogue to the conversation, then fuck off and I'll find it on the Internet."

Finian and Dalton stared at her as if she'd grown two heads—not that she gave a shit. They weren't clients; they were there because of the treaty and because they liked being there. She didn't owe either of them a damn thing. Trocar had the decency not to smirk . . . much. He stretched out his long, booted legs and slumped down in the couch, eyes closed, like a lethal, elegant poster boy for Elven *GQ* Casual.

Gillian straightened her shirt and started to sit back down, happy to have made her point, when Moose came in, escorted by Pavel. Trocar half opened an eye, then went back to resting. The two Sidhe, in contrast, bolted up and started out the door without a word. Moose and Pavel came around to take the seats they had vacated. The misshapen creature balanced precariously on the edge of the couch next to the beautiful Grael.

"What the hell was that?" Gillian said indignantly after the retreating backs of the Fey Lords.

"Sidhe prejudice in action, Gillyflower," Trocar mumbled.

"Because of what? Moose? Pavel? Er . . . sorry, Tuuli." It was hard to think of the creature sitting in front of her as a lovely Sidhe maiden.

"Yes, Gillian," Pavel said, disdain dripping from his voice, "a Wolf and a Moose are only animals to them. They do not look at us as Human or Sidhe."

"Well, fuck both of them. I'm glad you guys are here."

To her surprise, Trocar shifted, sitting upright, and turned to look directly at Moose. "As am I. It is good to have you here, Tuuli. My people have no such prejudices about one's outward appearance or what they shift into. Nor do we stigmatize anyone's heritage unless that being carries a portion of Grael blood. Only then is it a travesty of nature. Gillian is a master, she will help you through this, as will I if I can."

He rose fluidly and looked at Pavel, "Come, Wolf, I am not so particular about my hunting partners, and we need fresh game to feed this lot." He headed out the door in a swirl of cape, with Pavel tagging along behind him, smiling at the courtesy extended by a Dark Elf. Gillian was amazed. Kindness from Trocar, the king of the elegant insult? Who knew?

Moose sat, looking forlorn. Gillian got up and shut the library doors so they wouldn't be disturbed. She'd already had a few sessions with Moose . . . Tuuli. Dammit! It was slow and ponderous going due to her not being able to speak properly or write, but they were getting somewhere.

"We left off with you telling me about the curse," Gill started.

The creature nodded its heavy head. She wished she could speak or at least write. Gillian was tirelessly patient with her and her inability to communicate properly. Tuuli felt bad. She knew Gillian's quick mind would have understood everything by now had she been able to verbalize the sequence of events better.

"So, you were cursed because of your vanity?"

Again, the heavy nod.

Gillian muttered about Sidhe bullshit, pulling up some website links from IPPA's computer. "It says here that a Sidhe curse can either be inherited or cast on someone. Let's take this one at a time: Is your curse an inherited one that affects specific individuals in your family?"

Moose shook her head negatively. One down.

"Then you were the victim of hostile magic? A curse was placed on you and you alone?"

Affirmative nod.

"See? Now we're getting somewhere," Gillian said brightly. "Do you know who cursed you?"

Nod again.

"Do you know how it can be lifted?"

Nod and tears.

"Great! Oh, sorry, Tuuli. I mean, we're getting somewhere with this, a little at a time." She leaned forward and squeezed Moose's forelimb, radiating warmth and compassion. The hideous head rose, and the liquid brown eyes had a grateful look in them.

"We will figure it out together. Don't worry," Gillian said softly, wanting this being to know that she was valued and cared about. Leaning forward snapped her laptop shut and she had to reopen the case. Then her papers skidded off her lap again, so she stuck her pen behind her ear and bent to retrieve them, leaning over the computer. The pen slipped out, falling to hit a few keys, making the machine beep annoyingly at her. Gill stared at it for a moment, then looked up at Tuuli with a big grin. "Can you hold an item in your mouth?"

Moose nodded.

"Can you write in English?"

Nope.

"Russian?"

Still nope.

Shit.

"How about one of the Sidhe or Elven languages?"

Yes.

Yay!

"Wait right here." Gillian jumped up and hurried off to find an Elf, Fey or both, just in case. As she left the library, Tanis and Aleksei were just coming in from outside. It was early in the evening, so she figured they were returning from feeding. Anyway, she didn't really want to know what Aleksei was doing, nor did she care. He had yet to apologize directly to her.

She'd heard that he was sorry for his insensitive and shitty remark from Tanis but Aleksei had avoided her as much as she had avoided him. Looking at the two brothers brought a wrenching in her heart. The Rachlav family would have been spectacular even if they hadn't been Vampires. The Vampire conversion had only enhanced what they already had.

Aleksei. He was heartrendingly lovely. Six foot seven inches of sculpted muscular perfection. Raven black wavy hair past his shoulders, ice gray eyes, elegant brows and features and that sensual, kissable, perfect mouth.

Goddammit.

Just looking at him made her feel all gooey and tingly. Tanis was no less gorgeous. Black hair, a little longer and straighter than his brother's, golden eyes, six foot six inches of hot Vampire male, shimmering with power. She missed both of them and their easy camaraderie. Tanis was squarely in her corner in the situation they were in, but he didn't want to alienate his brother; Aleksei being a Vampire Lord of a Line, like Osiris and Dionysus. They needed him. Hell, they needed all of them.

Gill stopped in her tracks as they came toward her. Shit, damn, hell, she was trapped. Going back into the library was out; she needed to finish her errand in order to help Moose. Forward was bad because it went straight to Aleksei, who was staring at her, silvery eyes smoldering with some emotion. She didn't want to think about it.

Tanis saved the day. *"Buona sera, piccola sorella."* "Little sister." Good to know some people still thought of her as belonging here.

He moved away from Aleksei and offered Gillian a kiss on the cheek. "How are you? You have been noticeably absent from the library and the gymnasium of late. I take it your patients are doing well?"

"Yes, thanks. I appreciate being able to see them here, instead of traveling all over. Aleksei is very generous to allow it." She didn't look at the Vampire in question, who had halted and was hanging back, away from her and his brother.

"Yes, he is," Tanis agreed, winking at her.

"Would you mind going into the library and waiting with Moose? I'm trying to track down Trocar, Aisling or one of the Fey to translate for her. I have an idea that might get to the bottom of the curse."

Gillian and Helmut had made Aleksei's family castle into a therapeutic residence for Paramortal clientele. Aleksei had agreed instantly. Anything to keep Gillian there, where he could keep an eye on her. He hated the new aspect of her job, but he didn't want to lose her either. Everyone staying had to sign a confidentiality statement, and all the new patients had agreed to sign waivers and releases of information so that any and all possible sources of knowledge, as in Moose's case, could be utilized without a confidentiality breach.

Between Perrin, Samuel and Moose, Gillian's time had been tied up for the past few days. Perrin was making progress, getting used to talking to another living person nightly, getting comfortable with someone looking directly at him. And Moose, well, Moose was a special case that took a lot of time to decipher.

Samuel, the creature created by a proverbial mad scientist, was doing well. He was even venturing out to mingle with the other residents, taking walks to the nearby village and doing a lot of reading of the classics. There was nothing to be done for his appearance, but he wasn't abhorred. Some of the Sluagh had taken an interest in him, as had some of the townsfolk, and he was actually making friends, much to his delighted surprise.

The other client, the mystery Vampire, had been gone from the Inn every time Gillian had gone to meet with him. She had left word each visit that she would arrive about an hour after sunset to give him time to feed but he was still absent. It was beginning to annoy her but Helmut pointed out that he was there on his own nickel, and if he didn't avail himself of her skill and expertise, then it wasn't her fault.

Group therapy had been interesting. Moose and Samuel showed up constantly and were able to bond a little. The Vampire wasn't there, of course, and Perrin was simply too agoraphobic and anthropophobic yet to set foot outside the guesthouse, let alone subject himself to the myriad of beings living at the castle or group therapy. A Sluagh and a Dark Court Sidhe had signed on as clients as well, to Helmut's delight. Word was spreading about the Institute and he was getting phone calls daily, asking about therapeutic availability. Everything was actually going a little too smoothly and Gillian was suspicious that some giant shoe was going to fall out of the sky on all their heads.

"If the young lady will allow it, perhaps I can help with your translation problem."

Gill's head jerked toward the voice. Aleksei was looking at her instead of through her. It wasn't exactly a friendly look but he wasn't being hostile.

"Like how?" she said bluntly, not giving him even a hint of a smile or reminding him that Moose was at least a thousand years older than he was, and he was referring to her as a "young lady."

"Mind-to-mind contact. I might be able to access the source of her knowledge faster and with less stress for her." Aleksei paused a moment and something flickered across the perfect features—pain perhaps? "As I did for you once, if you remember."

He was referring to back when they had first met, almost two years before, and he had shared his knowledge with her quickly and efficiently. Yeah. She remembered. She remembered a lot of things, like them *not* fighting and making love all night. Too bad he'd fucked all that up. Oh well, she had a job to do.

"Let's ask her," Gillian remarked and turned back to the library without waiting for an affirmative. She was relieved when he followed her in and stopped just behind her, in front of the cursed Sidhe.

"Tuuli, this is Aleksei, remember? He owns this castle and is letting us stay here."

The sad eyes blinked and she nodded.

"What Aleksei would like to try, with your permission, is to enter your mind to help bring what you know out to me. It would be faster than you trying to type with a pen in your teeth, then having one of the others translate."

Gillian continued to explain gently. "Tuuli, he will have to touch your face since there is no blood bond between you. Is that all right?"

The pitiful creature looked up at the tall Vampire, measuring him up as a potential threat, then nodded slowly.

"He won't hurt you at all. I promise he is completely trustworthy and you won't feel a thing." Gillian sat closely to Moose, giving Aleksei room to pull a chair over and sit directly in front of them. She wouldn't look directly at him, but focused on Moose, pen and pad in hand to write everything down.

"You understand also that he will have access to *all* of your memories, good and bad. There may be some things you don't want known and he may find those. Is it still all right?"

She nodded again. She understood and they had consent.

Aleksei watched her tending to her patient. The wretched creature was shy and trembling, and he felt a surge of pity for what it was going through. No one would ever love her or want her in this state. She had been alone for over a thousand years, an outcast, unable to even communicate with her own kind. He remembered being alone, before Gillian came into his life. The emptiness. The void with no feeling. Gillian had given him back so much. He felt a twist in his heart. Everything she had given him might now be gone forever, all due to his thoughtless and selfish remarks. He might again be as lonely and unfilled as he once was, and Gillian just might go on with her life without him.

Perhaps that other male, the patient in the guesthouse, had felt the same way. Lonely, forgotten, hated. That one had never even known what real love was; the joy of making love to a partner who was everything to him; of having someone to share everything with. Aleksei forced that thought right out before it fully formed, or at least assigned it to the back of his mind. He'd offered to help here. Not there. Gillian and another male together was not a subject he wanted to acknowledge.

Slowly he reached toward the creature's face. "Just be very still and let me touch you. I will do all the work. You must relax and not fight me when I enter your mind. Do you understand?"

Moose nodded and sighed. She would cooperate.

Strong, elegant hands touched the long, grotesque face and she fell into immediate rapport with the Vampire. Aleksei pushed inward gently. He didn't want to go too fast and frighten her. A probe this deep would hurt her if she fought him. Smoothly he reached into her memories and found the information they were looking for.

"It is a curse put upon her by one of the Court of Light," he said softly, his voice still as magical and beautiful as always. "It will be lifted when she is loved by one lesser than herself and returns that love to its originator."

"What the hell does that mean?" Gillian whispered.

"How should I know?" Aleksei said. "I am only repeating what I have found in her mind. They are ritual words for a ritual curse."

Moose tensed with the voices being spoken somewhat harshly near her and Aleksei backed off as quickly as he dared. She nodded enthusiastically at them both and honked.

"You understood what he said?" Gillian watched her closely. The whole demeanor of the grotesque body had changed. Moose even felt different. She wasn't a whirling maelstrom of misery.

Again came the enthusiastic nod and she rose, waving a hoof at them both before hurrying out of the library and down the hallway, honking to herself. That left Gillian and Aleksei both in the same room with the last person on earth they each wanted to be with.

"Er . . . um . . . thanks, Aleksei. That was very generous of you to offer to help her." There. Polite couldn't hurt. Besides, he really had helped.

"It was nothing. The creature suffers. You had to know how to help her; it was a little enough thing to do for you."

He stood and walked away without another glance in her direction. Gillian might have yelled or thrown something but she didn't. She squelched every negative emotion. She still had a job to do and being a wounded puppy herself was not going to help those who were depending on her. Now at least they had somewhere to go with Moose, and it was time to visit Perrin.

As she walked up to the porch of the guesthouse, she could hear sorrowful music coming from the piano they'd brought in for Perrin to play. Music was all he'd had for so many years that to be without his familiar surroundings and his beloved music was part of his original trauma when he arrived. Gillian had spoken to Tanis, and the Vampire had immediately taken Jenna and Trocar to Brasov to purchase a baby grand for Perrin to use while he stayed there. It would remain in the house after he left, but there was plenty of room for it and it could be used anywhere on the estate.

She knocked on the door softly, shaking off the sad feeling the music was generating in her. Perrin was an agoraphobic and intensely shy. Add to that the post-traumatic stress from his childhood, his alienation from every living thing as an adult, his suicidal ideation from not wanting to live as a circus freak or a vengeful Ghost, his anxiety about being rejected yet again, his desire and fear about sex, and Perrin was a psychologist's dream come true.

Gillian mused about what he might have been like if he'd been raised in a loving environment with people who supported him, didn't judge him. He was intelligent, with a genius-level IQ; he composed soulful, breathtaking music, was as sensitive as anyone could be and was extraordinarily handsome on the undamaged side of his face. Perrin had all the components to be a whole person; he just didn't know how to put them together.

When he answered the door, she was ready with a handshake and a smile. They were moving excruciatingly slowly, but it was exactly what he needed. He was beginning to trust her and believe in her ability to help him climb out of the hell he'd been living in for over a century.

He looked better today, she thought. The mask was firmly in place; she was betting he even slept in it. He was wearing a soft cream-colored linen shirt with a loose, open neckline and a double line of ruffled cloth from the collar to his chest. The shirt had ties down the front but he'd left it open for comfort. Chocolate brown, tight velvet pants molded around his lower body. They were of the style he was used to, the waist high and tight, almost like a dancer's costume. The legs disappeared into a pair of shiny black leather knee-length boots that were so polished that they gleamed. Today his hands were bare for a change. Progress? Too soon to tell. Gillian noticed they were the hands of an artist or a musician—strong, slender, perfectly manicured. He had very nice hands.

Perrin watched her as she breezed past him into the living area and sat down so she could watch if he chose to play the piano or sit near her on the couch. She bewildered him and frightened him a little with her candidness and warmth. With no real, open experience with adult, sexually mature women, he had nothing to compare her to. The girls who were the cause of a great deal of his misery had been young—under the age of twenty-five—and in the tradition of the era, easy to guide and control. Gillian made it clear that this was a professional relationship of equals. He found the concept intriguing and exciting but still daunting.

She watched him as he walked closer after closing the door. It gave him a chance to observe her too. He was taller by over a foot but she radiated strength and presence, not intimidated at all by him or his masked face.

He loved her hair, he thought as he closed the gap between them. Golden as the candelabras in his home beneath the streets, it looked soft as silk though he hadn't yet mustered the courage to touch it. Lovely eyes; shining green and clear, they showed her every emotion freely. Gillian seemed to hide behind nothing. He admired her a great deal.

Curled up on the couch in her modern dress of jeans, boots and a T-shirt, she still looked feminine and lovely. She was his therapist, but the fact that a lovely woman wanted to give him back his masculinity and pride shook him to his foundations.

The hand he had grasped when she came in was strong yet small in his palm. It was the first time he had removed his gloves before her visit, the first time he had let his flesh touch that of another since the last girl, sending an unexpected heat racing through his veins.

Gillian had told him about being a soldier, an officer even. He had been incredulous until she showed him a gunshot scar on her shoulder and a machete scar down her arm. The world had changed above him, but Perrin was still very much a nineteenth-century man. It was hard for him to imagine anyone allowing such a pretty woman to be in any danger. Gillian had made sure he understood that women made their own damn decisions, thank you very much, and she was proud of her choices.

Moving to the piano, he sat, hands poised on the keys. "Do you sing, Gillian?"

She laughed and he ducked his head away. "No, Perrin, I'm not laughing at the question. I'm laughing because yes I do sing, but I also really suck at it."

Rising, she went to stand by him and ventured a hand on his shoulder. Instantly the muscles beneath her palm tightened. Time to share some of her own vulnerability.

"Perrin, I'm just standing here next to you. Please stop behaving as though I were a venomous snake that is going to suddenly bite you."

He turned his head and found her eyes warm and gentle. She was smiling and it took his breath away. The muscles relaxed a bit, but she didn't remove her hand. Abruptly, he began to play and she listened, watching him deftly cover the keys with his artistic hands. The music was beautiful but melancholy. Inexplicably it fostered strong feelings of loss and emptiness within her. Since she didn't recognize the song, she gathered it was his own composition. When it was over, he turned back to her. "I also take requests."

It took her a moment to realize that he'd made a joke and she laughed again. "Okay, hotshot, let's hear . . . Do you know any Beatles songs?"

Perrin shook his head. "No, I am sorry."

"Don't be sorry, we're just examining the possibilities. How about Three Dog Night?"

"Non."

"Shania Twain?"

"Non."

"Madonna?" Now he looked confused, but still shook his head negatively.

"Non."

She named several other groups and songs. Nope, not any of those either.

"Gillian, I can follow you if you can carry a tune." He was smiling when he said it, and she forgave him for being a smart-ass. He didn't have enough practice at it yet, but he showed promise.

"Okay, fine, but remember you asked for it, so if I horrify your perfect-pitch sensibilities, you have only yourself to thank." She hummed a few bars of "Let It Be," which was the only damn song she could think of that she might remember all the words to on short notice, and Perrin picked it right up.

She started to sing, instantly became self-conscious and stumbled over a verse. Laughing at her own ineptitude, she doggedly kept going, mangling lyrics and melody in equal proportions. Allowing him to see her ineptitude would offer him an opportunity to instruct her, level out the playing field as it were. Bolstering his confidence was one of her many tasks with the remarkable masked man.

He didn't know all the bridges between the lyrics, but he did well enough at following her with the tune. She'd bring him some CDs. Yeah. That would help.

When he stopped, she couldn't help herself. "Well, how was that?" she asked, with a gleam in her eye.

Perrin's mouth twitched and he smiled. Really smiled. Gods above, he had spectacular teeth too. It figured.

"That was . . ." he began, "possibly the most awful thing I have ever heard. I am sorry, Gillian, but it was truly terrible. You have pitch and your voice is good, but you need training, badly." The smile vanished as he waited for her reaction, unsure once more.

To his surprise, she cracked up laughing. "I told you I was bad, but did you listen? No. This is your fault that your ears have been assaulted. If you have been retraumatized by this incident, it is completely your fault." She poked him in the shoulder, giggling.

Her laughter was infectious, and he caught the backwash from her humor, powered by her own empathy. A grin split his face, then he chuckled. And finally, for the first time in his entire life, Perrin, the former Ghost of the Opera House, laughed out loud with another living being.

CHAPTER
6

As the giggles subsided, Perrin tentatively reached for her hand and kissed it. Gillian curtsied for him, and winked. "See? That was easy, wasn't it?"

"*Non*. It was easy for you. You merely brought me along into your fun and your humor."

Perrin took her hand in both of his. She noticed again how perfectly manicured but very masculine and strong his hands were. They were warm, calloused from years of manual labor, but not sweaty. Good, he was relaxing with her.

"I didn't bring you, Perrin. You willingly went. That's what I am hoping for. I may light the path, but you will make your own way along it."

He hadn't let go of her and she didn't pull away. Getting him used to touch, having him offer it, was one of her responsibilities. Spending casual time like this with him was doing a couple of things. First, he was acclimating to her presence, becoming less jittery. And second, it was helping her to really filter his glamour when it rose.

Perrin wasn't doing it on purpose to seduce her. He couldn't help it; it was inherent in his being. Most denizens of Fey and Faerie normally had to concentrate to remove their glamour. To them, it was as natural as breathing. No wonder the two human girls of long ago had wanted him to seduce them. He had influenced them without realizing it.

"You know, this gives me an idea. You seem to be more comfortable with music as a theme. Would you like to try singing to me or dancing with me perhaps?"

Enough of his face showed that she could see the thought pleased him. "I could try."

Their gazes locked. "May I kiss you, Gillian?"

She stepped back, adding her other hand to his and pulling him up off the piano bench to stand in front of her. "You may."

Perrin released her hands and brought his own up, cupping her jawline with only the tips of his fingers. A butterfly's touch, skimming the surface of her skin as though she were the finest crystal and might break in his hands. He leaned forward and right, keeping the masked half away from her so that she could clearly see the handsome profile. Gillian waited, letting him tip her mouth to his own, letting him control the moment. She kept her eyes open so that he could see that she welcomed his kiss, his touch.

The lips that tenderly pressed hers were silken soft, infinitely gentle. Again, she didn't push, only stood passively letting him cup her face and give her a kiss. All too briefly he pulled back slowly, watching her eyes. Gill mirrored him exactly. Not straightening too quickly, letting him tip her jaw back down. From her vantage point she could see the corded muscles on his neck, the result of over a century of singing, which terminated upward in the clean line of his jaw and down into the broad but slender shoulders.

Vaguely she wondered if his face was the only thing affected by the Gargoyle blood or if he had more disfigurements beneath his clothing. She didn't care; she had scars all over her body, the most recent from her last little misadventure in London with Jack the Ripper's surgery. Tanis and Aleksei both had been initially shocked by the evidence of her several near-death experiences, but neither had said anything. Smart Vampires.

"That was lovely, Perrin. Thank you."

Smiling, he reached down for her hand, then gently spun her around, facing away from him. Gillian felt the arm holding her hand wrap around her abdomen, his other hand gliding over the fabric of her shirt lightly, across her stomach then down her hip to finally grasp her free hand and bring it, palm up, cupped by his own to caress the undamaged side of his face.

Their bodies were separated by a small space. Perrin neither pulled her against him nor moved forward to close that gap. His arm around her middle only held her, didn't tighten to press her close. Gillian hardly breathed, afraid to speak or move and frighten him. Her hair ruffled with his breath and she realized he had brushed the masked side over her hair.

Perrin was sweet, tender, romantic, gentle. He had been denied the most basic thing people took for granted: simple physical contact. He cherished it. Craved it. She could feel his natural Gargoyle sexuality rising, only to be replaced by a driving need she couldn't yet name.

If she had merely been a woman in this compelling man's arms, she would have leaned back into him, closing the gap to weave her own arms around his hips and pull him to her. Because she was his Paramortal sex therapist, her better judgment overcame her instincts and she remained still, letting him experience what he wanted to, at his own pace. He radiated need, want, desire, longing . . . most of it wasn't even sexual. Just a stark, hollow craving of the most basic, simplest touch. Now she understood what it was. It had everything and nothing to do with sex. He was touch starved, beyond anyone she'd ever encountered.

Finally he released her with all the slow gentleness that he had initiated the contact with and stepped away from her. She turned to face him and found him looking slightly away, giving her full view of his left side.

"Thank you for letting me just hold you, Gillian. I am sorry it was for so long. I have never been able . . ." His voice tightened and he couldn't continue.

"You've never been able to just know what it felt like," Gillian said gently, feeling his withdrawal and pain swamp over her. It was getting hard for her to keep up with his emotional shifts and remain barricaded.

"Oui."

"And how did it feel, Perrin? To hold a woman in your arms, romantically?" She threw that word in to bring him back to why they were there.

Silence.

Unconsciously he raised his right hand and lightly touched the mask. "It felt warm."

He wasn't referring to temperature.

"Perrin, I have to go now. I have to see to my other patients. I do want to thank you for today. It was fun to sing with you, and I think you've got the part about holding a woman just right. I enjoyed it very much." He could see her with his left eye and she was smiling.

"Forgive me, Gillian, but could you see yourself out? I want to think about today."

"Good night, Perrin."

"Bon soir, Gilliana."

His French accent was lilting, warm, sensual. The diminutive of her name caught her off guard, but she let herself out and headed back to the castle as he began to play the piano again, soft and sad music. It surprised her when she hadn't gone but a few yards before she started to cry silently. She just couldn't stop the tears. This was bad. If she couldn't handle her own emotions around Perrin, this would not be a healthy situation for him. She needed to talk to Helmut and get his advice.

Back at the castle she located Helmut and together they went to the kitchen for some tea. Stirring sugar into her Lady Gray brew, Gillian wondered how she would broach this subject without sounding like an idiot. She'd been out of school a long time and hadn't consulted Helmut for years on a case. Briefly, she told him about how the sessions were going with Perrin and her seeming lack of control.

"I am having a tremendously hard time keeping my emotions managed around Perrin, Helmut." Well, blurting it out was good too. Sort of.

"And you believe that this may impair your effectiveness as his therapist." He made it a statement. Helmut knew her pretty well.

Taking a sip of tea, she leaned against the counter. "I don't understand it. I never have this level of vulnerability with a patient, ever. I know what I'm doing, Helmut. I am taking it slow, letting him make every move first. He needs to get in touch with his alpha side so I'm holding way, way back. He is calling all of the shots on how and when we proceed.

"Why am I reacting like this? Perrin is a patient. He trusts me, came to me for help, and I'm scared to death I'm going to fuck this up." She looked at her boss and friend. "What's wrong with me? Do I need to take myself off this case and let you reassign him to a more experienced sex therapist? Am I going to endanger his recovery by my own lack of control?"

Helmut watched her as she disclosed her concerns. He was proud of her in a fatherly sort of way. Her insight into even her own failings was what made her an outstanding Paramortal psychologist. Gillian would never allow them to endanger a patient's recovery and would absolutely take herself off Perrin's case if she felt his recovery would be compromised by her perceived weakness.

"Have you had many Paramortals needing sex therapy?"

"Only two previously, Perrin is number three. It's just not that common to be needed in that capacity with most of them. Why?"

"I don't think this is your fault. I think Perrin's own lack of control is what's causing your reaction," Helmut speculated.

"What? He had perfect control. There has been no sexual touching, Helmut. None. Today was the first time he kissed me and even then it was perfectly chaste. He's suffering from a level of erotophobia as well. It's like an elegant ballet except we dance around each other instead of with each other."

She set her cup down on the counter and started to pace. "Then I bounce from emotion to emotion, from feeling to feeling, like some rookie therapist, and find myself crying on the path away from the guesthouse. It's ridiculous!"

Helmut chuckled. "Hear me out, Schatzi. Perrin is part Sidhe, isn't he?"

"Yes, he is, but that doesn't explain my issues."

"Doesn't it?"

The thoughts whirled around on her face. Then she knew. "The Sidhe glamour is what I'm fighting, isn't it? He can't help it. He shifts feelings like you shift the gears on a car. Damn!"

"You've never had even a part Sidhe as a sex therapy client before, Gillian. Perrin doesn't know how the hell to control his emotions and glamour yet around other beings. He's been physically isolated most of his life from even the most basic touch. Give him time."

Helmut patted her arm as she kept pacing. "Besides, in your marvelous intake file, you mention that he is half Gargoyle. They are still part of the Fey populace and have their own glamour. That would account for the raw edge of the need that you feel."

"Shit, that's right. I need to read up on current research with Gargoyles then. It will help me know better how to buffer him and his emotions. I have to get him past this erotophobia thing or we're not going to get anywhere."

Gerhardt smiled kindly, patting her shoulder. "I have complete confidence in you, my dear. Perrin couldn't be in better hands."

"Thanks, Helmut, but I know that I'm going to have to set some clear boundaries for him. He's so starved for any contact that he's bound to let himself go too far in his feelings. I don't want to hurt him. He's been hurt enough for several lifetimes."

After finishing her tea, she put her cup in the sink and turned to go. "Good night, Helmut, and thank you. It feels good to confide in a colleague."

"Good night, Schatzi. You're doing our profession proud and lending credibility to it." Helmut put his own cup away, then remembered something and called after her, "Gillian! Wait!"

"What?" She reappeared in the doorway.

"I don't know if you've thought of it or not, but Perrin's mask is his final and most prevalent vulnerability. Be careful how you handle that."

Nodding, she agreed, "I have thought it over, but thanks for mentioning it anyway. I might not have, just because it's so obvious, so it's good to check. I'm going to leave that to him too, as I'm leaving everything else to him. If the damn thing comes off, it will be Perrin that removes it."

"Are you prepared for what might be underneath?"

"Nothing connected to that man could be that scary, Helmut. Perrin could have used his disfigurement and his powers as an excuse to be a sexually sadistic bastard getting even with the world, but he didn't. He didn't, because it would have been morally, ethically wrong. Frankly I'm impressed he's as sane as he is, even with all his hang-ups."

Her mentor smiled. "I was as well. From the time I first spoke with him to when he agreed to be your patient, I knew the least of your problems would be that he was a decent and kind soul."

Gill yawned, embarrassed. "Sorry, Helmut, I'm beat."

"Go on, get some rest. It must be very draining having to hold such tight control on your own shields against Perrin's power."

They said their good nights again and left the kitchen to go to their respective rooms. Gillian plodded up the stairs, ignoring the Brownie army that was carrying several trussed-up squirrels and mice, apparently on the way to a Brownie barbeque. She was too tired to go find Trocar and the other Elves. A clean, fresh, comfortable mattress was what she needed. If Aleksei was there, she'd bodily throw his ass out.

Head down and distracted, she hadn't taken two more steps before she collided with a solid form. Black boots, tight-laced black pants . . . her eyes traveled upward, ivory-colored linen shirt, broad shoulders, black hair, ice gray eyes. Aleksei. *Shit. Shit. Shit.* She did not need this right now.

"Oh, sorry. I wasn't watching where I was going."

She started to step around him, since he didn't seem to be

moving, when he gently took her shoulders. Her temper rose with her head as she tipped it back to look him in the eyes.

"Not now, Aleksei. Bad time, bad attitude. I'm going to sleep." This time when she pulled away, he let her, dropping his hands to his sides.

"Gillian, I do not wish to fight or argue with you. I merely wanted to apologize for my poor judgment and poor choice of words. I was wrong, an antiquated ass, and I am truly sorry."

Dammit. Shit. Hell. Fuck. His voice was still incredible. A sorcerer's black velvet voice that surrounded her with warmth and other yummy feelings.

Turning back to him, she met his gaze and dropped her reinforced shields a little. The apology was there in his eyes too. Okay. Fine. Still wasn't going to get him any blood or nookie tonight. "All right. Apology accepted. Thank you for finding me to say it. Now I'm going to bed."

Aleksei frowned. "Wait, *piccola*, you are exhausted. Let me help you."

"I don't want any help and I really don't want to talk about anything tonight. Good night, Aleksei."

She kept walking and got to her room without further incident. Thankfully he didn't follow her or press her further. Crawling between the sheets, she was asleep before her head fully contacted the pillow.

Leathery wings bit into the cool night air. The dragon banked sharper than necessary, its shape appearing to ripple then solidify once more. Rattled, Aleksei landed and shifted back to his Human form next to the ruins of an ancient castle. He couldn't think of Gillian and their relationship issues when he was flying. The expanse of feeling with too deep, too fresh and at the moment too painful for him to focus on when he needed to remember: how to maintain the shape of the legendary flying lizard. That partial shift in midflight might have been fatal if he'd lost it completely and fallen nearly a thousand feet to the earth. He might have caught himself in time; then again, he might not have.

Vampires were wondrous, powerful, magical creatures, but unless they were Masters, they couldn't shift shape, fly, dissolve to mist, like any run-of-the-mill movie Vampire could. In fact, most Masters could manage to become accomplished in only one or two talent areas. Vampire Lords like Aleksei, Osiris, Dionysus and Dracula had the ability to master several, and generally did, once they knew how.

Inferno, thought Aleksei. *If all of us could do all that, no one and nothing would be safe.*

Aleksei had become more than a Master. Now the head of his own Line, a true Lord—the lingering relationship with the Line of Dracula, which created him, shattered—he didn't know a thing about taking what was his or creating a Line of his own traditions and expectations.

Expectations. That was what this fight with Gillian was all about. Aleksei had expectations of what it meant to have a girlfriend, of being a couple, that Gillian seemed to take issue with. Even disagree with. Very significant issue, indeed.

Your own damn fault, his good Vampire side argued with his bad Vampire side, the latter being the one who was screaming at him to assert his mastery over the Human female and forget the implied chauvinistic rule breaking. No, he would never do that. It was more important to have Gillian's respect and trust.

Tonight's apology hopefully gained some of that back. He had been an idiot, as Tanis had implied. That really stung. Having his younger, more impulsive and definitely more chauvinistic brother lecturing him on the intricacies of his relationship with Gillian was humbling.

While Aleksei was arguing with himself and pacing through the woods like a chained tiger, a ripple in the atmosphere caught his attention. Senses focused, he tried to pinpoint it but it was gone again, as quickly as it appeared. Frowning, he headed swiftly in the direction of the village, where he thought he felt it strongest. Shifting into mist, he was there in moments, materializing in a quiet alley then pacing the busy streets, waving to the villagers who recognized their Count. It was still early in the evening and he needed to feed.

The villagers of Sacele had sent their mayor with a document to Castle Rachlav when the trouble with Dracula started. A document that listed the names of adults in the village willing to be donors to Aleksei, Tanis and any Vampire who was on the Rachlavs' side. Their homes would display a wolf of some kind outside to be easily identifiable. Since natural and Lycanthrope wolves were prominent in the area and Cezar, the Alpha pack leader of the Rachlav Werewolves, was the police chief's brother, any depiction of a wolf as a display piece didn't draw any undue attention. They were accepted here, even loved, as coprotectors of the area.

Aleksei turned down a less lively street and headed toward a neighborhood café where the local tradesmen gathered after their supper for coffee and conversation. Sacele was still fairly isolated in the heart of the Carpathian Mountains, off the main roads, still quaint and charming. It had all the modern conveniences such as the Internet and cable television. But when all was said and done, the residents rather liked their traditional values and kept the main part of town as their central gathering place in the evenings.

The men greeted their Count warmly. Aleksei and Tanis were well loved. They had never fed here, never killed here. The Rachlavs had kept the village as safe as they could. Silent, benevolent, but lethal guardians to the town and its surrounding areas. Nearly half of the businesses in the community owed part of their success to the Rachlav fortune seeing them through tough economic times.

The Rachlavs supported a large, viable network of local artisans who made traditional Romanian crafts and artwork. They were entitled to a percentage of the proceeds from the sale of the pieces and articles made, most of which they invested back into the town and its residents. Any person could directly petition the family for help if they hit a rough spot in their finances. All Aleksei had ever asked in repayment was that they give back into the community fund when they were able.

The town kept the Rachlavs' secrets as it had for more than four hundred years. It was a small price for the safety and support they had received. As Aleksei approached and returned the affectionate greetings, one of the men stood and extended his hand. "Count Rachlav, it is good to see you around the village again."

"Thank you, Mihai, I enjoy coming to the village as often as I am able." Aleksei made it a point to know each and every person by name and occupation. He saw the man's eyes light up as he heard his Count address him by name.

"How is the business going? Do you have enough orders or should we advertise a bit more?"

Mihai was a woodcarver of great skill. His woodcut panels, icons and signs were in great demand all over Eastern Europe, thanks to the webpage Aleksei had linked to the Village of Sacele's parent website. He fairly beamed as the Vampire asked him about his business.

"We have almost more than we can handle now, my Lord, but thank you for asking." He reseated himself with his friends, blushing a little to have been so bold as to speak to the reigning Vampire Lord directly.

Aleksei allowed his smile to reach his eyes, though he didn't feel all the warmth he should have with Gillian's newly disclosed occupation looming in the background. "You are welcome."

He looked over all of them, seated at the expertly carved tables drinking their evening coffee. "All of you must remember to tell me or my brother if there is anything we can do to help you. I am sorry we have not been as visible of late, but we have not forgotten our home and our people."

He bade them farewell and started to leave, but a voice stopped him. "Count Rachlav, did you come to visit or do you need . . . food?"

Everyone stopped talking as Aleksei turned back to the voice. A tall, slender, attractive dark-haired woman, only just beginning to show gray in her hair, stood in the doorway of the coffee shop, smiling. Esi Stanislaus had owned the local coffee shop and café with her husband for nearly thirty years. He had been an early casualty in the turf war, a victim of a preemptive Vampire strike when he traveled between towns purchasing the local gourmet items they stocked at their café.

Aleksei had personally tracked down the perpetrating Vampire and dealt with it. Esi had no reason not to believe in the Rachlavs, remaining loyal to Lord and village despite her husband's death à la Vampire.

She was a friendly, familiar face to himself and Tanis, and a sexy vision to the men of Sacele, but Esi was faithful to her husband's memory. While charming, she did not flirt with intent. She was known for being honest, honorable and mean as hell if provoked.

He went back to her, lifted her hand and kissed it formally, holding her gaze with his eyes. "Esi, you are as kind as you are perceptive. But I do not feed here, as you all know. You are my sustenance, but you are not food."

She blushed under the icy gray gaze and laughed. "Your hands are cold, oh great Vampire Lord. If you need your 'sustenance,' you have but to ask. Look . . ." She gestured to the tables.

At least five men stood up instantly with all the others rising next. None of them were hesitant, none were frightened, and they all nodded or vocalized encouragement. Aleksei looked them all over carefully. He could identify each one's intentions and found no deceit or hesitation. They were offering.

"Gentleman and Esi, please do not ask this of me. I cannot feed upon my people, those I protect. It is but a little journey to find an errant traveler or one whose heart is not as good as those who live and prosper in this village."

"It is for that reason we are offering, Count Rachlav." That was from Mihai again. "We do prosper and live here. In fact, we live very well thanks to the Rachlav family."

He stepped closer, having to reach up to put his hand on Aleksei's upper arm, feeling the coolness of the rock-hard muscles underneath the linen shirt. Esi was right; he needed to feed. "We are offering freely. You cannot take what is given to you."

Aleksei stared down at the smaller man. Mihai was fairly

tall for a Human, nearly six feet, but the Vampire topped him by almost eight inches. "It is not right," he said, almost helplessly.

"You cannot protect us if you are weakened, Count Rachlav," Esi pointed out. "It makes more sense to take what is freely offered here than to have trouble come while you are out looking for blood elsewhere," she added pragmatically.

In the end, Aleksei gave in. They were so insistent that he fed there from them. Several stepped up and went into the back of the coffee shop with Aleksei. He fed from each of their wrists, ritually, respectfully. When he'd fed enough, he thanked them sincerely. To his surprise, they thanked him for letting them be like his squires or vassals. It made them feel like they were important enough to help their benefactor, and as Mihai pointed out, technically he was their Liege Lord. That had brought a smile to the Vampire's lips, stunning them all for a moment with his sheer loveliness.

After he left, they gathered as many of the other villagers as they could find and talked with their fellows of their promise to the Rachlavs. It was agreed that every evening, alternate townsfolk would meet at Esi's to provide for Aleksei, Tanis and whomever else they might house who would need blood. A greater gift they couldn't have given.

Aleksei communicated what had transpired to Tanis through their link. They were trying an experiment since Gillian and Aleksei were staying away from each other as much as possible and he had more time. Since both brothers had come into their full power, owing to the dismantling of the dampening fields set up around Sacele, and Aleksei had emerged as the Head of his own Line, Tanis wanted to be free of Dracula's taint.

He was a Master Vampire in his own right, but Aleksei had the full power of a Lord. After much discussion, and consulting with their friend and ally, Osiris, they settled on treating Tanis like a new conversion. Four substantial blood exchanges initiated and given by Aleksei would hopefully clear Tanis's system of Dracula's strain. They simply couldn't afford the risk, especially after Dracula had kidnapped Tanis months before.

Aleksei wouldn't feed for the next two nights before nearly draining Tanis. Blood-volume consumption in Vampires was part of their inherent enchantment. Movie Vampires, who drained their prey to the point of death in a matter of seconds, were simply ridiculous. Victims could be killed because of blood loss, but it took more than one feeding and generally more than one Vampire to accomplish it. For a conversion, a single Vampire with enough power had to complete four massive exchanges with the intended.

Three significant but smaller exchanges would gift them with a mate or servant who did not wish to experience the full monty of the Night Life. It gave them many of the benefits of being a nightwalking Vampire and none of the consequences. Tanis was already a powerful Vampire but his lineage, like Aleksei's had been, was of Dracula's Line. He wanted to be free of it, especially now since he'd met Gillian and Jenna. He didn't know if Jenna was "the one" for him, but he never wanted to gift a potential mate with the blood of the Dark Prince. It would leave her, whoever she was, at the sinister Vampire's beck and call if he so chose.

While the Rachlavs were discussing the best way to get on with it, Gillian was headed toward the guesthouse. She felt pretty good. Moose's spirits had picked up considerably even though what Aleksei had gleaned from her thoughts made little sense to Gillian. The hideously ugly creature had practically skipped into the group session on her heavy hooves, horns waving happily. Samuel had even smiled, which for him was practically a miracle.

Still no word or sign from the Vampire at the Inn, so Gill had extended her session with Moose, Samuel, the Dark Court Fey and the Sluagh, who huddled uncomfortably in a dim corner of the room, behind Gillian's chair. It had been cloaked in some sort of shimmery gray fabric, and they got glimpses of too many limbs and eyes. Once they were through and her notes recorded, she'd moved on with her thoughts to Perrin.

It was a nice night. Just cool enough for most Humans to want a light jacket. Except Gillian. She reveled in the cool air, walking in tight black pants tucked into thigh-high flat boots. Her shirt was laced up from the chest, gleaming white, which cast a reddish glow over her blond hair. A heavy combat rapier swung at her left hip and black leather gauntlets, tucked into her belt, hung on the right. The plan was to spend some time with Perrin, then go in for a little sword-play with Finian and Trocar. She didn't want to take the time to change in between and looked like a short, blond pirate strolling through the dark verdant path adjacent to the parking area and entrance road.

As she was turning to climb on the porch, headlights moved up the road, toward her and the castle. She changed direction instantly, drawing the gauntlets on and putting her hand on the sword. No one should be coming right now. Glancing at the parking lot, she saw that Helmut's van was missing but she knew Helmut was in the castle. Who hadn't been there? Jenna. Goddess above, she was getting as attention deficit disordered as her friend. Tanis had told her earlier that Jenna had driven to Brasov to pick up Kimber and Daed, then Helmut had asked her about Perrin's progress, and "Shiny!," just like that, she'd lost her train of thought.

Argh! This was ridiculous. She was a trained professional, a former military leader; but the issue with Aleksei—being cut off from a regular diet of fabulous sex; the number of mounting casualties in the Fang Wars, as it was being called by the Human press; Perrin's situation; her missing client and generally not knowing where the other shoe would eventually fall were all getting overwhelming. She'd need therapy herself soon if she didn't blow off some steam. Hence the swordplay. Nothing like facing an opponent with a four-foot-long, steel barbeque skewer aimed at your vital bits to get your attention focused real damn fast.

Inside the guesthouse, Perrin waited by the window. He'd watched Gillian's progress down the path and seen the lights as she did. Amazed, he watched as she drew her gauntlets on and moved, hand on hilt, to stand on the path in front of the house where he waited. She was deliberately placing herself in the path of whatever threat she perceived and was shielding him, though he was safe inside.

The parking lot light that Aleksei had installed illuminated the area with a pinkish glow and turned Gillian's hair to flame. She looked so small out there, waiting alone. Perrin felt his heart rate increase and his breathing quicken. He was afraid for her and didn't know what to do about it.

The van pulled in and Jenna hopped out to hug her friend. "Hey I've missed you these last couple of days!" she said brightly.

"I know," Gillian murmured, patting her back. "I've been a lousy friend lately and I'm sorry."

Jenna held her at arm's length. "Knock that shit off, you hear? You've been doing your job. That's what you're supposed to do, so don't start the Jewish guilt thing or I'll pound you." Jenna's grin was infectious and Gillian returned it.

"I can't help it. I'm Jewish, by heritage anyway. The guilt comes along with it. It's like a legacy. I'm just a little overwhelmed and didn't want you to think I'd forgotten I had a gal pal here."

"Not a chance. Besides, if you do, I'll sneak in while you're sleeping and put purple streaks in your hair," Jenna smirked. "And I bet your rabbi would just love to know your best friend is a Pagan and your boyfriend's a Vampire."

"He's not my boyfriend!" Gill snapped.

"He is and he will be again. You're just taking a break, like Ross and Rachel."

Gillian opened her mouth to say something contemptuous about the *Friends* reference when she was grabbed from behind and tossed into the air. Instinct took over and she spun, not bothering to try to draw the sword in midflight, and dropped into a fighting crouch. Dimly she knew that if something really bad had been sneaking up on her, Jenna would have said something. Well, unless Tanis or Josh Holloway from *Lost* were standing in her line of vision without their shirts while the sneaking was going on. Then she'd be screwed for sure.

CHAPTER

7

DAEDELUS Aristophenes, M.D., Ph.D., was grinning at her full of Southern charm, arms wide, black eyes sparkling. Kimber had come around the other way and pounced on her from the side. Daed moved in to crush all of them in a group hug.

"Mmmmmmph! *Ow!* Sword!" Gillian squawked, feeling the hilt of the weapon digging into her diaphragm and prodding a lung. She sagged a little as Daed released them, and rubbed her abdomen. "Aristophenes, you moron! Don't you know weapon decorum, for hell's sake?"

Ever jubilant, her former boss laughed, rubbing her back, up to her shoulder, then gently kneading her tight neck muscles. "Hey, kiddo, you need a massage in the worst way."

"Not bad enough to get it from you, you snake. Don't ever do that again. If I'd had a *main-gauche* on like I usually do, I'd have pinned you like a moth," she said flatly, referring to the secondary stiletto-like weapon favored by Italian swordsman in the fourteenth century. But Daed didn't remove his hand, just moved it back to rest on her shoulder.

"Now, princess, don't be grumpy. We just got here!" Daed grinned, knowing he was playing with fire but he couldn't help it. The spark in her green eyes was just so endearing. Especially right before she tried to kill him.

"Yeah, Kemo Sabe, we got stories to tell, don't ya know!"

Kimber stood, arms on hips, a wicked gleam in her gold green eyes, her bronze-colored hair in perfect spiral ringlets down to her butt. She was taller than Gillian by several inches, slender, but strong and absolutely fearless. Gillian was secretly glad Kimber was on their side. Her lovely former second in command had most of the components of a garden-variety sociopath but fortunately had an ironclad conscience to go with her lethal skills.

Gill grinned at both of them. "Look, I'd love to sit around and do nothing but have a beer and shoot the shit with my friends but I've got a patient waiting. Go on up to the house, Helmut will have some confidentiality forms for you to sign. He decided to bring the patients here instead of me traveling around, so we have the Rachlav Institute of Paramortal Healing." She shrugged helplessly. "It works so far."

"Very nice," Daed said, smiling, still rubbing her shoulder lightly. "Can you use a good shrink?"

"Actually, yes, we can. I've got a Sluagh in there with some serious paranoia issues and I think it needs medication."

Daed's grin broadened. "Well, you need a psychiatrist on staff if you're going to run a legitimate clinic, so I'll be happy to lend my services." He leaned in a little toward Gillian and murmured to her, "In whatever capacity you need, darlin'."

"Cut it out, you egotistical fuckwit!" Gillian shoved him hard enough to stagger him.

Daed grabbed her extended arm and jerked her to him, dipping his body forward to catch her in the midsection and tossing her over his shoulder. Sword clanging against his side where she couldn't get it, he swatted her playfully on her black-clad derriere.

Jenna and Kimber were not helping; both were leaning on each other giggling. Great. Just great. Too bad she'd forgotten her gun; she could have used it to shoot herself. Note to self: Always bring gun and bullets.

"Now settle down, puddin'. I'm just playing with you." Daed's Southern charm was wearing very thin.

"Gee, Daed, I didn't know you were into Freudian kink.

You really should have that little quirk examined further . . . 'Daddy.'" Gillian's acid-laced voice zinged like the proverbial directional arrow and burned a little hole in Daed's ego.

He set her down in front of him and purred, "If I were into Freudian kink, dollface, I'd have tanned your butt more than once a long time ago for being a smart-ass."

"Right. Well, I'm a competent smart-ass, which is why you adore me. Now I've got a patient to see. So go fuck off or do whatever it is you do and poke some holes in people with your needles or invent a new psychoanalytic theory. I'm busy." She didn't back off or down but faced him squarely.

He gave her a mock salute and wheeled off, Jenna and Kimber following, still giggling and waving. Gill flipped them both off, which sent them into more gales of laughter as she turned back to the guesthouse, hopefully to finish what she'd started and do her nightly session with Perrin.

Perrin, who she didn't know had watched the entire scene from the window, was afraid that his physical appearance would make things worse if he ran out to save Gillian from that man who had hit her. He loathed himself more in that moment than he had in years and was furious with Gillian for her seemingly calm reaction to that ruffian. Did she like that? Did she expect him to behave like that?

She moved purposefully up the porch steps and to the door, adjusting her sword and hanging her gauntlets back on her belt. When Perrin opened it before she could knock, she was surprised, then embarrassed. "Good evening, Perrin. Guess you saw all that, didn't you?"

The tall, handsome man in the mask looked positively grim as he took her upper arm and literally marched her into the room, to the couch, anger clearly in the rough musical voice. "Is that what you want of me, Dr. Key? Do you want me to learn to manhandle a woman? I'm part Gargoyle; I have the capability of being brutal, I am told."

She was too surprised to speak at first so he continued, taking her by the shoulders and shaking her abruptly. "Answer me, because I will not do that. Is that what you want? Is that what women need? Or just what you need?"

Gray green eyes searched her face, confusion and pain etched on the classic features imploringly as he released her shoulders and cupped her face in his hands. "Why, Gillian, why?"

Centering herself, she opened her empathy to him, bracing for the overwhelming onslaught that was almost visibly whirling in the room. It hit her like a slap in the face. Perrin was furious, probably for the first time in ages, but beneath that was fear and worry for her. He had watched Daed "manhandle" her, as he put it, saw her put up a fight, then watched as they seemingly made up.

Holy Mother of Earth, he thought she and Daed were lovers. He'd never seen a man and a woman who were friends or lovers in real life. Perrin's only socialization and points of reference came from the elegance and formality of the stage and the opera, where people didn't act like that.

If a man put his hands on a woman's backside, either to caress or strike, it meant she had a relationship of some kind with him: father, brother, lover, husband. Then the man definitely didn't just let it go and walk off, nor did the woman just let it go with no tears, no arguments. Especially a woman like Gillian. It was all very confusing.

Gently she covered his hands with her own. "Perrin, please let me explain what you saw."

"He struck you, Gillian."

"Yeah, he did. But it didn't hurt and he didn't mean it to hurt. He was teasing me, that's all. Just friendly banter, nothing more than that."

The other side of his face seemed to freeze into a twin of the masked one and he stiffened, dropping his hands away from her. Understanding filtered into the marvelous eyes. Regrettably it was the wrong conclusion. "That man is someone important in your life, yet he allows you to be here, with me?"

It was actually more of a statement than a question, but Gill knew she'd better head all this off before Perrin became totally disillusioned and crawled back into his safe little shell. If that happened, she'd have to kill Daed for undoing her progress so far, and they really needed a psychiatrist of his caliber and expertise at the Institute.

"Perrin, sit down." She didn't mean to bark it like an order, but her patience was now officially shot so her voice was harsher than she had intended. His eyes widened, then narrowed, but he didn't move and remained standing, looking down at her. Hmmmm, maybe a little alpha there after all. Mexican standoff. Shit.

Power struggles with patients were always a bad idea. "Fine, stand if you want to. I'm sitting." She plopped onto the oversize couch, bounced once, then put her feet up, crossing her legs and arms and glaring at Perrin. "You want to yell at me, yell. Tell me you're disappointed in me, say whatever it is you have to say, then shut up and let me tell you what just happened."

She leaned forward a little for emphasis. "Because, Perrin, I am not giving up on you. I am not walking away from you, and we *are* going to resolve this, now. Tonight." She leaned back and rubbed her forehead against the headache she was getting.

Silence. She peered out at him between her fingers. He hadn't moved. "Perhaps tonight is a bad time, Dr. Key. Your lover is home; your friends are here. Why do you not go join them and we can pursue this conversation at a later date. I am certain they are missing you." Damn, he gave good voice, even when he was telling her to go to hell.

"Perrin, Daed Aristophenes is not my lover. What he used to be was my boss in the Marine Corps. Now he's just an asshole, but he's a psychiatrically proficient asshole and we need him. He's here to work with us at the Institute. We don't get along, quite frankly, so he goes out of his way to piss me off because I will *not* fucking go out with him nor will I be his lover."

The former theatre ghost didn't know whether to be more shocked by her language or by the content of what she was saying. "I will hear you out, then."

He sat down on the edge of the sofa and turned toward her for a change; elegant, handsome; clothes, hair, nails and boots spotless and perfect. He cut quite a noble and dynamic picture. She doubted if he knew it.

"Okay, listen until I get through, understand?" He nodded his agreement, his eyes never leaving her face.

It took about an hour, but she finally got it across to Perrin that Daed really was a phenomenally good psychiatrist as well as a devious, instigating shit, and that what he saw translated into play between friends and former service buddies. She also made it clear that neither Daed nor Kimber knew Perrin was in this house, so none of it had been a display for his viewing benefit. He visibly relaxed as she talked, giving her hope that this wasn't totally blown out of the water.

"I need to tell you, though," she went on, unbuckling her sword and laying it and the gauntlets aside, "that if you're unhappy with me, upset about this situation, want a new therapist, any of it, I'll get Helmut down here and you can make a formal complaint to him. We'll get you a new therapist, let you stay here, whatever you want." Reaching out, she meant to take his hand, but he jerked back. Now what?

"Why would you think I want a new therapist? Do you want to be rid of me?" He was genuinely surprised.

"No, of course not, Perrin, I love working with you. I just want you to be happy. If I make you uncomfortable after all this time, then I want you to know you have the option to reject me. I am certainly not rejecting you. Okay?" Her admiration for his courage, his nature, his beauty, his talent, all went into the intense look she gave him.

"You truly are not sorry you have taken me as a patient? No second thoughts? No disgust about my touching you?"

Now she was puzzled. "Perrin, why would you think that? I have never given you any indication that I was uncomfortable or that I dreaded us being together sexually."

A real smile graced his face, and she could feel the shift in him again. Then his eyes dropped and he said softly in a voice whose very pitch brought unrealized low heat to her, "I would like to be your friend and your lover, Gillian. I have never known the casual familiarity with anyone that you have with your friends. I have never had a friend."

The mask turned away. He wasn't feeling sorry for himself, just stating a fact. Gill's heart went out to him, but she kept it professional. He was too vulnerable right now for anything but the truth.

"I would like to be your friend too, Perrin, and your lover. I will tell you something that I have never told another patient." She shifted on the couch and pulled her legs up under her, her posture totally open to him. "If I had met you outside of this situation, at the theatre or at a coffeehouse, just a man and a woman, meeting one night, I would have been attracted to you and I would not have hesitated to show you that interest."

"Oh, Gillian, you do not know what lies beneath this mask or you would not speak so." Perrin rose and turned away from her. "If you are afraid that I do not understand this is a professional relationship, I do. I know you cannot care for me in the manner you speak of. I know that you are here to help a man who is hanging on to his sanity by a thread feel like a man and not like an outcast creature."

The mask. He'd brought it up so she went with it. "I'm glad you understand the nature of this relationship now, Perrin. I can't be friends or lovers or have any contact with you for a year after we terminate our professional relationship. After that time, I hope that you will have found your way in life and feel like a whole man, as you should." Now she got up and went to him, moving around in front of him so that he had to look at her.

"But understand that I wish that for you because I hope I am skilled enough to help you make it to that point. It has nothing to do with your face. I have to let you go at the end of therapy because it is my job to let you go." Slowly she reached up and lightly drew her fingers down the mask. It was leather and molded to his face. To his credit, Perrin barely flinched.

"If this comes off, it will be you who does the removing, Perrin. I won't do it. I want you to trust me enough that you will remove it without fear of my reaction. Because you will know for certain that whatever is beneath this covering can't take away from the whole man that I see standing in front of me."

Pain, gratitude, fear, disbelief, all flashed through his eyes and he moved to take her in his arms. Gillian allowed it, standing passive again but knowing she needed to move this along.

"Perrin, I am going to put my arms around you the way I want to hold you and because I want to hold you. I also want you to kiss me again, but I want to kiss you back this time. Is that all right with you?"

Wordlessly he nodded and she slid her arms around his waist. He wasn't as tall as Aleksei, but he was tall enough and she couldn't reach much farther without pulling his head down to her.

Perrin pressed her closer to his chest. For some reason he wanted her to hear his heart beat. An elegant hand stroked down her hair the way he had wanted to then dipped down to cup her face. When he looked down, he watched her smile, felt her arms tighten a little more around him. Small, but he could feel the strength in those arms. Their lips met and he felt a moment of surreal disbelief as her hand moved up his chest, then his neck, to twine small fingers in his wavy black hair.

Unexpectedly, she opened her mouth for him and he froze, unsure what to do. Gillian felt his hesitation and took over, sliding her small warm tongue into his mouth and slowly exploring it. Perrin was a quick study and mimicked her action. Gill let him take over the kiss, letting his tongue, a warm, quick wetness, explore her mouth. She molded her body closer to him, pressing against his perfect form, letting him feel every curve, every rise and fall of her breasts against his chest.

He moaned softly, his hand sliding from her shoulders to her waist to bring her against him more fully. Pliant in his hands, Gillian again let him lead. Perrin felt a bit dizzy as his blood supply diverted from its path to his groin. The erectile tissues filled in seconds, pressing against the confining pants he wore and against Gillian's hip as she leaned into him. He would have drawn away, embarrassed by his lack of control, but she shocked him again by sliding her arm down to his buttocks and keeping him pressed to her.

Since she didn't seem to mind having his aching sex pulsing against her body, he became encouraged and deepened the kiss, tangling his fingers in her hair and cupping her head, tilting her face a little more to fasten tighter to his own mouth.

Gillian was enjoying all of it but keeping her clinical perspective firmly in place. He needed to learn to be a little less passive and she hoped she was conveying that. She pulled back a little, breaking the kiss, and said a little breathlessly, "Now take me to the couch."

He froze and she cursed silently. "Why?"

"Because I want to kiss you from a better angle, and if we keep standing like this, you're going to have a stiff neck later," she said mischievously, grinning.

They were soon on the couch, Perrin a little taken aback when she slid onto his lap from the front, straddling him. But Gillian kissed him again, taking his face in her hands, which quelled any comment he might have made. To his delight, he discovered that her smaller size meant that she fit him perfectly; upper body molded against him, lower body . . . He felt a surge of heat and blood to his groin, swelling him to greater dimensions. She was astride him, as though he were a horse, and was pressing against . . .

If he could have gotten up, he would have, but she had him pinned with arms and thighs. So he suddenly pushed her back from him. "Gillian, we must stop. Please."

It was a plea from his heart. The ecstasy of release was looming before him. A feeling that he had never allowed himself, believing in the purity of high love, that it was wrong to masturbate or to erupt outside a female body. At the rate they were going, it would only be moments before he would reach his own fulfillment fully clothed without ever touching her as a man. And Perrin definitely and most urgently wanted to touch her as a man.

CHAPTER

8

GILLIAN wasn't at the top of her class for nothing; she knew what was the matter and got off him immediately. Settling herself into the curve of his arm, she rested against his shoulder, hip to hip, thigh to thigh. Perrin's pants were very tight, giving her a very defined view of his erection pressed halfway down his thigh by the material. Damn, that had to be almost painful. *Damn*, that was really, really large.

A brief thought of Aleksei in the same state skidded into her brain unbidden, reminding her that it had been a while since she'd had great sex, and she booted it out. Not. Now. Therapy. Professional. I. Am. A. Professional. A professional on a couch currently restraining herself from having wild monkey sex with a half-Gargoyle, quarter-Fey male whose special, potent brand of glamour was beating at both of them and testing their control.

"Perrin, I want you to listen to me again. We have done a lot tonight. Gone pretty far and gotten you to where you are all right with a woman feeling you becoming erect, even enjoying it."

Perrin blushed and turned his face away, leaving her looking at the mask as he cupped his hand over his hardened cock. She reached up and turned his face back, lifted his hand away. "No, don't do that. Erection, penis, vagina, masturbation, orgasm are all perfectly acceptable, clinical words. None of it is dirty or wrong, understand?"

He was mortified, but he tried to rally and listen to her. Trusting her this far had turned out well, but he couldn't quite get past his embarrassment. Gillian thought of what she believed was a brilliant idea. "I am going to show you something that I think you will like. Don't move, please."

Getting up from the couch was tricky—they were sunk in pretty far and he had her tucked under his arm—but she struggled up, having to put her hand on his thigh to push up. He gasped as she brushed his sensitized inner thigh with her fingers, but stayed put while she hurried off to the bathroom. There was a box of flavored condoms tucked away there that she had left before Perrin ever arrived, in anticipation of her client's needs. Finding what she sought, she grabbed several and went back to the living room. Perrin was as she had left him: hard, aching, thick and big.

When she showed him the foil square, he didn't understand what she held. Then she knelt between his legs on the floor and tore the package open, bringing out the latex ring. His eyebrows rose as she took it and deftly rolled it down over three of her fingers, then nodded toward his lap.

"You want to put that over . . . my . . . uh . . . me, then make love to me?" He actually stammered as he realized what she was demonstrating and sweat beaded on his forehead.

"Not exactly. I thought for the first time I would put this on you and show you how a woman can please you with her mouth. Later I will show you how you can pleasure a woman with your mouth . . ."

Practically leaping over her, Perrin was across the room in a heartbeat. "You cannot be serious! In your mouth?! I know I am ignorant, Gillian, but I never believed . . ." He ran out of words as he gestured abruptly toward his heavy sex, his vision gathering spots for a moment as the blood surged thick and hot into his already straining organ.

The thought of her lovely mouth wrapped around his

body . . . dear gods above, if he moved—moved, hell, if the slightest brush of air touched him now, it would kill him. The thundering in his ears was his heart beating frantically in time with the pulsing in his groin.

Exasperated, Gillian sighed, rolling the condom up and sliding it back inside its wrapper. She tossed it on the lamp table. "You do bathe, don't you?"

Had he heard her right? "What? Of course I bathe. I bathe daily. What kind of question is that?"

"Your penis isn't dirty, Perrin. You haven't been with another female of any species. You are perfectly clean. It's a sexual organ. Not just something you urinate through. I bathe daily too and I can assure you that you would find both aspects very pleasurable."

Perrin's face and mask disappeared behind his palms as he blushed even deeper. Apparently she had hit another Victorian nerve. Whoops.

"You speak so openly about things which are private." His voice was strangled but still held the roughness and the musical quality that she found so endearing.

"Gillian, I do not know if I can go through with all of this. I want to learn what it is like to make love, to feel the touch of another's hand upon me. To hold a woman in my arms and experience pleasure. I do not know if I can contemplate what you are talking about."

He moved gingerly to the fireplace, prepared to shatter at every step, and stood, one arm on the mantel for a moment, then sunk down to sit on an ottoman by the fire and prayed she wouldn't say anything else remotely enticing.

After another half hour of "Our Bodies, Ourselves," Gillian had gotten him not to blush when talking about sexual terminology. He actually smiled and looked more relaxed with her sitting in front of him.

"I do want you to learn to be a little more dominant, Perrin. Not forceful, not brutal, but confident, assured. Make sense? Don't be so afraid to experiment. It will all be good, I promise you. Do you understand better now?"

"Yes. I believe I do now."

Rising enough to put her hands against his legs, she pushed herself up. "I think that's enough for tonight. I don't want to overwhelm you more than you already are. I apologize for leaving you in an aroused state, but I just don't think it's a good idea after your reaction to carry this out tonight."

There. That was her clinical opinion. Good. She was keeping things in perspective. All right, so her body was screaming at her to fuck perspective and fuck him *now*, but her mind and will won the argument.

When he reached up for her, she leaned down for his kiss. Perrin instead braced her against his shoulder, kissed her, swatted her butt, then pushed her up to stand in front of him.

Gillian was annoyed. "Just what the hell do you think you're doing?"

"Practicing being more dominant?" Perrin was making an attempt at his humor skills again. Oh joy. She was going to have a long talk with him about his timing.

Sputtering, she couldn't think of anything appropriate to say. Perrin felt his heart melt a little at her discomfort. A blond beauty, intelligent, capable, so strong, yet so vulnerable, Gillian was a study in contradictions. Relinquishing control was completely foreign to her. He hadn't wanted to hurt her, just to tease her, copying what he had just witnessed. Seeing that it had backfired, he was instantly sorry.

"Forgive me, Gillian. I thought only to tease you a little, not harm you or humiliate you."

Glaring at him, she found her wits. "You didn't hurt or humiliate me, Perrin, it was just unexpected, that's all."

Her index finger poked him in the chest. "However, if you're one of those people who are interested in S and M, I will have to find you another therapist for that segment of your therapy."

In order to avoid another hour or two explaining sadomasochistic sexuality to him, Gillian referred him to the library in the guesthouse. It was much smaller than the castle's but fairly well stocked. He could damn well look it up, or they could provide him with a computer for research . . . maybe not. Exposure to sex via the Internet might just put his tender sensibilities into shock.

As she stalked back to the castle, her temper cooled. At least she hadn't yelled at him. Then she managed another epiphany, impressing herself since her brain felt like oatmeal and her body tender and sensitive all over. Perrin truly was an innocent.

He had all the needs and desires of a healthy male adult but none of the knowledge or skill. She had to remind herself that he had grown up essentially alone with no media, no contact, no observations, nothing to study that wasn't related to music, the arts or stagecraft. Growing up in the Victorian era had been hard on people, who were exposed to only general relationship knowledge.

Perrin hadn't been just sheltered; he'd been completely isolated until his first "angel" had come into his life and piqued his curiosity. Even then, with only the limited information base he had to rely on, he couldn't act on any of his impulses or feelings. Being as skittish as he was, he'd avoided anything related to what he couldn't have. Sex. Love. Lovemaking. Anything in the realm of a stimulating nature he had shied away from, believing there was no point in inducing desire for what could never be his.

Great Cronus, and he was how old? Over a hundred a fifty years old and still a virgin. Holy Mother Hera, it was unbelievable.

Sighing, she knew she needed to process with Helmut and keep her perspective. Patience was what Perrin needed, that and a healthy dose of experimentation. Deep in thought, she wasn't paying attention again and was startled to hear her name in a familiar black velvet voice. Damn, she was getting entirely too comfortable around this environment. No place was completely safe. Forgetting that could get her very dead. Reminding herself to be more attentive to surroundings was easy after she jumped at the sound of her name.

"Gillian?"

Aleksei. Great. Now the horror was complete. "Yeah, what do you need, Aleksei?" Clearly she wasn't in the mood for small talk. Perrin's sexuality aura apparently had lingering aftereffects because she wanted a very cold shower and a very quiet room.

Icy gray eyes took in every detail even in the darkness. Gillian was disheveled, her lips were puffy and swollen, her clothing rumpled and she looked tired. There was a familiar stomp in her step that was concerning to him. Anger swelled without warning inside the Vampire Lord's being and he started for her to confirm that she was undamaged from her encounter with the one in his guesthouse. He damn well didn't like this, but he would make sure that she did her job without being harmed or upset. If that male had hurt her, patient or not, he would pay for it.

"Come here, *piccola*, let me see that you are all right."

She waved him off. "I'm fine, Aleksei, really. I'm just very worn out." Suddenly she realized there was no familiar weight on her hip. The sword and gloves were at Perrin's. Lovely. They could stay there until tomorrow.

Catching up with her, he stopped her, his hand on her shoulder as he perused her up and down. "Truly, he did not hurt you?"

Several undiplomatic phrases were on her tongue as she felt the light brush of his mind on hers and hit "Delete" on what she was going to say. It was faster just to tell him and have it done with. Carefully segmenting the last few hours, she opened enough for him to see that Perrin hadn't hurt her in any way. Aleksei didn't need to know the details, just the facts. The fact was, she was fine. *Just doing my job, Your Excellency*.

Shit, he caught that thought and an eyebrow rose. "I am not your lord or your master, Gillian. Please do not make light of my concern for my lover and . . ." He stumbled over the word *girlfriend*.

This was not the time or the place to have this conversation that she'd been avoiding, but there wasn't going to be any good time.

"I have been your lover and I was your girlfriend. I know you've apologized for what you said, and I forgive you for that. But, Aleksei, we waited nearly two years, then moved really fast into a very intense relationship. I just want to take a couple of steps back, that's all. Really get to know each other before we get into full-blown commitment mode. Do you understand?"

"You are breaking up with me?" He wasn't insulted; he was stunned and stared at her in disbelief.

"See, when *you* say things like 'breaking up,' it sounds so silly coming from a Vampire Lord who is as erudite and concise in formal speaking as you are.

"We are on a break, Aleksei. Just a break. I don't want you to go away; I don't want to leave. I just want some space right now so I can get everything sorted out in my mind. I know that's selfish of me, but I need some time here. Are you okay with that or do you want to tell me to go to hell and to forget it?"

Tanis's voice suddenly rippled through his mind. *"Shut up. For the love of God, Aleksei. Just. Shut. Up. Do not say another word except 'All right, Gillian.' "*

With supreme effort Aleksei said exactly that. "All right, Gillian."

Suspicious, she looked at him carefully. "Just like that? No fighting, no arguments?"

"Just like that," he agreed. "I want you to be happy, *dolcezza*. Whether with me or not, I want you happy."

Because he couldn't help it, he embraced her, holding her as tightly as he dared, inhaling her lovely scent of snowy clover and sunlit meadow. And Perrin. The man's scent was all over her, but Aleksei couldn't smell sex. She hadn't made love with him yet. For a thousand reasons, he was relieved for the moment.

Her voice came muffled from his chest. "I am not unhappy with you, Aleksei. I am confused and scared to death. I do love you, at least I think I do, but I need to really know that this is *my* idea too."

Kissing her hair, he stroked her back. "I love you, *piccola*, and I am sure of that. I will continue with my life as intertwined with yours as it is and hope that your road will lead you back to me."

"Bravo, brother. I did not know you were capable of such sensitivity." Tanis again.

"Shut up, Tanis."

———◆———

This is the fucking night that never ends, Gillian thought crossly. Either that or she was caught in a goddamn time warp of some kind; she would look at her watch and discover it was still eight o'clock, and she'd be off to visit Perrin again for another night of idiot former bosses, gross misunderstandings with a patient, Vampiric relationship discussions in the moonlight and now this.

Cue X-Files *music* was the first thing Gillian could rationally sort out from her thoughts. She couldn't remember ever being this tired. All she'd wanted to do since leaving Aleksei on the path was to come in, get some coffee, read a few minutes then fall into a blissfully unconscious state where there were no demands on her time. But no. The truth was in here. In the library. Right smack in front of her.

"Gillian!"

Luis Clemente, formerly Captain Clemente, Pilot USMC and recruiting poster Vampire cover model, rose from his place on the couch beside, who the hell was that anyway? Gillian couldn't remember if she'd ever seen him before or not. Shit, she couldn't remember her own name right then, let alone whether or not she'd met someone.

Luis smushed her in a hearty embrace, dangerously wobbling the hot coffee she carried. He looked terrific. Six feet of bronze-skinned, built-like-a-brick-house, obsidian-eyed Puerto Rican Vampire. His hair was longer, she noticed. The last time she'd seen him, he'd been spelled asleep to travel via coffin to Dionysus in Greece to see if the Greek Lord could salvage his mind from Dracula.

Luis had been another kidnap victim with Tanis, but not being a Master, he had truly suffered at Dracula's hands. Finding out he was a "plant" while in the midst of their rescue excursion to Russia had been a very unpleasant turn of events. Luis had slashed his throat in an attempt at suicide, willing himself to die rather than harm anyone on their team.

Funny thing about Vampires—even a slashed throat won't take them out completely if they're at full strength and mentally healthy. Luis had been weakened by torturous draining and what amounted to mental rape. But Dracula, his tormenter, had seriously miscalculated Luis's level of loyalty and honor. Some of it was innate, Luis was just an outstanding guy; some was courtesy of the code and the measure of the USMC; and some of it was because Luis loved his friends more than he feared Dracula.

The handsome Vampire released her enough to look at her. "You okay, *muñeca de bebé*?" He was a little taken aback that Gillian wasn't more surprised or at least happier to see him.

Standing on tiptoe, she kissed his cheek, pressing him warmly in a one-armed hug to keep from jiggling the hot coffee over both of them. "Luis, I am delighted to see you whole, hale and hearty. I am whipped, so if my enthusiasm seems lacking, it's because I don't have the energy left to do anything except crawl into bed and die."

"Everything is all right, though?"

"Yes," she affirmed, "everything is fine, and I really will be all bouncy about this tomorrow evening. Now why don't you introduce me to your friend?" She turned back to the blond man on the couch, who rose and came toward them.

"Gillian Key, this is Oscar Gray." Luis remained at her side as his guest came forward. Gillian felt the cool empathic pulse of power that always registered on her radar as being from a Master Vampire.

"Oscar, I am always pleased to meet a friend of Luis's." She smiled as warmly as she could manage and shook his slender, pale hand, looking him over as she did so. *Striking* was the word that came to Gillian's mind. Soft beauty cloaked him, almost ethereal. She'd never heard of a Vampire Fey or Sidhe, and Elves simply couldn't contract either the Vampire or Lycanthrope viruses, but he looked like he hadn't been a full-blooded Human before his rebirth.

"How charming, Dr. Key." His voice was pure upper-class

Brit. "Luis has expressed great admiration for you and your profession, and I have looked forward to meeting you."

Oscar's smile was genuine and she couldn't pick up any deception from him. The crystal-clear starry blue eyes sparkled with warmth, complementing the shimmering blond hair the curled lightly at the edge of his collar and around his neck. His eyebrows were dark, but his hair was obviously naturally blond, usually interpreted as a genetic signature of a mixed blood.

"Thanks and please call me 'Gillian.' " Gillian wanted to cut this short and crash. "Look, I'm really glad you're here, Luis and Oscar, but I am just wiped out."

Keeping her arm around Luis's waist, she gestured with her coffee hand into the library, where they had been sitting. "Let's go in there for just a moment, Luis. A lot has happened while you've been away, and I promise one of us will explain everything to you tomorrow evening. Right now, I need you both to sign something."

She set her cup down, moved to Aleksei's large desk and riffled around until she found two confidentiality forms for the Rachlav Institute of Paramortal Healing. "If you would both read this over and sign them, we'll keep everybody's ass out of hot water with legal issues."

The Vampires took the documents and read them. Gillian fished out a pen from the top drawer and handed it to Luis.

"You and Daed are running a nut house for crazy Paramortals?" Luis laughed.

Gillian didn't want to strangle Luis, not on his first night back, so she settled for sarcasm. "Yup. That's why I'm having you sign a committal form by making it appear like a standard confidentiality agreement."

Luis laughed harder, but he signed. "I'm sorry, this is just an interesting surprise."

"No problem." Gillian sighed. "I'm trying to be witty, but my synapses aren't all firing at the moment."

Oscar took the pen from Luis. "I think this is a smashing idea, truly! We have needed something like this in our world. The Humans have help everywhere at their fingertips while we have quietly suffered our neuroses, psychoses, phobias and obsessions."

Signing, he handed the pen back to her. "Brava, Gillian, for being brave enough to offer help so openly to all of our kind." He bowed formally to her.

Oh boy, Gillian thought, *another pretentious asshole. Just what we needed more of.* Aloud, she said, "Thank you, Oscar, we are all very happy Count Rachlav has offered his family home as our sanctuary."

"Sanctuary?" Oscar purred. "What an interesting choice of terminology, yet how well you put it."

"Haven, refuge, safe harbor," she countered, not liking his tone and feeling a sudden cool twist in the atmosphere. "I don't like the word *asylum,* do you?"

"I was referring more to the avoidance of the word *retreat.* It is a retreat, after all, from the world at large, or perhaps from someone." Oscar was smiling broadly, showing perfect dentition.

"'Never retreat, never surrender.' Haven't you seen *Galaxy Quest?*" Gill shot back with a chilly grin that clearly said, *Do not fuck with me tonight or I will skewer you.* "Actually the quote is 'Never give up, never surrender,' but some people think of retreating as giving up. *Retreat* is just gathering strength for a new attempt."

Without waiting for a response, she hugged Luis, retrieved her coffee and excused herself. "Now if you gentlemen will forgive me, my bed awaits." Then she hurried off, grumbling to herself about ostentatious Vampires.

While Gillian was dealing with the castle's newest guests and trying to sleep after torquing Perrin's mind, Aleksei and Tanis were engaging in the first of four exchanges, hopefully to divest Tanis of Dracula's spoor and influence. Both of them would be vulnerable during this time so Aleksei had asked Trocar to watch over them. The Dark Elf liked Tanis well enough, but his opinion of the Vampire Lord was about on the same level as a goblin or troll. He agreed only because Gillian would be supremely pissed if anything permanent happened to Aleksei.

They met in the family crypt beneath the castle. Ironic to say the least, Trocar thought as he lounged atop a marble sarcophagus, back to the wall, long legs stretched out and crossed in front of him. A full wizard of the Grael, he was fascinated by what was about to occur. Vampiric magic was foreign to Elves of any variety since they couldn't contract the virus. Once in a while a single Elf might have dealings with a single Vampire, but as a rule, there was little reason for them to communicate.

Trocar knew the steps logistically, but he had never seen a Vampire feed before. The fact that these two were brothers made it just slightly twisted. It was for a good cause, certainly, but it wouldn't make it any less weird to see these two stunning specimens of sex-on-a-stick Vampires in what amounted to a lovers' embrace. The Grael propped one leg up and rested his arm on his bent knee, watching the show, a sword, stiletto and garrote next to him on the marble slab.

Aleksei wasn't fond of Trocar after finding him in bed, holding Gillian's breast as she slept. Gillian had confirmed that they weren't lovers and that, yes, Trocar was just that kind of instigating shit to do something like that knowing Aleksei was about to arrive. The two of them had maintained a level of nearly obsequious politeness that made one and all around them susceptible to diplomacy-induced toothaches.

Tanis stood in all his male Vampire glory three feet away from Trocar's perch. Aleksei came around and stood behind him. He was taller so he got to decide positioning. After confirming that Tanis was hell-bent to go through with this, he moved his brother's hair aside, leaned him back against that muscular chest and bit down. Tanis gasped audibly as Aleksei's fangs sank home.

Vampiric feeding was almost always accompanied by a glamour of some kind. It was like standard equipment on a car. They all had it, but with some of them it just worked better and sexier. Without it, feeding could be torturous, even cruel. It was not a good feeling when someone with inch-long fangs nailed you in your carotid artery without glamour to shield you from what he was actually doing.

Vampires used it when they fed, or word would have gotten around that it seriously sucked to be bitten and the donor dance cards would have been empty. When it was employed, the prey or victim, depending on your perspective, experienced the equivalent of speedy foreplay with a shattering climax at the end.

Since Tanis was his brother and Aleksei didn't care to do anything that would remotely bring sexual feelings into the situation, he didn't use glamour and Tanis felt the bite keenly. Every pressurized suction from Aleksei's mouth was excruciating, but it had to be done. They had regularly supplied each other with blood, generally via a proffered wrist. However, with this exchange, the volume and speed were what was important, so the neck was it.

Holding his brother in an iron grasp, Aleksei drained him as fast and fully as he could. Tanis was taking a risk, but so was he. Vampires had notoriously efficient survival skills. They could appear dead as a doornail then pop up like a macabre jack-in-the-box, rip your throat out, gulp your blood, then be back to fighting strength quick as you could wonder why there were red raindrops falling on your shoes.

If Tanis's consciousness wavered or if the process of reconversion was faulty, his instinct would take over and Aleksei could find himself on the business end of a very lethal pair of survival-oriented teeth, powered by two hundred pounds of steel-corded muscles and no higher brain activity. Things like that could ruin even a Vampire Lord's night. As Tanis's blood level dropped rapidly, he began to buck against Aleksei's grip.

Trocar sat up at that. He was there to intervene if necessary and prevent them from shredding each other if things went awry. Things were looking like they might be going wrong as Aleksei struggled to hold Tanis in place and complete the exchange. The younger Vampire's face was taut with agony as the cells in his body literally began to shrivel from lack of nourishment.

He didn't know that Aleksei felt his brother's instinctive panic beginning and had merged his mind fully with his sibling. Swiftly, he decided it was enough and closed the wounds in

Tanis's throat with his healing saliva, then in one motion tore his own wrist open and shoved it into Tanis's mouth, swearing in Romanian as his brother fought him. The Grael stepped forward to trace an archaic symbol on Tanis's forehead.

Aleksei looked up at him questioningly, but Trocar inclined his head toward Tanis, whose face had been etched with strain. Tanis's face relaxed, and though he was incapable of rational thought at the moment, he bit into Aleksei's wrist, taking his brother's rich and powerful blood back into his starving cells. The shift was obvious as Aleksei's face took on a more relaxed visage to mirror his brother's. He felt the change in his mind too. Whatever the Dark Elf had done had calmed Tanis from the panic he had been in and allowed him to feed without a fight.

"I am your Liege and Lord, Tanis Rachlav. With my blood, flesh and magic, I bring you safely into my House. If either has need, the other will answer, crossing land or sea to perform the obligation. In unity, family and honor, you are mine." Aleksei spoke the ritual words to bind another Vampire to him, modified slightly for his own Line. The last was whispered as Tanis was rapidly draining him and had not yet opened his eyes. Soon he'd be too weak to free himself. If he died, Tanis might too if the reconversion was successful.

"Enough!" Trocar snapped, sensing the danger and pulling Aleksei's arm from his brother's mouth. Aleksei gamely joined in the tug-of-war, but Tanis had a Reborn grip on him and he was weak from the exchange.

"Speak to him in his mind, Vampire," Trocar ordered, linking his fingers together in a double fist and swinging at Tanis's jaw. The force of the impact tore his mouth free, then Aleksei took his mind, holding him and ordering him to awaken.

Dark lashes fluttered a moment then opened with a blaze of golden fire behind them. Trocar dragged Aleksei back and away, positioning himself between the two, just in case. Tanis rolled on his side then got to his feet like a stalking tiger; slowly and inexorably. Trocar reached behind his cloak and brought out a small crossbow with an wooden bolt loaded and cocked. He drew down on Tanis, the one Vampire he could claim as a friend.

"Do not."

It wasn't a request.

Tanis wavered for a moment then seemed to find his voice as reason bled back into his eyes. "I am sound and sane, Elf. Thank you for your intervention. I fear I might have harmed my brother." The gold eyes shifted to Aleksei. "Thank you as well. I hope that we are successful, but we will know that we tried, no matter what the outcome."

Aleksei was getting to his feet while Trocar put his archery equipment away. No small trick for someone who had just donated most of his blood volume. Being the Head of a Line or House allowed him to regenerate faster than another Vampire. "I am glad you are well, Tanis. Only three more nights like this one and you'll be able to be right next to our dark enemy and not be affected."

"Go feed, Aleksei," Tanis said gruffly, leaning against the sarcophagus as a support. "I will make sure all is well around the grounds with the Grael's perceptive help."

"We cannot be sure this is working, what effects it will have on you in the interim before full conversion or even that it will work," Aleksei reminded him.

"Then we will have to 'stack the deck,' as it were, before we get the numbers up," Tanis shot back, leaning forward, seemingly to ward off dizziness.

"I can provide some assistance, Vampire," Trocar said to Aleksei. "There are spells my people use to ensure certain . . . outcomes, shall we say. I will think on it and be ready tomorrow evening."

On his way out the door he paused. "Go feed, Vampire Lord, so that you do not disconcert the fair Gillyflower. I shall think poorly of you if she is distressed." He vanished into the near dawn light.

"Do you have time to feed before the sun is fully up?" Tanis asked. Aleksei nodded and gained his feet as well.

Together they hurried out into the breaking dawn to feed Aleksei and settle Tanis in the healing earth until the next night.

CHAPTER

9

GRAY, Oscar Gray. Why should I know that name? Gillian crawled up out of layers of sleep with a name and a question in her mind. She lay alone in the enormous bed. Since she had announced that she was taking a break from Aleksei, he would leave her alone; that she was sure of.

Glancing at the clock, she noticed that it was after 5 P.M. Still keeping Vampire Standard Time, even without the Vampire, oh well. None of her other clients were much for sunlight either.

Still, "Oscar Gray" remained a puzzle that she felt would go better with cream, sugar and French Roast. After a hurried shower and starting to dress in her usual khakis, she remembered she had to see Perrin and changed into a slinky black velvet and lace shirt with buttery soft leggings, both of which hugged her curves; flat, calf-high, black velvet boots; and a matching ribbon woven through the braid that hung down her back. Looking at her reflection in the full-length mirror, she thought something was missing. Makeup. Sighing, she relented, slapping some mascara and blush on for good measure. She hated lipstick so didn't bother with it.

There. She looked . . . argh . . . cute. A pint-size musketeer. Shit, she'd been going for sultry. Oh well. She shrugged and gave her clothes a final pat. Fussing about her appearance wasn't like her. Surrounded by all the ethereal, metaphysical beauty that were the Paramortals, Gill opted for being just who and what she was: Human. Love it or lump it. It made things much easier on the ego.

Fortified with a cup of lovely New Orleans–style coffee and half a bagel, she was on her second refill when her synapses all came on line at once. "Gray" . . . Something Tanis had told her when they'd come back from England.

"Tanis!" she yelled, barreling out the kitchen door, knowing that if the Vampire was in the castle, he'd hear her. On the way, she nearly collided with Luis and Oscar, who were coming in from feeding presumably.

"Hi, Captain," Luis said, then seeing her rushing, asked, "Everything all right, Gillian?"

"Not really, but I need to find Tanis. I'll be right back."

She could have lied to Luis, he wasn't a Master Vampire so he might not pick up on it, but Oscar was and would certainly notice. Oscar nodded his head and smiled toward her as she breezed by. If she was right in her recollection of something Tanis had told her, Oscar was potentially a huge problem.

Mentally she reached out to Aleksei. She didn't want to, but Tanis might be with him, and instantly she felt his reassuring touch. "We will be there momentarily, *piccola*. Meet us in the courtyard."

Aleksei could feel her agitation and her reluctance to have contacted him directly. That bothered him more than anything. He wanted her to allow him into her life and thoughts more, but since their argument she had remained closed off and edgy around him.

"Gillian needs you," he said aloud to Tanis, who was strolling up to the castle with Jenna on his arm.

"Indeed? Why?"

"I do not know, but let us meet her by the castle."

"Are you all right, babe?" Jenna had gone out to meet Tanis in a pattern they had established since their return from France. There was something wrong; she could sense it but couldn't pinpoint what it was. He turned to meet her eyes, still breathtakingly lovely, enormously strong, but he felt "off" to her for some reason.

"I am fine, *cara mia*. Even Vampires do not sleep well sometimes." His smile took her breath away and dropped her IQ by several points.

"All right, you just feel different is all. I'm being jumpy, I guess." Jenna sighed and leaned into him as he tucked her under his shoulder and pressed her against him.

"I am different," Tanis agreed, kissing the top of her head. "I am happy."

She rewarded him with a brilliant smile. He felt a twinge of guilt. Nothing he had said was a lie, but he was skirting so far around the truth that he was nearly out of the country. Truth was, he felt like hell. Aleksei's blood was fighting with Dracula's strain in his system, and he wasn't looking forward to the next three nights of exchanges. He felt weaker than he had since leaving England but didn't want to alarm Jenna.

Gillian was walking down to meet them, Kimber and Pavel, whom she'd run into in the main foyer, beside her. Aleksei could tell by the aggressiveness in her stride that she wasn't happy about something. As if on cue, Trocar strode out of the woods by the guesthouse and gave a curt wave at them as they converged on each other. She waved at him and motioned him to come over. Good grief, this looked like a family reunion or something. All she really needed were Tanis, Jenna and Kimber, but Aleksei needed to know too, as did Pavel. Trocar, well, she just liked the Grael around these days.

The Dark Elf moved like liquid over the uneven ground, clothed in his predictable black leather from shoulders to boots. Reaching their group, he unobtrusively moved to stand between Gillian and Aleksei, effectively cutting the Vampire off from being near her even for the time being. He was still not in a forgiving mode and wanted to emphasize that his former Captain did not belong to the handsome Count. Aleksei wasn't sure that it was deliberate so he said nothing. Gillian wasn't paying attention, as she conveyed her question to Tanis.

"Tanis, where were you and Luis held in London? Did the estate have a name?"

"I believe it was called Windmere. Why do you ask?"

"Shit, well, that doesn't make sense. I keep remembering the name *Gray-something*, like Grayline, Graybridge. Hell, I'm probably thinking of Graystoke, like Tarzan's family name," Gillian groused. "I'm sorry I called you over; it was just a thought. I was concerned with Luis's new friend."

"Luis is here?" Kimber yelled, taking Gillian by the shoulders. "Why the hell didn't you say something?"

Jenna tried to speak, but Gillian interrupted her.

"Hey, it was like four in the morning when I went to bed, and I ran into Luis and his pompous friend Oscar. I couldn't shake the feeling—"

"Gillian!" Tanis exclaimed. "Oscar? Oscar Gray?"

"Uh-oh, why do I have the feeling that I am not going to like what you're about to tell me."

"I am about to tell you that you were right." Tanis smiled. "I did not understand why you were referencing the estate's name and the color gray. But you say that Oscar Gray is here with your friend Luis?"

"Yes, they were inside just a few moments ago. I talked to both of them last night when I had them sign a confidentiality agreement."

Tanis turned to Aleksei. "Oscar was the Vampire who owned the estate where Luis and I were held."

"Then he is in league with the Dark Prince and we need to confine him or destroy him," Aleksei said emphatically.

"Dammit, I hate being right all the time." That was from Gillian, who was starting to pace, then had a thought.

"Aleksei, why would you and Tanis not notice a Master in your own home? Because I've stood next to Oscar and I felt his power. Do you think someone has reinstated those nullification spells?"

"The dampening fields are down, Gillian, but Tanis and I slept away from the castle last night. We have only just returned," Aleksei said gently.

"Well, for crissakes, Aleksei, don't you people have a bad-Vampire distant early warning system? Or some kind of a force field?" Gillian stood with arms folded across her chest. "Come to think of it, how the hell did they get in the castle last night anyway? Doesn't that 'by invitation only' rule still work?"

"Oops."

They all turned to stare at Jenna, who was blushing. "I may have fucked up, guys."

"You issued an invitation to enter to an unknown Vampire?" Trocar tried to keep the "Oh my god, what a dumbass" out of his voice.

"I'm sorry. Shit, I mean it was Luis for fuck's sake! What was I supposed to say? You can come in, but your friend can't?" Jenna was upset. "Besides, no one was around to ask!"

Tanis pulled her closer and turned her to look at him. "You did nothing wrong, *cara*. Luis is your friend and someone you trust. It would not have occurred to you to question his visit or who his friend was."

"I'm really sorry, Aleksei . . . Gillian . . . I'll throw them out myself since I fucked up." Jenna tried to pull away from Tanis, but he wouldn't let her, pulling her into his embrace and stroking her hair, murmuring softly to her in Romanian.

"Jen, it's all right." Gillian and Kimber moved together to their friend. "Look, we're all in this together. No one knew Luis was coming back and no one thought to tell you, or hell, tell anyone what the rules are."

"Mainly because no one knows what the hell the rules are." That was from Kimber, who said it as an aside comment, but everyone in the group with superior hearing understood her just fine.

Pavel spoke up suddenly. "But was your friend not with the Greek Lord?"

Now everyone turned to stare at Pavel as if he'd just done something fascinating. "Yes, he was. Why?" Gillian asked.

"Did he not contact Aleksei before to say that Luis was healed or well, or that he was coming to you?" Smart Werewolf.

"No, he did not," Aleksei said, then closed his eyes, reaching out to his friend and ally. *"Dionysus, have you sent Luis back to us?"*

From across the miles the Greek Lord's voice came to him. *"Yes, my friend. I was able to stop the spread of Dracula's infection. Luis is whole and well. Quite himself, in fact. If he has reached you, then I am glad."*

"He has, but he may have gone to England before coming here. He is of your Line, Dionysus, can you determine what his true intentions are?"

There was a warm chuckle from the Greek Vampire. *"Of course, but you are Head of your own Line, my friend. You have the power to do this without me."*

"As long as we have the time to observe propriety among ourselves, I will do so. It would be impolite otherwise," Aleksei assured him.

Head of his Line or not, he still wasn't comfortable exercising his own rights just yet. He had been a Master Vampire for longer than he'd been a Vampire Lord.

There was silence for a few moments, then Dionysus came back on line in Aleksei's thoughts. *"Luis has great concern for what is happening. He is with this Vampire . . . shall we say his interests are truly personal? I can find no duplicity in my offspring, Aleksei. I cannot read the other one fully without drawing attention. He is Dracula's spawn and a Master. This I know. Be cautious, my friend. Maeti and I will come to you, if you have need."* Dionysus cut the mental link abruptly. He was wild and unpredictable, but at least he was on their side.

———◆———

Aleksei opened eyes that glowed silver from the powerful contact between the minds of two Vampire Lords. He was glowing faintly all over, Gillian noticed. Breathtaking even. *Stop it,* she told herself. "Well?" She was impatient. So sue her.

Smiling at her irritation, Aleksei answered, "Yes, Luis is healed and is safe for us. However, the other is Dracula's. We need to attend to this immediately. Tanis?"

Tanis leaned down and kissed Jenna. "Do not be troubled, *cara*, all will be well, then we will spend time together."

Jenna had rallied. Her friends were supporting her, but she still felt bad about letting a potential Big Bad Vampire into the castle. "Oh no, hotshot, I'm coming with you. I'll get Flicker and be with you in a minute." She hurried off to the side entrance of the castle, Tanis rushing to catch up.

"Flicker?" Aleksei said, puzzled.

"It's the name of her flame thrower." At his still perplexed look, Gillian explained, "It's a Marine thing. You name your weapon."

Seeing the handsome Werewolf standing by Kimber, lightly caressing her arm with his fingertips, she thought she should say something. "Pavel, you don't need to be in the thick of anything that might happen tonight. Kimber, Trocar and I will be there to back Jenna up. Aleksei and Tanis can handle this. We're just there for a show of strength."

Aleksei moved deliberately in front of Trocar to take Gillian's arm. "You have a job to do already, *piccola*. Pavel may accompany Kimber and me if he wishes."

"What?" Gillian stared at him in surprise, then realization dawned. Perrin. Well, she was needed elsewhere, he would have to wait. "I can cancel, Aleksei. Everyone's collective safety is more important, and until we find out what the hell Oscar Gray is doing here, we can't be sure of that."

Trocar noticed Aleksei's assertion and was pleased. Perhaps they would salvage this and Gillian would be less stressed and reactionary. "Gillyflower, what the fanged one means is that you rant about being pulled into soldier mode when you would rather heal the mind, yet you continually step forward and volunteer your services when they are better used elsewhere."

"I know you are not telling me to stay somewhere safe when my people are walking into a potentially bad situation." Gillian stared at him.

"You have a patient and they are no longer 'your people' since you have officially retired . . . again. A patient, I might add, that you were willing to sacrifice our relationship for, because it was so important to you to help him."

Aleksei was blunt. She needed to hear it. "Go do your job,

Dr. Key, and let us do ours. We will notify you if your services are required." Turning from her, he moved off after Tanis and Jenna, already communicating with his brother about their best plan of action and leaving Gillian openmouthed with Trocar, Kimber and Pavel.

"You heard the gorgeous bloodsucker, Kemo Sabe. We are free agents." Kimber shoved her toward the guesthouse. "Get going with your patient, and if there's any fighting to be done, we'll save you a head to crack." Kimber took Pavel's hand and went with him after Aleksei and the others.

"Well, fuck all of you," Gillian said to no one in particular, then realized that Trocar was still there. After he pointed it out to her. Compellingly.

"All of us? Would it not be more prudent for you to spend your time therapeutically with your patient rather than engaging in casual carnal relations with nearly half of the residents here?" Dear old derisive Trocar. He always knew just how to put the "fun" back in dysfunctional. Asshole Elf.

Gillian shot him a glare that would have melted metal and refused to dignify his witty repartee with an answer, stomping off to Perrin's temporary digs, angry at all of them, knowing they were right, frustrated beyond belief that she couldn't slip back into comfortable soldier mode and be the competent protector of her friends. Tears burned for a moment and she crossly blinked them away.

Focus. On. Perrin. He was entitled to her competent therapist self, her undivided attention, and every bit of compassion that she could muster. With effort, she slipped behind the familiar walls that she'd spent years erecting and put on her pleasant, professional therapist face. Anger still simmered with a touch of fear. Oscar shouldn't have been able to slip through their established net. Bloodsucking bastard. If he'd brought any sort of danger to her friends, Doctrine or no, she'd stake him herself. Right after she got past Aleksei and everyone else who would certainly try to stop her. A slight movement from the porch of the guesthouse caught her eye. Perrin? Outside? Holy shit.

CHAPTER

10

PERRIN had positioned the piano to give him a view of the deep forest outside the guesthouse. The house had windows aplenty, but he kept the shades drawn on most of them, being uncomfortable with the amount of natural light let in. Large paneled windows in the front provided him with an outlook on the shady copse. It was cool and green, inviting. Seeing the Dark Elf walk past made it a surreal moment for him. He was still getting used to Gillian's daily visits and knew that there were more people on the estate, but he'd never seen any Elf before and Trocar's dark beauty was enthralling.

He was half looking forward to Gillian's appointment with him and half dreading it. After her departure the night before, he had researched what she'd said about "S and M" and had been horrified to read that some people found sexual pleasure in pain. That was not going to be even a mild interest of his, he decided. Even though his Victorian sensibilities and inherent cultural characteristics of a Gargoyle were telling him that Gillian required a little strong-handed guidance, he was worried that she might think the light spank of the previous night was anything but a gentle, playful reprimand.

Watching the predatory grace of the Dark Elf, he dared to

open the front door and step out on the porch. It was after sunset, the porch wasn't lit and Perrin was used to melting into the shadows. He watched with interest the exchange between the group assembled some twenty yards away. Gillian. Her attention was completely captivated by the one very tall man. Then the Elf inserted himself between them as if staking a claim.

Perrin felt an uncharacteristic surge of jealousy at his observation and immediately stamped it down. Gillian had exhaustively explained their roles in his therapy, and he understood that she was forbidden any outside contact with him for a year after they ended their therapeutic relationship. He wondered if any of those assembled were her patients or if they had been and now were her lovers. The Elf perhaps? That tall, aristocratic man who even now stepped closer to her, looking down at her with desire plainly on his extraordinarily handsome face? Both of them? That notion twisted his stomach into a knot.

She was the kindest person he had ever known; she laughed openly with him and eased his discomfort. It was part of her job to be understanding and caring, but Perrin wondered, if she had such male bounty to choose from, if she would ever consider someone like himself in the real world. Someone that she already knew to be damaged and hideous. Secretly he hoped that someday he could return to her a whole man, and that she might be accepting of his interest.

Perrin didn't realize what a dangerous game he was playing with himself. They had not yet completed his therapy and yet he was still holding on to his old truths—truths that spoke of a magical, altruistic, esoteric love between fully dressed and proper people, rather than two naked bodies intertwined, sweating and straining toward the culmination of raw desire. He wanted her to care. She did. But not in the way he hoped.

As Gillian shot a scathing glance at the Elf and headed his way after the rest departed, Perrin's heart leapt a little. The Elf stood with all his heartrending beauty, and she just walked away, to come to him. He almost slipped back inside but braced himself and waited for her approach. Keyed up, he was more sensitive than normal to the night with all its sights, sounds and smells.

He realized it was the first time he had been near a forest. Beneath the streets of Paris, and even on his estate in Rouen, his world had been austere, delicate gardens, cold stone, cold courtyards and colder water. The scents he was familiar with were herbs, roses, damp rock, musty costumes, mossy passageways, dusty hallways and stale, long-closed-off rooms. Here, the night breeze was cool, gently caressing his left profile, ruffling the black hair as he closed his eyes and surrendered himself to the moment. He breathed in the crisp, fresh pine-and-loam scent of the mountains and felt alive.

"Perrin," Gillian said softly, not wanting to startle him as he stood relaxed on the porch, eyes shut and listening to the night noises.

As if in a dream, he heard her. Opening his eyes, he looked down and saw she waited, one foot on the step of the porch, smiling up at him. "Good evening, Gillian. Please come up." He moved down the stairs to take her hand and lead her back up again. She smiled at his courtly gesture and squeezed his hand warmly.

"You seem to be enjoying the night, Perrin. Would you like to sit out here or take a walk in the moonlight?"

No teasing in her tone, he noted. She was at her most pleasant tonight. Anyone who knew Gillian knew that if she was being overtly pleasant, it was time to take cover. Perrin was her patient; there was no way she was going to blow a gasket and scare him to death. But she was trying to tread lightly. If he opened up to her too fast tonight with her own emotions on edge, she would have to leave and see him later. Angry meltdowns were an inappropriate therapeutic tool for an oversensitive genius recluse to be subjected to.

Right now she was more interested in focusing on this new development. Perrin was an agoraphobic on top of everything else. Taking even a step outside his comfort zone was courageous and should be rewarded.

"A walk perhaps," Perrin agreed, not relinquishing his

hold on her hand. Glamour bubbled up like a frothy spray, unbidden, unnoticed by him.

Gillian braced herself internally, trying not to flinch as Perrin's emotive concept of the moment backwashed over them. Happiness, sensuality, confidence and more than a passing interest in how her eyes glowed in the moonlight.

Wait, confidence? Perrin? What had happened to bolster up his self-esteem? she wondered but said aloud, "Then let's go."

"You look lovely tonight." Perrin's voice was so unique, so mesmerizing that she turned to stare at him. It had a matchless timbre to it: part lilting, musical Sidhe, overlaid with his native French. On any day it was warm and inviting; with his glamour kicked in, it rivaled the vocal styling of the Vampires.

"Thank you, Perrin. So do you." She meant it. He was immaculately dressed as always in one of his period shirts with the heavy cloth ruffle parting in a deep V down his chest. Long, perfectly proportioned legs were encased in the tight black pants and tall boots he generally wore. The mask was a dull white by the light of the moon.

Everything was an easy formality for him. The way he held her hand, for instance: very courtly, very proper, her fingers curled lightly in an overhand grasp, over his forefinger into his palm. Only his thumb held her in place; the rest of his fingers were just a warm cushion for her hand. It felt like he was leading her down a grand staircase into a ballroom at a cotillion.

When both of them were off the steps, Gill shifted her hand, lacing her fingers through his. Perrin smiled at her softly as they began walking slowly. "That is very intimate, Gillian."

"It's one of the ways couples might hold hands. A little less formal than the way a gentleman from Victorian Paris might hold someone's hand."

She smiled up at him, carefully keeping her gaze warm, but squelching down her empathy; shielding, so she could remain in his company while he sorted through his emotions and not inadvertently trigger her own. Unlacing her fingers, she seated her hand firmly in his. "And that is another way. You're going to be dating eventually. I just want you up on more current methods."

Shyly he looked at her. "So you have hope for me to overcome my ineptitude in these matters?"

"Perrin, you are a lot of things but inept isn't one of them. You have been socially isolated, that's all. I don't expect you to know subtle nuances when you've never been exposed to them. That's why you're here. This isn't about you just learning sexual techniques, it's about socialization and all of it. You're romantic enough for three men, we just have to finetune that to bring it up into the present day."

She looked around suddenly. They'd been walking as they talked and had gone farther than she had intended.

"Look, we need to go back or at least back in the direction of the compound. It isn't safe out here right now."

Her empathy, even dialed down to be near him, was tingling, giving her a crawly feeling between her shoulder blades. Something was out in the night, not with them but close enough to issue a warning to her overstrained senses. Carefully she reached out with her senses but couldn't pinpoint a direction or a source. Automatically, her body tightened, preparing to flee or fight.

"What is it?" Perrin tightened his grip on her hand, looking down at her. He could feel her tension crackling against his glamour. Something was wrong and it wasn't just whatever she was sensing.

Gillian used her free hand to push him a little. "Move, Perrin, back toward the guesthouse." She wasn't looking at him, but scanning as best she could. Aleksei could link with her and probably pinpoint . . . *No*, she would not call Aleksei now. That would be just mortifying.

Gillian Key, former soldier, distracted by Fey glamour, got herself and a patient into a world of shit. Film at eleven. Cringing internally, she reached down to see if she'd remembered at least to put a knife in her boot. Nope. *Fuck.* And, of course, no gun. She was going to have to get better about remembering her "notes to self" and stop wandering around unarmed.

When he obeyed her but didn't pick up the pace, she said a little more harshly, "Perrin, we need to hurry. There's something out here. We're outside the compound, and I don't have a weapon on me."

Adrenaline surged through him at the thought of anything harming her. "Gillian, I may be a social phobic, but I assure you I am quite strong and am capable of defending you. I am part Gargoyle, you remember."

Goddess, he was so sweet. And a dumbass. He'd have a heart attack if they ran into some of the potential nasties that patrolled the area. Grabbing his hand firmly, she pulled him along, running lightly through the forest.

"Protecting me is not your job. It's my job to protect you, and right now I'm doing a shitty job of it . . . Hera's hells!"

Perrin almost ran into her as she stopped short, nearly impaling herself on Finian's arrow as he stepped out from behind a huge oak tree. The spectacular-looking Sidhe prince swiftly lowered his bow and brought a finger up to his lips.

"Quiet, Kynzare," he whispered. "Trocar and some of my people hunt the deep dwellers. There is a pack of them about tonight and the Wolves are herding them to us."

"Terrific, well, my apologies for not helping you, but we have to get . . . What did you call me?"

"Kynzare." He smiled at her then shifted his gaze back into the darkness. "Now go, we will watch so that none follow."

Gillian didn't argue. If the Fey were out, and Trocar was with them, the threat was real and she had to get Perrin inside. Thanking Finian, she continued on with Perrin until the guesthouse was in sight, then she slowed, realizing she was squeezing his hand. "Oops, sorry, I hope I didn't hurt you."

"You did not," he said quietly, stepping closer to wrap his right arm around her waist. "Come inside. You are very tense, I can feel you through my glamour."

Not giving her a chance to argue, he gently pushed her forward toward the porch. There was a little bit of an authoritative edge to his voice. A glance up at him, and she saw his jaw was set in a firm line. Uh-oh. Perrin looked a little put out.

Once inside, he locked the door and drew the heavy draperies across the front windows, then turned to find her pacing the floor, looking small and vulnerable. Something began to rise inside him, something protective and more predatory than he had known. "Sit down, Gillian. I will get you some tea, then we will talk."

"Perrin, I'm fine." More pacing.

"The doctor cannot admit that she is in no shape to handle her patient at this moment?" His left eyebrow rose and, with it, the temper he hadn't known he possessed. A stern edge had crept into his voice.

Gillian glared at him. "Fine. Look, I'll just go and come back later." She headed for the door.

Perrin was at her side in two strides, clearly annoyed, and had her by the shoulders. "You will sit down as directed and talk to me about what is bothering you tonight." He pointed to the couch. "Sit down."

"Okay, who are you and what have you done with my patient?" Gillian crossed her arms and looked at him, the slightest smile quirking the corner of her mouth. Bossy bastard.

The gray green eyes narrowed a little, joining the elevated eyebrow in giving him a vaguely edgy, dangerous look. "I might ask you the same thing. My doctor is a competent, brave woman, not a temperamental child."

That stung. "Hey! I am not being temperamental, goddammit! I wasn't paying attention while we were walking, and because of that, I led us out of the compound area, where it wasn't safe. I didn't even have a weapon on me.

"Shit, Perrin, I could have gotten you—hell, both of us—killed. Don't you get that? There are things out there that are not very nice, don't have a sense of humor about anyone encroaching on their territory and will eat you whether or not you are still screaming."

She pulled away from him and went to stand facing the fireplace. "You are trying to take care of me, and I don't need that. I am here to take care of you. How I feel or don't feel is inconsequential. How I help you feel is what is important. Don't confuse our roles, Perrin. I can't lean on you. It isn't right."

Tears burned again and she kept her face turned away, not wanting to inflict her tumultuous emotions on him. She had to get out of there. She was way too torqued up to be around someone who had as little control over his own emotions as he did. He was shifting emotions like gears on a Ferrari and it was playing hell on her nerves.

Silence reigned, then she felt him at her back. Quiet bastard too. Two strong arms wrapped around her from behind and pulled her against his chest, his glamour shifting to feelings of loneliness and longing. "You need looking after, Dr. Key."

"Stop using your glamour on me, dammit! And stop being so autocratic!" Pulling away was pointless. She could have broken his hold on her easily, but he was stronger than she was and she would have had to hurt him to do it. Besides, she wasn't afraid of him. She was afraid for him. Letting her anger with herself overwhelm her wasn't like her. It had to do with his specific magic and she needed to get a handle on it. She should not have come to him tonight.

"I am a vocal music teacher. I am supposed to be strict and authoritarian."

At this close range, his lovely voice rumbled a little through his chest but she heard the light teasing and relaxed a little in his arms, smiling despite herself. That was the first time he'd really given himself an identity other than her patient since he'd been at the Institute. She allowed herself a little internal "squee" at his progress.

Gently, he turned her to face him, noting with some surprise the iridescent sparkle of tears as she met his eyes with impunity. "Have I inadvertently discovered a chink in your armor?" he asked softly. The edge was out of his voice, but there was something very male and very commanding in his eyes.

"I need to go."

"No . . . you do not." The masked face bent toward her and he captured her mouth, one palm cupping her head, the tips of the fingers on his other hand tilting her chin up as he gained entrance between her lips.

Rather surprised at first, Gillian stood passively as he kissed her. Opening under his insistent lips, she was amazed as his tongue began to plunder her mouth. The fingers delicately poised under her chin moved and stroked lightly down her neck to her shoulder. That hand then glided over her collarbone and around to her back, where he pressed her close. Mind whirling, she tried to figure out what the hell was going on as he gathered her closer in his arms, molding their bodies together, the long, thick line of his sex hardening almost instantly against her abdomen.

Why the sudden dominance and aggression? she wondered as she moved her arms around him to hold him tightly. This was weird, but she'd go with it. No, wait, maybe not. Perrin was part Sidhe, a very sensual people, but he was half Gargoyle too. They were also highly sexualized, just very aggressive about it. Gillian at once realized that her inadvertent flirtation with vulnerability had triggered something in his inherent predatory nature.

Well, all righty then. It wasn't anything she couldn't handle. If he was ready to go for it, that's what they'd do. They could fine-tune his responses later. Right now, it was definitely time to push onward with his therapy.

Giving herself over to the kiss, letting him control it, Gillian consciously made her gestures less assertive. If he needed to feel a measure of dominance, she'd let him have it as long as it didn't go too far. Lightly, she ran her hand down his back, skimming his butt, then around to play her fingers down the straining outline of his erection.

Perrin made a guttural sound into her mouth, bringing his hand down from cupping her head to place it over hers, pressing it against his engorged organ. Gillian complied happily; he was initiating sexual contact and that was what they were there for.

Soon, getting into the spirit of it with him, she ran her hand around his butt, pulling him to her, wrapping her leg around him as high as she could. He responded instantly, hand skimming the outside of her thigh, leaning down a little then cupping her butt to lift her up and hold her tightly to him so that they were eye level with one another.

Through their two layers of clothing, Gillian could feel the deep pulse of his distended flesh against her core. Gently, she broke the kiss, whispering to him on his masked side, "Make love to me, Perrin. I need to know what you feel like."

Perrin needed it too. He could feel her damp heat through their clothing. His Gargoyle heritage gave him highly perceptive pheromone receptors, which scented her, telling him she was open and wet already. A surge of more blood to his groin, and he saw spots for a moment. Almost savagely, he took her mouth again as he carried her to the couch and lay her down on it, pausing to look at her, marveling at her dilated eyes, tousled hair and moist, parted lips. Beautiful, she was beautiful and passionate. And taking off her clothes.

Numbly, he watched as she removed her boots and pants. Her shirt was next, then her bra. No underwear. The spots came back before his eyes as his body insisted on pumping more blood into a space where there wasn't room for more.

Gillian watched raw need and desire flood his features. Well, the ones she could see anyway. The mask was distracting but added an element of mystery to him that was endearing and dangerous at the same time. Reaching up, she traced its edge, noticing that he looked at her warily, but when she made no move to take it off, he relaxed visibly.

She observed that the gray green eyes glittered with flecks of gold as part of his arousal. Also that he kept looking her up and down, not resting on any one part of her body, as if he were a starving man who was shown a banquet and couldn't decide what to eat first. He was beautiful to her, and she let him see it in her eyes as his rose to lock with her heated gaze.

"Now your clothes," she prompted and he began to unbutton his shirt, almost mechanically. Always helpful, she moved to unfasten his pants while he pulled his shirt free and off. Perrin stopped her at that point and sat on the edge of the couch to quickly remove his boots and pants. He wasn't wearing underwear either, she noted, smiling at his physical beauty.

Perrin watched her as she looked him over. If he hadn't been so sexually stimulated, he would have been embarrassed with her frank appraisal of his dimensions. He could tell that what she saw pleased her, and lifted a hand to her in invitation.

Gill took his hand and let him draw her to him, leaning in to kiss him and letting him roll her down and under him. Opening her legs, she moved his hips over her and gently grasped his rigid sex to guide him. Holy Mother Nature, he was as endowed as Aleksei, she realized when her fingers wouldn't meet around the thick shaft.

Condom! Shit! Where was a condom? They were in the box, in the bathroom . . . No wait; reaching back with her free hand, she found the ones she had placed on the table the night before and swiftly opened the foil container.

Watching her, Perrin's entire body stiffened in anticipation. Her touch was deft and sure as she placed it over the head of his penis, which was already beaded with pearly moisture, and rolled it down easily. Gritting his teeth, he felt her take him in her hand again, and position him against her wet, heated opening.

"Now, Perrin, make love to me." Her eyes were cool green pools for a man to drown in, her body a welcoming shelter for his battered psyche. Perrin wanted to kiss her but kept his eyes locked on hers as he sank gratefully into her, feeling the tight wet bands of silken muscle stretch to accommodate his size. She gasped as he pressed inside, the muscles of her canal tingling and stinging a little as he filled her completely, lodging finally at the very opening of her womb.

He couldn't breathe. This was how he was going to die. Asphyxiated during his first sexual experience. Perrin's mind and body were coming to terms with what it felt like to be sexually aroused yet have the potential to alleviate that need wrapped tightly around his rock-hard erection like a fist.

Gillian moved her hips lightly to encourage him and the dots were back in his vision. "Please . . ." His voice was guttural and thick with need. "Oh god, you do not know what it feels like . . . Gillian!"

It was suddenly too much for his overwhelmed, overburdened sexual sensory panel. Crying out, his body contracted, releasing a quick, hot torrent into the condom, leaving Perrin shuddering over her, trying to remember how his lungs worked and holding on to her with a death grip.

"Perrin?" Gill squeaked. "Can't breathe!" She was delighted he'd finally experienced what he was looking for, but he had to release his hold on her rib cage.

"*Mon Dieu!* I am . . . *Merde!*" Perrin found out his lungs worked after all and let go of her. Raising himself up on his arms, he looked down at the beautiful woman he was still sheathed within.

"I did not know . . ." Words failed him and his eyes sparkled with unshed crystal tears over the gold and green.

"It's okay." Gillian smiled up at him, smoothing her hand through his wavy, ebony hair. "Now we will take it slowly, let you see that you can be in more control."

Without waiting for him to think, she pulled him down to her, kissing him deeply. It registered to her that they needed to exchange the condom for a new one so she paused, detaching their bodies for a moment while she fumbled for a new foil packet on the table. He was still giddy with the tingling feelings of release and the monumental hope that crashed down over him. Perhaps there was a chance after all. He might live a normal life, like a normal man. She had given him that. Given him the manhood he thought he would never achieve.

Gill saw and felt that a maudlin episode was welling up. Oh hell no, not now. Now was for healing, not crying. Quickly she kissed him, stimulating him back into readiness and expertly situating the condom once more. Lying back, she guided him over and inside once more.

Perrin surprised himself by instinctively sliding his arm under her hips, lifting her, elongating her line, giving him a fraction of an inch more to fill, which he did with a light contraction of his hips. She responded, flexing her inner muscles around him, actually pulling him in deeper.

"Don't think, Perrin," she warned him. "Just go with it. You are part Gargoyle and part Sidhe. Your body is built for sex. It knows what to do, just let go; let it happen."

Now, fully seated within her, he was trembling with desire, uncertainty, need. He knew he had exploded like the untried male he had been only moments ago. Gillian was pushing him, trying to keep his mind off his ineptitude and focus him on what they were there for. He would love her forever, for her patience, unbelievable kindness and acceptance.

She waited, feeling the dial twisting on Perrin's emotional glamour; patiently stroking his back. Softly, she urged him on, "That feels just wonderful, Perrin. You feel wonderful, now move for me."

"Move?" He couldn't think. Move where?

"Move, inside me. Just go with your instincts."

Letting his body guide him, Perrin gave himself over to feeling. His hips flexed, shoving him against her womb, then pulling him nearly out of her. Experimentally, he thrust again, finding the pleasure intensified. Gillian whispered words of encouragement, shifting her body a little to accommodate them both and beginning to set a rhythm for them.

Perrin felt her respond and begin to meet his inexperienced thrusts. Quickly he caught on to her rhythm and began to take over their dance. Gillian let him, understanding that his Gargoyle blood needed to feel dominant in this situation.

He was thick, hard, angled just right; she felt every inch of him gliding in and out. Filling and stretching her, moving deeper. Plus, he felt good. Very, very good. Exquisitely good. Oh holy mother, *so* good. And getting better with every single deep stroke. So good, in fact . . .

"Goddess! Perrin!!"

The orgasm caught her unexpectedly and she bucked under him, her thighs holding him tightly as the rush hit her, and she clamped down on his turgid erection. The pheromones in the scent of her climax hit his Gargoyle sex receptors as her canal rhythmically clasped, then released him. All instinct diverted to his groin as the need to mate with her took him into a new realm of stimulation, swelling him to incredible proportions and flaring out evenly spaced circular ridges of flesh around the circumference and down the length of his engorged penis.

It heightened his sensitivity and hers because she responded with a fresh flood of liquid heat over him, drenching him in her scent. To his aroused senses, her aroma called to him to mate with her. Hard. Fast. *Now.*

Perrin literally growled and caught her tighter to him. His mouth clamped over hers and he swallowed her cries of pleasure, his tongue matching the motion of his pelvis, plunging, tantalizing, enthralling. Hips grinding, he couldn't get deep enough inside her. Electricity seemed to be pooling low in his body, winding him tighter and tighter as the newly formed ridges on his cock rubbed a delicious friction over her inner flesh.

She was exquisite beneath him. The silken velvet of her canal was hot and wet even through the condom; the tight grasp of her pulled him farther in with each clench around his body. Primal noises were in her throat and he enhanced his glamour deliberately, pouring his own raw sexuality over her and into her as she writhed beneath him, opening herself farther to welcome his magically enhanced erection. Tightening his fingers on her hips, he held her angled to give him the deepest penetration possible.

Anticipation rocketed through him as he felt himself coming to another pinnacle. Every stroke made the need to drive into her more frantic. This couldn't get any more pleasurable or he would die from it. Gillian was careening over the same precipice, but he didn't know a woman's body well enough to know it was coming.

When she bucked again, gripping him deeply inside her, moaning into his mouth, Perrin knew he was lost but had found what he had sought. He felt a profound jolt start a feeling that he had never experienced. Pure, primal mating instinct took over. His body knew exactly what to do.

A deep flex inside, then another, driving him up and against the back of her canal. A final hard plunge. Stars exploded in his vision as electric jolts of pleasure bowed his back from the base of his spine to his neck. Tearing his mouth from Gillian's in a primitive cry, he welded them together, pouring his essence against her womb but into the waiting condom.

Panting, they held each other, letting the aftershocks subside before Perrin realized he was lying fully on her. "Forgive me, Gillian. How crass of me to leave my weight on you."

He started to pull away, but she wrapped her legs and arms around him. "You stay right there and just enjoy your moment." She smiled at him and stroked his hair back behind his ear. "I'm not a delicate little doll, Perrin, so just relax and tell me your thoughts."

It took him a moment before he realized his brain was still functional, even with the prolonged blood and oxygen deprivation. Relief was evident in his voice. "My thoughts? I do not know what to say. I am overwhelmed with all of this. You . . . the sex . . . all of it is unbelievable."

His eye traveled down and rested on her breast. A hand followed, caressing her tentatively. "I seem to have forgotten something." The light smile that she knew meant he was unsure of himself ghosted over his mouth.

"You didn't forget anything. One thing at a time. Getting overly ambitious at the first experience would have overwhelmed you. This was exactly how it should have gone."

She stroked the back of his hand softly. "Now we do need to move and dispose of the condom before you completely soften. I'm on the pill so you can't get me pregnant, but you may be with someone who isn't one day. No sense in taking chances."

Slowly he pulled out of her, feeling bereft, and watched as she sat up and deftly removed it, then scooping up the first condom, walked to the kitchen to dispose of them in the trash. As she walked back, he admired her. Confident, poised, beautiful and temperamental. All woman.

What had she been upset about? "Come here a moment." It was an order, but she let it go and went to him.

Perrin wrapped his arms around her, pulling her back so that she reclined against him. "I do not know what to say. Thank you sounds so trite for what you have done for me." He kissed the top of her head, tracing her face with his elegant fingers.

"Thank you is fine. And I'm glad you seem to feel good about it."

"It was exquisite, Gillian. I never dreamed it would be so powerful and extraordinary. I will have to adjust my viewpoint of courtly love enough to allow a petite amount of base feelings into it." The softer lilting tone was back in his voice; he sounded satisfied and content.

They talked awhile longer, and Gillian let him hold her. She'd felt scar ridges on his back while they were having sex and asked him about it. Perrin was reluctant to disclose that they were lash marks leftover from his captivity of early childhood. Marks of enforced obedience from those who had held him captive for a number of years. He didn't want to elaborate, just bask in the glow of their shared experience. Gillian let it go for now.

Finally when it was time for her to go, Perrin produced a robe, watching her dress and go out into the night, alone. Bed for him was out of the question. He felt full of energy and delight. He moved to open the windows around the living room, letting in the night with its myriad of scents and sounds. The piano beckoned and he heeded its call; sitting on its bench, he began to write his first inspiring music in over a century.

CHAPTER
11

WISHING she'd had the sense to wear a watch, Gillian walked carefully toward the castle. A few pages of notes would be required to document Perrin's progress and, after his dimensions, a soft cushion to sit on and an ice pack. What the hell time was it anyway? She veered toward the cars, hearing music coming from the guesthouse, then punched in the keyless entry code to hers, opened the door and slid in to retrieve the key from under the seat, wincing a little as she did so.

Damn, Perrin's natural mating ridges had made him much more endowed than she'd anticipated. This was going to make things tender for a while with no special Aleksei interaction to alleviate it. A heated flush came over her thinking of how he had "healed" her before. The dreamy music continued from Perrin's and her romantic thoughts intensified, focused entirely on Aleksei's consummate skills.

Blushing, and cursing herself for wrecking a perfectly good memory of Perrin's evolution into sex god, she found the key, turned it enough to activate the clock. Nine o'clock?! Good grief. She'd been over there for almost three hours. Losing track of time was not something she was known for. Samuel and Moose would have been waiting. Shit. She needed to get to the castle, pronto, apologize to her patients and find out what had happened with Oscar after the gang had gotten hold of him.

As she eased gingerly out of the car, her empathy registered a weirdly hollow shift in the rightness of the world. What. The. Hell. Now? Remembering she had an extra gun in the trunk, she retrieved it without a qualm, quickly verifying that the Walther PPK was indeed loaded. The prickly feeling had long since gone from between her shoulder blades but this was a vague feeling of oppressiveness cloaking everything. It hadn't been there a moment ago so whatever it was, was alive and moving.

Closer.

Toward her.

Shit.

Psychologist, soldier, or dumbass, she was going to have to make peace with the different sides of herself or she was going to die. Not paying attention earlier because she was angry about having to be a psychologist when she wanted to be a soldier, then wandering off the grounds like a rookie; not calculating the level of Perrin's magic and losing her track of time with him, neglecting her other responsibilities. Christ. Maybe she could use that infusion of music teacher discipline. She was so going to kick her own ass for slacking off. That was if she lived through the next few minutes.

Something was wrong. Very wrong. Perrin's extra glamour boost had caught her in a very vulnerable preorgasmic moment, and her empathy was enhanced like never before. Briefly she considered getting back into the car, locking the doors and honking the horn until someone in the castle heard her, but she dismissed the idea. Perrin might decide he was brave all of a sudden and come out to look. That would get one or both of them killed for sure. Whatever was out there was stalking her. It had her on its radar; she could feel an indistinct nauseating undertone. Screaming was out. Gillian just wasn't a screamer . . . well, except in bed. Damn! Blushed again.

Where the hell were the Wolves? Generally there was a

Werewolf or two around the castle any given night. Backing around the side of the car, she tried to triangulate where the bad feeling was coming from. Not the castle, not the parking lot . . . the road? Maybe. The forest? Definitely. Turning slowly, she raised her gun and sighted down her arm, panning the area she thought was right. The car was behind her so she would be fine . . . *Aghhhhh!* She bit her own tongue to keep from screaming when something nudged her in the back. She whirled to face whatever it was.

The gun did not quite go off.

Moose. It was only Moose, who stood sorrowfully gazing down at her from widened liquid eyes, hideously twisted antlers bobbing a little in agitation.

"Goddammit, Moose!" Gillian whispered fiercely. "Don't sneak up like that!"

The tragic Fey dipped her heavy head in acknowledgment, then clumsily pointed toward the road with her hoof-like hand. "You want me to go over there?" Gillian asked, hoping she was wrong.

Nope. That's what the creature wanted. Baldour's balls. Sighing, Gillian started off, still angry with herself that a two-thousand-pound creature could get that close without her noticing it. Moose honked softly in fear and Gillian stopped.

"What?"

It moved in front of her and pointed back toward the castle, trying to convey something to her with its eyes.

"Wait, you just told me to go that way; now you want me to go back to the castle?" Gillian was trying to separate a portion of her empathy and focus on exactly what Moose wanted, but her own personal radar was having conniption fits about the danger it sensed and wouldn't free up any of itself.

"Look, are you saying you want me to see what's that way"—she pointed toward the road—"but you want me to go to the castle first?"

Moose nodded.

"For backup?"

Again the nod.

Relief. She understood. "Okay, look, I'm going to call

Aleksei, then you go back to the castle and stay inside. Don't come out and don't come after me. Just point whoever asks toward where I am. Aleksei will find me."

Vigorous shake of the head. No.

"Come on, Tuuli, I know something bad is out there. I just don't want you getting hurt is all." Gillian put her hand on the forelimb. "Please go inside. I'll be fine."

Again a negation of her thought.

"Are all of you Sidhe stubborn pains in the ass?"

Enthusiastic nod.

Gillian could have sworn Moose smiled. "Fine, hold on one second." Mentally she reached for the one person she knew would hear her. *"Aleksei, there's something very bad out here. Moose is scared but won't go inside. Send someone out right now because this is going to take more than me to handle it."*

Aleksei returned the thought after a moment's pause. Gillian sounded scared but in control, and she wasn't too proud to ask for help. *"I hear you, bellissima. Stay where you are; keep scanning around. I will stay with you until Tanis, Jenna and Dalton can get there. I am dealing with Oscar and do not want to let him out of my sight for the moment."*

Gillian hated to admit it but she felt better just hearing his voice. If he was dealing with Oscar for that long, she was betting it wasn't pretty. Tanis was suddenly beside her, materializing out of mist. She didn't care how he got there as long as he was there.

"Neat trick," she said, meaning it. "Now how about you and I go look and see what's scaring Moose so badly."

"The others are coming, *piccola sorella.* Wait until we are sure she is protected," Tanis said, ruffling her hair affectionately. "You smell like sex. Take a shower when you go in, before you see Aleksei."

Gillian glowered at him, blushing. "Never mind."

Great Zeus, she was overreacting to every thought about Aleksei. This was ridiculous. Thank all the gods, Perrin was still in his house, occupied at the piano. One less thing for her to worry about.

Ebony eyebrows rose. She didn't just smell like sex; she was emanating sex like a beacon and it was permeating the area. And where was that music coming from? It was remarkable. Probably her patient, the one Aleksei was so angry about. But the music was indescribable. It sang to every cell in his body. Tanis felt himself unwillingly reacting to whatever she was putting out.

Almost immediately he was full and needy, his ardor nearly tenting the tight blue jeans he wore. His focus on Gillian instantly became more intense. "Gillian, stop it! You need to stop it!"

He grabbed her shoulder and gestured toward his groin. Gillian's eyes widened at his tone and at what he was indicating. "How the hell did that happen?"

"You are giving off an erotic flare like I have never encountered, and you need to turn it off!" Frowning, he looked around as he picked up on the oppressiveness she was feeling. His face darkened even more as he closed his eyes, concentrating, scanning the area and trying not to think about fucking Gillian's brains out in the gravel parking lot.

"Feel that? What the hell is that?" Gillian ignored the commentary on her aura and watched him. Tanis had been her first lover in this Country and was now her solid friend. She trusted him to do whatever he needed to do but not get in her way either.

The golden eyes opened and he looked at her intently, his entire demeanor shifting. Tanis looked suddenly very dangerous. "Gillian, do not argue with what I am about to tell you now." His tone was soft, but his voice held a compulsory command. "Take Tuuli, get to the castle and remain inside. Find Aleksei and stay right by his side. I do not know if you are in more immediate danger from what is coming toward us or from me."

That statement and his using her actual name got her attention. She stared at him in disbelief. "Tanis, you would never hurt me. I trust you."

"Normally you can, yes. Right now, I am deadly serious. Whatever it is that you are inadvertently giving off has me literally fighting with myself not to tear your pants off so I can bend you over the car hood and fuck you senseless. I cannot divide my focus between you and whatever it is out there."

She had enough sense to step back from him a little. Tanis never swore, at least not like that. "Aw, shit! It's glamour. Perrin—!"

"I do not care what it is, get away from me, *now*!" Tanis interrupted, practically roaring at her, terrified that she wouldn't go while his aching groin was nearly weeping with hope that she would stay. "I do not want to take you by force, Gillian. I cannot control this feeling. Please. Leave."

His voice was strained and his golden eyes burned as they raked over her. Mentally he called to his brother, praying that someone else would get there in time.

When his hands moved to his belt, golden eyes burning with hunger for her, she backed up again, knowing with complete certainty that he was serious. She really should get away from him, but it wasn't right to leave him to fight alone. Reluctantly she took another step backward, bringing the gun around to a two-handed grip, keeping it lowered but between her and Tanis. Where the hell were Jenna and Dalton?

Tanis fought not to move, wanting to turn away from the little blonde in order to compel the disfigured Fey's obedience so Gillian would follow her. Gillian saw and felt what he was attempting, sensed something ephemeral winding through the atmosphere like a coiled spring.

"There's no time," she whispered to no one in particular.

A surge of metaphysical power wrenched the environment itself with a nauseating twist and three figures appeared out of the mist she hadn't noticed, in a large semicircle about twelve yards away. Gill brought the gun up and moved toward the trio except Tanis stepped in front of her, still fastening and unfastening his belt, trying desperately to focus on the potential danger instead of Gillian's shapely ass, but she elbowed him aside.

Placing herself in front of Moose, she ordered, "Stay out of my line of fire."

"Your bullets will not work, *piccola sorella*," he said flatly, then added, "You are like a sex goddess signaling to her devotees, Gillian. You are attracting them; however, it is not blood they want."

There was the sound of running behind her, then a gasp. "Good goddess! What is that?" Jenna. Flamethrower in hand.

Gill turned to watch her friend go from soldier to slut in milliseconds. Jenna's glassy-eyed, glazed look focused on her for a moment, then took in Tanis's tall figure. Practically drooling, she dropped the flamethrower and moved toward him.

"Tanis?" she said in a throaty whisper.

The Vampire turned her way, almost groaning with need. "Jenna."

His voice was deep, rasping and heavy with sex. As she ran to him, he caught her in his arms, fastening his mouth on hers as she wrapped her legs around his hips. Tanis turned to lay her on the car hood as he'd threatened to do to Gillian, tearing away her pants, opening his own, then thrusting hard. Jenna arched back, screaming, and it wasn't from pain. Gillian looked away as they commenced with a vigorous act of lovemaking, which rocked the car in the gravel.

Mother Gaia, now what. Gillian turned as Dalton came into her peripheral vision. There was no mistaking the gold, orange, blue and violet hair of the Prince of the Light Court. The three things were still coming but moving very slowly, almost as if they were in a trance. Dalton began singing in a remarkable voice, blending seamlessly with the music that was pouring from the piano in the guesthouse, staring at her. No, he was staring at Moose. Uh-oh. The prince had an unfocused look in his wonderful lavender eyes and a hard-on down to his knees from what Gillian could tell at that distance. Worse, Moose was staring at him with undisguised adoration and honking provocatively.

Ack! Gillian thought. *This is not going to be pretty.* She backed up farther away from what was going to amount to a sexual train wreck, knowing she did not want to watch but was not going to have a choice. There was nowhere to run to, and she really didn't want to leave the area or the music at the moment.

A whimpering sound distracted her and she turned. Pavel and Kimber were by the edge of the forest, engaged in what could only be described as puppy . . . love. They were nearest the woods across from the guesthouse, Kimber was on all fours and Pavel was behind her . . . Oh, well, Pavel was pretty happy from the looks of things. Kimber too if all the wriggling and squealing could be considered good.

Mind spinning, completely grossed out though completely turned on, Gillian bolted for the castle and ran into Aleksei halfway across the manicured lawn. Literally. They both tipped over and Aleksei rolled to take the brunt of the fall, turning so that Gillian wound up straddling him. Green eyes rose and locked with his icy gray ones. Between her legs she could feel him hardening, lengthening, as his arms tightened around her.

"Bellissima," he managed to pant before she fastened herself onto his mouth, small pink tongue teasing his own. He barely registered the astonishing music, singing and the indeterminate sexual noises that were going on, seemingly all around them.

Desire flooded him and overwhelmed every other sensation but the woman in his arms. Rolling her under him, Aleksei nearly ripped her pants away, tearing at the laces of his own to allow his rigid, aching sex to spring free, then penetrating her with no preamble, a deep flex of his hips, a primal growl coming from his throat.

Gillian had no reservations, no hesitation. Aleksei made her feel safe in every way. As he tore her clothes off and pushed himself into her, she was so grateful that she nearly cried. Hazily, she was aware that after having sex with a Gargoyle-enhanced penis, she should have been tender, but Aleksei just felt so incredibly wonderful that she urged him on, nipping his neck and ear and driving him into a turbulent act of lovemaking that put Perrin's newly acquired skills to shame.

Climax after climax hit her and she felt Aleksei come, straining into her time after time, pouring his heavy liquid heat inside her with each shattering orgasm. Both were insatiable in their hunger, rutting like animals on the lawn of the castle.

She felt limp as Aleksei positioned her again, crying out in delight as his mouth came down on her swollen flesh and he lapped at her, the rush hitting quickly and hard. The taste of her orgasm excited him beyond endurance as he lifted her and impaled her on his own body, still as hard and thick as the first time. Gillian leaned back, enraptured by the feel of him as he moved her up and down on his shaft. A glow in the corner of her eye drew her gaze.

Dalton was on his back not fifty feet away and something was on him. It glowed and shimmered, the shape vaguely familiar. Moose. He was obviously very happy as he bucked upward, crying out in the sweet voice that only the Fey have, blending with the music Perrin was playing in the guesthouse. The shape on top of him shifted, the glow dribbling down from the misshapen antlers, leaving nothing in its path as it continued down and began to form a woman's body. A woman who was crying out as Dalton was, in the throes of a titanic sexual peak, and he was calling out his love for her.

Dreamily, Gillian watched the transformation as Aleksei continued to drive up into her, then was taken by the feelings that he was producing and rewarded him with all her attention again. Straining together, they were on the edge of another explosion when she became aware that the music had stopped. Aleksei thrust upward again, finishing them both off with another near-blackout experience. Gillian collapsed on top of him and he gathered her close, kissing her, murmuring to her in Italian and Romanian.

"Listen!" she said suddenly, rising up from his embrace.

Aleksei looked around warily from his vantage point on the ground, ice gray eyes curious. "*Piccola*, I do not hear anything."

"Exactly. The music stopped."

CHAPTER

12

"THE music... it was the music?" Aleksei asked, as Gillian eased herself off him and gathered what was left of her pants and shirt. It was useless, they were shredded. Aleksei gallantly removed his shirt and drew it over her head, where it transformed into a dress as it came down to her thighs owing to their height difference. Oh well, at least her ass was covered. Aleksei managed to salvage the lacings on his own pants, assuring his modesty.

Gillian giggled, knowing she looked ridiculous, and pulled on her boots, which weren't in pieces, then belted the shirt so it wouldn't flap up and embarrass her, using a piece torn from her pants. Lastly, she retrieved her gun from where it gleamed dully in the grass and stuck it haphazardly in the makeshift belt.

"Well, it was at least partly the music. Look around at the assembled bodies. Pavel and Kimber, Jenna and your brother, Dalton and . . . oh Sweet Mother, Aleksei!" His eyes turned to follow where she pointed. "Is *that* Moose?"

They walked toward the entwined couple, Gillian not noticing when Aleksei took her hand, enveloping it in his larger one as they moved along. A remarkably beautiful woman was lying in Lord Dalton's arms.

Her hair was scarlet, shot with gold and framing a delicate heart-shaped face flushed with delight. The eyes opened and looked up at Gillian. They were liquid chocolate brown, framed by thick black lashes, the result of her being in animal form for so long, but they carried the signature Sidhe starlight. Above the eyes, dark winged eyebrows complemented the golden cast to her skin.

Dalton's golden locks were streaked with the colors of the dawn sun, his lavender eyes radiant with their frame of black lashes. His own dark brows were arched and perfectly complementary to his glowing ivory complexion.

The soft brown eyes continued to look at Gillian. "Dr. Key?" said the voice that was as soft and lovely as a spring day.

"Moose? Er . . . Tuuli?" Gillian managed to get out, trying not to stare at body parts.

Laughter like bells came then from Tuuli's throat. "Moose is fine. I rather like that name, Dr. Key. Thank you for what you have done for me."

"It's 'Gillian,' and I didn't do a damn thing!"

Aleksei nodded his head in agreement and both of them pointed toward Perrin in the guesthouse. "Him!"

Dalton joined his laughter with Moose's. "Him? I would say that 'him' is at least part Sidhe. Fertility magic woven into music or simply his heritage from a music Fey would be my guess. He is projecting his emotions into his music and it is affecting us all. I should like to meet him."

He lovingly smoothed his partner's hair. "Gillian, I believe you know Tuuli. Her curse has been lifted; she is loved by one lesser than herself and returns that love. We shall have to draw up a compact between the Court of Light and the Twilight Court, if we are to be married."

Tuuli's happy squeal was his answer, and they lost themselves in a rapidly heating embrace that had nothing to do with Perrin's music. Gillian and Aleksei kept moving, happy the lonely Fey had been relieved of her thousand-year-old burden but wanting to assess what had happened. Gillian was getting a pretty good idea based on what Dalton said and what they'd all just been through.

Aleksei's time sense was working better than a watch. It was about two in the morning, which meant they'd all been having marathon sex for the last four or five hours. She was so not going to be able to walk tomorrow. He related quickly to her the situation with Oscar now that he could think again. It had taken the blond Vampire quite a while to convince Aleksei that he was trying to distance himself from Dracula and was there only because of Luis.

When Aleksei had finally demanded a Blood Oath from him, he had complied instantly, offering his wrist to the newly evolved Vampire Lord and taking Aleksei's blood in return. Luis had stood near, pleased and happy that they all could remain.

Aleksei had no illusions about the other Vampire's motives. He knew that Oscar was there only because he'd calculated the odds and figured that Dracula was eventually going to come out on the losing end of the deal. As long as he was on Aleksei's turf, the Oath would hold him. Any deviation from it and his life would be forfeit by any Vampire loyal to the Rachlav Line.

Gillian wasn't crazy about having one of Dracula's progeny in the castle with them, but since Aleksei seemed sure that there was no danger, she let it go. It was his call and she'd trust it. Her inner rebel yelled at her to bitch and protest but she drop-kicked it to a corner and kept her hand in his as they walked.

Walking away from the castle and ignoring Tanis and Jenna, who were still sprawled on the car in the parking area, Gillian saw that the lights in the guesthouse were off. Perrin was probably having lovely dreams in his nice clean bed. She was starting to itch from rolling around in the grass and probably looked like hell.

Reading the surface thoughts in her mind, Aleksei picked a piece of grass out of her hair. "Truly, *dolcezza*, you look lovely."

He meant it. Rumpled, in his shirt, with grass in her hair, she was still the loveliest thing he'd ever seen.

"Thanks, Aleksei. That makes me feel a little better."

At least they weren't fighting, but she wondered how understanding he would be when he found out what had actually triggered the night's events. That is, if she was right in her assumptions. She, Helmut, Perrin and possibly Dalton needed to have a little chat if Perrin's therapy was going to continue on-site.

"No thanks are necessary; it is the truth." Glacial gray eyes warmed her as a smile made his face even more breathtaking. He looked up and around. "Where are we heading, by the way?"

"Moose wanted me to go down to the road before the orgasmatron broke loose and I want to check it out."

Dropping his hand, she drew the gun, made sure a shell was in the chamber and continued forward, her body adopting a more predatory stance. Aleksei watched her admiringly. She truly had no fear when it came to protecting those she considered hers.

"Ew! Goddess above!" Gillian veered away from a shapeless mass on the ground and Aleksei was at her side in a heartbeat. Both of them stared, unsure of what action to take, if any.

Trocar was in a tangled mass of tentacles, attached to . . . Dear Zeus, she couldn't even look at it. Sluagh. It had to be. Nothing else could possibly be that repulsive. In the faint light from the parking lot, it was part fuchsia colored, part pond scum green and in between—yuck! She couldn't even tell its gender when it drew back from their approach in a rolling movement that nearly turned her stomach.

"Trocar?" she asked tentatively, desperately hoping that he was all right and she didn't have to pull him out of *that*. If that thing was feeding on him . . .

One crystalline eye opened. "Not one word, Gillyflower, not one. I am not in the mood." The eye closed again.

Nope. Definitely not being eaten. Well . . . that line of thought wasn't helping. She really ought to not go *there*. At least that answered the question as to what one of the three shadowy shapes she'd seen earlier with Tanis was. Oh, dear goddess, that left two more unaccounted for. Great. Now they had to find those as well.

Trocar had been glaring at her, daring her to say anything, then shut his eyes, appalled that she should witness the scene. The juxtaposition of the heartbreakingly lovely Grael versus the monstrosity of the Sluagh struck her as outrageous and she could not stop herself.

"Sucks, doesn't it?"

Both crystalline eyes opened that time, and Trocar pinned her with an iridescent glare. "I am absolutely *certain* that you have somewhere else to be, which is not *here*."

Gillian couldn't help it. Having the elegant, annoyingly perfect Dark Elf in a position that she was sure would haunt him for a long time was so ridiculous that it doubled her over with helpless laughter. Besides, he looked like he was being molested by a giant calamari.

"You want some tartar or marinara sauce to go with that, dollface?" she snorted inelegantly. "Or are you two in the throes of Post-orgasmic Elf Dishevelment?"

Trocar's eyes shifted to Aleksei, who was now laughing heartily along with Gillian. "What did I tell you, Vampire? Abusing her extraordinarily lovely backside is a thought which eventually comes to us all," he said dryly.

That made Aleksei laugh harder, pulling Gillian to him, who was trying to get control of herself and failing. "It's a gift, really," came out in breathless gasps as Aleksei grabbed her wobbling gun arm and held it away from everybody. Not particularly effective since he was laughing just as hard as she was.

Trocar rolled his eyes, throwing his arm over his face and muttering about needing a mercy killing before he lost all credibility. Giggling against Aleksei's yummy bare chest, Gill allowed him to help her not shoot those immediately present.

"Yes, it is," said a uniquely accented voice.

Gillian and Aleksei spun, placing themselves in front of Trocar and his, er, lover. Gillian blinked and wiped tears out of her eyes while Aleksei helped steady her gun arm toward the voice. Her eyes cleared as Aleksei grew quiet beside her. Perrin. Oops.

"She does bring out very distinctive male qualities, such as a peculiar need to protect her, even while she risks everything to protect us. Impulsive, beautiful and in need of loving reproof occasionally, I would surmise," he remarked in a darkly musical, silky voice.

The extraordinarily handsome fusion of races walked smoothly toward them, head up, waves and whorls of ebony hair tumbling over his forehead and collar. He met her eyes valiantly, his mask a stark reminder of his difference. The black robe he wore was calf length with heavily embroidered lapels and sleeves; white shirt open to his chest with cloth ruffles that oddly looked more at home than lace on his skin. Long legs in those yummy pants and killer boots. If anything, he looked even more stunning than Gillian remembered. Had it only been last night? Shit, it *was* last night.

Gillian opened her mouth to retaliate and abruptly the oppressive air was back in full force, instantly shifting her thoughts and verbalization. The hairs on her arms and the back of her neck stood up as she pushed Aleksei behind her toward Perrin.

He was the most vulnerable of all of them, and because he was her patient, she was responsible for him. "Aleksei, keep him here and keep him safe!"

All trace of amusement and hilarity gone, she snapped at Trocar, "Get up. I know you're armed in there, I can't do this myself and I don't have time to unravel anyone else from their immediate paramour's clutches."

Trocar extricated himself immediately from the mass, fully clothed, which brought a quirked eyebrow in his direction from Gillian. He murmured something in one of his arcane languages and the Sluagh galumphed off into the darkness.

A flick of his right wrist brought a wicked-looking stiletto into his hand; the other drew a *main-gauche* from a slender scabbard strapped to his left thigh. Both blades were pure silver and had runes carved into them.

"Where, Kynzare?" Trocar was listening with all his

might and couldn't hear what was spooking her. He did, however, trust her empathy.

"That way"—Gillian indicated with her gun—"and what the hell does that mean anyway? Finian called me that earlier." She was moving forward slowly, trusting Aleksei to keep Perrin out of the way if things went badly.

" 'Soul healer,' Gillyflower," Trocar responded in a distracted manner.

He was starting to sense something. It wasn't magic, in the literal sense, but it was twisted and evil. Evil, he knew about intimately. He broke off from her to circle to the left. Gillian watched him go out of the corner of her eye. The Grael melted into the trees without a whisper of sound.

There was a slight sound of a scuffle behind her and Perrin's voice full of worry. "No, he is leaving her! She cannot go alone! Why are you not going? You must keep her safe!" Perrin felt the oppressiveness as well and was horrified, watching Gillian's short form dressed in an oversize man's shirt and boots, creeping down the drive slowly.

That question was apparently to Aleksei, who responded, turning Perrin's face gently to his own, his supernatural voice laden with a compulsion, "Look at me. Only at me. She is all right and will remain so. She knows what she is doing. Do not fear for her and do exactly as I tell you."

Gillian heard him but couldn't pay attention to what was going on behind her at the moment. She knew that Aleksei wasn't above using compulsion to keep Perrin safe. While he might bitch about it later, right now it couldn't be helped. Having the masked man running after her, loose in the night with whatever was stalking them, wasn't an acceptable outlook to either of them.

Aleksei was trying, his brow furrowing with effort. His place was by Gillian's side, but she had asked him to protect this man, and that he was now honor bound to do.

The man's mind was proving difficult to suppress as he had a steadfastness about Gillian that it was proving hard to sway him from. The top layers were there for Aleksei to read when he looked into the gray green gaze using his considerable willpower. He tried to avoid noticing the man's private thoughts, but nonetheless, he found out more than he wanted to know.

Perrin struggled in his grip, but Aleksei held the lighter-built man easily. "No, my friend. Let her go. If you distract her, you can get her or the Elf killed. I cannot protect her and you at the same time, you are in two different places." Satisfied that he had made his point when he saw the panic subside, then understanding come into the remarkable eyes, he let the other man go.

Perrin stepped back, looking up to search the taller, spectacularly handsome man's unique silvery eyes. "I will stay here, do as you say; just please keep her safe!"

"Gillian does not require me to keep her safe, *mon ami*," Aleksei said, partly to himself.

He surprised himself by realizing that he meant it. She didn't need him. She was perfectly capable and had other perfectly capable friends. What else could he offer her other than his protection, all that he owned and his love? Was it enough for her? Did she really want it? Any of it?

Shaking off those thoughts, he focused on the masked man in front of him. Perrin was grasping his lower arms; the perfect half of his face was full of worry and something else. He was also completely oblivious that he was standing near a half-dressed Vampire in the moonlight, Aleksei observed, then realized Perrin had no idea what he was, nor cared. He was concerned only about a certain little blonde.

Dammit all, he thinks he is in love with her, Aleksei grasped with uncomfortable clarity.

Complete understanding came crashing down then, as his normally very ordered but currently exhausted mind finally connected the dots: this was her patient. He must be more distracted than he'd realized. He'd not met the man before this so it hadn't occurred to him that this was the one she . . . no . . . that was dangerous thinking and he stopped himself from completing that particular notion. What little he had gleaned of the man's surface thoughts, by virtue of simply being in his mind, hadn't been pleasant.

Perrin was part Sidhe, which Aleksei assumed had produced his physical beauty, and part Gargoyle, which was a bit of a surprise. But the depths of despair and the level of utter loneliness that Perrin had known were things Aleksei had never encountered, even in maladjusted Vampires who had lived too long.

He didn't know what lay behind the mask that seemed sculpted to that otherwise perfect face, but he was gambling it had contributed to Perrin's isolation and continued solitude. Whatever Gillian had done or needed to do to help this elegant, lonely, tormented soul regain hope and maintain his sanity, Aleksei grimly knew he would support. He did not have to like it but he would not interfere again.

Perrin deserved compassion and mercy, if for nothing else than for not becoming a monster after how he had been treated by everyone he had encountered. The level of intellect Aleksei had stumbled on during the brief meld was alarming. Perrin was truly a genius, disciplined, creative, brilliant and fragile.

It was by the grace of God that he had chosen to use his talent in such an artistic and rewarding manner rather than being a vengeful psychopath. In an unaccustomed gesture of support, Aleksei warmly squeezed the other's shoulder and was rewarded by a ghost of a smile before Perrin's attention turned back in Gillian's direction.

Walking silently toward the road, Gillian felt rather than heard someone at her back. Powerful, familiar and Vampire. Tanis. On cue, he moved into step next to her, watching the woods on either side.

"Thanks," she whispered.

"I am sorry for before, *piccola sorella*," Tanis said just as quietly. "I hope I did not shake your faith in me for my lack of control."

"Of course not. You couldn't help it. But I think I know why it happened."

"I am glad to hear it. Please do not let it happen again."

A twig cracked to their left and both whirled. Not Trocar, that she knew; he'd have cut off his own foot before he made a mistake like that. Gillian nodded to Tanis, who misted out, moving to circle the noise. She squinted, trying to make out the erratic shapes of the forest and differentiate if there was a threat out there.

Giggling. *What?!* More giggling and a low voice chuckling in amusement. Another branch snapped and something moved in there.

"Whoever you are, come out slowly. Keep your hands where I can see them. You have beings all around you; they are armed and will shoot you if you do not comply," she ordered.

They were still too close to the compound. A glance over her left shoulder showed Aleksei and Perrin still watching her intently from the elevated hillside.

More crackling in the bracken and a very large shadow loomed. Gill tightened her grip on the gun, arms steady, her mind going to a very silent, still place, focusing only on what was immediately in front of her. To her astonishment, an attractive older Human woman stepped out, holding hands with . . . Samuel? Great Hera's peacock, it was Samuel. He was grinning from ear to ear, looking at the woman as if he could eat her up in one sitting. One thing was glaringly obvious—Samuel looked possibly more put together than he originally had when she'd first met him.

As he moved into the moonlight, out of the shadow, she could see it definitely wasn't the same face she'd been looking at night after night for the past week. Samuel was still very ordinary by any standards, but the terrible raw scarring on his neck and head appeared to be healing and his skin looked more evenly toned. Even the patchy reddish hair was grown in fully over his head. He wasn't ugly anymore. At seven feet tall and over three hundred pounds, he looked like a great, hulking, plain Romanian farmer. But he wasn't ugly. How had that happened?

"Gillian! How nice it is to see you this moonswept evening!" Samuel actually chortled. It was a scary noise.

"Oh, uh, hi, Samuel," Gillian managed to get out as Tanis materialized behind the pair.

She shook her head at his questioning look. "Look, I don't mean to be rude or dismissive, but do you think the two of you could hurry a bit and get back to the castle? It really isn't safe out here." There, another diplomatic brownie point for her since she really wanted to rant at them for being out in the night without anyone knowing where they were with all the potential hazards around.

Speaking of Brownies, she wondered where the local herd of them had got off to; she hadn't seen them all night. At least Samuel and his Human's presence answered what the other two dark shapes she'd seen the night before had been. Gill felt a small sense of relief in that knowledge, except the oppressive, nearly suffocating air was still hovering.

"All right." Samuel laughed. "This is Esi, she owns the coffeehouse in town. I think I am in loooove!"

The aforementioned Esi giggled and waved happily at Gillian before letting Samuel lead her up toward the castle, both whispering in scheming tones. They were still giggling like a couple of schoolgirls in a conspiracy as they passed Aleksei and Perrin, who waited at the top of the hill.

Gillian looked up at the night sky adorned with moon and stars. "Why? Why do I get all the weird shit on my watch?" It was more of a prayer than a statement.

"Gillyflower," Trocar's voice said over her right shoulder, making her and Tanis both jump. Lucky for Trocar he didn't smirk at being able to sneak up on a Vampire. Tanis might have just killed him. Gillian would have beaten him up first.

"Yes?" This was going to be another one. A night that just fucking would not end.

"Come with me. Bring Tanis, and prepare yourself," Trocar added cryptically, turning back to lead them through the forest to the road where Finian and several other equally beautiful Sidhe stood in the distance, about ten feet off the highway in a mowed field, weapons ready and faces grim.

Gillian had just glimpsed the others milling around and talking with each other when Tanis breathed in sharply, stopping her with a hand on her shoulder. "Stop, Gillian. I can smell the blood from here."

"Tanis, I have seen death before in most of its forms. Hell, I've even caused it more times than I care to think about. I can handle it."

He regarded her briefly. "As you wish, but I did try to warn you." The Vampire could scent the blood like a shark; he knew what the blood was from: Human. Female. Young. And that she'd died badly.

Gillian stuck the gun back in the makeshift belt as they approached the group of Sidhe. With that many weapons, Fey warriors, Tanis and Trocar around, she was overly armed. Finian stepped out to meet her. "Are you sure you want to look, Kynzare?"

"No, I'm not, but I'm going to because I have to."

Gillian moved slowly forward as the Fey parted. The grass wasn't particularly tall here, having been mowed recently. As the last Fey stepped aside, she could see the body clearly. Steeling herself as she had when she worked as an investigator for the coroner's office during her college years, Gillian walked close enough to see detail, but not too close to disturb any evidence.

To Tanis, she said, "Get Cezar's brother, Ivan, down here, please. Tell him to bring whatever people and equipment he requires, but we need him to collect evidence."

The Vampire obeyed her, shifting into mist and streaking off toward the small town. Ivan Jarek was the head of the local constabulary and the closest thing they had to a coroner or a CSI team. Their resources would be limited but it was better than nothing.

Gillian squatted down, tucking Aleksei's shirt around her for some modesty, and studied the body. Human, female, and about twenty from what she could tell looking at the mutilated face. Forcing herself to focus on the injuries one at a time, she tried to ignore the loops of intestines that had been eviscerated from the woman and tossed above the corpse's right shoulder, and the smell that came with them.

She ticked off the injuries in her mind: nose cut nearly off, face slashed, the entire right cheek cut open down to the bone. She held the sleeve of her shirt over her nose and mouth, trying to breathe shallowly. Throat cut: one hesitation cut, then the one that had probably killed her, that had severed all the major muscles and vessels in the neck. It was almost a decapitation, she realized, seeing white bone from the spinal column amid the deep red muscle tissue.

Rising, Gillian backed up a little, the Sidhe and Trocar watching her closely, but she waved them off. Gritting her teeth against the roil of her stomach, she continued looking at the body, knowing it was important somehow, that she needed to see something here. Something specific. The body had obviously been posed and left where it would be easily found.

The clothing below the waist was bloody with jagged tears, and while she wasn't going to touch anything until the police inspector got there, Gill was betting that, besides the disemboweling, the woman's uterus was missing. Nagging pinpricks of thought kept poking at her as she looked at the area around where the body lay.

It was virtually untouched, though the grass was high enough to leave a track. The lack of copious amounts of blood also bothered her. This woman had been effectively butchered yet there wasn't as much blood as there should have been. Absently, she tapped her front teeth with her fingernail as she worked through what was puzzling her.

She'd seen this scene before. But where? Where indeed. Not in real life. No. In pictures? Yes, that was it. Pictures. In a book, no, in several books. Bad morgue photos, old autopsy photos; grainy, sepia toned. Old case. Famous case. An infamous case.

No arterial spray, little blood at the scene, evisceration, mutilation . . . no, this girl's too young . . . couldn't be; face destroyed, intestines over right shoulder, ear sliced half off, uterus missing, nearly decapitated, hesitation mark, posed body position, not a lot of blood, where is the blood? Impossible; impossible . . . because he never left . . .

"*England,*" Gillian finished aloud as she talked herself through her thoughts and went white, turning toward Trocar with stark horror on her face.

CHAPTER
13

HE was at her side in an instant before he asked, "Tell me, Gillyflower, what has you, of all of us, unnerved?"

Trocar was shocked and put a comforting arm over her shoulder. He had never seen his former commander flinch, blink, blanch, throw up or run from anything in all the years he had served with her. This was new and very unsettling.

Gillian steadied herself on his arm but looked toward Finian. "There's another body. Somewhere close to here, probably near the road like this one. If none of you can track blood spoor, we need one of the Wolves or a Vampire. We need to find her right now."

Finian looked at her like she'd lost her mind but nodded and gave the order. The Fey spread out and started searching in both directions down the road. Gillian opened her thoughts to Aleksei. *"Get Pavel, Cezar or any Wolf you can trust down here right away. I need a tracker."*

"I can come myself, piccola. It would be faster. The entire pack seems to have been affected by Perrin's music and are still recovering."

"No, don't leave him, Aleksei, he's clueless about the world in general and would be a sitting duck for anything that crawled up there."

"We are coming together then. I will be your tracker, and he will be safe there with you." Before she could protest, Aleksei broke off. Soon, he and Perrin were running down the road to them. She knew Aleksei ran to keep his eye on Perrin and for no other reason. Aleksei could handle what lay behind her. Perrin . . . huh-uh.

"Keep back, Perrin, I mean it!" Gillian ordered him, her hand out in a "halt" gesture as they reached the edge of the field. He stopped at her command but was looking unhappy about waiting by the roadside.

"Aleksei, I sent Tanis for Ivan. They should be here shortly. There's going to be another body. It will be close by, and it will be a fresh kill but with very little blood around it. I want you to find it or listen to the Fey if they find it. Look at it carefully and tell me what you see."

The elegant Vampire Lord delayed a moment longer, crossing over to her in several long strides, his bare torso lovely in the moonlight. Ignoring the Dark Elf, who kept his arm over her shoulders, he bent to take her face and gently kiss her. "How do you know this, about the second body? Is that what has you frightened, *piccola*? What do you think you know?"

He drew back, staying close enough to examine her, then turned to stare at the body, taking in the scene. When he looked down at her again, the ice gray eyes were worried. She looked so pale; he had never seen her like this, and apparently Trocar hadn't either. The Grael hadn't spared him so much as a glance but was staring down at Gillian. That Trocar was concerned worried him most of all. The Elf knew her better than he did, and gauging his reaction, all of them should be panicking if Gillian was that unnerved.

"I need to be sure, Aleksei, *very* damn sure before I push everyone's panic button. As soon as Ivan looks at the body, I'll know for certain if I'm right."

"That is entirely too close to a lie, Gillian Key." Aleksei's rich voice was warm with love and concern but carried a wealth of reprimand.

Before she could answer him, the lights of Ivan's van

came toward them. "There's Ivan, and here's Tanis," she announced to no one in particular.

The other Vampire misted back in next to Aleksei. Gillian
stared at him a moment, a ghastly thought suddenly occurring to her and turning her blood cold. Tanis. Tanis was here;
Aleksei was here, Perrin, Trocar. Mentally she did a quick
head count of those she'd seen in the compound, then turned
back to Tanis. This time her eyes held absolute terror as she
grabbed his arms and asked in as level as voice as she could
manage, "Tanis, where is Jenna?"

Golden eyes narrowed, then widened with the same fear
in Gillian's face. *"Dio caro!"* he whispered and misted out,
streaking back toward the castle.

"Tell me, Gillian, right now," Aleksei commanded her,
but Ivan had hopped out of the van with two other people
and was coming toward them so she shook her head and
waved her arm in a semicircle, pointing, so they could see
where the edge of the scene lay.

"Good evening, Dr. Key." Ivan was as handsome as his
Werewolf brother but less graceful as he lumbered over the
ground to the body.

"Hi, Ivan."

"She's not a local, that much I can tell you." Ivan glanced
at the body, opening up a case with vials, instruments and
swabs, then snapping on latex gloves. He handed a pair to
his assistants.

"I figured that. Tanis and Aleksei didn't recognize her either or they would have said something."

"No, I mean I know she was staying at the Inn. Radu can
probably give you more information on her if you need it
right away." Ivan was Romanian through and through but
had gone to Cambridge for a couple of years and spoke English exceptionally well.

"Shit."

"Pardon?"

"Nothing. Look, without compromising your investigation in general, can you tell me if her uterus has been removed? Also, have there been any more murders around the

area like this recently? Like within the last few weeks, or even tonight?"

Ivan stared at her a moment, then turned back to the body, picking up a pair of forceps to gently lift the ragged cloth over her abdomen and peer down with his small flashlight. "Yes, it looks like it was almost surgically removed." He looked at her. "Why do you want to know about the other murders?"

"How many, Ivan, and where?"

"Two, in the village just North of us. Just like this one but not as mutilated. None tonight other than this girl."

"Goddammit!" Gillian swore, pushing free of Aleksei and Trocar. "Thanks, Ivan!"

Yelling for Aleksei to call Tanis and tell him to meet her, she was running for the road. Trocar was only a step behind her. He knew whatever her reasons for bolting or her suspicions about the murder and her missing friend, she'd never been wrong in a crisis as long as he'd known her. If she was running straight to the murderer with the intent of rescuing her friend, he would follow; he would follow her into the Abyss itself if necessary.

"Gillian, stop!" Aleksei's voice held a whip of authority. There was no way in hell she was running off to parts unknown without the rest of them understanding what was going on.

Perrin reacted and grabbed her as she started past him, then found himself facing the Dark Elf with a very sharp knife as Gillian struggled. "Let go, Perrin, I mean it!"

"Release her." It wasn't a request.

Perrin, however, was either very brave, incredibly stupid or had no prior experience with Grael Elves and their pointy knives, so shaking his head at Trocar, he pulled Gillian around to face him.

"Tell him what you know, *ma chérie*, immediately," he said firmly in a voice that said he expected compliance. He pointed to Aleksei, who had come after her and stood waiting, looking rather annoyed.

Gillian considered breaking Perrin's wrist to gain her

freedom, or knocking him out, but dismissed both thoughts. He'd been abused enough, she didn't want to hurt him when he meant well, but she needed to get Tanis and find Jenna. Now. Shaking her head at Trocar and gesturing to him to put the knife away, she informed them.

"Jack the Ripper."

Aleksei and Perrin looked at each other, then back at her blankly, but Trocar's breath hissed between his teeth. He knew whom she meant, intimately. He'd been face to face with the serial killer once, when he had indeed tracked Gillian through France. Tanis was suddenly there and they had another ally. An ally who would understand exactly what she meant without delay for explanations.

"Tanis, Jack is here and he has Jenna. I don't know how he's here, but he is. He found me in London; he tracked me through France. If we don't find him in a hurry, Jenna will be the second victim."

She pointed to the dead girl Ivan and his assistants were hovering over. "That's the Catherine Eddoes kill, I'm sure of it. I studied his crimes in college, I've seen the morgue photos and read the coroner's inquest report. That girl's injuries match the Eddoes kill, cut by cut. That night in eighteen eighty-eight, he killed two. A 'double event,' is what he called it. Jenna is going to be the Elizabeth Stride kill if we don't find her, fast."

She let that sink in. Aleksei was understanding her now, right along with Tanis, she was sure. Just as she knew Trocar would have followed her without question anyway. Perrin was looking more confused by the moment.

"There were two more murders in the area before this one, according to Ivan. He's re-creating his crimes from eighteen eighty-eight to remind me what he has in mind for me. He took Jenna to draw you and me out. It's his punishment for you escaping Dracula with my help and for me evading him the last two times we met. He'll be close by, watching. He gets off on all the hoopla surrounding the discovery of a body and seeing the reaction to what he's done to the victim."

She paused again. There was one way she could think of to draw the serial killer out and possibly save Jenna's life. Using herself as bait and taking a major potshot at his ego. The suggestion she was about to make wasn't going to go over well.

"We're going to have to use me as bait or we'll never find her in time."

"*If* there is time, *piccola sorella*." Tanis looked positively ill, beads of blood sweat breaking out on his brow.

"We have to try or she's dead. He's probably got her in the village. He'll want some sort of privacy while he waits for us to show up." Gillian's voice was flat but she had shaken off the fear. Now she was angry.

"Ivan!" she called to the police chief. "There's something very bad happening in the village. Please stay here with your people until we get back."

He looked up from his work. "I am the constable for the town, Gillian. If you know where the killer is and intend to confront him, I should be there too."

"Ivan, you've known me for a while, and you know I wouldn't ask you if it weren't important. So I'm asking you, please stay here. I'm afraid we're up against a very nasty customer here." She indicated the body as a reference.

"I want to avoid any more Human casualties if we can. It's nearly three o'clock so the streets should be deserted anyway. This isn't a suspect that you can take into custody and hold over for trial. We're not even going to try."

Chief Jarek considered what she said, then looked to Aleksei for confirmation. "You intend to simply kill him? No charges, no trial? Lord Rachlav? This all meets with your approval as well?"

"I agree that it will be safer for you to remain here while Gillian and her people track down this murderer. He is a rogue Vampire with a long and bloody history. They do intend to destroy him if at all possible under my authority. Tanis will be with them to verify his identity and see to it that he is utterly annihilated," Aleksei confirmed.

"Very well. You have never involved yourself with my position before, Count Rachlav. The Osiris Doctrine does state that violations of its principles will be dealt with through the respective Paramortal Courts or lawful honor systems. You are the Vampire Lord here, and you say that as a Vampire, on your Lands, he must answer to your justice. I believe in you, as do all your people, and I know Gillian to be honorable. We will do as you request," Ivan agreed.

"Thanks, Ivan. I just don't want to get you, any of your staff or a single villager killed. I give you my word that we'll find him and put a stop to this," Gillian stated.

Perrin watched her, amazement plainly on his face. As if by magic, she had evolved from an obviously frightened woman into a commanding presence with eyes that had gone from terrified to forbidding and cold. She stood squarely, shoulders back, intensity on her face. Then what she said sank in. Bait? She was going to use herself as bait?

Since he still had hold of her arm, he shook it, his grip tightening unwittingly. "Bait? For this killer? Is that what you just said?"

When she nodded, Perrin pulled her with him, past Aleksei, hustling her along, down to where the body still lay, Aleksei and Tanis following. Trocar stayed by the road. He'd seen it already. Perrin's eyes took in the horrific scene and he paled, his undamaged profile taking on the pallor of his mask. "You are going to attempt to lure the monster who did *that*?"

Unfortunately a light breeze picked that time to blow across the field, bringing with it the scent of blood, bowel and death. It was the smell of a slaughterhouse by an open sewer. The Vampires grimaced. Fresh blood was the only kind they were interested in. Gillian had pulled Aleksei's shirtsleeve up to her face already and was holding her nose, breathing shallowly through the material so she didn't get the taste in the back of her throat.

Perrin wasn't so lucky. As isolated as he was, he'd heard or read bits and snippets of news occasionally but, like most people, had never really comprehended the reality that comes with a personal, up-close perspective of a violent death. What he saw sickened him to the core. That Gillian was willing to place herself in mortal danger of winding up like the body that lay before him terrified him beyond his imaginings.

He was unprepared for what he had heard, completely ill equipped for what he was now viewing. But when the cruel authenticity that is built into the smell of fresh death crawled into his nose and mouth, he felt his gorge rise and turned quickly away as he began vomiting onto the grass, dropping to all fours before he fell.

Gillian shot the Vampires a look that clearly said, "Dumbass." But she went to Ivan, who glanced at Perrin, still retching his stomach out, and wordlessly handed her a travel packet of a menthol vapor rub. She took it to him, opening it on the way and gently rubbing his back as she knelt at his side, reaching around so he would see the packet but not so far that he would barf on her arm.

"Here, Perrin, rub some of this under your nose and up into your nostrils. It will get the smell out." Her voice was carefully pitched not to sound critical.

Nodding in understanding, unable to speak yet, Perrin did as she'd told him. The harsh menthol smell brought tears to his eyes but helped take away some of the horrible odor that he swore was still in his mouth and throat.

When he thought he could speak, he turned to look at her, feeling shamed by his reaction, but found understanding and kindness in her eyes. She hugged his shoulders.

"Experience is a bitch of a teacher. We've all thrown up the first time we saw a murdered body," she lied to him kindly, "and this one is particularly bad, so please don't be embarrassed, Perrin. It's a normal reaction. No one thinks less of you. Especially me."

"Even now, you are kind." He studied her face but found no censure there. "I want to help you find your friend, Gillian, but I cannot stand by while you risk your life as bait to catch a madman who could do such a thing to a young girl."

Struggling to his feet, he kept his face averted from the corpse. Gillian slid her arm around his waist to steady him and was pleased when Aleksei moved to support him on the other side. Together, they walked him back toward the road, upwind from the corpse, to Trocar and Tanis. Perrin was shaking like a leaf but he needed to be set straight.

"I appreciate your concern, Perrin. I really do. But I know how to handle this. Trocar, Tanis, even one of Aleksei's Wolves will be with me. Aleksei can't come because, as a Vampire Lord, Jack would sense his power immediately and run for it. There just isn't time to come up with another plan. Jenna is going to be dead soon, hell, she may already be dead while we're standing around discussing."

She gently turned him to look at her when they got to the bottom of Aleksei's drive. He was pale but seemed steadier on his feet, so the Vampire moved back to let her talk to her patient.

Perrin straightened and turned her toward him, taking her by the shoulders gently. "I do understand the danger to your friend, but I also understand the danger to you, *ma chérie*. If you throw away your life and she still dies, then all of us are lost."

His eyes were penetrating and direct, holding hers until she colored under his gaze. She felt like a raw recruit about to be dressed down by her DI, but it didn't sway her thinking. "I have no intention of being stupid about this, Perrin. Or of throwing away my life. Jenna is a Marine, as am I, as are Trocar and Kimber. We leave no one behind. Ever."

Perrin could see that he wasn't going to bully her into changing her mind and turned to Aleksei for help. "Can you do nothing with her when she is like this?"

The Vampire Lord's eyes were backlit with his pride in Gillian, and more than a little fear. He didn't like it one damn bit either, but short of literally holding Gillian pinned until the sun fully rose to make him retreat, there was little he could do and Jenna would die.

"I am afraid not. She is quite hardheaded when she makes up her mind."

The light ghost of a smile was there on Perrin's mouth and his color was quickly coming back. He looked beautiful, unyielding and stern as he squeezed her shoulders lightly.

"He is proud of you, as am I, though I do not have the right to be, for you are not mine to be proud of."

"I'll be all right. I'm scared too, but Jenna's more important than my being afraid. I know better than all of you what kind of a mind we're dealing with. And I do appreciate you saying that you're proud of me too, Perrin. I do value your opinion."

"But not my wishes."

"I don't need a caretaker, Perrin. Just support me in this, stay here and don't get in my way while I try to get my friend back. All I need you to do is just pray to whatever gods you believe in that we don't fuck this up and that we manage to get Jenna back alive."

Impulsively, she reached up to hug him around the neck. Perrin was so jaded in some ways but so completely innocent in others. She was so going to have to process all this with him. Helmut and Daed were probably both asleep in the castle like sensible people, not out seducing Gargoyles, having orgies, finding butchered corpses and chasing Jack the Ripper around Romanian villages at three o'clock in the morning to rescue a fellow soldier.

His arms went around her, holding her small body tightly sheltered by his taller frame, and he admonished her quietly. "What I ought to do is spank you until you promise that you will not do this insane thing, but I will pray for your safety and support you instead."

Despite herself, she smiled. He was so earnest and sincere, and he meant well; she just couldn't get mad at him. He'd come so far just being out here; actually asserting himself for fear of her safety was a major development. Hell, he wasn't even wearing his gloves.

"Is that how you handle all your female students, maestro, bullying them until they comply?" She pulled back, grinning, trying to interject a little levity into a very grim moment.

"Only the ones who need looking after as badly as you do." The gray green eyes were kind as he tucked an errant lock of blond hair behind her ear, but he returned her smile.

"And once again, she proves me right," Trocar, whose Elven ears had picked up every word, said to whoever was listening.

"Do not start with her, Elf. We need to find my lover." Tanis glowered at him.

Gillian moved to hug Aleksei tightly. "I will be fine and I will be back."

"You had better be. I am a Vampire Lord now. If anything happens to you, I will raise you from the dead for the sole purpose of allowing Perrin to carry out his threat."

He caught her to him, nearly cracking her ribs and lifting her so she was eye level with him. "I mean it, *bellissima*. You stay very safe. Perrin is right about one thing," he said firmly.

"What? The spanking thing? Sure! We can try it some night when we're getting a little kinky."

"It is meant to be a disciplinary action or an attention getter, Gillian, not foreplay." Aleksei glared at her, but the effect was lost owing to his looking a bit cross-eyed as she leaned in and kissed his nose.

"Ooooh, baby, don't tease me." Gill writhed against him, grinning like a fiend.

Aleksei developed a very wicked smirk suddenly. He cupped her butt in his large hands then squeezed playfully, kissing her as deeply as he could with Gillian squirming and giggling in his embrace.

"You need looking after, *cara mia*."

"*Rawr,*" she growled at him with an absolutely sinful gleam in her eyes.

He set her down, swatting her tush affectionately as she moved off toward Tanis and Trocar. She flipped her hair, then sashayed away for his viewing pleasure, waving backward as if she hadn't a care in the world, leveling off into a jog as Pavel loped down the hill in Wolf form to run at her side.

The Wolves had recovered enough for Cezar to hear Aleksei's call, and he'd sent Pavel. There was a pattering of another set of feet and Kimber ran to join them, several objects of wanton destruction in her hands.

After they disappeared into the darkness down the road,

Aleksei abruptly remembered that Gillian was wearing only his shirt, her boots, had no undergarments at all; had only one gun, one clip of ammunition, and now was about to go headlong into an encounter with one of the most vicious, sexually sadistic serial killers ever known.

A serial killer who had stalked her from London, through France, to his very doorstep. A madman from whom she had managed to escape twice, and who worked for Lord Dracula. Evidently she'd left out a few details when she recounted her adventures to him. They needed to have a discussion about her conveniently leaving out important segments of her stories.

Feeling dizzy all of a sudden, he wondered if there had ever been an incident of a Vampire actually fainting or having a coronary arrest. He steadied himself against a tree, hand over his heart, trying to calm his nerves. She was going to kill him by giving him a heart attack or aging him centuries before his time. That was probably her plan all along, little blond vixen.

Perrin was immediately there, patting his back. "Are you all right?"

"Do me one favor, Perrin."

"Anything, you have but to ask."

"When she gets back in one piece . . ."

"What?"

"Remind me to spank her for both of us. Even a Vampire's heart cannot take this level of emotional strain."

"Vampire? You. Are. A. Vampire?"

"Perrin, we need to talk."

CHAPTER

14

THE village wasn't that far but Gillian soon slowed and stood panting in the road. She was grateful for Aleksei's little bit of loving levity back there. It had helped get her head in order, calmed her anger, and made her realize how thankful she was that Aleksei was really, *really* trying to understand her and her many-faceted life.

He wasn't happy with her at the moment, but he was letting it go until a more convenient time. That was growth for a chauvinistic, old-school Vampire. She was inexplicably proud of him. How proud, she'd think about later.

Right now, she and her little group were headed down the darkened road toward Sacele since Saucy Jack had a proclivity for more civilized settings. He'd dumped the last body by Castle Rachlav to get their attention since they hadn't discovered the others. Well, now he had their attention. Pavel bumped her with his shoulder to move her along and she took a halfhearted swipe at him.

"Fuck off, Rin Tin Tin, I'm tired and I need to have some strength left in a very short time."

He subsided but sat next to her, giving her the Wolf version of a "what a wimp" look. Apparently Werewolves had better postcoital recovery skills than Vampires or Humans.

Kimber jogged up, panting as hard as Gillian was, and rested bent over, hands on her knees.

"What now, Kemo Sabe?"

"Other than we may need to consider quitting smoking, hell if I know." Gillian wheezed, twisting her back to pop a kink out but remembering her knickerless condition and not raising her arms up too high lest she moon Trocar.

"Tanis, I know you can hear me. Get back here for a second. You too, Trocar, and see if you can spot any of the Fey. Some of them went this way."

In seconds, Tanis was with them and Trocar was melting out of the trees with three Fey warriors and Aisling Crosswind at his heels. Gillian looked them all over objectively. She and Kimber were going to be the weak links tonight; she could tell that already.

First of all, they were both exhausted from their marathon orgy earlier, Gillian even more so since she'd had entrée de Gargoyle à la Fey as well. Second, their body clocks were still not fully adjusted to Vampire Standard Time, which the rest of the bunch lived with quite nicely. They needed to think or Jenna wasn't going to be the only other sacrifice tonight.

"Okay, look," Gillian started, getting into debriefing mode for the second time that night, "Jack the Ripper as a rule is an opportunistic killer. What that means is that he doesn't ordinarily target a victim, then follow her around until he nails her. He goes out hunting with the intent to kill. First woman he stumbles on in the right place at the right time is toast. It's that simple."

"Then why has he come here and taken Jenna?" Tanis asked.

"He's not switching his method, by any means, if that's what you're asking. I think this situation is so different because it's about a personal beef with both you and me, to be honest, Tanis. When he had Kimber and me in the basement of Oscar's estate house, we sort of didn't hit it off too well, if you know what I mean." Gillian winced, remembering some of her verbal sparring with the sexual sadist in question.

"I'm also reasonably sure he's pissed off that we sprung you from that basement right under his nose."

"How is it he did not come for you two then when we were all engaged in . . . our earlier activities?" That was from Trocar.

"I have no idea. Well, that's not quite right, I think I do but I need to talk to you, Finian and Perrin first to be sure."

Kimber lightly touched her arm. "Go on, give us your theory anyway."

"Okay, I think that Perrin's metaphysical music magic created a field of some sort. A geographically specific field folding outward from him as the epicenter, which both contained us while it was going on but also kept out anything that didn't have at least warm and friendly feelings at the time it snapped on. Sort of like a Fairy ring . . . or a rudimentary casting circle, but a helluva lot more powerful. Jack, of course, would have had murder and retribution on his mind so he would have been unable to approach the yard or us while it was active. I can't explain it better than that."

Trocar was nodding and spoke briefly in rapid-fire Elvish with Aisling and one of the Fey, a tall fellow with dark green hair and amber brown eyes. After a moment, Trocar switched to English.

"Actually, you are probably more correct than you realize. Perrin's lineage may be from a musical or fertility line of the Sidhe. Also a Gargoyle is a highly sexualized being with its own glamour abilities to seduce in a predatory manner.

"I believe he is unaware of this power, at least the level of it anyway, does not know how to control it and must be taught to do so if any of us are to have a moment's rest while he is still here."

Trocar bitching about the possibility of too much sex. That was a new one. This wasn't the time for jokes so Gillian refrained though Kimber covered her derisive snort with a cough.

Gillian elbowed her and asked the Dark Elf, "Can you, Dalton and maybe Finian get a small nullifying field up around the guesthouse then? Something to keep his magic contained so it doesn't spill over?"

"Yes, I believe we can. I will let you know when we all return alive," Trocar said unequivocally.

"Swell. All right. Jack has the problem with me or Tanis. He knows we've found the body, he left it near the castle on purpose since we didn't pick up on the two prior kills. I would stake my career on it. He knows we, or at least Tanis and I, will come after him to rescue Jenna.

"Remember, a serial killer like Jack is highly intelligent and can anticipate the next move of his presumed adversary with uncanny accuracy. It's a game to him, that's what makes him dangerous. If we fuck up this rescue, Jenna will die. If we don't attempt a rescue, Jenna will die. He doesn't care who gets killed as long as he wins. What I suggest is that we all spread out, circle the wagons if you will, and move in on him on all sides from the perimeter of the village."

"What will you do, *piccola sorella*?" Tanis came to her, apprehension and deep worry in his eyes.

"I am going to walk my happy ass straight down his throat. He is not going to come out willingly to fight. He knows I'm not so brainless as to face him without backup, so I'm going to have to provoke him to show himself. Hopefully I will piss him off so badly that he won't be the cold efficient killer, but will be so angry that he will make the proverbial 'fatal mistake.' If nothing else, it will give me a better chance of living long enough for one of you guys to take him out."

"I was afraid you would say that," Trocar muttered.

"I don't want to be filleted, Trocar. Jack is a blitz attack killer. He pounces, cuts, feeds, kills, then is gone again, melting into the scenery. I need a chance to confront him directly and find out where Jenna is before it's too late."

"What does he look like?" Aisling asked suddenly.

Kimber, Trocar and Gillian exchanged looks. They had no freaking idea how to describe him. Two of them had been under the influence of Pixie venom when they'd met Jack.

The venom, which was a mild hallucinogenic, had warped their perspective badly. Trocar had been dead sober, face to face with him, and realized he had no idea what the hell he looked like either.

Gillian was fresh out of surgery the second time she'd met him; weak and disoriented the third time. The fact that Jack was like a chameleon—he could blur his image and features so that anyone facing him wouldn't have been able to establish the difference between him and King Kong in a lineup—was one of the reasons he'd gone undetected for so long.

"Didn't he have dark hair?" Gillian was trying desperately to remember what the serial killer Vampire looked like.

Kimber stared at her. "I think so. Wasn't he sort of short?"

Gill had to think about that. "I'm not sure. Hell, I can't remember exactly what his eyes looked like and we were almost nose to nose more than once. Rusty brown, I think."

"I seem to remember looking down at him," Trocar added, "and I believe you are correct about his eyes."

Tanis was fidgeting. "Can you or can you not identify him?"

"No," the three of them chorused.

"This is not comforting, Gillian," Tanis snapped.

"We won't need to. He'll come to us." She gestured to herself and Kimber.

"How the hell did I get volunteered for this shit?" Kimber looked irritated.

"Because he knows you and me. Well, he knows Tanis too, for that matter, but Tanis kind of sucks as bait for a lady killer. Jack's only seen Trocar once, but I don't think he's after Elf tonight," Gillian said matter-of-factly.

"Yeah, but I'm betting that Tanis didn't get under his sensitive macho serial killer skin the way you did by calling him a 'sick twist.'" Kimber snickered while Gill made shushing noises at her.

"Please tell me you did not just say that Gillian deliberately antagonized Jack the Ripper on their first meeting." Trocar stood with fists on hips, eyes flashing a myriad of colors.

"Well . . ." Gillian shrugged helplessly.

Trocar threw both hands in the air, turning away in exasperation. "No wonder he stalked you across Europe. Did it not occur to you that he might come after you? That he would hunt you down and extract retribution? He is an egomaniacal killer and you have escaped him no less than three times. I did not understand fully why he was so determined before. Now I do."

"For crissakes, Trocar, you don't really think that I would deliberately provoke a nut like that while I'm lying there trussed up like a chicken and stoned on Pixie venom, do you? I didn't know who the hell he was until it was too late!" she retorted defensively, resenting her former Lieutenant's rant.

"*That* I believe," Trocar said, but his voice was still chilly.

"Hey, it's not like it was her fault. We were both hammered on Pixie juice and him with that little ability to blur and shift his image," Kimber countered. "I'm with you, boss. Let's do this."

Gillian beamed at her friend's defense, then immediately became serious. "All right, let's knock it off. We don't need to argue right now. Jenna's running out of time. Kimmy, you're going to have to lose the flamethrower and crossbow. We need weapons that aren't readily visible. He's not stupid—he knows we'll be armed—but there's no sense in advertising it."

"And then what?" Kimber asked.

"Then we are going to do it just like we said to do it before."

"I am terrified by what I believe you are about to say," Trocar said, supremely vexed.

"We are going to stroll right into town and demand the attention of Jack the Ripper."

Pavel snarled at her. Tanis and Trocar exchanged glances with each other and the Fey. Aisling stepped forward unexpectedly. "I will also be bait."

"Like hell you will," Trocar stated. "It is enough that these two have lost their minds. Your brother will dismember me if anything happens to you."

"No, he will not. He knows I have my own mind. I was a warrior in my clan long before you strapped on your first stiletto, Grael," Aisling argued and began to remove her outer cloak and visible weapons.

Soon she stood in her leggings, boots and cowl top, with only a six-inch knife secreted in her boot for a weapon. The Fey gathered her belongings and hid them off the side of the road.

"Lock and load, people," Gillian instructed. Calling to two of the Sidhe warriors, she pointed toward Aisling and Kimber. "You two pick a woman and shadow her. Stay close in case Jack goes for one of them instead of me."

To the third she said, "I would like you to circle around at the edge of the village perimeter and see if you happen to hear or see any of your friends. Then have them fan out and move in slowly."

"Tanis, you have an advantage he doesn't know about. He has no idea you can now shape-shift since his boss's nullification devices are down. Mist around and see if you can get a sense of where Jenna is then contact Aleksei. He'll contact me and I'll get to her, I promise." Her eyes were serious on the tall Vampire's face, trying to convey reassurance.

"All right, *piccola sorella*, we will do it your way, but I will also be watching over you, Aisling and Kimber from the air as well as I am able." Tanis was terrified for Jenna but almost more so for the other women.

Gillian turned to Pavel and Trocar. "Pavel, I need you to track her as best you can. Just go, stay out of sight and remember to bark, not howl, if you see or smell anything. We'll get to you. Trocar, I know you know what to do."

"Indeed, Gillyflower, I do. But first, take this." He pulled a shimmering cord about two feet long out of his leather shirt. "A garrote, my lady. It is of a material which, once wound round the neck, will continue to tighten and kill, even if you let go. I hope that you do not wind up in close-enough quarters to use it, but he if gets hold of you and you can get at least one arm free to use this, it will decapitate him."

He demonstrated the movement required to activate the cord, then waited until she secured it carefully around her wrist as he told her. One tug and it would come free for her to use without injuring her arm.

The Grael dipped his head, arm across his chest, in a gesture of respect for her, gave a mock salute and ran lightly ahead of them, Pavel for the moment at his side. The Dark Elf was silent, invisible if he chose and deadlier than the Ripper's wildest imaginings. He also had a score to settle with Jack for backhanding him across the room at the Chastel estate in France. He would hide among the buildings in the village, shadowing Gillian as she took her walk of death.

What she didn't know was that he planned to find this diseased creature first, hopefully while the Human woman was still alive. He would incapacitate him, make her safe, then return to leisurely finish a long overdue period of torment known only in the Halls of Anguish of the Grael.

Gillian actually prayed that Trocar or Tanis would find Jack first. She was no coward but she remembered distinctly how badly the sadistic Vampire had unnerved her. There was also no way in hell she could take him or any other Vampire in a hand-to-hand fight if it came to that. They were just too damn strong and fast for a Human to prevail in that situation.

The last thing she wanted to do was to walk down those moonlit streets alone, keenly aware that she was without a bra or panties underneath Aleksei's shirt even as she pulled and tucked the shirt and makeshift belt to make a suggestive-looking minidress. Putting herself into the role of a potential victim was not something she was used to.

It would have been more her style to storm the place with a fully equipped, armed unit who would kick ass and take names. Here there were just too many innocent civilians who could potentially get hurt. The streets themselves were clear since it was somewhere around three or three thirty in the morning. They had to find Jenna before the sun was high or Jack would certainly kill her then dump the body before he went to ground.

"Ready?" she asked the other two women, then moved off without waiting for an answer, gun hooked in her belt, resting in the small of her back, leaving her arms free.

At the edge of the town, Kimber peeled off down one dark street followed by one of the Fey and began singing, "I'm a bitch, I'm a lover, I'm a child, I'm a mother, I'm a sinner, I'm a saint . . ." Her voice wavered a little, but Gill couldn't blame her. They were all scared shitless.

Aisling lightly ran ahead and picked another alleyway to duck into. The Fey following her melted into the background as soon as he hit the shadows. Gillian heard her singing too. A rather suggestive melody, presumably in Elvish, from the sound of it. That was fine. Those two could sing all they liked. She had a different tactic in mind for attracting Jack.

Squaring her shoulders, Gillian adopted her most aggressive swagger and moved into the quiet streets, keenly aware that she was about to do the most idiotic thing she'd ever done in her life. The Ripper was about to be fucked with by a master smart-ass.

"Hey, Jack! Jack the Ripper! It's Dr. Key! I'm here, just like you wanted!" she called out into the night, her eyes shifting constantly for any sign of movement among the shadows.

"Come on, Jack, we found the body! I recognized the Eddoes kill so I know it's you! I also know you have Jenna, but she's not who you want, is she?"

Every ten yards or so, she'd stop to listen for a moment, her empathy on overdrive in a shell around her, feeling for any shift, any change in the quiet peace of the town. She trusted herself to know if he was sneaking up on her, but she turned around in the street anyway, noticing every shadow's position, every shiny surface illuminated by the moon and stars.

Still nothing after ten minutes. There were noises in the forest outside the village and some sounds of conflict but nothing near her. If any of them had found Jack, someone would have yelled by now. *Shit. Fuck. Hell. Damn.* She was going to have to do what all her training, knowledge and experience told her *not* to do: provoke the killer's wrath and hope to piss him off enough to flush him out. Without dying, that is. That was the tricky part.

"Hear me, Jacky! It's your favorite foulmouthed Dr. Key! All I want is Jenna freed, alive and well, then you and I will throw down, you sadistic, twisted piece of shit!"

Silence greeted her ears. The Inn was coming up on her right and she crossed to the left side of the street, her senses beginning to tingle a little. Slowly, she reached for the gun behind her back and grasped it, finger on the trigger, ready to draw and fire.

"What's the matter, Jack? You afraid of a woman with a weapon? Or do you only take on frightened, uneducated Cockney hookers, tranny men or young girls with no defensive skills? Come out, Jack, try fighting someone armed and dangerous for once, you fucking coward!"

Dammit, still nothing except a warning tingle. Okay, time to shelve the bitch and bring out the Marine.

"Jack, you cock-blocked, fanged-faced chicken shit! I'm walking these streets, Jonesing for you, baby! That's right! I'm half-naked, on display, and all for my favorite sick twist! Are you hard for me, you crazy fuck, or are you still so impotent with living women that you'll have to use a knife to get me off instead of that ineffective, limp wiener of yours!"

The rush of hatred, malice and evil that came staggered her back into a doorway, where she gasped for a moment, getting her shields more firmly stabilized. Evil: an evil so oppressive that she nearly gasped as it rolled over her like a malignant fog.

Bingo! Success! Great. Typical. She'd pissed him off by casting aspersions on his manhood, just like any other male. That was easy, now where the hell was he? Trying to home in on where the malice was originating from, teeth chattering, legs shaking, she kept moving, keeping up her tirade of the most vulgar, filthy, foul and downright nasty dialogue she could loudly produce, watching the Inn but knowing he wasn't in it. That was what he wanted her to think. Soon she was moving deeper into the town.

The heavy, stifling feeling of evil was getting worse. She was going in the right direction. Good. She knew his trigger and had an idea of his location. Now to turn it up a notch.

"Come on, Jack, did I rattle your cage a little back in England? Did I upset you by escaping you in France? Or did I do it just now, when I mentioned your inability to fuck any woman due to your unfortunate erectile-dysfunction problem? You're nothing but a run-of-the-mill rapist with a knife, Jack, not a genius serial killer. You're ridiculously common and you know it."

Yeah, like I know this is the stupidest, most suicidal thing I've ever done in my life, she thought as the oppressive, evil presence in the air grew more intense, but she continued her verbal harassment. She wanted him so blind with rage that he would reveal himself, giving her time to call for help before he attacked her. She prayed that Trocar, Tanis or Pavel was somewhere near. Maybe then she'd live through this.

Gill also had her mind consciously and completely closed off to Aleksei. First off, he'd be way pissed off with what she was doing at the moment, probably fly to her side to yell at her, which would abandon Perrin, who was with him, and blow their rescue by tipping off Jack to a Vampire Lord's presence.

Second, if things went badly, she didn't want him to feel her die. Shit, if it came to that, she'd send him a last thought and let him know it wasn't his fault if she bought it out here tonight.

"Feeling your love there, Jack! Trying to scare me off after you went through all the trouble to get my attention? Well, fuck you! Oh wait, you can't! That's it, isn't it? That's why you killed all those women in Whitechapel and those transvestite hookers in Soho!

"You couldn't deliver to a woman, so you killed them. Then, when you finally understood that you're a raving homosexual, you tried the boys but you couldn't get it up for them either, could you, Jacky? They had to die so they wouldn't spread it around that Jack the Ripper, Master Vampire, legendary serial killer, has got a broken dick!"

Lucky for her, with her senses on autopilot, she felt the strong disturbance that came with a new wave of his rage, pinpointed it and looked up. The Vampire in question was poised on the sill of an upstairs window several buildings down.

Gillian skittered out into the street, away from the building, to give herself room, then leveled her gun at him.

"Jack, how good it is to see you again," she said in her sultriest voice. "Now get the fuck down from there, you sick son of a bitch." Into the night itself she yelled for Tanis and Trocar.

CHAPTER
15

"DR. Key," Jack said pleasantly when the reverberations from her shout had faded, "how good it is of you to come. I look forward to teaching you better manners and vocabulary before you die."

He floated effortlessly down and stood several yards in front of her, dressed completely in stylish black clothing, hands behind his back, apparently completely calm. Gillian knew better. His rage flooded over her, and the essence of absolute, chilling evil continued to beat at her through the night air.

Seeing him face to face, it all came back to her and she remembered him. Dark curling hair, cut fashionably short, rust-colored eyes, an ordinarily handsome man about five feet nine inches tall. One thing was for sure: Either one of the others had to show up, or she needed to figure out how to kill him now with just a gun.

There was no way in the nine rings of Hades that she was going to let him get close enough to engage in a fight, though she would dearly love to rip his balls off and shove them down his throat. She had to keep him talking, try to get Jenna located. Then someone with more hit points than she had would arrive. Hopefully he wouldn't kill her in the meantime.

"Jenna had better still be alive, Jack."

"Your friend? I believe so. She was just now when I left her." He half turned and flicked his eyes upward toward the window that he had just vacated.

"Jenna!" Gillian yelled, not taking her eyes off the Vampire in front of her. Not hearing a response, she narrowed her eyes. "She's not answering me, Jack. Why is that?"

"I truly cannot tell you, Dr. Key." Jack smiled at her, the otherworldly beauty of the Vampire immediately suffusing his ordinarily handsome face. "Perhaps she is unwilling to attract my attention."

This was getting her nowhere. She needed to get Jenna and get the hell out of there. And where were Trocar, Tanis and Pavel? If Jack had injured her and she even now lay bleeding to death upstairs, Gillian would never forgive herself.

"I want my friend released, right now." To anyone listening she yelled, "I have him! Come down the street from the Inn!"

"I want you, Dr. Key." His voice hit a previously unknown sensual register, sending shivers down her spine. Vampire voice foo from a sexual sadist. Oh yay.

Ew! Ew! Ew! Touché, Mr. Ripper. Terrific. Now she was seriously creeped out.

"Fine, you can have me, but let her go first." To herself, she was praying silently, *Please, everybody, get the hell here, now!*

Stylish eyebrows arched. "Just like that, you would surrender yourself into my tender keeping?"

"Just like that," she agreed. "Jenna would do the same for me."

He looked at her askance, turning up the volume on his hatred, rage and evil, smiling that eerily lovely smile, and tut-tutted at her. "Dr. Key, you know better than that. I am a Master Vampire and that is very close to a bald-faced lie. I am quite sure you would come along, but you would be fighting and screaming. So no, not just like that."

Hera's hells. *When did he ever shut up long enough to kill anybody?* Gillian speculated, then had another thought on how to extend her lifetime a few more minutes.

"Look, Jack, you know I said those things just to get you out here but I think I might be able to help you if you let me." Where in the name of all that was holy was the rest of her party?

"Really?" One eyebrow arched. "Help me in what way?"

"Well, how about if we start by figuring out why you're so pissed off at everything sex related."

Gillian tried putting on her understanding therapist face while stalling for time. "I mean, you're not that bad looking; you're handsome even. It's not like you couldn't get a date. So I'm wondering, what happened to you to make you like this? If someone molested or abused you when you were a child, that's not your fault. You don't have to take out your anger on others. You don't have to be like this. We can work through your anger together if you are interested in getting better."

He laughed then. It was an unnerving sound and felt like broken glass slicing across her aura. "Oh, Dr. Key, I am not a stupid man, I assure you. The only interest you have in me at the moment is to delay me long enough for your friends to arrive so you all might kill me. You think to coax me into your clutches with promises of redemption and salvation. To lure me in like a fish? A baited animal?"

The laughter cut off like a switch, which was even more unsettling. "And you are very wrong about one thing in your assumption of my proclivities."

"Really? How am I wrong about you?"

"I do not wish to be cured. I like what I am." Something in his eyes changed to a look that was so dark, so terrifying, so absolutely-without-hope-for-redemption evil, that Gillian knew she was about to die.

"Then you'd better ask yourself one last thing." The expression in her own eyes grew so cold and so completely without emotion that his face registered surprise as he looked at her. Women . . . Humans never looked like that, they feared him.

"And what, pray tell, is that, Dr. Key?" Gods above, his voice never changed timbre even though his rage was pounding at her.

"Is this the hill you want to die on?" She quoted a regular Marine saying, cocking her head to look at him, a very chilly smile creeping over her lips.

"We are not on a hill, Dr. Key." The Ripper was taking in the picture of her. Dressed like a wanton slut, but her eyes and smile were as cold as his own. Her hands were absolutely steady on her gun. They each meant to kill the other. This night one of them would die.

"You are. You just don't realize it yet."

His eyes dilated as his gaze raked over her from head to foot, taking in the short skirt, her nipples visible under the white linen, the boots which made her legs look muscular and firm. The way she stood with her legs apart was tantalizing. He could detect her scent from where he was; smell the sex all over her.

She'd been with someone earlier when he'd come for her. He hadn't been able to enter the castle compound, something had kept him out, but he could hear the cries. Yes, she and the dark-haired whore he held prisoner had been fucking tonight. Too bad he'd had to settle for the other one when he could finally enter the yard. Just seeing the foul-mouthed bitch standing with her legs apart, open to the night under that flimsy garment, knowing that someone had already put a cock up inside her tonight, excited him beyond what he thought possible.

"Do you remember the Mary Kelly kill, Dr. Key?"

"Sure do."

"My masterpiece. You remind me of her."

Involuntarily licking his lips, he fixed his eyes on where her legs met under her shirt, imagining what he was going to do to this little tart's body, much as he had done to Mary Kelly over a century before. His hand trembled as he reached down to fondle his groin through his pants.

"Are you really without undergarments under that man's shirt?" he rasped at her, clearly excited as he grasped his concealed organ, moving his hand up and down its length rapidly.

Ye gods. That was so gross. Gillian immediately wanted

to take a shower to wash off that look he was smearing all over her. Completely disgusted, she managed to keep her face absolutely neutral except for the chilly smile.

Jack the Ripper hell, more like Jack the Wanker. At least he wasn't taking it out to beat off. She definitely couldn't have handled that.

"You bet, wanna peek?" Practically gagging but wanting to keep him doing anything except killing her or Jenna, she kept the gun trained on him with one hand, while she slid her hand suggestively down her breast, stomach and to the hem of the shirt, his widened eyes following her all the while he continued stimulating himself.

Gillian wasn't about to flash him so she only lifted the hem farther up the side of her thigh, just high enough, then let it fall. To her horror and disgust, his eyes glazed momentarily as the hand moved faster, hips thrusting forward. The Ripper's face flooded with relief as he groaned heavily in release, breath hissing through his teeth, emptying his seminal vesicles inside the sober black cloth. His eyes never left her, still stroking himself as the aftershocks made him jerk and gasp.

"Oh yeah, *that* was real attractive," she said mostly to herself. Unfortunately he heard her.

"You loathsome *whore*." The word was hissed as his face became suffused with the rage that she'd known was there all along. He brought his other hand around to the front. There was the scalpel—his substitute penis. She stared. The blade and his hand were stained dark with blood. Jenna's blood. Shit. Shit. Shit.

"You perverted son of a bitch." It was ground out between clenched teeth as she fired at his head.

Vampires are fast. Ask any Human who's ever pissed one off, and actually lived, just how fast. They can move in the blink of an eye, which was what Jack did when she fired at him. Gillian saw the blur and moved, but he materialized in front of her, backhanding her across the jaw as he formed, throwing her a good eight feet. *Fuck, that hurt!*

Rolling as she hit the ground, scraping head, arms and

thigh, knowing that she was going to hurt later, she ducked her head between her arms, which were still held stiff, pointing her weapon. Sighting him as best she could from her prone position, she fired as he headed for her, hitting him twice in the upper body. The concussion from the nine-millimeter weapon knocked him backward, giving her time to get to her feet and move.

"Tanis! Trocar!" she bellowed in her best Marine Captain voice, circling around from where she had been standing as the Ripper snapped back to his feet and started for her, scalpel poised to kill.

Gillian had the benefit of some of Aleksei's mystic Vampire foo in her veins and used it, moving faster than the Ripper thought she might and avoiding his blade. He still could have killed her easily, but like any good sexual sadist, he wanted her pain and fear first. That was good and bad for her.

Unbelievably, he overbalanced when his thrust didn't connect and stumbled. Maybe she accidentally had hit something vital. Nope, he was still after her. Gill dodged the other way and started to run as if every demon she'd ever faced were on her heels, then realized her leg was bleeding. He'd managed to clip her after all, but she couldn't worry about it right now. In the distance, she thought she heard someone running toward her. Too bad they'd get there too late.

This was it. She wasn't going to make it so she sent Aleksei a frantically apologetic thought that she was sorry to break her promise and to please take care of everyone, especially Perrin, for her. Most especially she wanted him to know that her death wasn't his fault. It had been her choice; she was an adult and she wasn't sorry. Clanging the barriers back down, she closed her mind again to everything but her immediate survival. She kept moving, praying that her luck would hold out for a few more seconds.

A noise far too close behind her made her flinch, then fury roared through her. Dammit, she was not going to die running away. Dropping to a crouch as she spun, she leveled the gun at every monster she'd ever faced, praying she had time to fire just once more and maybe give the bastard a bullet in the brain before he killed her.

Tanis's back filled her vision as he dropped from the sky to stand in front of her like a big Romanian wall. She jerked the weapon up just in time and avoided accidentally shooting him.

He stood like a rock between her and certain death. The Ripper was only a few feet away, staring up in surprise at the much taller Vampire as Tanis's hand shot out and grabbed him by the throat. Jack struggled and tried to cut him. Tanis slapped the scalpel out of his hand almost casually, golden eyes blazing as he lifted the smaller Vampire off the ground by his neck.

"Where the hell have you been?" Gillian gasped, happy to see him.

"He had a few friends with him," Tanis replied softly as Gillian came around to his side. His clothes were torn and there was blood on his pants, boots and shirt.

"Are you hurt?" she asked.

"Nothing important," he replied, still holding Jack, who was tearing at Tanis's hand with his nails. "We have all been busy with revenants, lesser Vampires and ghouls. Kimber and Aisling are a little disheveled but safe, we got to them in time. Pavel is helping the Fey round up the rest of his servants."

"Where's Trocar?"

"Here, Gillyflower," the Dark Elf said as he strolled into the street from yet another alleyway. "I apologize for being detained."

She looked him over. Trocar was, as always, immaculate except that the knives he held in both hands were dark with blood and other bits of things that she didn't want to think about. He looked her up and down too. "We need to bandage your leg, Captain."

"I'm all right. We need to get Jenna."

Tanis hadn't moved. His eyes were locked on the Ripper in front of him, who was bucking in an undignified manner in the air. "Jenna?"

"She's in that room on the second floor; he jumped out of it. He says she's still alive."

"You are injured, Gillian. I can smell your blood. Take Trocar and get her out of there, then get back to the compound." Tanis's voice was low and full of rage.

Gill didn't argue with him but did as he asked, giving the Ripper a wide berth as Pavel ran panting into the square and, seeing her, ran to follow her. He looked a little worse for wear. There was blood around his muzzle, he had a knick in his right ear, and some of his lovely fur had been yanked out in chunks.

They found the door to the upper-story staircase easily enough and one kick from Gillian and Trocar splintered it. Racing up the stairs, blood running down her leg to squish in her boot, she followed as Pavel located the room where Jenna lay tied and gagged on a bed with bloody sheets. Trocar slashed the bonds as Gillian helped her sit up. There were sounds of a struggle outside; they needed to hurry.

"You okay, honey?" Gillian asked, brushing her friend's hair out of her face.

"Yeah, now," Jenna said, then burst into tears.

Gillian and Trocar held her, offering comfort while quickly checking her over for injuries. Jack had slashed her wrists and breasts lightly, presumably to attract Tanis, but the wounds were superficial. Gillian tore pieces from Aleksei's already ruined shirt and bound the wounds up. Trocar insisted on doing the same for Gillian's leg. The Ripper had sliced the muscle of her thigh straight down the length. The wound wasn't particularly deep but they didn't have a field medicine kit so it would have to wait till they got back to the castle. At least he had missed the femoral artery.

"I knew you guys would come. He said you wouldn't, but I know my friends," Jenna said definitively.

"Leave no one behind." Gillian smiled. Helping Jenna off the bed, she flinched as Trocar gently turned her toward him with his fingertips, examining her face.

"He struck you?"

"Yes, but I'm lucky that's all he did."

"Damn, Gill, you've got a helluva bruise going on there. Somebody's gonna be pissed," Jenna said, wide-eyed.

"Not as pissed as I am for being sucker punched by a psycho," Gillian joked.

They helped Jenna downstairs and out the door, where Pavel placed himself squarely between them and the two Vampires who were locked in combat in front of them. Tanis, in a rather brutal move, had released Jack, allowing him a chance to fight him. He had been beating, biting and tearing the shit out of the Ripper ever since. The problem was, Tanis was just too honorable simply to hold Jack helpless as he ripped him into pieces and was done with it, so he let the serial killer have some kind of a chance.

Gill noted that Jack's clothing was mostly tattered and he was dripping blood everywhere as he staggered out of Tanis's reach. She brought her gun up and leveled it at the back of Jack's head, waiting for a clear shot.

"No, Gillian. Let them be. This is now a matter of honor. Take Jenna and Pavel and leave," Trocar ordered her as she turned to stare at him. "I have plans of my own for Jack the Ripper, and I will share them with Tanis. Now trust me and go."

Tanis heard him. "Stay out of this, Elf. Get them back safely."

"I do not take orders from you, Vampire," Trocar purred, stepping into the street, twin long knives flashing dully from the blood on them. Expertly whirling them, he slashed across the back of Jack's legs, hamstringing him. The Ripper went down hard, screaming until he felt the cool edge of Trocar's knife at his throat. "Gillian, I will take my garrote if you don't mind."

Nodding, she unwound it and tossed it to him. She'd quite forgotten she'd had it. Having gotten Jenna on Pavel's back since he was the size of a pony and could carry her easily, they headed in the opposite direction, toward the castle. They hadn't gotten far when Kimber and Aisling joined them with their Fey bodyguards.

All were bloody, bruised and bandaged, but Gillian won

the unofficial prize for looking like hell. Her roll on the pavement courtesy of Jack had given her a shallow cut on her head, which had bled and matted her hair on one side, road rash on one shoulder and hand, and a twisted ankle she hadn't noticed until they pointed out she was limping. Not to mention her sliced leg, which had bled enough to make her boot soggy.

Then, there was her jaw. The left side of her face hurt like a bitch, but at least none of her teeth were loose. Just a split lip and a bruise from where Jack had clocked her. Bastard. It would have been a pleasure to get one good hit in on him, but she was just glad to have Jenna back and the rest of them in one piece. Killing Jack herself would have made her happy but she wasn't that egotistical. Tanis and Trocar would finish it. That was fine with her. She just wanted to take a shower.

Footsteps behind her made her turn. Tanis. "I did not want to alarm you, so I made noise," he said apologetically.

"Nice. Where's Trocar?" Gillian asked, looking past the Vampire for the Grael.

"He wanted to have some private time with Jack. He said you would understand. I decided that after I had nearly removed his heart, the Elf deserved a turn." Tanis was positively smirking. Oh great. Trocar had a new buddy.

Gillian grimaced. "Jack is about to meet Hell itself."

"I cannot imagine what else Trocar will do to him," Aisling remarked.

"I can," Gillian said flatly and continued limping along with a grim expression on her face.

No one asked her for details.

CHAPTER
16

IT was dangerously close to dawn by the time the tired and battered group of Ripper Busters slogged down the road near Castle Rachlav . . . er . . . Rachlav Institute of Paramortal Healing. Tanis was carrying Gillian by now. After watching her limping next to Pavel, who was carrying Jenna, the Vampire hadn't taken no for an answer, scooping her up in his arms and carrying her down the road.

Hearing a shout, everyone looked up to see Aleksei, Perrin and, oh joy . . . Daed and Helmut, all running down the road toward them. They seemed to be upset about something, goddess only knew what.

Please, oh please, let it not be another goddamn crisis, Gillian thought wearily in Tanis's arms. The collective groans from her companions indicated everyone else felt pretty much the same way.

"Shit, please tell me nothing else happened while we were gone," Jenna said, folding over onto Pavel's furry neck, echoing Gillian's thoughts.

"Gillian!" Aleksei called out. He had heard them tramping up the road, singing "The Night Jack the Ripper Died" to the tune of the Irish drinking song "The Night Pat Murphy Died" to give them something to do after they had discussed the likelihood of everyone being cross with them when they got back since they all looked like shit.

His heart had leapt with joy when he'd actually seen the ragged little group. With blurring speed, the Vampire Lord was at Gillian's side and lifting her from Tanis and into his own arms. Gillian flinched in his embrace, discovering for herself and alerting Aleksei that she had a bruised rib cage. He set her down to look her over, his face alternating between joy at her being back and fury at her injuries.

The rest followed as they had expected. As they were hustled back to the castle and relative safety, with Aleksei cradling Gillian in his enormously strong arms like a child and Perrin pacing rigidly next to them, there was collective and individual swearing, hugging, welcoming back and scolding of their band of rescuers. When everyone settled in the great hall area to attend to their assortment of injuries, Tuuli, Dalton, Samuel and Esi came in with Finian, the Sidhe and Gunnolf Crosswind to thank Gillian and the others for everything they'd done.

She waved them off, embarrassed, insisting that it was a team effort and that all was well. They lingered in the great hall, sitting among the returning walking wounded, wanting to share the light of camaraderie with all the residents. Even the Brownies pattered downstairs to see what was happening. They'd been staying in the upper attics of the castle and were vaguely miffed that their help had not been required after the Perrin-inspired orgy. Yup, the Brownies had been exposed to the magic and had been reveling, as it were, on their own.

Luis and Oscar were notably absent, but it was near daylight, and since they'd spent the evening in the castle watching movies with the Brownies after Aleksei's confrontation, no one gave it another thought. Until proven otherwise, Aleksei insisted that everyone receive the benefit of the doubt. The lovers had done nothing wrong to his knowledge, so no one should assume anything different.

Tanis and Aleksei had to leave as the dawn was beginning to streak the night sky with pale shadows. They could have stayed long after it had actually broken since all windows of the castle were heavily draped and the great hall itself was completely shielded by stone and heavy tapestries. With their awesome new Vampire powers, neither of them was as susceptible to sunlight as other Vampires of their age range and could remain awake far longer than most. However, they still had an exchange to complete for the second night of Tanis's conversion from Dracula's subordinate to Aleksei's House.

Both had blood that was old and powerful, but as full brothers, one a newly developed Master and the other a newly evolved Lord, the reconversion process stood a good chance of succeeding and they didn't want to miss a night. Aleksei had been reluctant to leave Gillian until Tanis practically dragged him off physically.

"I do not wish to leave Jenna either, Aleksei, but I am going to because this is important if I am to have any kind of relationship with her," Tanis reprimanded his brother.

Jenna smiled and pressed his hand to her cheek. She understood as well; he'd explained what he and Aleksei were trying, and she supported him in it. Also, she wasn't as badly hurt as Gillian was, even after being in Jack's hands for several hours before her rescue. The Vampire had wanted Gillian in exchange and intended to keep her alive as a bargaining chip unless they hadn't come for her.

"Go on, Tanis, I know this is important. I will be fine," Jenna substantiated for his benefit.

Gillian was rather glad they would have an opportunity later to process, particularly with Aleksei and Perrin, the whole of what had happened. Both men were furious with her and Tanis for not letting them know that they were all right and breathing after the Ripper fight. When Gillian had sent her frantic "good-bye" thoughts to Aleksei, he had feared the worst. His agonized reaction had alerted Perrin that everything was not all right. They'd started toward the village, Aleksei forced not to shift and thereby abandon Perrin on the way.

Seeing her alive, seeing his brother walking strongly

along, holding her petite bruised and battered body, had evoked a tapestry of emotions within his very soul. Deep dark impulses roared through him. She was his. He had the right and the glorious responsibility to protect her, shield her, cherish her . . . lock her up for her own good, if necessary. Civilized urges warred with those instincts. He respected her and her abilities. He wanted her to know that. That precluded any need he had about enforcing dominance. Gillian wanted a partner, a lover, not a keeper. He was going to have to deal with it, bottom line.

For Gillian's part, she was delighted and encouraged that Aleksei hadn't flipped the fuck out on her. She could feel his restraint, feel the seething emotions he was holding firmly in check, for her benefit. It added a new layer of respect to her thoughts about him. His culture demanded that he take care of her—see her as a possession. His evolving relationship skills were allowing him to see her not only as a woman but as a partner. She was proud of the old fossil. He was trying.

Right now, though, she hurt in every muscle and bone of her body after getting knocked across the street by Jack, and she wanted to die quietly in her bed after a steaming hot shower. She lifted her face to see frosty gray eyes examining every inch of her and held out her hand to him.

Aleksei took it, raising her scraped knuckles to his mouth and laving the injuries with his tongue before kissing each abrasion. When he smiled at her, it was with warmth and concern rather than anger. Gill took the next move and leaned over to bestow a kiss at the corner of his lovely mouth.

Kissing Aleksei good-bye gingerly with her split and swollen lip put renewed fury and sorrow in the Vampire's eyes. Instinct told him to stay with her; responsibility for her and Tanis tore at him. He wanted to stay but needed to go more. That evoked a brief argument between himself and Gillian until Perrin stepped in and promised to take care of her for him during the daylight hours, his eyes and that of the Vampire's locking for a moment in perfect understanding of what he meant.

Keep her out of trouble; see that she rests. Aleksei and the disfigured genius had shared a long conversation while Gillian and the others were away. They had come to a few basic understandings and Aleksei now trusted Perrin as he did few others, despite the level of the man's professional relationship with Gillian.

There was simply no duplicity in Perrin. He didn't know how to lie, was incapable of flirting, had no emotional filter. Gillian had awakened something in him, something raw, primal and protective that superseded his own desires. He was evolving into what he should have been all along: a man who could be a partner, not a teacher, not a keeper, but someone who could live his life, rather than merely exist.

Gillian strenuously disputed her need to be looked after until both of them stared her down, ice gray and gray green eyes burning into her own, each pair beautiful yet insistent and a little ominous in its demeanor. Since she was too tired to fight with both of them at the moment, she relented but insisted Daed look after the others first. Her injuries could wait.

Tanis led Aleksei away after kissing Jenna softly. Perrin remained seated on the arm of the sofa next to Gill, a quiet, slender presence, holding her hand. Pavel was at her feet, still in Wolf form, healing himself more efficiently than medical attention could have. His injuries were relatively minor. He needed rest and the camaraderie of his friends.

Daed and Helmut were, as she predicted, royally pissed off, mostly at her. Daed had run upstairs, then returned with his proverbial doctor's little black bag with syringes of wonderful substances. After bandaging their various wounds, giving injections when needed for pain, Daed finally got to her own injuries.

"C'mere, darlin. Let's see how badly you're hurt." His voice dripped Southern charm but his black eyes were shooting sparks. That was a very bad sign.

Helmut was angrier with her than she'd ever seen him about her organization of a rescue effort without more backup and planning. "I understand how you couldn't have known about Perrin's ability, Gillian. Hell, even he didn't know; but afterward, after everything had stopped, especially with Tuuli's and Samuel's transformation to consider, you should have gotten myself or Daed to process through everything before you went out to investigate further. You could have been killed!"

He was pacing and slapped the back of the couch opposite her in frustration. "Goddammit, we can't afford to lose you at the IPPA! *I* can't afford to lose you!" Pausing a moment, he looked around the room. "We can't lose any of you."

Gillian let him yell at her, getting it out of his system. When he stopped to take a breath, she took her chance at an explanation. "We were rescuing Jenna, Helmut. There wasn't time for a caucus on the situation and you guys were sleeping," Gill said tiredly.

"Look, I am well aware that you all are entitled to an apology for me and Tanis fucking up and not checking in after Jack was . . . killed. To tell you the truth, I simply didn't think about it. I'm trying to adjust to a lot of things too. Direct mental communication isn't something I normally do on a daily basis." Looking around, she could see that she had everyone's attention. Oh boy. That wasn't necessarily a good thing.

"But that isn't an excuse," she continued. "I don't know why Tanis didn't think of it either, except he was really happy that Jenna was still alive and that distracted him. Anyway, I am sorry for worrying everybody here and I am sure Tanis won't mind me offering an apology for him either."

Helmut had stopped pacing and was looking at her with eyes that were softer than they had been a few moments before. Even Daed was looking a little less pissed off. At least he'd stopped jerking on the bandage he was applying to the sprained ankle they'd found she had after the adrenaline rush wore off.

Encouraged, she went on, "I am a soldier as much as I am a psychologist. Being one doesn't negate being the other. I didn't get involved in all this Fang Land bullshit by choice but I am involved; we all are."

Turning to Daed, who was injecting anesthetic in her leg in preparation for sewing it up, she pointed out, "You called on me to be a soldier again, not too long ago. Said that the Paramortals needed better publicity, and even blackmailed me into going.

"This isn't any different. I couldn't sit by and let Jenna die because of protocol and rules and decorum. There wasn't time. Be mad at me all you want but I would do the same thing again, for any of you." She looked around at the assembled faces. Daed had the grace to look sheepish, and Helmut was starting to look embarrassed about his rant.

"I am a good psychologist, but I am also a good soldier. Let me be who I am. I know *when* to do either job. Trust me to know the difference and stop getting pissed off at me when my current events list doesn't exactly match yours or because I didn't check with someone first."

There. She'd made her point. Gillian watched as Daed finished stitching up her leg. When his eyes rose to meet hers, they were softer, twinkling, and he smiled a real smile.

"You know, I tend to forget, when I'm away from you for a while, just how big a pain in the ass you are, girl."

"Yeah, well, I'm a competent pain in the ass, which is why you keep me around," Gillian growled back.

Helmut laughed, making everyone jump. "Gillian, when you came into our program to help put Paramortal psychology on everyone's radar, I said to myself, 'That little girl is going to shake up what has been a rather stodgy occupation and breathe some real life into this profession.' I knew what we were getting when we took you on."

"Then quit bitching about it if you know so goddamn much." She glared at him, arms folded across her chest as Daed put the final bandages on her leg.

"I didn't say I was sorry we took you, did I?" Now it was Helmut's turn to glare at her, then he softened again, coming around to sit next to her on the couch.

"We are all still learning new things about this job and our clientele. There is so much we collectively don't know about so many of the Paramortals we try to help. I am glad that you're here, that you're willing and able to do every part of the business so well."

He took the hand that Perrin wasn't holding. "I am sorry, Gillian. I was angry because I was worried and afraid for you, as were we all, but it's because we all care, don't you see that? You are so strong, so capable, yet you're this lovely looking little thing that everyone wants to take—"

Gill interrupted him. "I know you are not about to say anything stupid like 'take care of,' because that would really piss me off right now." She took her hand back.

Perrin laughed behind her, a rich and lovely sound. "Allow me, Dr. Gerhardt." He turned farther on the sofa arm to face Gillian. "You are a small, lovely, spirited woman that everyone wants to take . . ."

"Knock it off, Perrin." Gillian glowered at him.

". . . in their arms and protect." Perrin smiled warmly at her, finishing his sentence.

"Maybe . . . take you to task?" That was from Jenna, who was grinning like a fiend, bandages on both wrists and around her chest. *Fuck you, Jenna.*

"Under their wing?" *Thank you, Tuuli.* Gillian shot her a beaming smile.

"Out behind the proverbial barn?" *Double fuck you, Kimber.* Her friend's left arm was in a sling.

Gill flipped her off, bringing peals of laughter from everyone. Pavel was making god-awful noises in his Werewolf throat as he tried to laugh from where he lay on the rug in front of her. Gill booted him in the ribs with her unbandaged foot, and he huffed at her but didn't move.

"Over their knee?" Daed was sitting much too close to make smart-assed remarks like that so she shoved him over backward with her good foot.

"You guys are assholes," Gill griped under their good-natured teasing.

He rose, laughing to shake his finger at her. "Now, now, sweet cakes, that's just not neighborly. Besides, a friendly little ass-whuppin' never hurt anyone." Sometimes Daed was a Southern-fried jackass. Too bad everyone was now laughing themselves sick.

Helmut was beside himself. "Oh, I would truly pay to see something like that." More gales of laughter from everyone. This was just getting better and better. What happened to being a competent professional and a Marine? Where was her gun anyway?

Gillian had the decency to blush and covered her face with her hands. "I am in hell. Testosterone hell."

Perrin slipped down beside her on the couch, gathering her into his arms and hugging her close. *"Non, ma chérie."*

"No, sweetheart," he said in French, stroking the top of her head. "You are with people who care about you and who will take care of you, as you take care of us. That is why we tease you so brutally."

She let him hold her, letting herself, for the moment, enjoy feeling sheltered, hearing the laughter of her little group subside into conversation and more giggling. A mixture of sandalwood, cedar and candle smoke was what Perrin smelled like. His scent wasn't quite as comforting as Aleksei's, but it was masculine and clean.

Without thinking, she opened her mind to the Vampire, who answered her unspoken need to know that he was all right and not mad at her. *"You are safe and alive, that is all that matters. I am proud of you despite being angry that you were injured. Let Perrin give you comfort as I cannot be with you. Rest and recover. I will see you this evening. Buona sera, piccola."*

He cut off the contact just as quickly, sounding tired. She knew he was with Tanis in the castle's crypt. They would rest safely shielded from the day, hopefully adding another victory in Tanis's effort to free himself of Dracula's taint.

Gill shuddered in Perrin's arms, the events of the long night finally catching up with her. Her head hurt, her face definitely hurt. The only reason her leg didn't hurt was that Daed had shot it full of painkillers before he stitched the slash that Jack had put there. She felt like shit and was beginning to feel sorry for herself. She just wanted to sleep.

Perrin felt her tremble. He shifted a little, his fingertips tilting her chin up so she could look at him. Gillian pushed his hand away but not before he noticed rings of exhaustion around her eyes.

"I'm tired, I hurt and I want to sleep. Let me go, Perrin." It was a whispered plea.

"Never," he said softly. "Now behave yourself and let me take care of you." Without giving her a chance to protest, he pulled her farther onto his lap, then rose with her cradled in his arms.

"Put me down, goddammit, I can walk!" Gillian fairly snarled at him, embarrassed at being carried in front of everyone but a little grateful since her back was killing her.

"Now, baby, don't you give that young man any trouble or I'll have to fetch a switch, ya hear?" Daed's smoky voice called to her. He'd just made the top of her "he needs killing" list.

"She will not," Perrin assured him, not pausing in his stride, carrying her toward the staircase. "She is overtired and needs a hot bath and sleep. I will see to it that she gets some rest."

"Perrin, I swear by all that is holy . . ." Gillian said through her clenched teeth.

"Doctor, you need to heal thyself." Perrin smiled, scolding her gently as he walked up the stairs. "If any of us were in your condition, you would insist on helping. Do not try my patience tonight, mademoiselle, you are going to do exactly what is best for you. Rest and heal."

"Fine."

"I mean it, Gillian. Now cooperate." The authoritarian music teacher was back as he set her on her feet in her room and stood looking down at her, that secret smile ghosting across his features.

"Take off what is left of your clothing and get your robe. I will draw you a hot bath, then get you some tea while you sit in the tub."

At her affronted look, he laughed. "You are hurt, Gillian. There is no way I would look on you with desire tonight. Get ready for your bath." He smoothly turned and left her to change.

Therapy. He is doing well in his therapy, she reminded herself, quashing down her resentment over her vulnerable position of the moment.

Muttering about chauvinistic attitudes in survival situations and about males in general, she tore the shirt and boots off, throwing them in a corner. She got her robe on and went into the bathroom, where Perrin waited by the tub, still fully dressed, making sure the water wasn't too hot.

"Get in, *bébé*," he told her, holding her robe so that she could slip out of it and into the heated water. She winced when the heat hit her numerous cuts and abrasions. Perrin reached over, got a bag from the sink, extracted a small glass vial, then poured some of the contents into the tub. It helped immediately and the stinging went away.

"Thanks, what's in that?" Gillian asked, indicating the vial.

"You do not think all of my time was spent by my lake mooning over singers and writing music, do you?" he teased her gently, going down on one knee by the tub and dipping a washcloth into the healing water. "I studied some Fey magic after I found out about my heritage." Gently, he washed her face and split lip, his touch butterfly light as always, completely attentive to her possible pain.

Gillian watched him. Perrin gained confidence when he was able to assert himself a little. Probably owing to the Gargoyle genes. They were an aggressor species. Made sense.

He was completely in control of the situation at the moment and enjoying himself thoroughly. It wasn't at her expense; it was for her that he was doing it.

The mental lightbulb flashed and her tired brain understood now. He was cracking out of his victim chrysalis and becoming what he was supposed to be. Perrin was definitely finding himself.

Later, after he'd gotten her some tea and lit candles with

calming aromatic scents, he dried her off, then dressed her in one of her oversize T-shirts. She had given up objecting to his pampering her. When he tucked her into the great bed, she surprised herself by asking him to stay.

A myriad of emotions crossed the half of his face that she could see. The mask stared at her, stark and cold, but the living flesh of his perfect left profile finally stabilized into a soft smile.

"Of course, *mon amour*, as you wish."

He was so perfect, so correct in his movements and actions. Every gesture and step was like watching a dance as he moved fluidly to recline next to her on top of the covers when she scooted over to give him room.

Looking at his raven black hair, always so perfectly tousled, she reached up to handle its texture, entranced by the silky feel of his curls. Absently, her fingers continued to trace the angle of his jaw and his perfect mouth.

Perrin caught her hand, kissed it gently, his eyes holding hers. "None of that, *ma femme*. You need to sleep," he admonished her lightly.

Gillian stared at him. "Cut it out, Perrin. I really hate that."

Chuckling, he drew her just a bit closer, then stroked her damp hair until she relaxed against the pillow. He longed to gather her in his arms but she would never allow that.

"Good night, Perrin," came her soft, sleepy voice.

"Bon soir, mon amour," he said quietly in return, taking in her scent of clover and snow-tipped meadows.

Perrin stayed with her long after he could have left. He slept lightly in the chair, having moved from the bed once Gillian was asleep. He startled at every movement, every sound she made. When she cried out angrily during her rest and struggled against the covers, he went to stand by the bed, whispering in French, singing softly as she settled back into sleep, never waking to know the dreams that tormented her.

Affectionately, he smoothed her hair back when she snuggled deeper into the blankets. He loved her hair, the way it shimmered in the candlelight. He wished he could simply look into her eyes for a while, see the compassion and stalwart courage there. After the events of this night, he knew those lovely eyes, so green and warm, had looked upon horrors that he could not imagine; did not want to imagine.

Delicately, he traced the edges of her face, lingering over the bruised jaw and the cut on her lip. The protective and aggressive instincts of both an adult male Gargoyle and Sidhe reared their heads knowing that monster had struck her.

She had brought him out of the darkness of loneliness, given him hope, gave him back his pride, made him believe that he might actually have a real life outside of his marginal existence.

Perrin resolved that he wouldn't dishonor her effort by exposing to her the level of his interest, the depth of his heart. She was right. He wasn't ready; for her, for anyone. He wasn't whole yet but he was less fragmented than he had ever been in his life. Gillian and he still had some work to do, more of his issues to resolve. He understood her better now. She was a soul healer, just as the Sidhe had said.

" 'Tears, idle tears, I know not what they mean, / Tears from the depth of some divine despair / Rise in the heart, and gather to the eyes, / In looking on the happy Autumnfields, / And thinking of the days that are no more.' " He quoted Alfred, Lord Tennyson quietly to her, kissing her forehead then returning to his chair. One happy tear trailed down his unblemished cheek, sparkling in the candlelight. Aleksei was a lucky man, er, Vampire.

CHAPTER
17

"Mmmmmm, that feels wonderful," Gillian sighed, stretching like a cat and wriggling a little in emphasis as the strikingly handsome, naked man massaged her back and shoulders, getting the kinks from her fencing practice out. They were working on his skills as usual, but she was reaping the benefits of his determination to be good at everything related to being devoted to women.

A smile quirked his gorgeous mouth, the skin around his eyes were shadowed by the mask he wore, but she could see that skin crinkling in mirth at her responses. He enjoyed doing something for her for a change.

The upper half of his perfect face was covered by a black leather stylized mask, formed to fit his features; covering every part of the disfigurement his mixed parentage had given him. Most days he wore only the white partial mask on his disfigured right side. Today he wore the black, making him look like a roguish French Lone Ranger.

Gillian said it was for him to know when he trusted her enough to take it off. It was part of his therapy. She was still waiting several weeks later.

Perrin continued his ministrations on his lovely sex therapist. Gillian had been dedicated, patient and understanding with him. Helping him make more progress both in sexual situations and in socialization than he'd ever thought possible.

He'd been a shy, trembling, suicidally depressed wreck of a male when he'd first come there to the Rachlav Institute of Paramortal Healing, sponsored ever so lushly by Aleksei Rachlav.

Gillian's kindness and abilities with her natural empathy had seen him through the worst of it. She'd taken him from someone too terrified to meet another's gaze for fear of their reaction to a confident man who could initiate sex or a conversation with equal ease and grace.

"A little lower and to the left," came Gillian's muffled voice from the pillow. She shifted her hips, pushing her cute and curvy bottom against his thigh. "Or do I have to fuck you blind before I get a decent massage?" She was teasing him.

A few weeks ago, such ribald humor would have devastated him. Now laughing with her, he swatted her sheet-covered bottom, making her squirm. "You are scandalous, *ma petite femme*," he scolded her in mock severity.

"You love it when I talk dirty to you." She rolled a little and looked at him through the hair that was over her face, one visible green eye sparkling at him.

Perrin tried to look stern; he was an autocratic music teacher after all. Instead, he brushed the hair from her face. "I love it when you are open and honest. Do not shut me out, or try to get yourself killed."

Perrin had come a long way, and she was proud of him. He was open with giving and receiving affection, had been coming to group therapy at the castle. Hell, he and Aleksei were positively tight now. Even Trocar was kind to him.

Once Trocar and Finian designed a suitable magic-dampening field, Perrin had been freer to compose his haunting, erotic, magical music; with or without the windows in the guesthouse open. His musically enhanced glamour was contained to the house itself with no spillage, thus preventing another orgy like the one weeks earlier. Since then things had progressed rather rapidly in his therapy.

He watched Gillian as she studied him back. As always, he was amazed by her ability to be so completely altruistic, so completely absorbed by what her patient, in this case himself, might need or want. It reminded him strangely of the night she'd taken on Jack the Ripper.

Perrin still had dreams about that night. How close she'd come to dying at the hands of that psychopathic monster, using herself as bait to find her friend. Since then, his level of respect for her had grown along with admiration for her skill and bravery.

He, like Aleksei, loved her for everything that she was. Only Aleksei was free to express that feeling for the little blonde; Perrin could not. To do so would be to risk being banished from her forever. When he was stable and could function, he would be discharged from her care. Then there would be no contact whatsoever after that for at least a year.

Perrin was secretly a little daunted by the prospect of being without her sheltering presence. At the same time, he was beginning to actually think of a life outside the safety of the compound as a possibility. Thinking like that scared him but it encouraged him too.

Right now, he didn't have to think about being without her. Gillian was here, in his bed, in his arms, warm and alive. And squirming. "Perrin, don't have a death grip on the woman, let her know you want her close, but don't cut off the blood supply to her brain," she instructed him crossly.

"I am sorry, *ma bien-aimée*. I wasn't thinking," Perrin said softly.

Gillian turned and looked into those wondrous gray green eyes. "That's the problem, you *were* thinking. Is everything all right?"

Perrin met her gaze easily now. He loved to see the genuine compassion and concern in the emerald depths. Only now he had an inkling of the horrors those eyes had seen; it brought the instinct to keep her safe and sheltered roaring to life.

"Everything is fine, thank you," he assured her, skimming the backs of his knuckles down her throat to lightly tease her coral nipple. He bent his dark head to taste her; tongue now expertly flicking it to pebbled hardness.

Gillian gasped as his hot mouth closed on her. Heat flooded her pelvis as he teased her breast with his teeth. Her hand moved between them to his semierect flesh and felt him spring to full hardness at her touch.

Perrin had been shy about initiating contact but even worse about her touching him. It brought a small flash of victory to her, to know that he wasn't afraid anymore, that she could touch him at will and have him be comfortable enough to respond to it.

They'd been experimenting with all aspects of sex. Perrin had had an enormous problem with the thought of oral sex until recently. Once she convinced him to try it, both giving and receiving, he had been an enthusiastic pupil, adding another accomplishment to his growing repertoire of expertise.

At the moment, however, Perrin's Gargoyle sex receptors snapped on line with the sensations of touch, taste and scent he was getting from her; diverting all his thought and a certain level of his blood supply to what Gillian referred to as the "battle bridge."

Instincts honed from thousands of years of Gargoyle evolution and time immemorial in the Sidhe demanded that he mate with her immediately. Fully erect, his penis was enhanced by the equidistant ridges that were characteristic of a sexually mature Gargoyle male.

Though Gillian insisted on using a condom, Perrin longed to enter her freely, feel her actual flesh around him, carry her scent on him after she left. Gods above, she was wet already. A new surge of blood tidal waved into his penis, and he groaned.

"Condom!" Gillian gasped as his fingers stroked inside her and she moved restlessly against his hand.

Perrin had hardly turned over to retrieve the latex covering from its foil pouch before Gillian pushed his shoulders back, and straddled him. His glamour was filling the room, pouring into both of them, and they hurried to slide the condom on. Gill rose up, first taking his hand to show him, then letting Perrin position his body under her own. They hadn't tried female superior yet and this was as good a time as any.

As he gripped her hips to lower her over him, Perrin locked eyes with her, loving the look she got whenever he filled her completely. Gillian's head was back, exposing the line of her throat, her breasts tantalizingly before his eyes. The feeling of her tight and hot, opening slowly as he pressed inside, brought a fresh rush of blood to his now aching flesh. The bands of muscle in her canal gripped him like a fist, beginning the friction that would send them spinning into orgasm.

He was gentle, holding back on his instinct to thrust until he was sure she was fully stretched for him. He wasn't quite sure what to expect from this new position and gritted his teeth to wait for her example. When Gillian began a slow, sexy ride on him, he was undone.

Over the weeks he had learned to read a woman's body, to gauge her reaction and time her climax with his own. He found himself having to think of everything but what she was doing on him to keep from exploding right away.

"I never dreamed you could be more beautiful than I thought already." The musical deep voice with its unique lilting French-Sidhe accent was strained as she leaned back, letting him see their bodies parting and joining.

Panting with restraint as she moved on him, he gritted his teeth, admitting to her, "Gillian, it is too intense, feeling you and watching you like this. I need . . . I need . . ."

Before she could answer or he could finish his sentence, a growl started deep in his throat. Then he was dragging her arms up over her head with one hand, rolling her under him, his other arm going under her bottom to lift her line higher and open her farther until he was pressed against her cervix. He held there, breathing heavily, tension obvious on his face.

"I need to mate, Gillian. I am trying to cooperate, but the Gargoyle in me demands something else today."

"Tell me." She was breathing heavily and shifting up against him, eyes dilated and lips parted.

Perrin's voice was guttural, deep, full of sex. "I have yet to know what sex is like without a barrier. Let me mate with you, *ma bien-aimée*, truly mate. Allow me the experience of your true flesh. Permit me release with no impediment."

The term he used: *mating*. He was the product of a rape between a Gargoyle and a half-blooded Music Sidhe. When he said *mating*, he meant it. She was a female; the male was dominant in the Gargoyle species. That meant sex to deposit seed. He'd been studying up on his blended physiology apparently.

She couldn't get pregnant by him; she was on the pill. Perrin hadn't been with anyone but her and was disease free, as was she. Aleksei couldn't contract anything back from her; being a Vampire, he was immune to illness and disease. Maybe once wouldn't hurt.

Stroking his hair, caressing his back, feeling him trembling with desire, and his instinctive, cell-deep need hammering at her empathy, she relented. He needed this for some reason and she was all right with it.

"All right. Let's do it."

The perfect, sculpted face rose, and once again she felt the shock of the distraction of the mask against that beauty. His eyes held all of his anguish, all of his joy. They mirrored his soul and gave it to her in that moment.

"Are you sure?" He hardly dared breathe for fear he hadn't heard her right.

"Take off the condom, then get back here."

He eased out of her, practically tearing the condom off once he was withdrawn. Elegant fingers, artistic hands, which could command the most beautiful music from a violin, piano or pipe organ, softly caressed the inside of her thighs as he looked at her dark pink glistening folds. Dipping his head, he tasted her sweetness, reveled in her.

The sensation was powerful as he plied her with his lips and tongue, making her writhe as he held her hips down with one arm across her pelvis. Fresh blood surged to his groin as he became aware of her impending orgasm. Abruptly stopping before completing the act, he lifted his head and started to crawl up her body, gently probing at her opening with his unencumbered flesh for the first time.

"Perrin!" Gillian complained, moving her hips. "Don't stop now!"

Taking her mouth, he kissed her deeply, relishing the sensation as his ridged erection found the perfect angle to slowly press inside her. It felt . . . incredible. The tight silken bands of her passage were slick with arousal, gripping his hardened flesh, welcoming him into her heat. Something wild and predatory reared its head within him, knowing that he was sheathed within her with no barrier between them.

Perrin wanted to make this perfect moment last, but the awareness of his unprotected state overrode his intentions. He groaned into her mouth. That was what he needed. What his body needed. He felt a brief emission of semen like a jolt through his groin as he pressed against her cervix. Instinctively he knew what it was for.

Gillian felt it too. The abrupt orgasm his semen caused overwhelmed her in a rippling, gasping rush. Perrin felt her come, the scent of her orgasm rocked him, driving his hips and tightening his hold on her.

"Like that, *mon amour*, yes," he encouraged her, turning her face to his own and looking into her eyes, reveling in the pleasure he found there.

Perrin tensed, feeling another brief jolt of semen against her Human cervix. His body was impatient and demanded her cooperation.

"*Ma passionnée*, relax for me. The fluid will open your body to me. Trust me, I would never hurt you." His voice shook, and his glamour flared, pouring into and over their bodies.

She felt him going deeper, then understood what he meant. Her cervix was softening and thinning, the result of his semen leaking into her. Her newly opening body was taking him in farther with each thrust.

Perrin pushed her hands back up, holding her in a submissive posture under him. His instincts took them into a turbulent Gargoyle mating frenzy. The waves of delight washed over them as his glamour intensified the experience.

Incredibly at that moment, her cervix acquiesced to the insistent probing and allowed him complete entrance to her womb. The imperative need to ejaculate slammed into him like a freight train as his ridged cock slipped through the widened opening. His body knew and responded. Instantly the hard ridges flattened out, extending his length by several inches and sliding him fully inside her womb.

He cried out, his now smooth erection skating over the cervical ridge to its final destination. The sensation brought the completion of their mating surging upward through his shaft hot and fast. Their bodies were welded together, his locked tightly within hers, his glamour enhancing every nuance of sensation.

Gillian crashed over the edge first, watching the tension in his face as he arched back, straining into her. His body expelled heavy jets in a torrid wave, the liquid heat and literal vibration from his climax triggering her again and again in a breathless rush as he poured into her.

Perrin could hardly breathe. The feeling for him was like sex and fellatio all rolled into one. A sensation so strong that he nearly blacked out. As the final shudders left his body, he gathered her tenderly in his arms, kissing her with gentle fulfillment and watching her eyes come slowly back into focus, the aftershocks shaking them both.

"Are you all right, *ma chérie*?"

"If I get any better, I'll be dead," Gillian said when she could breathe again and form a coherent sentence.

They were still welded together as Perrin rolled gently onto his back, still holding her pelvis pressed firmly to him, not wanting to relinquish the barest fraction of his place within her yet.

"Are you uncomfortable? Do you want me to withdraw?"

"If you do, I will kill you," Gillian said, eyes closed. "At least I will when I get my energy back."

Chuckling with deep male satisfaction, Perrin stroked her

face, kissing her eyes, her mouth. "In a short time, you'll be ready for me again. Your body will want more sex. A gargoyle's semen is like an aphrodisiac. It triggers need within the female, opens her to the male and ensures pregnancy."

"That's not funny. I'm not going to be able to walk as it is with you nearly in the back of my throat."

"Gillian, have I hurt you?"

She opened an eye to see if he was kidding; he wasn't. "No, Perrin, you were wonderful; that was wonderful. I am not complaining, all right?"

Pleased, he gathered her to him. "I wanted to do something for you after all you've done for me. I read up on Gargoyle sexuality and wanted to know if it was possible to bring you that kind of delight."

Returning his embrace, she kissed along his jaw. "You can bring a woman delight like that anytime. It will soon be time to turn you loose on the world of females, and I'm sure there will be no complaints."

Perrin grew instantly quiet. She reminded him that his place was not with her. Intellectually he knew it; emotionally he dreaded it. He could never repay her for what she'd done for him. The money he'd spent for his time at the Institute was marginal. Perhaps she would allow him to take her out to dinner, or he might donate a substantial sum to the facility as a very meager thank-you.

Isolated for so many years, denied even the basest contact, he was almost obsessive in his observation of others. Now, he was acutely aware of the feeling of their joined bodies, the silk of her hair in his hands, the softness of her skin. Her unique scent, like snow on a clover meadow, blended with their combined fluids, which now stained his sheets. Listening to her breathing, he knew she slept, and he stroked her hair carefully with his characteristic delicate touch.

Gillian was exciting, intelligent, exasperating, obstinate, brave, hardheaded and kind. She triggered his protective and dominant side inadvertently, coaxed his tender and artistic talents purposely. She had managed to bring out the best in him.

Perrin smiled unconsciously, thinking of how he'd never known he had any "best" in him. Thanks to Gillian, now he did.

Things had been a little strained with Gillian following Jenna's rescue, after Trocar had returned with the Ripper's heart in a leather bag. He had initiated some arcane ritual at the great hall fireplace, culminating in dissipating the evil of the fallen Vampire. The heart was magically dried, ground up and burned. Then Trocar scattered the ashes to the winds. He also destroyed the scalpel Jack had used in his crimes and the knife he'd used to remove the heart, saying that the weapons were dishonored and could never be used again.

Gillian had solemnly helped Trocar every step of the ritual, but was noticeably withdrawn. Aleksei finally took her aside into the library, to give her a gentle but firm talking-to. Testing his mettle was becoming a regular occurrence, so he put on his best diplomatic hat and broached his concern.

She had listened to him. She could feel that Aleksei's own heart was aching for her, and her empathy demanded that she respond. He had reminded her how much she'd taught him about trust and sharing, admonishing her gently for shutting them all out.

Finally, she revealed to him that she was trying to come to terms with how Jack had really unnerved her. Being stalked by the legendary serial killer, having other women die because of his misplaced hatred and determination to finally have her, had shaken her more than any other threat she'd ever faced. It was the first time she'd ever felt like a victim and she didn't like it.

Working on processing those unfamiliar feelings was unintentionally shutting them out. She was unhappy with how she'd handled the situation, unhappy with the fact that her friends had been hurt ultimately because of her. It was great that they had been successful but she felt she had caused the circumstance in the first place.

While she talked, her voice was level but tears welled in her eyes. Aleksei was shaken by her stoic resolve; she needed comfort, needed someone to look after her, but wouldn't ask. She would never ask. She wasn't fragile; she was the bravest person he'd ever known. But she still needed someone. She was handling it characteristically in her own way. Alone.

"*Cara mia*, you are not alone in this. I am here to help you, as are all of your friends. You do so much for others, Gillian, let me . . . let us, do something for you." Aleksei's eyes were warm with affection and his sincerity was completely evident in the way he felt.

The concept was alien to Gillian's basic psyche. She could instruct it, teach it, but not live it. She'd had no one she could depend on emotionally when she was growing up. In her adult life, she honed her skills of keeping others just far enough away so she wouldn't impose her needs on anyone. Being "the Helper" was her purpose. Being helped . . . that she fought tooth and nail.

"Aleksei, I am trying." She managed a weak smile.

"I want to understand, *il mio amore*. Why is it so hard to trust me with your heart? You trust me with your body, with your thoughts, with your safety. Let me help." There was no pity in Aleksei's face. He wasn't feeling sorry for her. Just honest compassion and a desire to have his girlfriend back up on her stabilized pins again.

"My family was rather distant from each other," she said, taking a deep breath.

"Were they harsh with you?"

"No . . . more like . . . preoccupied," she continued. "My parents both had their own interests, their own careers. And I wasn't a problem child, believe it or not."

She grinned up at him and he laughed. They were sitting together on the couch. Gillian was pressed up against the back and arm of the sofa; Aleksei was next to her, just holding her hand, lusciously sprawled on his part of the sofa.

"I do find that difficult to believe." At least the sparkle was coming back to his eyes.

"I bet you do. Anyway, I was alone a lot. We didn't live near anyone with kids, I was an only child, so I had no one to talk to or process things with. There was a housekeeper who kept up with all the little chores like the laundry and general cleaning."

"So you had little responsibility."

"No, I had homework, my horses . . . We had a small acreage . . . and I was alone."

"I did not know you were an equestrian." He sounded surprised.

"I have many skills. You just haven't discovered all of them yet."

He laughed at that. "All part of your mystery and allure, *dolcezza.*"

Gill continued, "Yeah, right. Well, part of the family dynamic was that if you fucked up or made a mistake, you were essentially ostracized."

"Shunning? In this day and age?" Aleksei was taken aback. "I thought that outside of a few religious groups, Humans did not practice this."

"I'm not talking about minor debacles with denting the car fender or bad grades, more like . . . Well, for example . . . I had an uncle who was trying to put his life back together after being a prisoner of war. It was hard for him; he wanted some distance and he wanted to work things out.

"My father was determined to be involved in his recovery, so he tried to get my uncle a job at a local business. It was a good job, right up his alley for his skills and abilities."

"I take it your uncle was not pleased."

"Not in the least. He took the offer, basically to shut my father up, instead of just going ahead with his plans. He wound up doing a not-so-great job, leaving the company and then finally sharing that he wanted to be a police officer. Dad wasn't too happy about it and said so.

"What we didn't know was that my uncle had tried to tell my dad what kind of help he wanted—for tuition, so he could get his degree and be a cop—but it was the wrong choice, in my father's opinion. He never approved of my uncle's choices. It sort of started a family feud.

"My uncle went on to become an outstanding police officer, got married and carved a good life for himself and his family out of the shambles he had been in. When he tried to reestablish contact, my dad cut him off."

"So you lost contact with your uncle."

"Yes, but so did a lot of others who took my father's side in the argument. No one was allowed to discuss it or even bring it up. I thought the whole thing was stupid."

"Family arguments usually are." Aleksei sighed.

"Yup. But the point is that anyone who countered my father's position was booted out of the family circle. No explanations, no railing and ranting; they were just gone. It happened with my grandfather, my cousins, and I was scared it would happen to me."

"And you believe that if you ask for help, you are weak . . . because . . . ?" Aleksei was trying to keep her on topic.

"I just don't want to let anyone down . . . have you think less of me because I asked for help or for the wrong help. It sort of undermines my credibility, don't you think?"

Aleksei studied her face, reaching out his hand to caress her cheek and cup her chin before he spoke. "What I believe is that the only person you are letting down is yourself."

"Maybe . . . but when I decided to join the service, go to college on the GI bill, it did happen. I was told I was making a mistake, and not to expect any help from my family in the future. So far I haven't."

"That is terrible!" Aleksei was outraged. "How can a parent cut off a child because of their choices?"

"Aleksei, you had a great family. A wonderful warm family who loved each other openly, supported each other completely. Not everyone is lucky enough to have that dynamic. Some of us just have a comfortable living in a nice neighborhood with decent people for parents who are emotionally barricaded.

"I'm not bitching, my folks are good people. They just didn't know how to show it in the right way. Or at least in the way that I would have liked. It doesn't make them bad."

"I understand, *piccola*, but it also does not make them right. You needed to be shown love, not just lauded for your accomplishments, or punished because of what was in your heart." He watched as emotions flickered across her face. He could feel her turmoil through their link but he wouldn't interfere or pry.

"When I joined the Marines and then the IPPA, I got a family, Aleksei. Those people are my friends, yes, but they're more than that. They're all I've got."

He pulled her to him, tucking her against his chest and under his shoulder. "Not all you have, *innamorata*. You do have me."

She relaxed against him after a moment, thinking about that. "Yes, I guess I do. Now I have to decide what to do with you."

Aleksei chuckled and pulled her up so he might kiss her. "I have an idea."

They kissed and he thought. He thought about what she'd said. Growing up in a family where no one paid attention unless you did something amazing or wrong . . . love being measured out in increments . . . no wonder she was so barricaded. They would have to work on that.

"Gillian . . ."

"Mmmm-hmmm?"

"Gillian, if you let me, I would like to help you get over these bad feelings about Jack."

Silence.

Crickets.

"Gillian?"

"How, Aleksei? I keep going over it in my mind. No matter how I slice it, it is still my fault."

"No, *angela*, it was not. Nor was how you handled it. I want to take you to the village, revisit the place where you confronted each other. Maybe that will chase your demons away."

"It won't work."

"It might."

"All right, I'll try."

18

ALEKSEI arranged with Pavel, Kimber, Helmut and Trocar to accompany him in taking Gillian to the village. Jenna and Tanis were off getting acquainted again, but Gillian needed a night out. It would be good to finally have her demons about Jack exorcised. The rest of them were going to help support her and she was going to let them. Gah! Her stomach was in knots over the idea.

He found her in the library, poring over some Internet documents that reported recent attacks on Humans by Paramortals. They were listed by country, crime and alleged attacker.

There was starting to be some pressure on all law enforcement, mental health professionals and even mercenaries to form a cooperative to share information and start second-guessing the attacks. Gillian was swearing under her breath, understanding that the tactical problems involved in such a measure would be insurmountable.

Another article announced that a few televangelists of varying denominations were reiterating their objections to legalizing the Paramortal community in general. They dubbed anything not Human to be godless creations of evil and were calling for revolution. There were the predictable countering broadcasts from several others, insisting that all were divinely created creatures and we were better coexisting than fighting each other.

Gillian wished they'd all stop proselytizing and realize everyone had to inhabit the same space together, like it or not. It was better to live peaceably and with everything out in the open than looking over your shoulder every moment, being afraid of shadows in the darkness. Frowning at the screen, she looked up when Aleksei spoke.

"Come, *piccola*, be with your escorts for the evening." He'd held out his hand and she took it shyly.

Damn, she thought. They all looked like a smorgasbord for Sex on a Stick. Aleksei was breathtaking. He wore his customary black boots but the deep burgundy velvet of his pants and jacket were different. A black shirt with a black lace spill was left open down to the middle of his impressive chest. The colors set off the arctic gray of his eyes. His black hair was loose and spilled over his shoulders in soft waves.

Helmut was out of his usual tweed for once. He was tall enough that Daed had been able to contribute to his evening wardrobe. The dove gray European-cut suit he wore brought out the intense blue of his eyes, toning down his ruddy complexion and the red in his sandy hair. His shirt was blinding white, fitted and elegant. Platinum cufflinks sparkled at his wrists and Italian leather loafers graced his feet. Since Helmut was more slender than Daed, the clothes were a little loose on him, but he looked splendid nonetheless.

Trocar was out of the one-piece black thing he generally wore and looked resplendent in glossy dark Aegean blue leather pants and matching boots. A surprising silvery blue shirred tunic, made from some obscure cave spider's web, molded over the obsidian muscles in his upper body but managed not to conflict with his shimmering white crystalline hair. Iridescent eyes twinkled at her and he bowed formally.

Perrin glided down the hallway to join them. Aleksei had invited him, thinking it would be good for the masked man to get out with a group of friends for one night. The Frenchman would be leaving within a day or two, and everyone wanted to give him a nice send-off. As it was, he quite took everyone's breath away with his entrance.

Tailored, flat-front black pants fit his long spectacular legs like a glove. He wore his boots underneath, the bottoms of the material brushed over the shining leather. A black cut-away tailed jacket fit his slender but nicely muscled upper body to perfection. The high-collared white shirt was mostly behind an expensive embroidered vest. His cravat was gold, matching the needlework on the vest and the flecks of gold in his eyes.

Still masked, but this time it didn't distract from the overall picture but seemed more part of him. The perfect left side of his face turned toward Gillian as she took in his gleaming hair; tonight he had groomed it straight back so as not to detract from the mask or the perfect side. The slight curl at the ends brushed his collar, contrasting the black against the white.

No gloves. Interesting. Perrin might just be permanently out of his shell. Shorter and lighter built than Aleksei, he was as tall as Trocar and had the same sort of "put together right" finished look as the Dark Elf. There was no denying there was hard muscle under either of their clothing.

Seeing the approval in her eyes, Perrin said, "Thank you," in his exquisite voice. "You are lovely tonight, *ma chérie*."

Aleksei and Trocar nodded in agreement. Gillian moved to take Aleksei's arm and Perrin's hand. Trocar and Helmut wouldn't be offended. Both preferred walking unencumbered by anything or anyone.

Kimber bounced down the stairs in an adorable, skintight, denim outfit. The pants fit her like a glove, as did the golden, sparkly vest and tailored jacket. Girlfriend was tall but wore four-inch gold stiletto heels. You had to admire confidence like that.

Moving out, Pavel fell in step beside them, his arm around Kimber's waist, looking like he'd raided Aleksei's or Tanis's closet. The Lycanthrope was dressed in brown leather pants and a matching leather jacket, plus an old-world ivory silk shirt. He looked yummy, and Kimber's leer made certain he knew it.

Gillian did look good. She'd traded in her usual casual attire for something a little flashier. Her tunic was one Trocar had given her years before. It was forest green and made from a soft pettable silky Elven fabric. Tight black pants curved over her legs and her boots were on display. Black crinkled pigskin leather, they resembled pirate boots, folded over beneath her knee. Her hair was down for a change and picked up every ray of light.

Together, they all walked to the parking area and squeezed into Gillian's car. She drove, preferring her own hand on the wheel. As they approached the village, she stiffened and gripped the steering wheel tightly as she pulled over into the first side street she could find and parked.

Piling out of the car, Aleksei, Pavel, Helmut, Kimber and Trocar fanned out a little, sensing their surroundings for any danger. Perrin came to offer his hand and waited until she considered for a moment before she took it. He moved with a Sidhe's grace, fluid and controlled but far from delicate.

Dressed in the black formal attire, which complemented his raven hair and the one exposed ebony eyebrow, Perrin looked sensual, masculine and a little dangerous, the mask lending to his mystery and beauty. He led her slowly from the car, walking carefully, turning to make sure she wasn't going to balk.

Soon, Gillian dropped his hand and moved away, looking up and around at the streets, deliberately walking to the place where she'd confronted the Ripper and stopping there, rubbing her upper arms as if a sudden chill gripped her. Aleksei was behind her in an instant, his arms going around her, locking her back against him. This was one thing he could give her that she could accept—his support.

"Now, *piccola*, we will all face this together."

She felt something coalesce around her . . . strong, good, warm feelings . . . glamour. This wouldn't do.

"Perrin, stop it. I need to feel this with my senses open like they were that night," Gillian ordered him.

He complied but stayed close. The only reason she had agreed to bringing him along was to help him feel incorporated in a busy social setting outside the castle grounds.

After they confronted her feelings about Jack, the plan was for everyone to stop by the coffee shop or the bar at the Inn for singing, tale telling and general fun. Gill hoped that his self-assurance would receive a final push from being included as their guest, knowing he was accepted publicly and welcomed, so he could leave with confidence.

She'd argued with Helmut about it at first. He wanted her to go ahead with it; she disagreed, thinking it was crossing a therapeutic line. After a call to her former mentor, Dr. Cassiopeia Delphi, a Master Vampire Ph.D., and Director of the Miller-Jackson Center for Intimacy, who also encouraged her to follow it through, Gillian had relented.

Cassiopeia had pointed out that it would be in his best interest to empower him a little outside his safety net. It cost her nothing except a moment of vulnerability at the beginning of the evening and would give him so much more overall than she would relinquish. Gill agreed but had no intention of involving Perrin as anything but an observer in her moment of facing her fears. She didn't want to encourage his protective feelings toward her any further than he'd already imagined them.

Aleksei moved to flank her on the left as Trocar did on the right. Helmut was there to offer any therapeutic support but knew Gillian wanted to work through this on her own. Pavel and Kimber stayed behind her and the Grael near Perrin. All eyes were turned on her, expecting what, they didn't know. They were just there if she needed them.

"Perhaps if you talked about your encounter with him, *piccola*," Aleksei suggested, taking her hand in his own. "Tell us what happened, how it occurred."

"How did you happen to find him before we did, Gillyflower?" Trocar suddenly asked, realizing that she wasn't going to come to terms with it easily.

No matter, he could help, and he had an idea just how to do that. Piss her off, let her get good and mad at something, banish her own demons.

"There were three of you out here alone, all of you bait. I was following you, then Pavel veered off on the trail so I chose to follow him, believing that he would lead me to Jack before you."

"You wanted to kill him yourself," Gillian said absently.
"So did I, so I made sure he found me first."

Perrin was stunned. Aleksei had been filling him in on the various varieties of Paramortal, Vampires and Jack in particular since that had been whom Gillian had been hunting. She could have been killed, nearly was killed in fact. She knew better but she had set herself up.

"Gillian," Perrin said softly when she didn't continue to speak, "what did you do?"

"Give her a moment, Perrin. Leave her to her thoughts." Aleksei slid his arm over her shoulder and pulled her into the shelter of his own body.

Kimber had a vague idea of where Trocar was going with this and chimed in, "Look, you people need to leave her alone. She will deal with this in her own way."

Trocar ignored the suggestion, and put his hand on his former Captain's shoulder. "I believe you said that you verbally sparred with him . . . before you knew who and what he was, of course. I recall you and him taunting each other in France as well. Did he truly unnerve you that badly? More than every other monster I have seen you face?"

"Careful, Trocar." Helmut's soft voice carried on the night air. "Don't push her faster than she is willing to go. Remember, Gillian did nothing wrong. All bets are off when a life is at stake. She did what she had to do."

Gillian bit her lip, looking anywhere but at her friends. She wasn't necessarily proud of what she'd done; it had been an unpleasant necessity to rescue her friend. As it was, she was struggling with her choices, actions and decisions of that night. All of it had gone against everything she knew or had been taught.

For the first time that she could remember, she'd acted solely by relying on others to come and save the day. That wasn't like her. She handled things herself, never second-guessed her decisions. Great. Now she knew what was dogging her ass. It was herself.

"He didn't unnerve me, Trocar." Gillian finally turned to him. "It was just that in order to find him, to get to Jenna . . . I had to go against things I knew. Things that I . . . I had to compromise who I was to get to him. I'm not proud of it, but I did it."

"Of course, Petal, keep talking and you will convince yourself eventually." Trocar knew he was treading dangerous ground, antagonizing her. Truth was, he was afraid for her, for the first time in their long friendship. She had to pull out of this or she'd never trust her own judgment again.

"You taunted a killer, used yourself as bait. What else, Gillian?"

Gillian slapped a hand over her eyes and blushed furiously while she contemplated various methods of killing a certain Grael Elf while he was sleeping. She didn't want to talk about this, right now, or ever.

Kimber wasn't embarrassed at all. "Damn straight she did. Kemo Sabe got him to come out, didn't she? She made sure Jenna was found, didn't she? So she provoked him to get him to show himself. So what if that's against procedure and protocol? We've broken the rules before. Isn't the result what's important? Why are y'all ragging on her?"

"What did you call him? Cock blocked? Impotent? A fanged piece of shit? Did he pleasure himself because of your discomfort? Do enlighten us, Petal. I know how you dislike being misquoted." Trocar was a little too close to be smirking in her direction.

It was the last thing he got out before Gillian's right hook caught him in the mouth and he found himself looking up at her from the very hard pavement of the street. Even reaching up from her poor angle of nearly a foot shorter than himself, she managed to land him on his ass on the road.

"Shouldn't have gone there." Kimber grinned at the fallen Elf, then investigated her manicure.

From where he lay, Trocar, though momentarily shaken, stared up at his former commander; she still looked short. Damn. He had forgotten that was how she normally won a fight. Someone usually underestimated her because of her size and gender. Also she wasn't afraid of him or of serial killers or of much else either.

That was what he wanted her to remember, that her strength lay in her ability to use her anger productively, just as she had the night with Jack, to make judgment calls of her own accord, stand by them. Not feeling as though she had to make excuses for her actions. They owed her respect, not their mollycoddling.

"Yes, Trocar. Yes, you're right. I also called him a 'motherfucking, perverted son of a bitch.' And yes, it was right after he finished getting himself off in the middle of the street while he was staring at my crotch under my flimsy little Aleksei-dress. Probably because he was fantasizing about sticking his stiletto into my vagina. Is that what you wanted to hear?" Gillian vented at him, fists clenched and legs braced in case he got back up and she had to drop him again.

"You want to hear why I used myself as bait to flush him out? Because he wasn't going to come out, Trocar. He was going to stay up in that room and murder Jenna like he killed that girl we found by the compound. Like he murdered the other two before, that we found out about later. Jack was here because of me. The responsibility of stopping him was mine. Just mine." She had started pacing back and forth in front of the three vertical individuals and Trocar.

"Oh boy, she's wound up now. You started this; you all get her calmed down again. I am getting a drink." Kimber waved her hand dismissively at all of them and ambled off toward Radu's bar at the Inn, Pavel striding up to flank her as she crossed the street.

Gillian was wound up all right. Something cracked inside her. She was tired of having to defend her actions and choices in that situation. She was tired of thinking of Jack and how much he had bothered her. She was just plain tired and wanted everyone to leave her alone.

"He would have killed Jenna, then he would have come for me, or for Kimber or Aisling for that matter. He would have kept butchering women, and I saw a chance to stop him. Hell, I thought you and Tanis were dead or prevented from coming so I really would have had to kill the son of a bitch myself or die in the process. There at the end, I thought I was going to die, but I dealt with it.

"You saw what he did; you knew what he was capable of. Tell me that I was wrong for doing what I did. Stand there and tell me that I was wrong." Green eyes blazing bright with tears, she turned away.

"I made the right choices, whether anyone else agrees with me or not. I made the right choices for the situation." Her voice was overlaid with emotion, but it was stronger than it had been. She turned back to her friends with an announcement of her epiphany. "We all lived, that's what is important. I did the right thing."

"Yes you did, Schatzi. You did indeed." Helmut squeezed her shoulder in support. "No one could have done a better job, nor expected a better outcome."

Aleksei hugged her close, grazing his hand down her hair, whispering sweet nothings, then looked her square in the eyes. "I am proud of you, Gillian. No one should have had to face what you did alone. Your friends didn't come to your rescue, they came to your aid. There is a difference, *cara*."

"Thanks, Aleksei." Gillian had the faintest of smiles as she looked up at him. "I guess I just needed to really understand that."

Trocar gracefully got to his feet, rubbing his jaw ruefully. He glanced at Aleksei, who now had a genuine smile on his face. The Vampire was astute enough to understand the pretext for this whole charade.

Gillian had found her way through her own mental maze. She would never be victimized in thought or in dreams by Jack the Ripper again. Perrin, however, looked a little pale. Poor creature probably thought Trocar and the fair Gillyflower were on the verge of killing each other.

"My apologies, Petal. I did not mean to hit such a sensitive nerve, but I am glad to see that you came to the conclusions which we knew all along." Trocar dipped his head and drew his left arm across his chest, fist to shoulder. It was a gesture of respect among the Grael from a subordinate to a superior caste member and left the originator open to attack.

She turned in Aleksei's arms, the beginnings of a familiar grin forming. "Go fuck yourself, Trocar. I ought to kick your ass for pulling that shit. You're not exactly qualified to do flooding therapy."

"Welcome back, Captain," was all he said, but he smiled when he said it.

"I would have handled this eventually, Trocar, but I know you meant well."

"You are correct, *piccola*," Aleksei murmured gently, pulling her back against his chest and kissing the top of her hair. "You would have found your way through eventually. Unfortunately you have people who love you and who could not bear to see you punishing yourself for making the only decisions you could have made at the time."

Helmut interrupted at that point. "You never were at Jack's mercy, Gillian. This was simply your first encounter with a truly evil Vampire. If nothing else, you come away with a better understanding of what you have been facing."

"Now you can appreciate why Dracula is so feared. Jack was only one of his subordinates. The actual Dark Prince is far, far worse," Aleksei added quietly.

Gillian turned in his arms and searched his face. He felt sincere; seemed to believe what he was saying. Could he really have made this leap of faith? Believing in her without question? Tentatively she touched his mind, wanting that connection with him.

"I mean every word, bellissima. *You are a remarkable woman and I am a very lucky Vampire."*

She cleared her throat past the lump in it and said aloud, "Lucky man, Aleksei. The term is lucky *man*."

He laughed and embraced her tightly. "*Sì, piccola.* I am indeed a lucky man."

She turned to look at the Dark Elf. "I did read all of this right, didn't I? You were trying to piss me off so I would get past the Jack issue?"

"Aye, Captain. I rather hoped you might become angry enough to shake yourself out of it.

"We have a Blood Oath, my friend. I am honor bound to protect you, and on the night that you needed me more than you have ever needed anyone, I failed you. I came too late to prevent your injuries and your humiliation. That is my shame to live with. I was hoping to help you and to resolve my guilt as well," Trocar finished finally.

"So the bottom line of your little show tonight was to alleviate your guilt and to help me overcome my perceived victimization about how I handled the situation with Jack."

"Aye." Typical Grael. There had been something in it for him too. Oh well, she couldn't fault him, not really.

Once again, he saluted her in respect: left hand across his chest, fist to shoulder and a deep nod, taking her out of his vision, offering his neck to her. This time she returned the gesture correctly, superior to subordinate. The Elf's obsidian face visibly relaxed.

She turned to Perrin, still standing nearby. He looked very confused. "See what happens when you develop friendships? I have friends like this who will stop at nothing to bring me back to myself. Once a Marine, always a Marine."

She visibly straightened her shoulders and walked back to them, taking Aleksei's arm and offering Perrin her hand. "Let's go have some fun. I could use a little levity at the moment. How about you guys?"

Perrin still looked a little bewildered, but he smiled and nodded. They all headed to the Inn to find Kimber and Pavel already hoisting pints of the local ale and singing with a rustic-looking group.

Once inside, they grabbed a large half-circle booth, carefully seating Perrin next to Trocar and Gillian. Aleksei, Helmut, Kimber and Pavel completed the circle. They spent the next few hours talking about everything but Jack and plans for the Institute, and they also avoided telling war stories.

To everyone's surprise, Esi and Samuel came in during the course of the evening and joined the party. The night was filled with laughter, fun and companionship. It was exactly what Gillian needed and what Perrin had always wanted to experience.

It was getting close to dawn when Perrin turned toward Gillian during an infrequent lull in the conversation.

"I am in your debt, Gillian. I never thought I could learn to be anything but a social outcast. You, your therapy, this place . . . your friends have been wonderful, and I cannot thank you enough."

"We are your friends too, little brother." Trocar dipped his head toward the masked man and smiled.

Perrin's eyes misted, but he rallied and offered his hand to the Dark Elf. "For that I am forever grateful."

"Okay, enough of the male-bonding buddy bullshit," Kimber butted in to the moment. "We're having fun. Let's not start crying in our beer."

A month ago, Perrin would have been shattered; now he joined in their laughter, lifting his glass in a toast to his new confidence and his looming freedom. He might just be able to make it. He hoped he could make it without them.

When they left the Inn, everyone headed toward the car. Aleksei hung back, keeping Gillian close to him, whispering to her conspiratorially, nodding toward Perrin, who was enjoying the night air and admiring the stars.

"Go with him, *piccola*. He needs a fairy-tale end to the evening. Let him be your knight in shining armor tonight."

"Aleksei, his therapy is essentially finished. I've done all I can for him . . . Well, all except one thing."

"The mask?" Helmut joined them, overhearing Gillian's comment. "He never removed it, I take it."

"Nope. I never insisted and he never offered. I know it's his shield against the world but eventually he will have to let someone in." That one thing had frustrated her. She hadn't been able to broach his final defense.

Aleksei leaned down, kissing her softly. "Long ago, when you were here on an enforced basis, I did not have to give you up when our therapeutic time was completed. After our time of waiting, I thankfully did not have to let you go.

"He knows it *is* time to acknowledge the end of your therapeutic relationship and go his own way. He knows that he can bring nothing to your table, not now, not in the future, and he fears what life outside of our sanctuary and his will be like.

"Make it easier on him and on you. Say your first goodbye to our enchanted angel so that your last good-bye will not tear out his heart. I will miss him as well; he is a remarkable man." Aleksei dropped his hands from her shoulders, giving her the freedom to go.

"One last time, Gillian, give it a try," Helmut agreed. "He leaves in two days. He told me tonight."

Nodding, she tossed Aleksei the keys to the Opel, and ran after Perrin, catching him as he was walking past the car, toward the compound. "Come on, you and I have a date," she said, grasping his hand.

Perrin stopped dead and stared at her. "Now? I believed our therapy was completed, so I thought I would walk a little tonight."

"I can walk with you," she offered.

"Why?"

"Why what?" Now she was confused.

"Why the extra attention tonight?"

"It is supposed to be a night where you get to feel what your life is going to be like when you get back home. Fun, friends, maybe dating . . . a few drinks, music, singing. All the things you enjoy and have become adept with, in an actual multibeing, social setting."

She smiled up at him, matching his stride, letting the night breeze ruffle her hair. A car's motor buzzed so she waved to her friends as they drove past them toward the castle. Trocar was driving. That should be interesting.

Perrin walked with her quietly for a moment, enjoying the feeling of normalcy which she seemed to gift him with every time they were together. "Home is supposed to convey thoughts and feelings of safety . . . of belonging."

"Yes, it is."

"I have felt at home here, *ma chérie*. I hope I can feel this way when I am back at my estate or at my lake house."

"You will, Perrin. You have come a tremendously long way during your stay here. You worked really hard and I'm proud of you."

That stopped him midstride and he stared down at her. "No one has ever said that to me before."

"Well, I'm saying it, because it's true. I am very proud of you. You faced down over a century of preconceived ideas, feelings and fears. That is a huge accomplishment." She smiled up at him and squeezed his hand.

"Perrin, whether you want to believe it or not, you have brought a great deal to all of us. I was pleasantly surprised when you and Trocar became friends. Even Aleksei discovered new things about himself because of his association with you. I learned new things about my own abilities because of who you are. I just wish I could have helped you realize that your mask doesn't define you, any more than my having blond hair defines me."

He visibly flinched when she mentioned his mask, and his emotions ran their usual gambit. Having been around him so much, she was better able to shield and filter it, but it still affected her. She desperately wanted to help him with this last hurdle, but if he wasn't ready, he wasn't ready.

"I want to believe you, *ma chérie*, but I do not know if I can risk that step just yet."

"I know. It's all right. You'll find your way in your own time." Her smile was as reassuring as she could make it. His emotions were rioting all over the map. With her earlier confrontation of her own issues, she was more susceptible to him than she'd calculated.

He noticed the extra moisture in her eyes. A gentle touch of his hand brushed her hair back from her face, then tilted her chin up when she tried to duck her head away.

"Pity, Gillian?"

Her head shook in negation. "No, there is no reason to pity you. I always wish I could have done more."

It wouldn't do to let him know he was still playing hell with her empathy, despite her statement that she was shielding better. She wanted this to be a pleasant walk, a memorable, nice moment for him.

She kept her voice carefully level. "If I had the power, I would give you the life you should have had with that girl you loved. You deserve happiness, Perrin."

"And you believe I can truly have it, if I allow a woman to see behind this." He gestured toward his mask.

"I think that loving someone is about trust. I also think it's about learning. I learn things at the damndest times myself." The last statement was more to herself than to him. She was amazed to find that she actually meant it.

"Since I cannot love you, but I have learned from you, learned to trust you, where does that place your theory?"

She stared at him, then realized he was trying out humor again. The skin around his exposed eye crinkled and he smiled at her.

"It's a conundrum, Perrin, what can I tell you?"

They laughed together and continued their walk back toward the compound. As they left the edge of the village, Perrin stopped suddenly, turning Gillian toward him, tipping her face up in his characteristic fingertip gesture.

"We may not have another moment alone before I leave, and I need you to know something."

She raised her eyebrows questioningly but didn't interrupt.

"When I came here, I was a lonely, frightened, disfigured shell of a man. Now I am full and have something to give to a relationship or at least I believe you when you say I do. I am no longer frightened, Gillian. But lonely and disfigured, I remain.

"I believe I have come as far as you can take me; that it is time for me to make a place for myself among the world and its inhabitants. There is only one thing left for me to do, one last hurdle. If you say you can take it . . . take me . . . as I truly am . . . I will indeed be a whole man."

"What do you need me to do?" Gillian's empathy was flaring to beat hell. She had a fair idea of what he would ask, but he needed to vocalize it.

Perrin took her hand and led her to a tiny egress that wound deep between the buildings at the edge of the village. Once inside, well secreted from the street, he pressed her gently against the wall, looking down, holding her gaze, the question still unspoken.

When his mouth crashed down on hers almost savagely, Gill's head spun from proper and gentle Perrin apparently finding his Testosterone Ocean Water Wings and it had nothing to do with his Gargoyle heritage. Her response was automatic at first, then it became real as sensitive nerve endings fired.

Perrin's tongue was suddenly in her mouth and he was lifting her farther up, pressing her against the bricks as he wedged his hips between her legs. The thick length of his sex was squarely where it should have been, but she had pants on. Grinding on him, she broke the kiss for a moment.

"Wait, Perrin, let me take these off." Gillian reached for the waistband, but his hand got there first, pushing between them and tearing them from her. Her breath hissed through her teeth and she arched back against the wall as his fingers stroked her open heated flesh.

"Sweet Jesus, you are already wet." His breathing was ragged as he continued to tease her with his fingers, reaching down to open his trousers and free his heavy erection, placing it at her opening, listening to her breathing grow faster and shallower.

Gillian gasped, closing her eyes and leaning in to kiss him.

"No, look at me," he commanded, his voice velvety and erotic. "*Je t'en prie* . . . look in my eyes."

As her eyes opened, Perrin's face held a hunger that she'd never seen. It was dark, primal, accusing, and aching with something neither of them understood. Elegant hands pulled her against him and brought their bodies completely together.

Buried within her, he shuddered with effort not to thrust. He wanted this moment with her. He had to have it or he would never be completely whole. He had to be as open as she was, as courageous as she was.

"Gillian." Perrin's voice was low, thick and full of sex; oh, so very compelling. "I want you to truly witness what you are having intercourse with."

She understood. She'd known before he broached the topic. He was picking a hell of a time to test her nerve and ask his question, but she'd be damned if she'd flinch, no matter what was behind that leather covering.

His hand rose to the edge of his mask. The moonlight was fully on his face from a beam of silvery light that had found its way into the darkness they coupled in.

"Can you look at the monster with desire, make love to it?" He pulled the mask off, dropping it at his feet, then he lifted his eyes to lock them with hers, his voice harsh and guttural. "Do you still want this carcass inside you now, Gillian?"

The night was still except for the pounding of their pulses and the harsh, quick breathing from both of them. Perrin waited as she stared at his face. He waited for her to scream her disgust, for the horror that would make her push him away. He waited to prove her idealistic viewpoint wrong.

God help him, if she rejected him, he wasn't sure he could stop, pull out of her and go home before he became a rapist and took her with or without her consent. If he crossed that line, if he hurt her because of his weakness, he would destroy himself.

The Gargoyle gene had indeed left its mark upon his face. It was as if stone and flesh were carrying out a war . . . fighting for supremacy on his facial canvas, carving almost a full third of his face out of living rock.

Gillian took her time to observe him with clinical eyes. It was bad. Very bad. Mottled gray granite interspersed with raw skin, flesh and bone, leaving ulcerated, angry-looking, glistening places back as far as his hairline.

The boundaries of fleshy ribbons strained to meet and close across the rough stone but couldn't make it. His right eye socket was flesh and was pulled down a little from the stone occupying the area near its space. Both eyelids were flesh and sported thick black lashes just like the left side; the perfect gray green eye was just that, perfect. He even had a perfect ebony eyebrow, curiously growing out of pure stone.

Brow, cheekbone and nearly half of his forehead area the mask had covered were granite. Most of the right side of his nose appeared chiseled off, lending a cadaverous appearance to it. He looked as though something had raked huge dull claws unevenly across his face in an effort to rip through and expose the stone. The hairline itself was intact and perfect; no stone intruded there.

It was very, very bad, but she'd been prepared for much, much worse. Having seen battlefield injuries, murder victims, violent death in all its forms, she was braced for something truly horrific, but she would have completed this act with him, no matter what. He needed it. Needed to know that she could still make love to him, even if she saw everything. She put that knowledge into her eyes and let him see it.

"Yeah, I want you, Perrin, with or without the mask." Gillian took his face in her hands, gently kissing the damaged side, not sure if she might cause him pain on the raw-looking cheek, whispering to him.

"You are a whole man, a beautiful, wonderful, gifted man, not a monster or a carcass. A small area of your face does not determine who you are or what you are. We're here, we're joined, now take us both where we want to go."

She kissed him and she put all her passion, need, desire and warmth into that kiss. He was passive for about three seconds, then his hands moved, tears of relief in his eyes. He responded to her kiss with the same dark hunger as before but the savagery was gone.

Having her total acceptance, knowing she knew what she was making love to, made the moment all the more important to him.

"Gillian, *mon Dieu*, you are beautiful," Perrin gasped as he felt the powerful rippling of her climax. His own release followed instantly. The gift she had given him was immeasurable. Now he knew for certain that he could manage out there. Everything she had told him was the absolute truth.

"You're beautiful, Perrin. Beautiful, sexy, and you've become quite the thrilling lover." Smiling at him, she stroked his face, wiped his tears away; obviously in no hurry to have him withdraw. He needed to know she was in no rush to end the moment. The shift in him was immediately apparent. Desperation and despair had turned to satisfaction and contentment.

Perrin hadn't realized that he'd been crying. His face and neck were wet, and he touched them with his fingertips almost reverently. "What you have done . . . I did not think could be done. I cannot express . . ."

Drawing back a little, she smoothed his hair, tracing the line around the granite-edged part of his face. "Perrin, do you realize that you just made love to me with no glamour whatsoever?"

He hadn't. In his desperation he hadn't used his talents. "But you responded, you climaxed . . . How?"

Great Hathor, he really was shocked and wide-eyed with the revelation. "Because you have become a wonderful lover. You don't need glamour to go to bed with a woman. You are all the man that you need."

Laughing, she kissed him again. "You have skill and technique now, not to mention finesse!"

The lovely green eyes glowed and Perrin felt satisfaction, pride, completely whole, for the first time in his life. Gently disengaging from her, he helped her straighten her clothes, which necessitated removing the torn and ripped pants, and let her tuck him away behind the elegant black cloth and fasten everything back up.

Once again, Gillian stood in Sacele with only a tunic-size shirt and a pair of boots. Perrin was back to looking extraordinary and elegant in his formally dressed attire. Coat and tails, perfectly pressed pants, even after their encounter. All he needed was a cape.

He touched her face almost reverently, a smile ghosting across his own face for a moment before he bent down to retrieve his mask. Gill watched as he turned away from her to affix it back to his face.

"Why, Perrin?"

Turning back, he cupped her face delicately as always, impressed by this woman who was willing to give so much because she believed. "My angel, you have given me back my soul and my heart. I can never repay what you have done for me this night, but I have worn this mask too long. I cannot throw it down forever, just yet."

She blushed, her eyes flicking down, and he brought her face back up with a gentle hand. "Do not turn away, *ma chérie*. Learn to accept a compliment, Gillian. It is all right to be pleased and proud of yourself. You gave life back to a dead man. I had no hope, no faith; you gave it back to me because you believed. That is something to be proud of, fair one, not embarrassed about."

"I'm not very good at this."

It was his turn to laugh, deep and low, no glamour, just pure sensual Perrin. "*Ma petite belle*, you are very good at this, I assure you."

He turned serious suddenly. "I would like to come to the castle again, play a little concert for your friends and for the other clientele. But I know that it is time for me to go and discover if I can have a life without Gillian Key by my side."

Wordlessly she nodded; her throat was a little tight from the pride she had for him and his courage. Perrin's face was full of compassion as he brought her hand to his mouth to kiss.

"Thank you for your acceptance of everything I am. I think that is what every man truly desires. Now it is late and I am being most ungentlemanly by keeping you out here in this place."

Gallantly he offered her his arm. "May I escort you home?"

She nodded and took his arm, keeping her face away so she could unobtrusively wipe the tear away before he noticed. But Perrin had noticed. He knew it wasn't sadness. She felt proud of him, but didn't want to talk about her contribution to his success. He knew she cared. It was what made her good at her job.

Walking back in the near dawn, he managed to make her

smile, then laugh. By the time they turned into the drive, they were enjoying a lively discussion about the CDs she wanted to give him with soundtracks from various movie musicals on them. They held hands till the path diverted to either his guesthouse or the castle.

Perrin took her hands, a full smile gracing his mouth for a change. "This one night will you stay with me? One final night of instruction to know what it is like to hold a woman in my arms all night?"

"Only if you promise to take off the mask as soon as we're inside and no glamour."

"That I believe I can do, now."

"Good because I think you've forgotten that I am not wearing any underwear under this very short tunic."

The curtsy she made was comical, but it flipped the edges of the shirt up enough that Perrin knew he hadn't remembered.

An uncharacteristic gleam grew in his eye and he moved toward her slowly, sensuously. Gillian's eyes widened and she backed up a step, giggling. Then he had her, sweeping her up and tossing her over his shoulder. Gillian half shrieked as he reached up and smacked her bottom playfully as he carried her to the house in long strides.

"Perrin! What the hell is this?" Torn between laughing and being annoyed, Gillian kicked her feet and tried to make sure her butt was covered. He rewarded her by carrying her in straight to his bedroom and tossing her onto the bed.

"I have wanted to do that for a very long time, *ma chérie*. Being able to relax, be playful with a woman . . . You have no idea how good this feels."

Her eyebrow arched as she looked at him with the most wicked smile he'd ever seen on another being. "So you want to . . . play? Be playful? As in a little role-playing? Like pretend?"

Getting the gist of what she was hinting at, Perrin sat properly on the edge of the bed, holding out a hand to her and shifting his look from playful to stern. "I think that is a lovely idea. I think I will be the autocratic music teacher and you may be the young impetuous student."

"No mask and no glamour."

Complying, he removed the stylized piece and laid it on the table next to the bed. He never thought about the light still being on as Gillian rolled off the bed and ran to the living room to hop up on the piano, ready for her voice lesson.

CHAPTER
19

I⊤ had been so dark in the alley that Gillian hadn't even thought about being observed. Her empathy had been solely focused on Perrin's needs, but the watcher, a lone, black-clad figure, had looked down from high on the rooftops, secluded in plain sight by his own power. A power that she had never before encountered. A power hundreds of years old, with the ability to mask itself from her with little effort.

Long, straight black hair, shimmering as it gathered starlight, waved in the gentle evening breeze. Gillian's mystery patient decided that he definitely needed the services of this petite blonde after watching her with the man in the alley. It had been a surprise to see what it was that she welcomed into her arms and between her legs when the man she embraced so passionately had taken the mask off.

The Vampire had watched with eyes that could only be described as pale glacial green. The man she'd coupled with was a monster, yet she had been docile, compliant, a lovely receptacle for the semen that the Vampire knew had been expelled.

Her own scent was lovely, snow on mountain clover, sunshine and wet, hot sex. That she had the compassion to take such a being in such a loving embrace confirmed what he had been told. Her innate empathy was powerful indeed and she used it well. She truly was a healer, though he had no need of that particular brand of her services.

He had done the right thing by coming. Her abilities had not been overstated or exaggerated. Perhaps he had been wrong to wait so long. He'd avoided her, wanting to know that she was as good as her agency and press said she was. Now he knew.

The Vampire had turned away from the couple mating in the darkness, hearing their cries of completion from a distance and catching their combined scent on the light night wind. He was no voyeur. Watching others make love was not what excited him.

Tomorrow night, he would introduce himself to Dr. Key. If there was hope for that creature she had held, there may yet be hope for him. Spreading his arms, he'd stepped off the roof, becoming a night-flying raptor and spiraling lazily away into the darkness to hunt for his own prey.

Gillian hadn't come home last night. Aleksei knew what had happened and where she had been the instant he stepped inside the castle, which was devoid of her presence. Part of him was torn apart with jealousy but not because she'd had sex with Perrin in the alley. That was part of her job with him. The other half of him was tremendously proud of what she had done for the dynamic yet tormented genius.

In the short time that Perrin had been at the Rachlav Institute of Paramortal Healing, he had made so much progress that Helmut Gerhardt, Ph.D., IPPA's director, was considering asking Gillian to do a paper on the case. Bravo, Gillian.

The problem plaguing him was that Perrin was able to do what he, a newly anointed, immensely powerful Vampire Lord, could not. Perrin was able to hold her all night, wake with her in the morning, see her hair shine in the full glare of the noonday sun. Haunted and damaged as he had been before he started therapy with Gillian, Perrin would always be able to walk in the daylight with her.

Grimly, Aleksei wondered if Gillian had missed having a lover who could be with her all night. He could remain conscious long after the sun rose with his age and level of power, as long as he remained out of its direct rays. She woke alone since being with him. He always left her, allowing her to get the amount of sleep her Human body required, instead of waking her too early in the morning before he went to ground.

Her code of ethics would prevent ongoing contact with any patient for a year after their professional relationship terminated. Somehow he suspected that Perrin might consider finding his way back to Romania after that time. Aleksei would cross land or sea himself to reach her; Perrin was no different.

Aleksei had recognized the hard truths about the limitations on their relationship before he ever got involved with her. Waiting two years, knowing that she was having sex with his brother Tanis in a nontherapeutic sense for part of that time, had made it agony for him.

Tanis. He wished he could talk to Tanis, but he was off in Egypt with Jenna, and Aleksei didn't want to intrude on them. The close call with Jenna nearly being Jack's serial killer fodder had shaken his younger brother badly. Jenna had been remarkably brave and stable afterward, but it had haunted him. A visit with his friends Anubis and Osiris would be healing and allow Jenna an up-close-and-personal view of Tanis on a night-to-night basis.

They'd been gone a week but Aleksei knew they couldn't be safer where they were. Dracula would never dare try a direct attack in Osiris's territory. He missed his brother but refrained from contacting them via their link.

Tanis had survived the conversion from Dracula's Line to his own. Now he was free to love Jenna if he chose or, if they didn't work out, to have a relationship with another. Free of the taint of the Dark Prince, Tanis had his Reborn life back, as Aleksei did.

Neither would have chosen to become Vampire if they'd been allowed the choice. However, if this was what they must be, then it was better to live without the corrupting shadow of their former Lord.

He missed Tanis but he missed Gillian being there when he rose and returned to the castle from feeding. Rationally he knew that if she'd stayed with Perrin, then she had good reason. He trusted her; he knew that without mentally kicking himself this time. Perrin would be gone soon and they could try to work out the kinks in their relationship.

Gillian was right about one thing—they had rushed headlong into this and needed to be more attentive to the details. Aleksei fervently hoped that Gillian would still find beauty in the night and passion in his own arms.

On cue, the heavy front door opened and Gillian came in, disheveled and wearing very little clothing. She was still in the green tunic and boots but her hair was wet, her pants were missing and she was shivering.

"*Piccola*, come to me," Aleksei said hoarsely as she shut the door.

Gill's head snapped up and she saw Aleksei sitting by the fireplace, which had a crackling blaze going. Willingly she went to him as he stood to enfold her in his arms.

"I am glad that Perrin will leave us a whole person, Gillian. Truly you have worked a miracle with this man's psyche and soul." Aleksei's voice had a black velvet quality which got inside her and warmed her from her toes to her head.

"I'm sorry, Aleksei. I know this has been rough on you but I really appreciate your support in all this." Gillian had wrapped her arms around his waist and let him hold her.

Surprise registered across the Vampire Lord's face. "I am sorry if I have been that obvious with my level of discomfort. I have tried to remain distant to give you room to do your job."

Smiling, she looked up at him. "You've been great, Aleksei. Thanks. I mean it."

"You are cold and we are talking about my magnanimous nature." He scooped her up in his arms and carried her swiftly through the hallways and up the stairs to their shared bedroom.

"Woo hoo! Door-to-door service." Gillian laughed as he set her down and moved to the bathroom to turn on the heat and start the shower running hot for her.

"Come, *bellissima*, your hair is wet so I assume that you have bathed, but you are cold and this will warm you quickly." He held out his hand to her.

Kicking off her boots and pulling the shirt over her head followed by her bra, she took his hand. "Will you join me?" she asked shyly.

Ice gray eyes widened a little, then crinkled at the edges as he nodded. His clothes were soon on the floor next to hers and he followed her into the shower, where she stood luxuriating in the warmth. Strong hands were soon rubbing the tension out of her neck and shoulders.

"Thanks, Aleksei, that's just wonderful."

"My pleasure, *piccola*. I am glad to be able to do something for you."

Maybe his voice sounded more forlorn than he'd intended, maybe Gill was feeling guilty, but she turned and reached up to kiss him. Aleksei happily complied, enjoying just being able to hold each other before something else happened to interrupt.

Gillian's hands wound their way down his iron-hard arms, skittered down his rib cage then moved toward his groin. She broke the kiss in surprise when Aleksei captured her wrists and held her away from him.

"What? I've been neglecting you lately and I want to start something I'm sure we both want to finish."

"Do not do this, Gillian. Do not come from his bed into mine because you feel guilty. You do not owe me anything. We are here because you need a hot shower and I am giving you a massage. You have circles under your eyes. You are pale, and I can feel your weariness."

Catching her around the waist, he lifted her to him and kissed her thoroughly before she could protest, then put her down. "I am an adult, I can wait until you are through with Perrin and his demands on your time. And for the record, I want you to know how proud I am of you, of what you have done for that man. You have given him his life back, Gillian, much as you gave me mine and that is no small thing."

"I am not too tired and I am not feeling guilty." She leaned against the wet tiles. "However, thank you for saying that. It doesn't make me feel any less like I'm flaunting Perrin under your nose, but I appreciate it." The Nile green eyes that she raised to his were anxious.

"You have not flaunted anything, especially not Perrin. He needed you last night, *piccola*, it was not about the sex. He needed your kindness, acceptance and your strength. I am glad that you could help him."

Coloring in memory, she said, "I am sorry about that, you know. I intended to just walk home with him, then come to you, but he needed to cross one more hurdle. It was actually his idea, and as it turned out, if I had pushed him away, it really would have destroyed him."

"Think no more on it. We were well away from the village while you two were still strolling down the road. You do not need to be embarrassed."

"That was sort of a first for me too. He seems to have discovered a more assertive nature."

"Truly? In what manner?"

"He took his mask off in the alley," Gillian said.

Aleksei searched her face for any sign that she was traumatized by what she'd seen. "How bad?"

"Actually, it was very bad. He looks like someone tried to rip the living flesh off stone, chipping the stone in the process. It's not remotely as horrifying as some things I've seen in combat or in the morgue, but I understand why he's so terrified of sharing it with a lover," she mused, remembering last night's activities.

"Do you think that his glamour and music might eventually heal him the way it improved Samuel's appearance and transformed Tuuli?" Aleksei mused.

Gillian perked up. "You're a genius! I wonder if that would work!"

He laughed, warm and comforting. "You are an eternal optimist, *cara mia*. I too hope that Perrin would be fully

healed if such a thing were possible, but please take care in
how you approach the subject. You have just convinced him
that he is worthwhile as he is."

"Damn straight. I have to believe my patients are going
to get better. And yes, I will be delicate." She smiled. It was
nice to have a conversation with Aleksei without fighting
or worrying about what next bad thing was going to happen.

"Are you warm enough now, *piccola*? Even a Vampire
gets wrinkled after too long in hot water."

They exited the shower, Aleksei drying her off and insisting that she rest while he ordered her something to eat.
Gillian was too tired to argue. He threw on a robe and left her
briefly to consult the Brownies about food.

The little beings had taken over the attic, the uppermost
floors and the kitchen, insisting that a castle needed a staff.
Now they were the obtrusive chefs, housekeepers, butlers
and concierge for the Rachlav Institute of Paramortal Healing, with Aleksei's blessing. The Brownies were cheerful,
underfoot, helpful, noisy and conspicuous, but everyone
rather enjoyed having them around, especially at odd hours
when someone wanted a snack or beverage.

Perrin was still up and pacing, long after Gillian had left.
They'd had an enjoyable time together, but since he knew he
was leaving soon, he'd wanted to stay as close to her as possible all night, savor the experience with her just a little
longer. He'd barely slept.

Happy, feeling proficient in his ability to try to have a
semblance of a normal life, Perrin still felt conflicted. He
didn't want to leave but knew he had no choice. Gillian had
been more than accommodating, more than patient with him,
in his weeks there. He felt more for her than gratitude, he was
certain.

Love? Was it *really* love? Surprised, he realized he didn't
know. Limited exposure to anyone his entire life, with the
exception of the two protégées he thought he'd loved and his

misguided notions from the theatre, had left him unprepared for the myriad of feelings he was experiencing.

They hadn't spent all their time in sexual situations. The majority of their time had been in straight therapy, getting him used to talking, sharing his thoughts and feelings; used to initiating touch and accepting it in return. His depression and suicidal thoughts had evaporated like brut champagne on the tongue.

Gillian had been brilliant, caring and patient but always challenging him to rise higher than he'd thought possible. With a jolt, he also realized how much she'd suppressed her basic nature for his benefit. Gillian was a strong woman; a leader, a commander with a very dynamic personality and manner.

Perrin let his thoughts solidify. She had been utterly passive in all their physical encounters until after the first time they'd had sex. Only then had she begun to acclimate him to a woman's appetites and needs. Helping him understand that two people concerned with pleasing and enjoying each other was the ultimate turn-on.

Yes, she'd pushed him along a little when he needed it but mostly allowed him to make all the decisions regarding the speed at which his therapy had progressed. Letting everything be his choice, remain in each newly acquired comfort zone until he was ready for each step.

With her complete acceptance by making love with him unmasked, she forced him to consider the possibility that there might be one or more women who would take him as he was, if he let someone get to know him. It was a frightening yet exciting thought that he might have something to offer, something he could bring to a relationship.

Perrin's epiphany crashed into his logical mind like a bullet. He needed to shift his thinking, focus on his own life, not the thoughts of what he might or might not feel for Gillian. Her job was done. He wouldn't know if he had a life until he actually started to live one.

She hadn't prepared him by making him dependent on

her; she had prepared him by increasing his self-esteem in small, significant ways, producing a rock-solid base for him to build on. Whatever came his way, he could handle it.

Encouraged by his private pep talk, Perrin had made a call to Helmut Gerhardt, asking for travel arrangements back to Paris. His therapy was over; it was time for life. The curtain had fallen on the wounded patient and risen on the man.

———•———

When Aleksei returned with some soup and soda for Gillian, she was asleep. Lying there alone in the huge bed, she looked so small and delicate. There were light shadows under her eyes and she was still pale. He woke her gently to let her eat. She needed to keep her strength up.

Remaining on the edge of the bed, still in his robe, he kept her company while she ate. They talked about how they were handling the current situation and if Dracula knew that his number one psycho was dead.

Sated with food and feeling her strength return, Gillian reached up and pulled his dark head down to hers for a deeply sensual kiss. It felt nice to be next to Aleksei again. He was comfortable, he smelled familiar and she didn't have to give him instructions. He responded to her, gathering her closely to him, and plundering her mouth with his tongue.

When Gillian reached inside his robe to grasp his rapidly hardening erection, he rolled toward her, pressing himself into her hand. He was hungry for her, and all his good intentions about letting her rest went right out the window. Her small strong fingers couldn't meet around his thickness but she was doing a damn fine job of driving him crazy by slowly stroking him up and down.

Aleksei's large hand deftly untied her robe and slipped inside to caress her hip and bottom. Moaning, she shifted closer and moved her legs apart in invitation. He didn't disappoint her. Laying her back, he covered her with his larger frame, sliding long elegant fingers through her dark golden curls to find her wet and hot. Cupping her bottom, he slid into her without further preamble as she positioned him hurriedly at her opening, making both of them gasp from the shock of his sudden deep entry.

As her body gripped him eagerly, Aleksei held still, allowing them both the glory of being conjoined once again. They realized how much each of them had missed the other as Aleksei brought them together again and again. Gillian made appreciative noises in her throat as his hand found her breast, his mouth moving hotly over her neck and shoulder.

She grasped him tightly, enjoying the feeling of him caressing her from the inside and out. Goddess, she had missed his skillful touch. The orgy in the compound didn't count; this was the first time they'd really been together in weeks.

Raising his head, he looked down at her, watching her eyes dilate in passion. "I have missed you, *piccola*," he said hoarsely. "You and making love with you."

"I have too," she agreed, running her hands up his back to his shoulders.

He fit inside her perfectly, every velvety inch sliding insistently within her. "Give yourself to me, *innamorata*, let go, let it come." His voice was deeper, more urgent, as she became more vocal beneath him.

Their eyes were locked as he shifted forward to bring them both to the pinnacle they so insistently sought. Gillian deftly raised her hand, moving her hair back, away from her neck.

"Penetrate me," she whispered, and watched his eyes blaze with banked fires.

Aleksei nearly growled at the sight as fangs exploded in his mouth. Having her like this, completely open to him and offering him her blood, sent the pressure at the base of his spine upward and outward.

It had been so long since he'd been inside her, too long since he'd tasted her spicy sweetness. He swelled fuller and tighter as his seed began its explosive journey up and out. He bent his dark head dutifully to her neck, praying he could hold on for a few more moments.

She tensed a little as his fangs scraped gently, then she

nearly screamed as he drove them home. It was instant, excruciating pleasure that flooded her as he began a rhythmic pull at her neck, timed perfectly with his imperative thrusts while she climaxed with an inarticulate cry.

Aleksei's own moan of completion came from deep in his chest as he felt her bear down around him. He locked her to him; the sweet, spicy taste of her on his tongue jolted through him as he erupted in heavy jets. He shuddered as his sex-starved body found satisfaction with the one woman he wanted to remain with.

Even as overwhelmed as he was with her gift, he stopped himself before he took too much blood. His velvety tongue swirled over the pinpricks from his fangs, instantly healing the tiny wounds. He returned to her mouth to kiss her deeply, passionately; holding her body as tightly as he dared, their hips still welded together.

As he drew back, Gillian whispered to him, her hands smoothing back his long, black hair, "Don't pull out. I want to feel you a little longer."

He was overcome and dipped his head again to kiss her so she wouldn't see the deep emotions roiling in his eyes. Aleksei held her awhile longer, then withdrew to lie beside her, tuck her in and stroke her hair. Gillian was too tired to argue about being babied and let him. Later, she stirred, coming out of her sleep to find him resolutely watching over her. For once exercising discretion on her possible comments, she snuggled deeper into his arms and let herself enjoy him caring for her.

When she could delay getting up no longer, she sat up, intending to get dressed. Aleksei had other thoughts. He pinned her to the bed, and they were soon involved in a rapidly escalating erotic wrestling match, culminating with a firestorm of passion that left them both breathless but fulfilled.

He let her up then and watched as she transformed from a small defenseless woman into a capable healer of souls. Dressed simply in a pair of khaki carpenter pants and an olive green T-shirt, Gill brushed her hair and applied a light coat of mascara without really looking at herself in the mirror. She had no vanity and no fear. She'd expunged and settled her issues with the Ripper. He was unable to haunt her thoughts anymore.

Aleksei waited until she was finished, then told her that her new patient had contacted the Institute, saying he was ready to meet with her that night at ten o'clock at the Inn. She had plenty of time to get there, and Aleksei said he would go with her, to make sure she felt safe. Everyone was still a little jumpy after the Ripper incident. An anonymous Vampire patient insisting on complete and utter privacy made everybody nervous.

Pavel had taken the call so Aleksei had no immediate impressions to provide her. Gillian interrupted to explain that he couldn't go as the patient had asked Helmut for total anonymity. She'd take Daed and Trocar instead. There was no chance they would have any knowledge about the Vampire they were about to meet.

With Aleksei's newfound power level, he might recognize the individual and they couldn't let that happen. Daed would go as medical director of the Institute. Trocar could come as ... well, Trocar was sort of a heavily armed, lethal security blanket in case there were any further unpleasant surprises leftover from Jack or his Master.

Aleksei wasn't happy with the idea and insisted that she remain in the bar at the Inn, where Radu also could keep watch. The Innkeeper, Radu Smirnoff, whose name always caused double-takes and giggles, was one of Aleksei's loyalists. Human and reliable, Radu had always been a trusted wellspring of information and sharing.

Thankfully, Gillian agreed. Gathering her notepad and the forms she'd need, she took Aleksei's hand and they went downstairs together. When they reached the hallway, Pavel was there to tell Aleksei that there was an urgent message regarding an attack consisting of several Vampires and Shifters on a communal farm homestead near the village. There were over a hundred men, women and children under attack.

Swearing, Aleksei excused himself to take the call while Gillian waited by the fireplace, watching a little procession of Brownies coming down the hallway from the kitchen. They had a fairy-tale version of a flatbed trailer which they were pulling. On it was a cup of coffee, creamed and sugared just like she made it herself.

"Gillian Big, we know that you have not visited the kitchen today, and to prevent any personal mishaps, we bring you . . . your awakening beverage!" the closest to her shouted. The others drew the cart around to her feet.

She dropped to one knee to take the cup and thank them seriously. "Thank you. The Brownies of Castle Rachlav are kind and wise."

Gillian knew they weren't being obnoxious; they were just being nice, so she'd let them. Aleksei would be proud of her, letting the little creatures help her out like that. Maybe she was making progress. Nah. Too soon. She sipped the coffee gratefully and lit a cigarette.

"Are you recovered, Gillyflower?" Trocar's dulcet tones crawled down her spine.

"Well enough."

"I rejoice."

She had to smile. Trocar was so unbelievably deadly and so wholly without remorse generally that she forgot sometimes when he was truly just being kind. She was feeling more awake with caffeine in her system.

"What about you, Trocar? Everything all right?" Turning, she set her paperwork down and continued to enjoy her coffee.

"I could quip something delightful about 'squid happens' but I suppose I really do not understand the Human sense of humor," he said dryly.

Gill spit coffee on the fireplace, coughing, laughing and trying not to drown. "Goddammit, Trocar!" she gasped when she could draw air into her objecting lungs. "Did you have to bring that visual back up on my mental screen?"

"Perhaps it will make your day a little brighter, knowing that I was not sure if I was being digested or molested." He scowled at her. No mean trick for an Elf with his remarkable beauty.

"Oh gods, Trocar, I am sorry. It was just the most ridiculous thing I've ever seen. You, with hair still all perfectly yummy amidst that Sluagh. It was a nightmare version of an oxymoron." She was still giggling in between sentences and the Dark Elf rolled his eyes, leaning against the wall, waiting for her to get control of herself.

Aleksei came out just then. He glanced at Trocar, who was wearing the look of the long suffering, and Gillian, who was still giggling and wiping something wet off the fireplace. They seemed fine so he went ahead with what he wanted to say. "*Piccola*, I am sorry but I must rally my Vampires and the Wolves and take care of this problem."

"I'll be fine, Aleksei, I have backup. You go do what you have to do and I'll go see my patient."

"I am glad that you are taking Trocar and Daed with you, *cara*. Jack is well and truly dead but the Master who controlled him will know he is dead and want retribution. That may be the purpose of this particular attack."

Momentarily she bristled. She'd already agreed to accompaniment; his restating it over and over was getting on her nerves. It occurred to her abruptly he wasn't really trying to be bossy. It was just him, being hundreds of years old and a fossil.

"Aleksei, I promised I would be careful and take backup, but just this once. I don't want to get used to someone else watching my back. It's not healthy for me if I get complacent."

Sighing, he grasped he wasn't going to win this in the long run. "Very well, *bella*, I understand, but I appreciate you agreeing to be careful."

Kissing her quickly, he was off to round up his own Vampires and attend to the problem. Gillian would have two very powerful beings with her in case there were more—What was the term she used? Oh yes, "fuckwits"—to contend with.

Daed came downstairs willing to join the happy little group, all smiles. "Not going off to play hero with the big guy, darlin'?"

"Daed, if you fucking start with me tonight, I will kick your ass back to Brasov. You're along for PR as the Institute's medical director, but what it comes down to is you are muscle in the event anything spills over. That's it."

"Oh god, sugar, I love it when you say things like 'comes,' 'muscle' and 'spill' in the same sentence; gets me all hot." He grinned wickedly at her. It was just too much fun to yank her chain.

"You know, for a Freudian shrink, you have a lot of unresolved penis envy," Gillian said glibly as she sauntered out with a grinning Trocar on her heels. Daed followed with a somewhat deflated look.

CHAPTER

20

THEY parked down the road from the Inn so as to orchestrate a better entrance for Gillian. Trocar got out and melted into the first available shadow, literally vanishing. Gillian had seen it before, but it never failed to amaze her how the Grael could become a piece of the darkness. The Dark Elf would enter the Inn and be the silent guardian for her meeting.

Daed would walk directly in with her. If her patient was there, Daed would introduce himself as the medical director for the Rachlav Institute, then excuse himself as his cell phone rang in exactly ten minutes, courtesy of Pavel back at the castle.

Gill finished her cigarette, stubbing it out in the car's ashtray, and got out. Daed refrained from saying anything; she needed to focus on what she was doing. Damn Vampire boyfriend of hers ought to be on her ass about her smoking. Nah, probably didn't care if she got cancer or emphysema; he could fix that for her.

Together they walked directly into the Inn and into the bar. Gillian waved to Radu and they got seated in one of the circular booths in the corner to wait. Daed sat close to the edge of the bench, but Gillian scooted most of the way around to the middle. Close enough to be within Daed's reach but far enough away that, when he left, she wouldn't feel vulnerable.

"Be careful, pumpkin. After that ordeal with Jack, Aleksei may be contending with one form of retaliation at the farmhouse and you may be walking into another one. I've heard from Luis and Oscar that the Prince is not the forgiving type." Daed was suddenly serious, and it tweaked her alarm bells.

Laughing to cover up her nervousness that he might be right, Gillian shook her head. "I'm not worried. That individual has probably forgotten all about me by now. He doesn't know how his sidekick died or who helped him along."

"Darlin', you are the boob that fell out of Janet Jackson's top, the bullet that shot J. R. Ewing and the pretzel that choked a president. You are not forgettable."

Sparkling black eyes winked appraisingly at her. Daed definitely was a handsome man . . . er . . . Shifter. Telling a Minotaur that he was full of shit when he was along to help out didn't seem like the wisest course of action. Oh well, she never was the Princess of Tact.

"Great! I'm a sex toy, a projectile and a snack! How kind of you to notice." She propped her foot up, leaned back against the wall and cocked an eyebrow at him.

Daed shook his head. "Snack maybe, but you have never been anyone's toy, honey. I don't think you qualify as a projectile unless you count your rapid-fire wit."

"Oh, *touché*, Dr. Aristophenes. I salute your smart-assness. Now flash your gonads, and show me what else you got for Christmas."

Gillian snorted and Daed had to laugh with her. God, she was a pain in the ass but competent and funny. He had missed working with her and fighting with her.

"Dr. Key?" The lush velvet voice turned both their heads. The man who stood by Gillian was nothing short of breathtaking. All conversation in the bar had stopped and people were staring. Even Daed felt a sensual jolt go disturbingly through him.

Oh shit, Gillian thought. *I hope neither of us starts drooling.*

Long hair that looked like spun black liquid silk hung over his shoulders to midway down his chest. He had the most remarkable eyes that she had ever seen. Glacial green, lightly hued but full of color at the same time: ice green, frost green, the cool welcoming green in the heart of an iceberg. Pale but ringed with a darker hue that emphasized the color perfectly.

Those eyes were fringed with long, thick black lashes, a perfect frame for the two jewels they sheltered. Twin arches of onyx rising on his forehead were the backdrop for the beautiful orbs. His nose was straight and perfectly proportioned. His mouth was full, not feminine but sensual and tinged the most delicate of pinks.

He was more slightly built than Trocar or Perrin and not quite as tall either—Gillian figured he was right about six feet—but his otherworldly beauty was over and above any Vampire she'd ever seen, including Aleksei. Hell, including Osiris and Dionysus, she realized in astonishment.

His face and body seemed sculpted from the finest translucent alabaster, virtually glowing with an inner light. The green velvet tunic he wore was so dark it was nearing black; the color brought out his eyes, and it was difficult to look anywhere else *but* at him.

He had a heavy linked chain of gold around his neck, which sported an emerald the size of a quarter that picked up the green of his tunic. Matching dark green velvet pants and dark brown calf-length boots completed the splendor. He looked like a cover model for the entire Reborn community or the poster boy for a "Get Your Own Vampiric Makeover" recruitment ad.

The entire picture was enough to wrench a Human heart or bring a tear to a Human eye. He had been Human, Gill realized with a jolt, and must have been spectacular even in his day-walking years. The faintest of crow's-feet by his eyes made her guess his Rebirth to have occurred around his Human age of forty.

Her empathy was used to Vampirism and didn't flare in response to his presence, but the level of sensuality he generated made her natural shields snap into place. All her exposure to Perrin had been good for fine-tuning that instantaneous reaction.

"Yes, I'm Gillian Key." She rose and held out her hand, which he took gently.

"I am called Csangal, and would like to apologize for taking so long to get into contact with you."

Crap. Even his voice was spectacular: all low vibrating tones implying sweaty bodies entwined on silk sheets by candlelight. Bet he didn't have a problem with finding prey. Not a comforting thought.

"Chahn-gell?" Gillian asked, pronouncing it phonetically back to make sure she'd heard him correctly. "That's a lovely name and there is no need to apologize. I am glad we are finally getting together."

"Thank you, I am pleased to meet you at last, Doctor."

"Me too, and please call me Gillian." Turning to her companion, she introduced Daed. "This is Dr. Daedelus Aristophenes. He is our medical director at the Institute."

The two men shook hands. Daed had a strange expression on his face, sort of like lust combined with an "Oh. My. God. I'm feeling hot toward another man" expression. Daed wasn't homophobic, but, being heterosexual, anything besides a female was a nonoptional choice.

On cue, Daed's cell phone rang. Damn, Pavel was on the ball as usual. Daed excused himself on the pretext of the phone call, leaving Gillian alone with Csangal. He seated himself after she said he might, and settled into the spot that Daed had vacated.

"You do not have to shield from me, Gillian." Csangal spoke in tones meant only for her ears. "I am here as your patient, not to feed."

"It's habit, I'm afraid. Spending as much time as I do around people like yourself, I have to, to keep my sanity." She smiled at him, her best professional "you obviously don't know who you're dealing with" smile.

Csangal's smile literally lit up the booth they were in. Gillian fought to keep her jaw hinged just the way it was and not have it flop down to the table. Holy mother of the gods, he had been merely breathtaking before; now he transcended into the realm of wondrous, spectacular, inhuman . . . the word flashed in her mind. He was too lovely to be real, but there was no glamour. It was just his own special, regular Vampire du jour. Good thing he wasn't trying to impress her. She didn't think she'd survive it.

"How kind of you to think of us as 'people,' Gillian. A great many Humans do not, you know. They prefer terms like 'creature,' 'monster,' 'thing' or 'bloodsucker.' The last of which, while accurate, is somewhat disappointing to dwell on."

What the hell had he been saying? Shit. She'd been so distracted by his sheer physical beauty that she hadn't focused. Um . . . oh, yeah, "people." Right.

"If I didn't, I couldn't do my job properly. You're sentient beings. A good number of you were Human once. The Sidhe weren't, of course, nor the Elves, but they're still people. I try to respect our similarities while remembering our differences. We all have moods; feel joy, sadness; have thoughts and ideas. All of us can act in either self-serving or altruistic ways. Paramortals have stress, anxiety, depression; you fall in love, suffers losses, have victorious moments.

"Being Human, I try to remember that there are differences unique to each of the Paramortal cultures which don't necessary coincide with a Human perspective on the same issues. I can't bundle everyone up in the same box. I keep firmly in my mind what the perspective is of the patients I have. It makes group therapy interesting, to say the least."

Now it was her turn to smile. She realized that she'd been rambling. That wasn't like her. Csangal was affecting her with his sheer presence. Double shit. Well, she'd get a better handle on it after one or two sessions with him.

"Thank you, Gillian. I had a certain respect for your reputation before I came. It has been solidified even more so now. I believe that you will help me. Remain unbiased yet compassionate to my situation."

Crikey, he dropped his eyes for a moment, then turned the

full force of their beauty on her. Gillian felt her IQ slip by several points. She had to watch it or she'd start babbling like an idiot again.

"Perhaps if we began," she said, getting her forms, paper and pen out. "If you could tell me what you'd like to focus on, that would be great. Oh, and I need a copy of your insurance card as well if you want us to bill for these sessions."

"I hope you have a bit of time, Gillian. This might take an hour or two to explain. And thank you for the offer, but I am a private, cash-paying client. I made the arrangements with Dr. Gerhardt to do it this way since I am a Romanian national and Count Rachlav or his brother might recognize me. I prefer to hold our sessions here at the Inn or perhaps we could meet elsewhere."

"That will be fine and please don't worry about confidentiality. Here is a form for you to sign regarding that very thing. All patients, residents and staff are required to sign it and to abide by its rules. We have a less restrictive policy than most agencies as the Paramortal field is still growing and we occasionally have to utilize resources we may not realize we have."

Smiling that devastating smile again, he took the pen from her and signed "Csangal" where she indicated. He had ornate, elegant handwriting, she mused.

"No last name?"

"People of my era rarely used them unless you were from a noble house," he replied, handing her back the pen and the forms.

Two hours later, Gillian had everything she needed from Csangal. He was paranoid in the extreme, believing he was being targeted for murder by stalker or stalkers unknown. Another reason for his request for total secrecy. He had anger issues, some body dysmorphic problems, which she had found hard to believe at first, but he did—he was convinced there was something seriously wrong with his height. His sense of self, paradoxically, was fine, if you called bordering on megalomania "fine."

Csangal had Risen as a Master Vampire since his Rebirth,

over six hundred years before, his extreme physical beauty lending itself to finding prey easily. He had amassed a lot of money over the years in various enterprises and traveled a great deal, leading the quiet life of the fabulously wealthy immortal. He didn't like attracting attention to himself, the exception being with prey; kept little to no company with anyone; and generally spent his time researching ancient religious art and artifacts.

What bothered him a great deal was that he said he could not name one person he considered an actual friend. He'd formed some rudimentary attachments to Humans and Paramortals alike over the centuries, but nothing had ever lasted. Everyone either died or just left him eventually. He wanted to share things with a confidant, a lover, just have someone to talk with.

"Surely with this face, I would merit one friend, but alas, I am lonely and wish to form my own empire of loyal friends and fellow outcasts. Perhaps if I were less attractive, more would flock to me." Those ice green eyes sparkled with his personal egocentric brand of humor, Gillian noticed.

The contrast that popped into her mind unbidden was of Perrin. Sweet, kind, disfigured Perrin, who would sell his soul to have a whole face that matched his lovely Fey side so people would want to know him, and Csangal, who wanted to look a little less spectacular so others wouldn't feel intimidated by his physical beauty. Egotistical bastard. Life really sucked sometimes.

"What do you think, Gillian? Should I stage a coup for all the beautiful people of all the races in the world? Force the rest to accept us as their new icons?" He laughed warmly and reached a hand over to squeeze her arm in a gesture of camaraderie.

Ye gods, his touch was electric and sent waves of his inherent sensuality skipping across Gillian's nervous system. *Ack! Shields! Shields!* Well, hell, at least he was honest. She felt no deceit, no duplicity from him. Plus he had a great laugh. Oh yeah. A really great laugh.

"I think we can fix it so you can live without your own fan club but still have a fulfilling life and gain some real friendships." She chuckled with him.

"I am delighted to hear that, truly." He squeezed her arm another time, gently. "I must say farewell for now, and thank you, Gillian, for your time. May we meet again the night after tomorrow? I assume you will need time to process your reports."

"The night after tomorrow will be fine. I'll meet you right here." Gillian offered her hand, which he took. For one horrible moment she thought he might kiss it, since he took it much as a courtly gentleman would, but instead, he pressed it between his own hands.

"I will be here then, at eight o'clock?"

"Eight will be fine. Good night, Csangal."

"Pleasant evening, Gillian."

He rose with that extraordinary grace that all Vampires possessed, went through the doorway and up the stairs toward his room as she admired his stellar-looking backside while he climbed each step.

Gill realized she was staring and shook herself mentally. *Stop it. Stop* it. *The Vampi— man is a patient.* She reached for the glass of water that Radu had placed earlier, dipped her fingers, then flicked the water in her face.

No staring at non–sex therapy patients' asses! she admonished herself sharply. Oy vey. This was going to be difficult. Csangal was a phenomenal Vampire, and it wouldn't do for her to be drooling all over his soft, yummy boots.

"I can get some ice from Radu and deposit it down your pants if you like, Petal."

The sudden voice made her heart leap in her chest. Trocar. Asshole Elf. Odin's hells, where had he come from?

"Although the ripe blush on your lovely face is most stimulating."

Gillian palmed her face. "Blessed Hathor, I couldn't help it. Did you *see* him? Look at him?"

"Indeed I did. You are correct; this one is truly remarkable.

He rivals even the Elves and the Fey in their beauty." He slid in beside her, putting his arm around her and pulling her close.

She peered at him from between her fingers. Trocar wouldn't be flirting, he just couldn't be. "What the hell, Trocar?"

In response, he turned his equally devastating megawatt smile on her and caressed her cheek with his obsidian-hued finger, leaning his head toward her in a conspiratorial manner.

"We must leave, Gillyflower. The Vampire's visage and touch have left you quite ripe for the picking. I caught your scent as I came into the bar, and I believe the various other night walkers are making the same observation. You are advertising your need for sex with your scent, blush and body, Captain. I am staking my claim so the others will not bother you as we leave."

Sliding out of the bench, Trocar pulled her along with him, keeping her tight against his side. As she scooted out, she was treated to a significant bulge in the Dark Elf's leather-clad groin.

No, no, *no* . . . Trocar would never be so blatant or déclassé as to allow himself an erection in a public place, especially because of her. She peeked again; yes . . . yes he did. Bigger than Dallas and twice as obvious. Great. Just great.

Gillian was blushing furiously as she climbed out and swept her arm around his slender waist, not knowing how to argue this one with him. He was right. Csangal had some powerful sex foo going on there, and despite how much she'd blocked, some of it had leaked through. Speaking of leaking . . .

"Goddess above, Trocar, I don't know if I can walk," she whispered to him. The more she moved, the worse it got, and the thought of pulling a *Harry Met Sally* real-life moment in a bar crowded with various Lycanthropes, Vampires and Fey who all knew the state she was in was mortifying.

"Trust me, Gillyflower. I will get you out of here," Trocar assured her, reaching down to lift her effortlessly in strong elven arms.

"Go, Elf!" and "She's ready for you; we can taste her scent!" were two of the milder commentaries from the assembled males in the bar.

"Don't you people have wives or girlfriends of your own to fuck?" Gillian snapped as Trocar carried her past. "I suggest you quit running your mouths and fantasizing at the bar and go get some real action for a change." That shut them up. Sort of. But it did tone the tittering down a bit as they left.

As soon as they were outside, Trocar sprinted for the car with Gillian in his arms. Taking her keys, he got the door open and deposited her in the backseat, then slammed the door shut and got in the driver's side.

"Hey, you can't drive!" Gillian said sulkily from the back, still nearly writhing from the overabundance of Vampire sensuality.

"Watch and learn, Petal." Trocar was fairly growling as he cranked the engine, threw the car into gear and sped off into the night.

Half turning, he said over the front seat, "I do not wish to be indelicate with you, Captain, but please take care of your need immediately, I give you my word that I will not watch you."

"What?!" Gillian turned a deeper shade of pink. "You are not suggesting that I basically get myself off here in the car with you driving!"

"That is exactly what I am suggesting. You have just been in the presence of an obviously exceedingly powerful Vampire. You teeter on the edge of lust normally around Aleksei as well when you are not fighting with one another, but fortunately he is there to remedy it. Without him available at the moment, you are once again broadcasting sex and need, and while I would happily volunteer to ease your suffering, I do not want to have you suddenly uncomfortable with our relationship."

Gillian would have responded, but she was too busy covering her eyes with her hand and gritting her teeth as the car bounced and vibrated down the road. She just couldn't do what he asked. Not here, not in front of him.

Maybe Trocar could help . . . It would just take him pulling over and climbing back here for maybe two seconds. Unleashing that lovely obsidian shaft . . . Gah! What was she thinking?

"*Aleksei!*" she yelled through their link. She knew he was occupied at the moment, but . . . but there was another possibility. Of course! There were always alternatives.

"Perrin!" she ground out. "Get me to Perrin."

"Done," he said and sped up.

The Dark Elf pulled up almost on top of the front porch of the guesthouse and leapt out, running up to knock on Perrin's door.

"*I cannot come to you, piccola, but if you have been affected like this by your new patient, you must work on better shielding. If Perrin is not there, let the Elf help you.*"

Aleksei had instantly read everything she fed him. They would discuss her problems with her shielding later; right now, she needed relief and to get out of his mind.

"*I can't do that!*" Gillian insisted.

"*Yes, you can. The identity of your patient is safe, you managed that much, but the sexuality he was projecting did indeed cause you to invade my thoughts and it is a distraction to say the least.*

"*Be reasonable, bellissima. Dionysus, Osiris and the Egyptians have thousands of years of practice shielding from others. You respond to me because you care for me; Tanis does not affect you normally nor do most of the others of our kind because they are simply not that powerful nor do they rely on that ability to form relationships or seduce their prey.*

"*This Vampire would be a very old, very strong Master. He is using his power as a food resource; it probably keeps any lesser beings he has contact with enamored of him. I would assume he doesn't realize it is automatic and does not tone it down to a comfortable level. You are merely overwhelmed after being so sensitive to Perrin for so long. There is no shame in this; so please do it. I will be with you when I can.*"

Nice to have a boyfriend who could answer even your un-spoken questions. Gill had been wondering why she was re-acting so strongly to a Vampire she didn't know when even their most powerful, Osiris, didn't affect her in that way.

"*Aleksei, no, I am not fucking Trocar!*"

"Piccola." Aleksei's dark, sultry, velvet voice plundered her thoughts. "*I can bring you to climax right now if you like. It will take the pressure off, and you will be able to shield.*"

Trocar had turned from the door and shook his head. Per-rin wasn't home. Lovely. She was so not going up to the cas-tle like this.

"Trocar, put the keys on the hood and leave, please!" Gillian yelled through the window.

He nodded and did as she asked without inquiry, disap-pearing into the darkness.

"*Okay, Aleksei, but this had better work,*" she grumbled, getting increasingly edgy as time passed. This was so damn humiliating. That was it; she was back on a meditation schedule to get her control back where it should be.

"*Relax, cara, I will help you.*"

Gillian felt the deeper brush of his mind on hers. Quite amazingly, she felt his hand between her legs and his fingers, stroking and probing. Jerking back, she arched into the feel-ing and could have sworn he was plundering her body, stroking the swollen flesh with his thumb. Biting her lip to keep from screaming, she rocketed over the edge of a tumul-tuous orgasm.

"*I hate to leave you like this, dolcezza, but I must. There are injured here.*" Aleksei abruptly broke off the contact, mind and ghostly hand suddenly gone.

She lay in the backseat of her car, shuddering in after-shocks, embarrassed and damn glad to be alone. This could not go on. Always priding herself on a remarkable level of control for an empath, she knew she'd been slacking off on her routine, but hadn't realized it had gotten this bad.

Several weeks of exposure to Perrin's auto-glamour and short-circuiting emotional scale should have boosted her ability to shield, not weakened it. Well, it didn't matter, she'd call her mentor in for some extra skill building in preventing near-orgasmic reactions to strange Vampires.

Backing the car away from Perrin's doorway, she parked it in the graveled area and headed for the castle. As she entered, she could hear laughter from the great hall and went to investigate. Kimber, Pavel, some of the Fey and Brownies, Trocar—who had evidently taken the long way around to the castle after leaving her—and Perrin were all by the fireplace, laughing merrily, enjoying tea and tiny Brownie cakes. The little menaces were proving to be very helpful and could cook better than a Cordon Bleu chef.

Perrin looked luscious. Tight nutmeg brown pants that left little to the imagination and matching jacket, rich copper silk shirt, black boots, black mask tonight . . . no gloves . . . hooray! He was sitting next to Trocar and a couple of Brownies, arm over the back of the couch, legs stylishly crossed. Gloriosky.

It was a good thing Aleksei had . . . er . . . relieved the pressure or she would have jumped him on sight. Decorum. Professional. Like hell. Trocar raised a crystalline white brow, and she nodded just enough so he'd understand all might not be well but it was better.

Kimber waved from under Pavel's arm. "Come on in, girlfriend!"

She looked cute with the gorgeous blond Lycanthrope, all one hundred ten pounds of her skinny self against his six-foot-three, two-hundred-pound bulk. They looked charming together.

"Hi, everyone, I will be back in a few minutes. I have to make a couple of phone calls," she said cheerfully, waving at them all and leering appreciatively at Perrin, who winked at her, smiling.

It was good to see him more relaxed and beginning to enjoy real camaraderie. He was less clingy and insecure too. Trocar and Aleksei especially had been trying to include him in excursions around the property and in the inevitable male-bonding chats.

Even Daed had positive comments about the fascinating masked man. Since he was the new team psychiatrist, she and Helmut had staffed Perrin's case with him and Daed had spent some one-on-one time with Perrin himself. He'd remarked proudly how well-adjusted Perrin had become under Gillian's care. Helmut was all for making sex therapy a regular option at the Institute, a thought which Gillian negated rather forcefully. She'd had quite enough of that for a while. It was too draining in too many ways to run those clients one after another.

Watching Perrin now, as he looked directly at the others when they spoke and laughed openly with her friends, was all the reward and thanks she needed. He could leave without her worrying about him. That brightened her thoughts somewhat as she went to the library.

Turning on her computer, she opened her browser and initiated chat. Almost at once there was a cheerful chime.

"Darling, Gillian! What can I do for you?"

The chime and the typed words were from her mentor at the Miller-Jackson Center for Intimacy, Cassiopeia Delphi, Ph.D., and Master Vampire, whom she'd called for advice regarding Perrin's inclusion in social outings. Cassiopeia was honest, blunt and occasionally as tactless as Gillian. Ever since they'd discovered their similarities, they'd been fast friends.

"I am having a hell of a time maintaining my shields," Gillian wrote quickly after she had explained the situation.

"You have not been observant with your meditation and practicing your healing, especially with having that Fey-Gargoyle for a client, Gilly. You have better discipline than that," Cassiopeia scolded, but she did it nicely.

Gillian knew her. Her mentor had never in anyone's knowledge raised her voice above her normal sultry tones. She was also one of two people who could call Gillian "Gilly" and not be shot.

"Yes, I fucked up." No sense in denying it.

"And I assume that you would like me to come there and give you a refresher?"

"Please, if you have time, I would appreciate it."

"I just finished a class yester eve, so I am free for the next few nights. I will get there if you will take care of my accommodations, darling."

"You can stay here at the Institute, we have plenty of room."

"Wonderful, Ducks, I am looking forward to meeting your Lord and this patient who has had you all atwitter. Please introduce me only as your former instructor who is now your meditation guru. I would rather not actually work while there."

Cassiopeia had been Reborn during the late 1930s. She was of Dionysus' Line, looked like a thirty-year-old violet-eyed Greek goddess, spoke like a forties USO girl and was a delight.

"Thanks, Cass." Gill signed off. Cassiopeia was completely reliable. She also hated being called "Cass," but let Gillian get away with it occasionally for the same reason she was allowed to use "Gilly" as a pet name for her protégée.

Great, now she had to tell Aleksei they were having more company. That was fine. Perrin was leaving with Helmut night after tomorrow, which would coincide with Cassiopeia's arrival. That thought stopped her. Gods above, she was thinking in "Vamp speak," using their terms in how they related to time passing. She really needed to get up early once in a while and remember what a sunrise looked like.

CHAPTER

21

"BELLISSIMA, *can you gather anyone you know amongst our fair company who is a healer? The Humans are all safe, with the exception of minor injuries, and are being looked after in the town hall. We have a number of wounded Vampires, Sidhe and Shifters with us. Most will heal naturally in due course but I fear that some of the injuries are rather serious as the enemies were armed with silver, iron and wood. We simply do not have enough blood between all of us to heal them quickly."* Aleksei's thoughts skated into her mind on silvered glass.

"I'm on it." Gillian didn't waste his time or hers questioning him on the situation. As a soldier, you generally had only minimal information at your disposal and you acted on it until told differently. She took off at a dead run, nearly stomping some Brownies outside the library, and bolted for the Great Hall, yelling for Trocar, Dalton and Finian.

"Gillian, what do you need us to do?" Luis was unexpectedly beside her, running with her, Oscar flanking him.

"We need healers, Luis. And why weren't you two with Aleksei? You in particular, Oscar, since you took a Loyalty Oath," Gillian said curtly, glancing at the blond Vampire over her shoulder.

"I am sorry, Gillian. You are right, of course. I had taken Luis away for a few days, we've only just returned." Oscar gave off nothing but complete honesty. There was no tingle, no flare from him to indicate a lie.

"Okay, fine, take it up with Aleksei then. Meanwhile, get any of the Fey in the area that can heal." She skidded around the corner into the Great Hall while the two Vampires ran past her and out the front door to follow her command.

Thud is quite descriptive of the sound that occurs when a fast-moving Human takes a corner too quickly and plows into a Dark Elf, who, while not running, was hurrying with one of the Sidhe Princes she'd asked for right behind him.

"Ow! Dammit! Sorry, Trocar," Gill said as he steadied her with a glare. She took that moment to unwrap herself from his sheathed sword and check for accidental puncture wounds.

"What is it, Kynzare?" Finian asked, his hand on his own blade.

"Aleksei's coming with wounded. The attackers used silver, iron and wood so we've got wounded Vamps, Fey and Shifters, and I don't know who else. Can any of your people heal?" That was to Finian. She knew Trocar was a healer and quite capable of assisting.

"Yes, let me call to them." Finian unhooked a small silver horn from his belt and went to the front door. Several of the other Sidhe in the Hall heard her, coming forward to announce themselves as healers.

Two or three spriggans, it was hard to tell, lumped over. "We do not heal, but we are magic and can help the cause," one said in its gravelly thick voice.

"Thank you. We can use all the power we can get," Gillian thanked it gravely. They were even worse-looking than the Sluagh that'd had Trocar in its clutches the other night, but she kept her face pleasant and pushed accepting and grateful feelings toward all of them. They collectively nodded and moved back to a darker corner of the Great Hall.

Perrin was abruptly at her side. "What can I do to help?" Shit, he looked magnificent, but the gray green eyes were worried. She could feel his need to be useful to his newfound friends beating at her.

Thinking quickly, she had an idea. "Tell you what, we need your music."

Turning to Pavel, still seated with Kimber, she asked, "Pavel, get whatever Wolves you can and get the piano from Perrin's house, please, then bring it here. Kimber, Perrin, help me move these couches out of the way."

They all moved to obey her, Perrin grabbing the opposite end of the couch she had. "What good can my music do anyone in this situation, *ma chérie*? It caused so much trouble before."

"I have an idea. Can you tone down the erotic part of it and make it about healing? Dial up the glamour to respond to curative magic?"

He set the couch down, nodding in understanding. "You want me to amplify whatever healing the rest of you can do. I am not certain, but I will try nonetheless. You must tell me if it causes any discomfort among the wounded."

"Yeah, that would suck to have a bunch of bloody, dismembered people trying to screw each other." Gillian laughed; Kimber laughed; even Trocar and Pavel laughed. Perrin wasn't laughing; Perrin was abruptly pale. Oops.

"Look, Perrin, I'm sorry. The situation is bad, so we make bad jokes. It's called 'gallows humor.' It's a defense mechanism, nothing more. We're not making light of anyone being injured or killed. Understand?" She'd stopped rolling up the rug with Kimber and focused on Perrin's distress.

"I know, Gillian. I really cannot joke about any kind of pain." He turned away from her and went off in the direction of the foyer.

"Dammit, I keep forgetting he's not used to us." She raked her hair back. "He just fits in now, you know?"

"Yeah, he does, honey, but you know you can't think like that." Kimber was right, as usual.

"I know. It just sucks. I'm trying to keep my own objectivity, but he got to me. First client in all my years of practice that actually got to me," Gillian admitted, more to herself than anyone else.

Trocar put his arm around her. "It is only Human of you, Gillyflower. He is no longer in the pain he knew when he first arrived. Now, it is a joy to see him as he should have been all along and now can be. Be glad of what you have accomplished here, keep that perspective, then let him try his wings. He is not as fragile as you might think."

She hugged him for a moment, allowing herself to be comforted, then stepped away. "I know he's not fragile, he lived for over one hundred fifty years with not one kind word or thought or deed from anyone. It just amazes me that he's adapted so well. I guess he was just waiting for the time when everything would be all right. I can let go, guys, really. I've just gotten used to him being around, but I can let go."

"We know you will, Kemo Sabe, but we worry about you too, that's all." Kimber hugged her friend.

"Thanks, Kimmy. Now let's get this ready for the incoming."

Soon, they had the room cleared as Perrin returned with all the linens, pillows and towels he could find on a cart he'd pilfered from somewhere in the castle. Pallets were laid out from one end of the hall to the other with the help of the Brownies to straighten out wrinkles in the blankets and smooth the corners. They didn't know how many were coming back—Aleksei hadn't been specific—so they decided to take no chances and go for possibly too many rather than not enough.

Daed was there with his proverbial little black bag. He had ordered a generous amount of various pharmaceuticals from Brasov after the Ripper incident and felt confident he had enough types of drugs to handle any being who needed medication.

Finian returned with a small assortment of Sidhe, both Seelie and Unseelie; there was even the tentacled Sluagh that had been with Trocar the night of the orgy. Seems it had some sort of strong healing abilities built into its slimy body. Who knew?

"Thanks, Finian. I have an idea on how to pull all of our talents together," Gillian said gratefully.

"You are welcome, Kynzare, we are allied, and it is our pleasure to help one another."

"As it is ours." That was from Gunnolf Crosswind, who stood in the entry with his sister, Aisling. She was looking at Trocar with undisguised desire in her face. The Dark Elf went to her and kissed her fingertips. Gunnolf rolled his eyes but said nothing.

"Thank you, Gunnolf, Aisling. I know from experience how powerful the healing skill of the First People are," Gillian said politely, giving the Grael gesture of respect that she'd learned from Trocar long ago. Gunnolf's eyebrows rose but he said nothing, nodding and returning the movement. Aisling was too busy staring into Trocar's iridescent eyes to notice.

Just then Pavel and another Wolf came in carrying the piano from Perrin's guesthouse. One of them could have managed it alone easily but it was less awkward since they didn't want to scratch it. Gillian indicated they should put it down in the foyer, facing the Great Hall.

Perrin watched as they angled it and raised the lid, propping it up with its shiny brass arm. "I am to play, while people are lying here, hurt and possibly dying?" Perrin's voice was lovely but held a rough edge that it got when he was in the beginnings of anger.

Gillian turned to look at him. The amazing eyes were determined yet held a thread of fear. "Perrin, you're not going to throw up again, if that's what you're worried about. You'll be in here while they're all in there so you won't have to look at any of it. And yes, I would like you to play, use your talent and enhance the healers in this room. That seems to be part of your magic, at least the way that we've interpreted it."

Taking his arm, she patted his hand. "But I would like it if you waited in the library until we're all ready in here. Once we get everyone situated and inside, I want to try something which I hope will work with the addition of your skill."

Looking down at her, so earnest and intent in her need to

help everyone, he smiled. She was so lovely, so clever and sweet. He could refuse her nothing. "All right, *ma chérie*, I will wait until you call for me. My talents are at your disposal."

"Thanks, Perrin. You're a prince." She impulsively squeezed his hand, then she was gone, off to open the door and wait outside with Pavel, Trocar and the Wood Elves with her.

"Only a prince without his lily-pad kingdom," the masked genius murmured softly before turning to wait in the library.

"Aleksei's almost here," Gillian announced, feeling his presence growing stronger.

Trocar took the hint and called to everyone to come out and help with the wounded. Almost immediately the yard was full of the returning fighters. The strong helped the wounded; races that weren't supposed to get along were helping each other, stanching wounds, offering comfort.

Kimber, Trocar and Gillian directed traffic, forming a makeshift triage. The worst of the wounded were settled nearest to the front of the Great Hall and the less–seriously injured farther toward the back. Blood of all different shades and varieties trailed over the yard and in the foyer. The Great Hall soon resembled a slaughterhouse in smell and appearance.

Vampires wounded with wooden weapons lay convulsing and bleeding. Lycanthropes pierced and slashed with silver whimpered and fought not to shift back into their Human form to die, knowing they had a better chance in animal form to heal the terrible damage. Sidhe injured from even a glancing blow of a cold iron weapon huddled together in groups.

Aleksei misted in and appeared next to Gillian, sweeping her under the shelter of his shoulder and kissing her when she looked up at him. "Thank you, *dolcezza*. I do not know if we can save them all, but I would like to try."

"I have an idea, Aleksei. Don't give up on them yet. I'm going to need your help. You're a Lord; can you focus the talents of everyone who is capable of healing here?"

At his puzzled look, she explained, "I think I have an idea

about how to help everyone, but I need your mind to direct the others."

Nodding, he crowded her with his body, nudging her inside. It was a purely alpha thing to do, but Gillian realized she was getting less reactionary about it. He didn't mean it as an insult. It was just him. A four-hundred-year-old Vampire who was going to help keep her safe and out of harm's way. Hell, if she had his powers, she'd do the same thing to him.

She allowed him to guide her into the foyer and to the Great Hall, where they witnessed the carnage, he for the second time that night, she in the artificial light of the castle's huge room. She missed Perrin's gaze following them as Aleksei maneuvered her protectively across the rooms in front of him. The masked man had come out of the library, watching the upcoming drama get under way.

Seating himself at the piano, where he could be unobtrusive but still watch everything, he realized this was his final night at the Institute. He hoped he would have time to say good-bye to Gillian privately, cursing himself for being selfish while there were so many injured.

From his vantage point, he could hear every word she spoke in a clear, strong voice to the assembled and watched how all of them relaxed, trusting her. She was such an admirable woman.

"Everyone, please listen for a moment. We have healers who are going to place themselves at various positions among you. Our maestro"—she half turned to motion toward Perrin—"will play the piano. He has the capability through his music to enhance the natural thought processes, feelings and abilities of anyone. What we are hoping is that with Perrin's help we will be able to heal all of you collectively. So please clear your minds if you can and listen to him play."

Winking at Perrin and nodding encouragement, she went on, "Aleksei will explain his role."

"If the collective of the Vampires, those who are mine, those who are not, will allow it, along with my Wolves and the other Shifters, I will be the conduit to link all of you with Gillian.

"The Sidhe, Brownies and Elves are welcome to use their own manner of communication, but please focus on Gillian and myself. She has a plan that may help you all." Aleksei's magical voice rolled over all of them, seductive, warm, inviting them to merge with him.

Those that were not his wished that they were. This was a Lord that they could believe in. He was one of the reasons they had risked their lives tonight, the reason they now lay in his Hall bleeding from difficult-to-heal, nearly lethal wounds.

Aleksei and his Human female had already proven themselves worthy of trust and respect; rumors about them were already spreading far and wide. All eyes turned to him, then closed to focus their abilities.

Gillian watched them listening to the Romanian Lord. Aleksei was honest, powerful, spectacularly lovely and had a certain noble charisma, an elite quality which inspired allegiance. They wanted to be by his side. They had supported him during the conflict and would do so again.

"Okay, Aleksei, bring me in first, then gather the rest of them," she whispered softly then signaled Perrin to begin.

Haunting, heartrendingly beautiful, yet joyous music flowed into the room. Perrin looked enraptured as his elegant, aristocratic hands danced over the keys and he played one of his compositions. Focusing on his former pain and loneliness; thinking about how his attitude had changed because he felt healed. He worked the thoughts over and over. Remembering what he felt like after he'd kept company with Gillian; healed and whole.

He had it then. He could call it up at will. The music swelled somehow, got bigger within itself. Perrin wasn't playing loudly; the magic he was bringing to the table was significantly more powerful than more than a third of the beings there.

Some of the Sidhe gasped in shock or stared at him openmouthed as he played. He was one of their own. They could hear their magic in his song.

Gillian dropped her shields and felt Aleksei ghosting in her mind. *"Show me what you want to do,* piccola," came his wordless command.

She showed him. Focusing, drawing on the astonishing level of power he had recently acquired, Aleksei drew in the ones he could reach. Following the pattern Gillian was imagining, he took the single threads of thought and wove them together in a gleaming, shining net of healing light. A net fueled by the power of Perrin's music and glamour, the healing abilities of Trocar, the Sluagh, the Elves, the Brownies and the Sidhe; the innate ability to rapidly heal that all the Paramortals possessed.

Allowing Perrin's music to consume her, Gillian let it flare her empathy to a glowing orb around her body, completely open to him and his power. As it pulsed through her, her hand inadvertently strayed to the open top of the piano, fingertips brushing the vibrating strings. In indirect contact through his hands on the keys and her hand on the lacquered wood, his glamour and her empathy merged fully.

Aleksei felt the surge through their own link and reached for her free hand, putting his other on the piano beside hers, and completing the circuit. Mentally he reached for Perrin, drawing the masked man's phenomenally brilliant mind to him. He couldn't waver his concentration from the vast array of life forms whose thoughts and abilities he kept. There was no way for him to shield either Gillian or himself or warn her away from what she was gathering her strength to do.

Around his waist, he felt powerful arms enclose him as Luis dropped into rapport with the rest. Oscar was behind Gillian, adding his own cool strength to the mix, pulling her close and bracing her against him. Aleksei didn't think, he simply wove them into the threads that made up the enormous net of light that pulsed, thrummed, surged and sang over all their heads.

There were Brownies everywhere, the gods only knew

when they'd come in, scattered among the wounded, around their feet and the legs of the piano, the tiny strands of their inherent magic anchoring the entire array. Those he couldn't have brought in on his own, like Kimber and Daed, reached into the general feeling and added their considerable will and intent.

Gillian illustrated the thought of her intention to Aleksei a heartbeat before she acted on it. Fueled by Perrin's unparalleled ability, with the full concentration and power of the Vampire Lord behind her, all the strands and threads Aleksei had gathered to make the metaphysical mesh joined back through them. She waited until the precise moment of a powerful surge when its light was brightest and Perrin's music crescendoed, then flared the net and dropped it over all of them.

A blinding flash seared through the Great Hall as the web of light whiplashed through everyone in a titanic burst of power. Simultaneous cries and screams echoed through the ancient stones of Castle Rachlav as the two hundred or more occupants jerked and rebounded in a cataclysmic paroxysm of absolute ecstasy and warm bliss.

For those who were touching, it was beyond orgasmic but without the body fluids and sweating. Those who were without benefit of touch still shuddered through the aftershocks and waves of energy that cranked through them as though they were individual conduits for the power.

When Gillian opened her eyes, she realized that she and Aleksei still held hands. Everyone was on the flagstone floor of the castle. The only reason she wasn't flat on her back was because she was sitting on Oscar's lap and he was leaning, seemingly boneless, against the leg of the piano. There was a deep, throbbing warmth between her legs that she couldn't explain.

Aleksei was on one knee in front of her, braced with one hand on the piano, the other arm across his thigh, holding her hand; he was the only being in the castle who hadn't been nearly flattened by the event. A virtually comatose Luis's arms were still around his waist, his body half sprawled out behind him.

Turning her head, she strained to see around the piano to where Perrin was. She tried to stand, but her legs wouldn't hold her and her bottom molded to Oscar's lap again. From what she could tell, he had one hell of an erection under her butt.

"Please, darling, have mercy and do not shift your weight again or we will both be embarrassed."

The richly cultured English accent brought her back to the present. "Oh, sorry, Oscar."

"No worries, love, but the slightest movement from you and I will explode, so give me a moment."

"All of us are similarly affected." Aleksei's molten silver eyes took her in. Gillian glanced down, yup, the long thick outline of his erection showed in bas relief, straining against his thigh in the laced-up black velvet pants he wore. She realized she was rather . . . damp. Hooray for Perrin and his magical musical world of wonder.

Apparently everyone was "similarly affected." There were gasps, bitten-back screams and deep moans from those who had tried to move too soon and found a secondary enjoyment out of their experience. Gillian and Aleksei were staring at each other, pure heat coursing between their linked hands. The deep warmth in her groin grew more intense and insistent. Shit and double shit, how were they going to get out of this?

Grinning lazily, Aleksei arched a brow at her and nodded.

"No," Gill said in a breathless whisper, her eyes wide.

"Yes," Aleksei countered and yanked her off Oscar's lap, fitting her against his own body. His mouth covered hers and she instantly forgot about Oscar, who arched upward as she brushed over him and was now convulsing behind her. Luis, who had let go of Aleksei's waist, was now writhing on the floor in perfect sync with his lover.

Other than the kiss, there was no sexual touching, but Gillian jackknifed in Aleksei's arms, the warmth within her becoming a pulsing heat. He joined her in delight, the force of their passion fed from the afterglow of the healing net.

Both of them were still in contact with the piano and heard

Perrin's answering gasp. He was draped over the keys, suffused with satisfaction and unable to move.

Gillian broke the kiss simply to breathe and let Aleksei hold her tightly as she rested her head on his shoulder. That brought her eyes in line with the scene in the Great Hall. Abruptly, she started to laugh. Aleksei turned her a little in his arms, rising from the ground to look at what she saw, then started to chuckle.

All of them, every creature who was coming out of the throes of the healing pleasure they'd all experienced, were moving, shifting or getting shakily to their feet. All except a pile of bodies in the archway to the Hall. Trocar, Aisling, Gunnolf and the squid Sluagh all lay as if piled together. Specifically, Trocar and Aisling were one pile, right next to the Sluagh and Gunnolf. The Sluagh had a tentacle on Trocar and Aisling but its massive bulk was wrapped around Gunnolf as it had been around Trocar.

"Sweet mother, that is a big sucker," Gill quipped, still giggling. She was rewarded by an offended glare from Gunnolf, who said nothing but slowly extricated himself from the Sluagh's clutches. He was rather shaky on his feet and backpedaled into the wall, sliding down it, where he rested wearily.

"It was good for him apparently," Trocar muttered from his vantage point on top of Aisling, who giggled, making the Grael shudder in a rather sensual way.

"And for you," Aisling managed around the snickering.

"And for me," Aleksei murmured into Gillian's neck as he held her tightly, sending a quivering shimmer down her spine.

Before she could answer, there was a deep moan from Perrin, "Gillian . . . please . . . it hurts . . ."

Hurts? Nothing should hurt. Gillian and Aleksei staggered to their feet as best they could and stumbling, holding each other up, made it back to Perrin. He was holding his hands tightly against his mask, rocking on the piano bench in obvious agony.

"Healer!" Gill bellowed as she reached him. Aleksei

brushed her out of the way and scooped Perrin up off the bench like a child, cradling him in powerful arms, then knelt so Gill could get to him.

"Perrin, talk to me." Gently she placed her hands over his own; her voice was tight with worry. What the hell had happened? He shouldn't be in pain; it shouldn't have affected him at all.

"Un cher Dieu qu'il blesse!" Perrin gasped.

Trocar was suddenly there, bringing with him a female Sidhe warrior with curly lavender hair, light blue skin and soft pink eyes. "Gillian, please move aside."

When she didn't respond right away, he touched her arm gently. "Captain, let us help him."

She moved, but kept her hand on Perrin's shoulder. The Dark Elf and Fey ran their hands lightly over Perrin's. The female touched his hands, which still clutched at his mask.

"Allow me to look. We can help." Her voice was light and gentle as a spring day.

Reluctantly Perrin moved his hands away, then reached back for Gillian, who took his hand and held it to her chest. Trocar stroked his hair as the Sidhe removed the mask. There was a collective intake of breath. Most of the living stone on Perrin's face, which the mask had covered, was rapidly being enclosed by raw muscle and encroaching skin. It looked like pure scar tissue, very pink, shiny and tough.

Seeing what was happening, Aleksei intervened. "Perrin, look at me, my friend. Let me have your mind for a moment."

Perrin's eyes opened and were riveted to Aleksei's. The Vampire Lord waited for no other invitation but brushed aside Perrin's normal defenses and took over, shielding the other man from the agony he was experiencing and helping him relax for the healers to be able to do their job. It was abrupt and sent a shudder through the man in his arms, but he had no choice; the pain and fear were paralyzing him from any rational thought.

As she watched Aleksei, Gillian smiled. It was comforting somehow to see his acceptance and kindness toward Perrin, considering what his attitude had been at the first. Perrin's return of that trust was equally heartwarming. He lay in the arms of the most powerful being in the region, letting a Grael Elf and a Sidhe work on him, completely accepting of whatever they were about to do.

Trocar was murmuring an archaic chant while the Fey sang softly. Both of their hands were positioned over Perrin's ravaged face. The Grael moved forward; sculpted, obsidian fingers wound around the Sidhe's light blue ones. They steepled their hands over the area and continued chanting and singing.

"*Bellissima*, he wants to know 'How bad is it?'" Aleksei's voice, though pitched low and soft, made everyone jump. He was firmly in Perrin's mind, holding back the pain, reading the surface thoughts from the musician.

"It's not bad, Perrin. It's remarkable," Gillian said, tears in her voice. "There is flesh growing over the stone. Trocar and . . ." She paused, not knowing the Sidhe's name.

"Kestrel," the Fey said.

". . . Kestrel are doing what they can," Gillian finished, still pressing his hand tightly to her.

Perrin seemed to struggle for a moment, but Aleksei's hold on him was firm. The two healers kept up what they were doing for what seemed like ages. Finally both pulled away from each other and sat back.

"We can do no more, Mellina," Trocar stated, using Gill's Elf Friend name.

Hearing that, Aleksei released his mental hold on Perrin, who blinked, his eyes coming back into focus, hands going up to touch his newly re-formed but scarred face.

"May I . . . look?" His voice was shaky but still lovely.

"Of course, my friend." Aleksei stood, raising Perrin with him and steadying him.

Gill scooped up his mask then joined him to take Perrin's other arm. Together they led him to a mirror in the bathroom off the foyer.

Perrin stared at his reflection in the mirror. The left side of his face and bottom right side were as they always were: perfect, lovely, astonishingly beautiful. The upper-right third, devoid of the mask, was now without the gray stone bursting through it on cheek, nose and forehead. Everything was covered by pink, shiny scar tissue.

There were newly filled in black lashes around the right side's gray green eye, but part of his nose was still missing. Perrin looked like he'd been burned in a fire, then had skin grafts afterward. It wasn't much of an improvement from the gray stone, but it was an improvement.

"Flesh from stone . . ." Perrin whispered. "It is a miracle." A single tear, wept from the right-side gray green eye, its lower lid no longer twisted from the growth of living stone, trickled down the newly scarred cheekbone. He forced himself to look at it critically.

His face wasn't cured but rather healed; the stone deformity was merely covered up with flesh and skin. The mask would continue to be necessary in public, but he felt the shock of its removal would not be as great should he ever have occasion to take it off again. Still, not having magical rock growing out of his face was an improvement he would never have hoped for, never dreamed about as possible.

"Thank you, all of you," Perrin said softly, still not quite believing what he saw. "All of you, this place, you have given me back my faith, my hope, the ability to live and love; now you have granted my most secret wish. I do not know how to thank you."

He turned, clasping Aleksei's arm in one hand and cupping Gillian's chin with his other, his remarkable eyes searching her face, "*Mon petit ange,* I know that you will be embarrassed if I thank you directly for everything you have done so altruistically to bring me back to life, so allow me to say this: If ever you should have need of me, for whatever reason"—he lifted his head and included Aleksei and Trocar in his statement—"any of you . . . you have but to ask. I would move heaven and earth for each and every one of you."

Perrin drew Gillian to him, then Aleksei, hugging them both tightly. When they stepped away, Trocar unexpectedly moved forward to embrace him.

"*Eluvano,*" the Grael said in his beautiful voice, "you already have."

"He called you his 'lovely little brother,' Perrin," Gillian informed him, hoping that she was correct in her memory of High Elvish.

The gray green eyes, which had been sparkling, overfilled, spilling tears down both sides of his face. "I am honored, Trocar." He looked at all of them, knowing it was a tender moment that would likely never be repeated.

"I do not have any friends, but if I did and they had problems such as I had, I would recommend them coming here. You people cannot know what you have done for me." Perrin took his mask from Gillian, pushed past all of them out the door and hurried out of the castle.

Gillian started after him, but Trocar stopped her. "Let him go, Mellina. He needs time to adjust." She nodded and turned back to take Aleksei's hand. Everyone's eyes were damp, even Trocar's, but now they needed to see to the others.

Luis and Oscar were sitting together against the archway, watching the activities of everyone in the enormous room. They waved and nodded to them as they passed, seemingly all right after their shared ordeal. When Aleksei and Gillian appeared in the archway, followed by Trocar, the noise in the room stopped and everyone turned to look at them.

"We are healed, Lord Aleksei." That was from a phenomenally handsome, tall male Vampire with very long dark hair and equally dark eyes. He continued, "I am not of your Line, but I will, this night, take your Oath and sign your document."

There was scattered consensual comments from around the room, including Sidhe, Sluagh, Spriggan and Lycanthropes. "We were here for our Oath to our Liege Lord only, but now we will remain for our Lord Aleksei, who gives us another way to govern his people." That was from a female Lycanthrope, with a lovely heart-shaped face and spring green eyes.

Cezar, Aleksei's Alpha Wolf, looked on proudly. "My friend, there is a consensus. Most here are not of your Oath or Line nor mine, but they are willing to sign, swear and seal this bargain tonight."

To Aleksei's utter horror, Cezar dropped to one knee. The rest of the room followed suit. Only Gillian, Trocar, Daed and Kimber remained standing.

Gillian glanced over her shoulder. Luis and Oscar were both kneeling behind them. "Good grief, it's fanged obsequiousness!"

"Please," Aleksei implored all of them, embarrassed and appalled, "please get up. I have never asked for nor expected fealty like this!" The marvelous, deep, rich baritone voice cascaded over all of them. No one moved.

He tried again, "That you all are healed is enough. That you came at my request is enough. You have shed your blood, that is enough. I do not wish to govern you from your knees. Please get up and be our partners in this endeavor. Be our trusted friends and comrades, watch our backs as we watch yours."

"Forgive me, my Lord, but that is not how it is done in our world, as you well know. You may consider us whatever you like, but we will be yours in name and deed." That was from the first handsome Vampire. "My name is Teo, and I swear Oath to you."

He rose and went to Aleksei, kneeling again at his feet and offering his wrist. The Vampire Lord was transfixed for a moment.

Gillian whispered in his mind, *"Do it, Aleksei. They're expecting a ritualistic acceptance. It's being offered freely. I'm not picking up any duplicity and I know you aren't either."*

"Piccola, I—"

"Just do it. It will give us a tactical advantage that Dracula won't expect or know about. You're not recruiting; they're making their own deal with who they think is the best leader on the best team. We'll sort out the details, about bowing and kneeling, later."

"Teo, I am honored to have your allegiance," Aleksei said formally, taking the other Vampire's wrist, then raising him to his feet before he put his mouth to the offering.

Aleksei looked into the other Vampire's eyes before he bit

into the proffered wrist. It was quick; Gillian couldn't be sure she'd actually seen it, just Aleksei brushing his mouth over the other's flesh, then lowering the arm.

Teo blinked. "Your touch is gentle, Lord Aleksei. I felt nothing but pleasure from your bite."

Ew! Gillian thought but kept her mouth shut. When Teo turned to her, she braced herself. Surely not.

"My lady, may I offer my allegiance to you as well?"

O-kay. She was so not going to suck anyone's blood, and she was so not going to stay in Romania forever as Aleksei's ... consort ... girlfriend ... mate ... *Ack!*

Wide-eyed, she turned to Aleksei for guidance. "Aleksei?"

"Gillian does not need a blood exchange, Teo. She is Human, but I am certain she will accept your hand and your word." Aleksei deftly rescued her from any sanguineous activities. She shot him a grateful glance and offered her hand to the Vampire.

"I will gladly accept your friendship, Teo, but I am not in a position to accept your allegiance. Alek ... er, Lord Rachlav is in command here on the Paramortal front. I just work at the Institute."

The Vampire shook her hand and bowed. Gill smiled at him, then stepped back next to Aleksei. A strong arm went around her shoulders and she looked up into bemused ice gray eyes.

"Captain Key, or Dr. Key, as some of you know her, has a gift for understatement as usual."

He cocked an eyebrow at her, making her feel suddenly nervous. "While Gillian does work for the Institute in her capacity as psychologist, she will continue to be an invaluable resource in tactical and military matters. I encourage all of you to seek her out for her wisdom and advice should you require it. You may speak to either her or myself if you wish to organize any offensive effort. I trust her and so should you."

Gillian stared at him openmouthed, mirroring the astonished faces of Kimber, Daed and Trocar. By the look of things, all of them were shocked. They could all see that she too was floored by the news. Aleksei hadn't discussed it with her; this was definitely a surprise.

"She is your chosen then?" Teo asked.

Either Teo was the unofficial spokesman for the lot of them or he needed to find another goddamn hobby besides worrying about what her place, her business or her anything was with Aleksei, and he needed to find it really fast, in Gillian's opinion. *Chosen?* Baldour's balls. *Chosen* sounded a little too much like shopping for drapes.

Nile green eyes rose to his own once more, but this time they were flashing a definite warning to tread carefully. Aleksei stared at her for a moment, drinking in the view of her as she started to tremble under his arm, and her cheeks took on that delicate coral flush he loved so much when she was in the beginnings of a temperamental episode.

"While she would be my chosen, if she wished it, Gillian has her own mind and will make her own decision about her personal relationship with me in her own time. Meanwhile, I expect all of you to afford her the courtesy and respect which you would give me, always. I also expect you to be courteous enough not to inquire as to the nature or status of our relationship. Gillian will remain here in whatever capacity she chooses for as long as she chooses. She is under my protection, as are her friends."

Aleksei gestured toward Kimber, Daed and Trocar, then to Luis and Oscar. "All of these people are to be given deference, and treated like the finest crystal at every moment. That includes Dr. Gerhardt when he is in residence, and any patients or guests who lodge here."

He looked around the room, holding each of them with his gaze. As long as he had their attention, he decided to get one or two other things straight.

"Cezar remains my senior Alpha to any pack or lone Wolf who remains here to serve me. He is not to be questioned nor challenged, as he has my trust and my ear. The same goes for any Shifter wanting to remain in this area of Romania, not just the Wolves."

There was some undertoned muttering and grousing at

that among the assembled. One of the Shifters, a big man
with amber eyes and auburn hair, stepped forward.

"The Bears do not answer to Wolves, Lord. We are a sovereign nation ourselves. Nor will we answer to your female.
If you want the help of the Bears, you may call upon us but
we will not be subjugated to lesser beings."

Aleksei's eyes flashed and he started to glow softly. *Shit,
it's Smokey the Werebear,* Gillian thought. *"Careful, Aleksei,
he's testing you."*

"I am aware of that, piccola," he sent her assuredly.

"You will answer to Cezar as if the order comes from me
directly if you are called upon. If you are not needed, you will
certainly remain a sovereign nation and I will not involve
myself in your affairs unless necessary. As for Gillian, I
strongly advise you that I will support her in whatever decision she makes, and if you cross her, I will consider it a personal insult."

He held the massive Shifter's eyes in his, their wills bat-
tling it out. It was the Shifter who dropped his first.

"As you wish, Lord Aleksei."

Once the Bears threw in their lot, there was no bickering
at all. One by one, the Vampires all came to Aleksei, offering
their wrists. The Sidhe offered nothing but a bow and an
Oath, as did the Brownies and Elves. The Shifters all went to
Cezar, who kept Pavel at his side as he was greeted by and
acknowledged by all the Lycanthropes in the room. Not one
of them had any lingering pain, injuries or scars.

Soon, the Great Hall emptied, except for their original little group. Gillian turned to Aleksei. "Thank you for being
diplomatic and for what you said."

"About you?" he asked and she nodded.

"I am learning, Gillian. You have taught an old Vampire a
few new tricks these past two years."

He raised her hand and kissed it, which earned him an
"Awwww!" from Kimber and Daed.

Trocar shook his head and smiled one of his unreadable
smiles before heading off to watch over Perrin on his last
night. Gillian watched him go. She would stop by to make

sure her soon-to-be-discharged patient was all right but
thought it might be a good plan for Trocar, Kestrel or Aleksei
to stay with him to make sure there were no magical aftereffects that none of them had foreseen. Since Kestrel had vanished with most of the Sidhe and Aleksei wanted to stay with
her, she agreed to let the Elf go since he was the magic expert
on-site.

CHAPTER
22

WHAT had happened was nothing short of a miracle and the whole of the Paramortal community in the area was talking about it. That Aleksei's phenomenal power had been inspired and aided by his Human lover. All had been healed in a most agreeable manner and everyone was impressed.

Csangal had heard as well. Waiting unobtrusively in the bar at the Inn, he listened to the recounting of the situation. Aleksei Rachlav had unexpectedly grown in power. Intriguing, to say the least. Csangal had not been in the area for over a century but he was certain that the Vampire Lord would remember him so it was best to keep a low profile. No use in spreading the word around that a formerly local Vampire was crazy enough to be availing himself of Dr. Key's skill.

Still, healing on this magnitude was something to be reckoned with. He knew that Gillian wasn't a magical being so all or most of the power had to have originated with Aleksei. Apart from her ability to conjure some mild spells and her enormous level of actual empathy, Gillian was still just a Human female. A brilliant, talented Human female, but Human nonetheless.

Looking around the room, Csangal recognized some of the Vampires. It had been a long time and was interesting to still see a familiar face or two. He kept himself cloaked to Human and Paramortal alike, blurring his edges slightly, so that even after a direct stare into his face, no one would be quite able to remember him.

Times were dangerous for everyone these days with the War going on. He had seen the evidence of it around the county and the Country. During his travels, he was finding there were beginning to be some very clear-cut loyalties and divisions growing among all that were not Human. It was to every person's advantage to lie low, not draw undue attention to themselves, and try to focus their efforts on the side most likely to prevail.

After tonight's activities at the castle, Gillian probably wouldn't come to the Inn this evening. He was free to wander about the area, leaving a note with Radu that he would return tomorrow evening, in case she did come again that night.

Aleksei waited for Gillian on the porch of Perrin's house. They'd stopped by to make sure he was all right. He was; Trocar was with him and they seemed to be getting on well. He even had his white mask back on. It was a familiar comfort to him, and after all, while the healing had helped a great deal, the upper-right quadrant of his face was still a grotesque parody of his exquisitely handsome left side.

Aleksei and Perrin said their good-byes with a handshake and a brotherly embrace. Since Aleksei wasn't his therapist or an employee of the Institute, Perrin had no restraints on keeping in touch with the Vampire Lord. By mutual agreement, if letters were exchanged, they would be without any pertinent Gillian information. It wouldn't be ethical, and since both men held honor in high regard, they would follow the edicts of her profession and let the time frame run.

Gillian would be driving back to Brasov with Perrin the next afternoon, returning that night with Cassiopeia and Helmut. She wanted Perrin to have his time to say good-bye however he wished.

Perrin held her close for a fragile moment; Gillian's eyes became deceptively bright. Perrin smiled at Aleksei over

Gill's head as he watched, hoping that whatever was best for all of them would come to pass. Perrin knew he needed to live his life before he could hope to compete for Gillian's affections with Aleksei, if it should come to that.

There was no hope if he stayed here or close by. Finding new experiences and new relationships was high on his agenda. If he came back to her, came back for her, he wanted it to be for the right reasons. There was a twinge of guilt at that thought.

He knew Gillian and Aleksei were lovers. The Vampire Lord was his friend. Someday, after he had determined what real love was, not just the hero worship, gratitude and admiration he was sure he felt for her, he would seek her out. The chips could fall where they may; she may not want anything to do with him on a personal level, but he would have tried.

Trocar politely left them for a moment as Perrin enfolded her in his arms. After watching her be so calm, commanding and strong tonight, it was a revelation to see her so openly vulnerable if only for a moment. He marveled at the feelings that had wound through him: pride, admiration, for her strong presence, her leadership skills, the way others looked to her for advice and guidance.

Now with her in his arms, her eyes moist with joy as she looked at his improved but masked face, he spoke softly to her in French. *"Ne pleure pas, ma bien-aimée, s'il vous plaît . . ."* "Do not cry, sweetheart, please."

Seeing her feelings exposed brought every protective male instinct clamoring to life. Tough, commanding, honorable, intelligent and gentle of heart, she was all woman, the best there was of her gender, in his opinion.

"Okay," Gillian choked out, trying to laugh and keep things lighter. The tears did not quite spill over. She was so proud of him. Now he truly had a chance at a possible normal life and she knew he intended to be strong and take it.

"I'm just so proud of you, is all, Perrin. You've come so remarkably far. I just wish you every wonderful thing imaginable."

A gentle, elegant hand rose as Perrin caught a tear shimmering on her lashes with his knuckle, smiling affectionately down at his little therapist. "*Merci*, Gillian." He inclined his head to her. "*Tu as toujours besoin qu'on prenne soin de toi, ma bien-aimée*," he murmured in his lovely deep, musical voice, cupping her chin in his hand.

"What?" Gillian said, wiping her eyes and smiling.

"I said, 'You still need looking after, sweetheart.'" He chuckled as she went from vulnerable to affronted in the blink of an eye.

"Do not start that shit again, Perrin. Just go have a good life. Worry about yourself for a change."

Gillian reached around and swatted his butt, winking at him as she turned and went out the door. That single sexy ebony eyebrow arched and he shook his finger at her, his rich laughter following. "*Tu es une petite peste, mon ange*. Until tomorrow, *ma chérie*."

That brought an inelegant snort from Aleksei. Perrin watched as the Vampire Lord linked hands with Gillian and walked off into the darkness.

"Do you think I might have you to myself this evening, *cara*?" Aleksei asked, pulling her under the shelter of his shoulder.

"Maybe," Gillian said happily, "if you tell me what he just called me." She was fairly skipping over Perrin's triumph.

"He said you were a 'little brat' . . . '*angel*.'" He emphasized the last word, looking at her skeptically as she laughed, unsure if she really was all right. He decided to change the subject.

"Tomorrow you see him off, then you will bring back your mentor?" Aleksei slowed his pace, wanting just to spend time with her in the moonlight.

"Yes." She altered her stride to match his. "Cassiopeia is coming in as Perrin is leaving. Wait till you meet her, she's a hoot."

"I cannot wait. If she is a friend of yours and taught you all she knows, we are in for a few days of excitement," he said dryly, earning him a poke in the ribs.

"Hey, you don't seem to complain too much about my

knowledge and skill level." Gill gave him a sidelong glance.
"In fact, I think you've benefited more than once."

"Indeed I have, *piccola*." Aleksei laughed. It felt good
just to be with her with nothing pressing at the moment. He
was still charged with energy after the miracle of the evening and wanted to expend it doing pleasant things.

Suddenly he stopped and turned to pull her more tightly
to him. "Fly with me tonight, Gillian."

"Um . . . I'm not quite equipped, if you haven't noticed."

Smiling, he stepped back from her. His outline wavered,
then expanded. Before her was his dragon form—sleek black
scales glittering with iridescent color in the moonlight. The
massive head dipped and turned toward its back, ice gray
eyes shining against the dark scales. The leathery wing
folded farther against the lustrous back muscles, the forelimb and shoulder lowered in invitation.

Gillian laughed and clambered on board. As soon as she
was seated and had a firm hold on the silky hair that grew
along the heavily plated neck, the great beast moved. It
took two galloping, undulating leaps then the immense
wings pumped once, launching into flight. She suppressed a
shriek and held on. Aleksei wouldn't drop her; she trusted
him, felt safe with him.

As soon as the thought crossed her mind, she frowned. Oh,
how the mighty have fallen. Consorting with fanged friends of
all sorts, sex therapist to the preternatural.

She remembered a less than flattering news article or two
when she'd first started out as a Paramortal psychologist.
The IPPA had picked her as sort of their unofficial poster
girl for the up-and-coming field and all that it implied.

Gillian had found herself at the center of an ever-
widening gulf. Humans in general were divided sharply in
the recognition of the Paramortals as beings. She'd gone
public with rousing support for the affirmative side and had
helped bring about some swift, positive changes in everyone's thinking. Anyone with emotional pain was entitled to
her undivided attention and skill; it didn't matter if they used
to be alive or not, or if they'd recently gained the ability to

grow fur. She even opened her doors to the Sidhe, the Elves and most of the dwellers of Faerie. All notoriously resistive to the idea of a Human having the skills necessary to help them out of their respective funks.

Gill reminded everyone very publicly that her crack unit in the USMC was made up of only three Humans. The rest were Paramortals who performed heroic acts daily in order to protect the very people who were bitching about them. That was when she'd stopped seeing Human clients altogether. The decision had cut into her income, but it was the principle of the matter.

Because of her bold moves, more therapists, counselors, psychologists and psychiatrists came out of the proverbial closet and admitted to having been treating "the others" all along, since before legalization and recognition. It had been a crowning victory for the IPPA, its fellows, the Marines and Gillian.

It was also what brought her to the attention of Aleksei Rachlav in the first place. Now, good grief, she was like his . . . his girlfriend or something.

"You are not my girlfriend. You broke up with me," Aleksei reminded her in her mind.

"We. Are. On. A. Break. And get the hell out of my thoughts." Gillian seethed right back. Chuckling to himself, Aleksei dipped a shoulder midflight, making her wobble and clutch more tightly to him.

"I am taking my ex-girlfriend on a moonlight flight so that we may enjoy the stars and the moon together."

She kicked him in the ribs for being a wiseass, and he rewarded her by swirling lazily around, then nose-diving for a large, ruined castle. Gillian gritted her teeth and held on, knowing he was playing with her. At the last moment, the medieval beast backwinged and brought them lightly to the ground. Aleksei waited until she climbed down and was far enough away before shifting back to his tall, dark and stunning self.

"Now what?" Gillian was looking at him, half provocatively, half challengingly. He took a moment to admire her.

"You are quite lovely, *bellissima*." The voice held both humor and heat. Icy gray eyes raked her up and down as he circled her like a shark, his intentions obvious from the smoldering gaze to the thickening outline down his thigh.

"Haven't you had enough tonight?" She folded her arms and stood at parade rest, refusing to take the bait.

He didn't give her a chance to breathe before he moved with blurring speed, capturing her in his arms and crowding her up against the wall of the derelict structure. Pinning her against the stone gently, he plied his fingers through her silky hair. Leaning over her, he brushed his lips across hers, a butterfly's touch. "There is never enough of you, *dolcezza*."

Eyes flashing, she shoved at his shoulders. "Down, boy!"

Aleksei heard the laughter bubbling beneath her words. "As you wish, my lady."

Using one of her own fighting tricks, he hooked a boot behind her ankle and yanked. Catching her deftly, he rolled as she fell so that he took the brunt of the impact. Gillian wound up on top, looking into bemused silvery eyes.

"One of these days I am going to shoot you just on principle," she said, laughing.

"I doubt that, *piccola*." He captured her face in his hands and brought her down to kiss her. His hands ran down her back to cup her butt and pull her tighter against him.

"You do not want to damage your favorite plaything."

He meant it as a joke, but Gillian's eyes clouded briefly. "Aleksei, you have never been a plaything."

Realizing his mistake, Aleksei backtracked. "Please, *innamorata*, let us not be so sensitive with each other. We have never had a problem communicating before, Gillian. Tonight was a very special, extraordinary experience. I do not want to fight with you. I was joking as you so often do but I do not appear to have your strategic timing."

She looked down at him. He hadn't moved. His arms were still tightly around her, one hand cupping her butt, his keen eyes watching for any shift in her face. He looked beautiful lying there on the ground, his black hair blending with the grass on the mountainside. Shit, she was being overly sensitive.

"Sorry, I'm a little touchy, I guess."

"Nothing to worry about, *piccola*. Now kiss me."

Smiling, she figured he was right—there was no reason to debate the issue further so she kissed him. The sudden heat that had lingered in her pelvis since the healing intensified and she squirmed against him, straddling him and locking his hips between her knees.

Aleksei responded to her instantly, his own groin still full and heavy. Tongues dueled as he enjoyed being able to kiss her unhurriedly, running his hands up to tangle in her hair then sending one down her back, feeling the solid muscle of her form. The heat between them rose and their bodies pressed tight, needing to find solace in each other.

Moving her hands around his shoulders, Gillian pulled his upper body tightly to hers and sat him up with her on his lap. She wrapped her legs around his waist, and they pressed together, grinding against the clothing that separated them. Aleksei groaned, rolling them so they were head and shoulders upward on the incline of the slope and Gillian was beneath him.

She shifted her hips as his large warm hands unfastened her pants, pulling them away. Her own hands were busy unlacing his velvet ties, freeing him from the tight confines of the soft black material. Aleksei shuddered as she caressed his length, and he tucked a hand under her hip, tilting her to receive him.

"Guide me inside, *piccola*." His voice was magical, pure silky sex, and she felt her body respond with a fresh wetness as she positioned him at her opening. Reaching up, she took his head, drawing him into a kiss.

He started to enter her, then froze as she gasped in pain, lifting his head from the kiss to stare at her, silvery eyes wide in surprise.

"Gillian . . . ?"

Frustrated, she frowned and tried to push upward onto his shaft. *"Ow!"*

That hurt. What the hell?! It never hurt.

"Easy, *tesora*." Aleksei was frowning too, but a niggling idea was clawing at the back of his thoughts. "Relax, and let me see what the problem is."

Experimentally, he withdrew completely from her, then lightly flexed his hips forward again. Gillian gasped, "Ow! Damn! Why would this hurt all of a sudden?"

Confusion was plainly on her face. Gently, he pulled back, resting on his hip, and softly probed her with a long finger. Gillian watched him carefully, feeling his examination of her. He was being extremely tentative and gentle, but she felt the same pressure as she had when he'd tried to enter her.

"Aleksei? What is it?"

He knew then. He'd felt a resistance when she'd yelped. His fingers confirmed it. He knew what the problem was and it suddenly made sense.

"I do not know if this is good news or bad news, but it seems our healing affected all of us more than we realized."

Now he was looking at her again, part amusement, part something else in his eyes. He pulled away from her and tucked himself back inside his velvet pants.

"Goddammit, what *is* it?" Gillian was thoroughly confused and getting pissed off. She wanted to boink Aleksei's brains out, and having sex that hurt was not on her agenda.

"You seem to have regained what you lost a long time ago." Aleksei leaned over and retrieved her pants, handing them to her as he rose and lifted her from the ground.

"What the fuck are you talking about? What did I lose?"

"Your virginity, *dolcezza*." The smile he gave her wasn't mocking; it was sweet and tender.

He wasn't making fun of her, but it took a moment for what he said to sink in. "My virgini— You mean . . . ?"

"Indeed I do. You are intact once more."

Her eyes went wide as she made the same connection he had. "Oh shit! That is not funny!"

"No, it is not, but it is a fact." Aleksei took her pants away from her and held them out for her to step into.

"Wait, what are you doing? Don't you want to finish what

we started?" Gillian looked at him, realizing that the Little Transylvanian Train that she wanted to ride was locked up behind Aleksei's relaced pants.

Aleksei's eyebrow rose and he scolded her lightly, "*Cara mia*, you are a virgin. I realize that until a few hours ago you were not, but now you are. I will not have sex with you out here, in the grass. It is not right."

"Have you lost your mind?" She stared at him, more than a little annoyed. "What difference does that make? We've been having sex for months now, just do it and get it over with!"

"Gillian Key, I am astonished!" he reprimanded her. "I do not know what your first experience was like, but I do not take a virgin out into such an unromantic place for her deflowering. This is something that deserves courting and the proper atmosphere. Now please put your pants back on so I may take you home."

"My first experience was at three o'clock in the morning on a deserted construction site when I was eighteen," she snapped, still coming to terms with where this had degenerated to. "I can't believe you are stopping in the middle of sex because I grew back an insignificant piece of flesh thanks to Perrin and his musical mojo!"

She grabbed her pants and put them on herself. When she straightened, he was looking at her. "What? What did I say now?"

Aleksei was nearly speechless, hands on hips, glaring down at her. "*Il Perrin aveva ragione, lei potrebbe usare del raddrizzare fuori, piccola,*" he said under his breath in Italian. In English he snapped, "Are you ready?"

"Not until you tell me what the hell is bothering you and what you just said about Perrin." She stared back at him, just as stubborn.

"*Il damn di dio esso!*" he swore, raking his hand through his hair. "I said, 'Perrin is correct, you need to be straightened out on a number of things, *piccola*.'"

"Such as?"

"Gillian, being the first man to be with a young woman is a special thing for them both. I want to treat you as I would have treated you if I truly had been your first lover. Why is that so hard for you to understand? Will you not allow me to treat you with the respect this situation deserves? Like the woman I love?

"Must you always be the brash Marine and make light of something that could be so exceptional for us both? This is a miracle for you, *cuore dolce*, your own sort of rebirth. Do you want to just give it away to a Vampire you have already broken up with on a mountainside or would you like it to be a beautiful, special event?"

Gillian had stopped listening when he'd dropped the *L* word again, her insides tightening with nervousness. Dammit, dammit! Did she want that? Did she want to have *this* "special" moment with him? How far and deep would that tie them together in his eyes? Would she be betraying him if she just found someone to have sex with if he wouldn't? No, she couldn't do that. She was fine with her sexuality but she wasn't just going to pick up someone to get laid. Shit and double shit.

What had he just said? Broken up . . . oh yeah. "We are on a break! Just like Ross and Rachel!" she retorted. "And isn't it up to me where I lose my cherry and to whom?"

The moment she said it, she realized her mistake. Something dark and heartbreaking flickered across his perfect features. The silvery eyes dulled for a moment, then lightened to nearly white ice. He straightened to his full height, invisible walls almost audibly clanging down.

Whoa, she felt that, even without her empathy switched on. She had hurt him, deeply. Great. This was just getting better and better. Vaguely she wondered how badly it would hurt to cut out her tongue before she did any more damage.

Amazingly, Aleksei spoke first. "My apologies, Gillian. I presumed too much. Of course it is your choice as to who will be the honored man, and when it will happen."

He turned away from her. "Perhaps Perrin would oblige if you are in a hurry to get on with it."

Ouch. That hurt, but she really couldn't blame him. "Perrin has nothing to do with this."

"Neither do I, apparently," he said softly, still with his back to her.

Gillian had half a dozen smart-assed remarks ready to fire, but his last comment completely disarmed her. Shit, all they'd done was argue for the past couple of months. No, scratch that. All she'd done was argue. Aleksei had been pretty decent, after he'd redeemed himself for his negative interpretation of her job as a sex therapist. Hell, he'd even taken Perrin under his wing, literally. And she really did lo . . . lov . . . um, like him a lot. Not going to go there, dammit.

Swearing under her breath, she kicked a clump of grass, then moved closer and put her hand on his arm. "Look, I'm sorry and I'm not trying to pick a fight. I would be honored if you could be my . . . first."

Aleksei looked down at her, his eyes boring into her, but he could feel no duplicity, no reservations. Sincere feeling was in her lovely green eyes, and it moved him. She was trying. She was just unbelievably blunt and said what was on her mind. Maybe working on the filter from her brain to her mouth would be in order.

"I do not want to pressure you nor fight with you either. I was only trying to think of your feelings, *cara.* To give you a lovely romantic evening as you should have had in the first place rather than just 'doing it' as you said. That was my reasoning for refusing you right now, nothing more," he said earnestly, taking her hands as he turned back to face her.

"I know. I should have realized that. You're always very considerate of my feelings, and I usually forget to notice. I appreciate it, Aleksei. I truly do." There, that was nice. Polite even. High road. Nosebleed.

Immediately, his face softened and he pulled her close, hugging her in the shelter of his arms. "I am four hundred years old, *piccola.* In that time I have been with a virgin or two, even if it was before I was turned. It was always very important that the setting, the time, the mood, all be just right for the moment. I simply wanted to give you something which no one else thought to do."

Allowing herself a moment of honest vulnerability, she

responded, "I know. I always wished that the first time could have been different. I just never admitted it to myself before."

Smiling and stroking her hair, Aleksei whispered, almost to himself, "And we reach another milestone in the growth and development of Gillian Key."

"I heard that."

"I love you." He chuckled, reaching down to pat her bottom affectionately.

"I know," she muttered against his chest, gritting her teeth. She was now a virgin with a guaranteed date for Aleksei's Vampire version of prom night. This was just simply fucking fascinating.